Chao.
A Warlocks c

Steve K Peacock

*For Nigel, the most resilient and inspirational person I know,
and a pretty great uncle too.
Still think you should get an eReader, though…*

Published by Magister Books

Copyright © Steve K. Peacock

One

'Get her up, we can't stay here!'

A javelin of pearlescent power zapped past my ear as I shouted, obliterating the plasterboard wall behind me. On the floor next to me, Sophie Preston, former warlock, was bleeding from a nasty wound in her head. Romsey, another former warlock, was doing his best to hoist her up.

Sorry, dropping you all *in medias res* here. I'll catch you up shortly.

A flurry of javelins slammed into the table we were using for cover, the shock reverberating up my arm and rattling at my shoulder. The spell I was holding to keep the upturned table in one piece was robust, but that energy had to go somewhere, and it was already starting to take its toll.

'I don't think I can shift her,' Romsey said. 'Her fucking brains are all over the floor, if I try and move her—'

'What's left might slosh out, yes, I know,' I shot back. I risked a glance over our makeshift parapet and loosed a wild spell of my own. 'But if we don't move her, we're all fucked. So, use those meaty Scouse muscles and get her to the door.'

Romsey's expression turned to stone as, with barely a grunt of effort, he lifted Preston up and onto his shoulders, one arm and a leg thrown about his neck like a scarf. He gave me a nod and set off at a sprint for the door. I gave him two steps and then followed, pulling my spell from the overturned table and angling it in the air to deflect any incoming spells. There were a lot of them.

Harried and under pressure, we made it to the door, and I seized the lock with a flake of power. We didn't dawdle to watch the sparks it spat out – we could hear them on the other side already, throwing spells and fists and furniture in the hope of breaking down the door. They'd succeed, but we had enough of a head start to be able to escape before they did.

Probably not enough to catch our breath, though.

*

An hour later, and Romsey was setting Preston down on a cot that had, at one point, been the dancefloor of a night club. Another ex-warlock, one I didn't know by name yet, immediately shoved the man out the way and set about working their magic on the young woman. I didn't stay to watch.

I slipped out the fire escape, out into the concrete quadrangle that had once served as the smoking area of the premises – hundreds of tiny ash marks on the bricks of the walls spoke to that. I picked a corner and slumped to the floor, reminding my lungs that it was their job to breathe, my heart that its job was to beat. The adrenaline was wearing off, so I figured the vital organs would need a bit of bossing around.

'Hey there, handsome. How'd it go?'

Charlie didn't waste time. Couldn't even give me a minute to stew. 'Shitly.'

'Looks it, yeah.' She had been leaning on the frame of the fire escape door, but already she was moving to sit across from me. 'No progress?'

'None,' I said, shaking my head. 'They're too angry right now. They're in that space where any words at all are going to sound like lies. Barely got through the introduction before they turned on us.'

'But Sophie—'

'They played her too,' I interrupted. 'Apparently treating your informants right doesn't do as much to create a bond of trust as you'd expect.'

Charlie dropped her chin to her chest. 'Will she live?'

'No idea. Ask the warlock patching her up.'

Charlie's cheerful demeanour faltered for a second. She had improved by leaps and bounds since being liberated from the control of The Rider – she had some colour in her cheeks again and had finally regained enough muscle mass to use a proper belt on her jeans rather than a bungee cord. Every now and then, though, a haunted look flashed across her face. She was becoming better at hiding it, but I never missed it.

In fairness, she hadn't been given the safest place to heal. From the moment word got out about The Rider taking the Vault out of play, things had gone to shit. The free wizards had mobilised, organised, and started really kicking off – targeting anyone associated with Whitehall. They'd done some damage to the suits, sure enough, but they'd also turned on the warlocks.

No mercy for collaborators. As a motto, it had all the slick gravitas of something whipped up in an advertising agency boardroom, but it was the driving force for most of the free wizards now. We'd been trying to talk things out with them, at least get them pointed at the real enemy but, well, all they could see were the treacherous turncoats who had gone against their own.

We had sown a lot of distrust over the years, and now it was time for the reaping.

See, told you I'd get you all caught up.

'You've got a visitor, by the way,' Charlie said without looking up. 'Again.'

I sighed. 'She won't take no for an answer, will she?'

'Stubbornness has worked well for her so far, no reason to change her approach now I guess.'

'I'll give her one.'

I stood up slowly. There was a dull ache in my shoulder, the aftermath of holding that shield against the attack. As I went to walk past Charlie, the pain flared. She had grabbed my hand to stop me.

'Jim,' she said, her voice quiet and delicate. 'You're doing good. Remember that.'

I looked down at her and nodded, unable to come up with any other way to respond that didn't sound trite or insincere. As if sensing what I was feeling, she let go of my hand and looked away, and I went back inside.

Kaitlyn van Ives was waiting for me in the manager's office behind the DJ booth. She had really taken to the whole revolutionary uprising thing – which, I suppose, is just a small pivot from *freedom fighter* when you think about it. Her fire-red hair had been tied back so as to accommodate an honest-to-God beret, a crimson band tied around her upper arm, and she had started swapping out her shabby-chic combat trousers for something a little more photogenic. She was wringing every ounce of political legitimacy out of the Zapatistan aesthetic.

She crossed her arms as she watched me enter. 'Parker.'

'I don't want to hear it, not now.'

'I told you it wasn't going to work.'

My eye twitched. 'I don't need you here gloating about how your untethered army of angry proles have pushed me and mine back to hiding like rats, Kaitlyn. I've got a woman bleeding out down there whose only crime was trying to *talk* to these people.'

'Not her only crime,' Kaitlyn said, her tone measured. 'Not to them.'

'It wasn't like Whitehall gave us much of a choice. If they had been in our place—'

'But they weren't, so you can't go thinking that way. It's going to take time before you can bring them to the table, you're pushing them too hard.'

'I don't need a lesson on politics from the face of the revolution.'

She bristled at my words. 'Now, that's not fair.'

'Neither is your people trying to hound us to the ends of the bloody earth. And yet, here we are.'

'They're not my people,' she said. 'You can't steer a revolution, it does that itself. You just hold on tight and wait for it to calm just enough to tug the reins a little.'

I laughed. 'I never thought you'd be giving a politician's answer.'

'Me neither.'

'Why are you here, Kaitlyn?'

She went quiet, her jaw trembling a little. It jabbed me right in the heart, which made me think that it had been designed to do so. Van Ives had been to see me every day for a week now, trying to talk me into something, but I had shut her down each time before she could even explain what it was. This was the first time she had tried the waterworks strategy, and it was a little disappointing to find I was still that easy to manipulate.

'We're splintering,' she said. 'At first, everyone was happy to be one big force for change, but it was only a matter of time before factions started forming. I can work with most of them, but there's one in particular—'

'Not interested,' I said, cutting her off. 'I'm not going to go from hated warlock to hated union buster.'

'They're supremacists,' she continued, undaunted. 'The worst ideologies of the dark times, all mixing together into one horrible mass of hate. They are gaining more support every day, pushing me out. If they keep gaining traction, I won't be able to tug the reins anymore.'

'Fat lot of good you've done for us so far.'

Her eyes blazed. 'I've done everything I can to keep this contained! It's my influence alone that has kept this discontent to the magical community. It is a daily struggle to talk them out of going for the families of warlocks to draw them into the light. Without me blunting their edges, you're looking at an all-out civil war.'

I took one long breath. The free wizards had us outnumbered ten to one, but the reason they had been able to remain free for the most part was because they weren't as magically adept as the people who had been dragged in to make warlocks. They were minor talents, low priority. We had the muscle to beat them in open conflict, but they had the numbers. Any victory we managed to eke out would be Pyrrhic at best – especially as we didn't have the *will* to fight them.

'Why do you need me?'

'They know all my agents,' Kaitlyn said. 'I move against them, they'll use that as an excuse to force me out. That happens, there's no-one else to be the voice of reason.'

'And I'm the most famous warlock in the country, apparently. They'd lynch me as soon as look at me.'

'Not if you play your part right.'

She had kept her eyes right on the cusp of bubbling over, of tears streaming down her face, for the entirety of the conversation now. It was such a transparent gambit, so overly rehearsed and artificial, that it was almost insulting. This wasn't just manipulating me to accept her request here, it was *knowing* that I wouldn't be able to turn her down and was laying the groundwork for *how* I would justify it to myself.

Shit, I bet she even planned how many visits it would take me to break.

Worst of all, she was right – things were currently very bad indeed, but it didn't take a substantial amount of imagination to see how much worse things would be with a true zealot at the helm of the good ship Uprising.

I pushed my thumbs into my eyes a little and groaned loudly. 'Tell me everything I need to know.'

It took her a long time to get me filled in, and the more she talked the more impressed – and intimidated – I was about the sheer scale of her network.

I had never been under any illusions about how dangerous Kaitlyn van Ives could be. Working for Whitehall, her position at the top of the Most Wanted list had come parcelled with entire hard drives full of documents about her activities. And yet, even after having met her, it had been hard to see her as anything but an underdog eking out her living in the spaces between the gears of government.

Turns out, what she had been doing was constructing an entire bloody shadow state.

The dossiers she had put together for each of the key members of the supremacist faction were scarily detailed, rivalling anything I had ever received from government agencies. In a different life, she would have been a deadly spymaster.

After a few hours, I put down another stuffed file folder and sighed. 'These are some bad dudes.'

'That's putting it lightly,' she said. 'Honestly, that they've shown any restraint at all amazes me.'

'From what you've shown me, looks like their leader has been keeping them in line.'

Kaitlyn shook her head. 'I don't think so. Efraim Kingsley is old-school, knows a lot about how to organise properly, but he doesn't have the charisma to command.'

'He's not the leader,' I said. 'A lieutenant, maybe. But we both know who's pulling the strings.'

'Ah,' Kaitlyn said. 'I did wonder if you'd make that connection.'

'Of course, I'd make the connection! He flat out told me this was the sort of shit he had planned!'

For a moment, there had been the tiniest hint of enjoyment on Kaitlyn's face. She got pleasure out of testing me, seeing what I could work out on my own and where I needed some gaps filled in. My outburst had wiped that away, though. I realised that she hadn't been prepared for me to be quite so business-like about things, and a dark knot squirmed in my belly as a result.

It wasn't her fault that The Rider was such a sore spot for me. I do have a problem when it comes to holding grudges, and someone manipulating me into taking the greatest deterrent to magical uprising off the board was always going to cut very deep. But it wasn't just that – he had shown me things, what he claimed to be the future, and how he wanted me at his side to help deal with what was coming.

Kaitlyn didn't know – *couldn't* know – that these supremacists were most likely the tip of a spear that The Rider had been very keen to place in my hand.

'If it is him,' she said gently. 'Then surely you see why we have to get in there and shut this shit down?'

I nodded. 'He's done enough damage.'

'Come see me tomorrow,' Kaitlyn said. 'I'll have my guys tidy you up so you can make your grand entrance.'

'How did you know I'd want to make a grand entrance?'

That spark of joy returned to her face for an instant. 'Because I've met you.'

She rose to leave, and I declined to do the gentlemanly thing and stand to see her off. I don't think she minded. Besides, I wasn't done yet.

Kaitlyn left, closing the door behind her, and I waited until her footsteps had finished fading away, lost among the cluttered soundscape of our little hideaway. When I was sure she was gone, I let my eyes wander to the corner of the room. Shadows had been gathering there slowly over the last hour, cottony wisps of darkness congealing like cobwebs. It was subtle, slow, and not something anyone would think to notice if they hadn't seen it before.

But I had. The damned thing had been haunting me for weeks.

As if reacting to my gaze, a face formed quickly in the darkness, followed by a body, and stepped out into the light. The sickly light of the bare bulb hanging from the ceiling caught her hair instantly, a tight braid of auburn flecked with highlights of red. No matter where we were, the light had always found a way of catching her hair like that.

'I don't think she gives Efraim enough credit,' she said. 'Given enough media coaching I think I could make something pretty special out of him.'

'Piss off,' I spat back, trying to resist the urge to look her in the face.

'Come on, Jim, don't be like that.'

'I'll be however I want,' I said. 'Especially when you wear that face to fucking mock me. I've given you your answer, so piss off.'

My resistance wavered and my eyes crept from her hair to her face. The gentle chin, the smile like a crooked stream in a renaissance painting, the nose just a little too pointy for her own good. And then the eyes, red-ringed irises on black, burning out the core of all my good memories of her.

The Rider had been wearing Robin's face every time he had paid me a visit since the incident at the vault, and it never stopped hurting.

'I should let Efraim know you are coming to relieve him' The Rider said. 'Because that *is* what will happen if you try your hand at this cloak and dagger business. We both know it. We've *seen* it. The only way you can stop all of this is to take charge, just as I've wanted for you from the beginning.'

I pulled my gaze away from The Rider's eyes. 'Ever the devil on my shoulder, aren't you? Keep wasting your time, see how that goes for you.'

The Rider opened their mouth to respond – Robin's teeth were an off-white, one canine adorably wonky – but I had no patience left. I pulled a scrap of paper from my pocket, held it tight in my fist, and blew a mote of power into it. When I unfurled my fingers, a starburst of pure white light flashed as the paper burned away in an instant, scouring the shadows from every corner. The Rider was gone, and I was alone.

My heart thumped in my chest for a moment or two, and my palm tingled from the results of the spell. I let myself feel both those sensations, allowed the rest of the world to drain away while I regained my centre.

So, yeah, things had been a bit weird and stressful and, if I'm honest, thoroughly *shit* since the vault fell. And it's not like they were going to get much better any time soon.

Still, makes for good reading for you, I suppose. How's that for a silver lining?

Two

Charlie took me clothes shopping. It wasn't that I didn't trust Kaitlyn and her team of guerrilla stylists, but if I was going to do this then I damn sure wasn't about to go in solo. Besides, I had chopped up all my debit cards after Whitehall had sent a technologically savvy assassin after me within days of the Vault falling and I'm not one for carrying cash. You just end up with pockets full of useless slag.

Being considerably smarter than me, Charlie had cashed out all of her accounts immediately – and they had been *vast*. I felt not a pang of guilt for sponging off her.

'No ties,' she said, slapping my hand away from a rack of shimmering velvet nooses. 'You don't even like them, why are you mooching around here?'

I shrugged. 'I want to look professional when I crash their meeting. I need to look powerful enough that they won't just cave my face in before I can get my pitch out.'

'*No ties,*' she repeated. Taking me by the shoulders, she turned me around and shoved me out of the *casual-smart* section of the shop and into the *smart-casual* zone. Within seconds, she was plucking shirts and trousers from hangers and throwing them into my arms. 'You want to command respect, you need to rock a *Zelensky*.'

Before I could respond, she had press-ganged me into a changing room, snapping the curtains shut behind me. I laid the clothes out in front of me, sighed, and began to change. 'A Zelensky?'

'The Ukrainian guy,' she said from the other side of the curtain. 'Goes a whole war in cargo trousers and a tailored hoodie, looking like a man of the people. It's simple, solid PR, and it'll buy you enough time to lay on the charm.'

'You're good at this,' I said with a small chuckle.

'Handling an asset means making sure they are fully prepared,' she said, her voice suddenly cold and flat. 'The right outfit for the right job. There's a science in there.'

I slipped on a second pair of trousers. The first pair had been too tight on my thighs, but these ones were perfect. 'Actually, I wanted to talk to you about that. Fancy being my handler again?'

A head shot through the curtain. 'What?'

'I... oi, excuse me!' I sputtered, practically swallowing my own tongue. 'Eyes up here, you. And, well, yeah, if I'm going to do this then I want a support team. I need that whole James Bond back-up team with the supercomputers and the gadgets and the superstar hacker that can pull facial recognition off the blurry reflection of half a face reflected in a window on a photograph from the 50s. You were always pretty good at that sort of thing.'

A joke crossed her mind – I saw it on her face – but it got batted away by something else. She had been different since her time enthralled to The Rider, obviously, but it was still a little unsettling to watch. I'd expected banter, a little back and forth, playful repartee. That was how our relationship worked, and sometimes it still did.

And then other times, ones like these, Charlie was unable to keep reality at bay long enough to savour those little moments of joy. She had worked something out, and it had cut any merriment off at the knees.

You're scared, her face seemed to say. *You want someone in your ear keeping you on the level, and I don't know why. But I do know you don't want me to know that, so for your sake I will pretend I don't. But we both know that I do.*

'Will last year's smartphone and a Swiss Army Knife be enough for you?'

'I suppose it will have to.'

She smiled softly. 'Then you've got yourself a handler. Get dressed. You're only going to sign up with a group of bolshy minor talents, anyway. You're hardly going to need all that tech.'

Her head slid back through the curtain, leaving me alone again. She was, of course, right – I didn't need all that tech. I only needed one thing to help me get through this.

And now I had her.

*

After a fraught bit of last-minute coordination with Kaitlyn, I chose that same night to make my introductions to the group. Apparently, they had been through enough names for their little association to fill a rolodex, but as of that night they were going by The Aegis. It was all I could do not to roll my eyes whenever I heard it.

The Aegis – ergh – did their meetings in the backroom of a working men's club on Grafton Street. It was the last grasping vestige of the 1970s, the ghost of a labour movement and the perfect place for a man like Kingsley to whip up a little fervour. I didn't know shit about him before I arrived at the club but watching him for a few minutes told me everything I needed to know.

I had expected the backroom to be set up for a lecture, or at least for the self-aggrandising proselytising of a champagne socialist at a trade union conference. Instead, Kingsley had arranged something much more lowkey – a loose circle of chairs, like a group therapy session but with better turnout, his own chair differentiated only by it being the only chair with uneven legs.

You show them you can be trusted to make the bigger sacrifices by making the small ones first. Not many sacrifices smaller than making sure you're the one to take The Wobbly Chair.

Lingering by the doorway, I waited for the best moment to make myself known. There's a fine line you need to consider, take my word for it. Go too early, the crowd won't be warmed up enough, their brains not squishy and malleable enough, for your words to lodge in there. Let the revolutionary love-in continue for too long, though, and they'll be too rabid. Got to hit the sweet spot.

The trick is not to listen to the words. Words mean next to nothing; you want to map the energy of the room. You surf it, ride the waves and troughs, probing for the moment where things stagnate for just an instant. Pinpoint that eye of the storm, the split second as the wave breaks on the shore and it stops, reaching as far up the sand as it can, before it collapses back into the ocean. That's not in the words.

Kingsley was not a masterful orator, but I could surf his energy well enough to pick my moment.

I snapped my fingers and killed the lights, stopping Kingsley stone dead in the middle of whatever it was he was going on about. There were some hushed murmurs from the assembled group, which I tolerated for a couple of seconds before kicking open the door in which I had been lurking. The light from the other room splashed along the floor, painting me in a rather cutting silhouette.

Feeling their eyes on me, I peeled myself off the doorframe and let them stare. Someone would break first, I just had to milk the moment until they did.

Within seconds, a voice piped up in the darkness. 'Who the bloody—'

I reached out with my power, found that voice in the darkness, and snatched it up. The speaker coughed into silence. That's little more than a parlour trick really, provided you have some real magic at your disposal – with this lot being minor talents, it was enough to let them know they were dealing with someone important.

Another snap of my fingers and the lights came back on.

'Come now, I'm sure you've all heard of me.'

This was the moment. The awe-filled silence, the squirming thoughts wriggling in the back of their minds, the confusion and, yes, even a little bit of fear. It was written into their DNA by this point that a warlock is a Big *Fucking* Deal. I'd put them on the back foot and that meant…

It meant…

It meant that I was very confused when laughter rang across the room with all the force of a peal of thunder. Every single person was looking my way and laughing a full, raucous, lung-splitting chortle right at me. No matter how secure in yourself you are, that sort of psychic assault is going to cut deep, so I'm not ashamed to say it knocked me off my stride. I goggled at them for far too long, letting what little majesty my entrance had achieved melt away.

Something bubbled up in me, something dark and unwanted and far too familiar. I pushed it down and locked it away, but my fingers were tingling from the magic I had drawn in just those couple of seconds. It did serve to stop the laughter, however.

'You see, I told you,' Kingsley shouted from his chair. 'Look at how hard he had to try to not obliterate us all for the simplest matter of disrespect.'

There were mumbles of agreement from the group, their faces so serious now that it was hard to believe they had been laughing at all. They kept mumbling as Efraim Kingsley slowly got to his feet, puffing with the exertion, and started to walk towards me.

'And he could, we all know it,' he continued. 'The only chance any of us would have at stopping him is if he *allowed* it. Exactly as it should be. Power is power, my friends, and the discomfort of pretending otherwise hurts all of us.'

He closed to within a couple of metres before stopping, his girth obscuring a fair amount of the group. His breathing was a loud rattle between sentences, and his face was so ruddy it was bordering on purple. A heavy-lidded eye aimed a lazy wink at me.

'I take it you heard I was coming, then?' I said.

Kingsley shook his head. 'Not really. We've had suspicions that *someone* would come as we started to open eyes, but not you specifically. Come here, let's get you a drink and we can talk about this like adults, yes?'

Before I could respond he had already turned and began walking to a refreshments table nearby. Cheap plywood covered with a cheaper plastic tablecloth and the *cheapest* of snacks – party rings, pink wafers, off-brand crisps. Pouring a drink from a thermos on the table, Kingsley filled a paper plate with his spare hand before offering it to me alongside a steaming mug.

'This is big *kid's birthday vibes* for the meeting of a group of magical malcontents,' I said, studying the liquid in the mug. It smelled warm and tart.

Kingsley shrugged. 'Why should we eat and drink the things we are told to enjoy?'

'Oh, I see. You're embracing your inner children now? I've got to say, I wasn't expecting something so new-age touchy-feely.'

'I don't want to give you the speech, Jameson Parker, former warlock of Her Majesty's government. I'm also sure you have no interest in hearing it.'

I placed my drink and plate down on the table. 'You'd be correct.'

'I'll just ask you the one question that brought all of us together and leave it to you to answer however you wish. So, what are you so afraid of?'

I blinked. 'That's it? Not very insightful.'

'I mean, you came here because you think we're a threat, right? We get together and talk about wizard supremacy, and that scares you. It scares all of you with real power. There's not a man or woman in this room with the magic to stand against you, and yet *we* scare *you*. Something to think about, that's all I'm saying.'

It was becoming rapidly clear to me that Kaitlyn had been underestimating Efraim Kingsley. The words weren't his own, he wasn't *that* far above what she thought, but he knew exactly where to aim them. A solid and skilled application of doubt and rhetoric, it was easy to see why he had risen to the top of this little group of misfits.

And they were misfits, I could see that now. There was something in their eyes that marked them, they were a little too wide and far too hungry, driven by a parasitical thought that had burrowed in deep and gnawed away at the shield between the mind and the real world. Empty eyes in hollow faces, all watching me and Kingsley conversing quietly by the Bombay Mix.

If I let myself blink again, they'd close the gap between us before my eyes opened again. There was no doubt in my mind of that.

Through the door behind me, I heard a lock clicking shut. I didn't need to turn around, I knew what that meant: the few people that had been in the main bar area were gone, and I was sealed in with the people I had come here to see. The hair on the back of my neck bristled, as if I wasn't already aware I was in a dangerous situation.

'I'm surprised you haven't tried to smash my face in,' I said. 'Aren't warlocks traitors as far as you all are concerned?'

Kingsley snorted. 'That's a bit of a simplified view. But yes, overall, that is a good way to describe you. I think the point where a lot of people get confused is who it is we think you betrayed.'

'Not you, then?'

'You can't betray us,' he said. There were traces of Mancunian in his accent, slipping out from between the East-End Cockney twang he had been using. 'You don't owe us shit. It's yourself you've been betraying, letting yourself believe the lie that you weren't made to rule.'

'Ah, ok. Cool.'

'Don't be so dismissive. What's the point of power if not to wield it? You have a lot of it, and the fact you don't let yourself *use* it is the biggest betrayal of all.'

I didn't mean to snort in amusement, I really didn't, but how could I not? 'Are you serious?'

'Excuse me?'

'You lot aren't supremacists,' I said, flinging my arm in a wide gesture. 'You're bloody groupies. Not one of you has the juice to put a rabbit in a hat, let alone pull one out of it, and yet you think you know how proper power should be used? Mate, that's sad – cranking the hog to your ex's Facebook page levels of sad.'

Rage I would have expected. Frustration and concerted dislike, too. Hell, even disappointment would have made sense. But instead of all that, Kingsley smiled a little and nodded softly. 'You need to remember who you are, that's all. We need you to retake your rightful place, it's the only way this can all end – strong leaders, chosen by the flow of magic itself.'

I groaned. Kaitlyn had really fucked up here – she had seen what she had wanted to see, a political movement. Perhaps The Aegis had elements of that, enough charisma and talking points to turn some heads, but surely this brand of bullshit wasn't going to sway the majority of the factions. To them, warlocks were collaborators to be shunned at best, and not even a skilled hype man would be able to break down that perception any time soon. Hell, I'd been given the credit for taking down the Vault and they still tried to blow my head off on sight – no way these guys were talking them around.

Which meant, what, Kaitlyn's little shadow government looked the part but had the covert intelligence gathering skills of a cartoon squirrel? That didn't track. She was too competent to fuck up this badly, which meant lying to me had been intentional.

I wasn't a big fan of that realisation.

'I'm leaving,' I said and turned my back on Kingsley.

'You're welcome to,' he said. 'We haven't the power to keep you anywhere you don't want to be. You're always free, that's what power is.'

I was at the door when something hit my shoulder. At first, I barely registered it, but it was quickly followed by another three impacts, then a fourth. I glanced over my shoulder to find out the cause, and saw my hoodie was already darkening with blood. That was when the pain hit me.

Shimmering needles of force jutted from my flesh, grouped so tightly that only a military education or a misspent youth chucking darts in a pub could have resulted in such skill. I traced their trajectory back to Kingsley, who had another dozen flicking in his grip. With a quick flick of the wrist, he sent another pair my way, but they were easily deflected now I knew they were coming.

I brought up my other arm and drew on enough energy to form a shield at the point of impact. The needles shattered against my power, and Kingsley's smile widened. 'Yes, there he is! There's the Dark Lord of Hampshire! Swat us aside like flies, stop pulling your punches!'

'Are you trying to get me angry or something? Make me lash out?'

Another needle, another deflection. 'We're trying to get you to remember just how powerful you are. That's what we want for every warlock, to heal their confidence.'

I missed the second volley because it came at me from the side – a dozen needles of magic from the group of wild-eyed zealots who had been watching the whole exchange. One caught me across the cheek, opening a small cut that stung like fire. I scarcely had time to turn my head before the third volley came, more needles this time, every member of the congregation bearing down on me. A rain of razorblades, too many to deflect all at once and not enough time to conjure a more robust shield.

There was little danger of the onslaught killing me – minor talents have very little magic to work with, and while shaping it into needles is a very smart bit of combat casting, it's going to be largely superficial damage. Each needle that slipped through my attempts at deflection sank deep enough to hurt, but never so much that any arteries were at risk. But then, that hadn't been the plan, of course.

They wanted me angry, an excuse to flip off the safety catch and lash out. I could feel the hand of The Rider on the tiller here, hoping the stick would do what the carrot couldn't. And, I daresay, it would probably work. Get a warlock angry enough, shove enough pointy shit under his skin, and like any wounded animal he'll lash out with what he has at his disposal.

But what Kingsley didn't seem to realise was that I had been there before. I'd flayed men alive in a petrol station a continent away because they had made me angry, I'd crushed the love of my life to death because I let my temper take the wheel. It was interesting that The Rider hadn't told him that this approach was going to be futile.

Still, all that said, I really did need to do something about all the *horrible needles piercing into my flesh.*

I dropped my shield and started to weave a new one that was less deflective and more destructive. If you're skilled, you can swap spells in a fraction of a second – it's all about compartmentalising thoughts. The thing is, a fraction of a second can still be a hell of a long time when you're under fire. Dropping my shield to recast it stronger was a risk, but considering the needles were already making it into my delicate flesh, it was one worth taking.

The instant my shield went down, I felt the full force of those magical flechettes. More of them caught my face, peeling away skin, as I tried to keep my focus. The new shield expanded around me, a barely visible bubble that neutralised the remaining volley, unravelling the energy and leaving only twinkling motes to pass through.

With the assault curtailed, the pain flared – my body was now acutely aware that more damage was not immediately incoming and had decided it was time for me to address the *current* injuries. And there were a lot of those; so many needles were poking out of me that I looked like I'd had a very entertaining evening with one of those crystal hedgehogs seemingly every grandmother has on the mantelpiece.

Another impotent wave of flechettes disintegrated against my shield before Kingsley waved off the assault. He had one heavy-lidded eye closed while the other was open wider than before, a crooked brow heaving it upwards.

'Look at that,' he said. 'And he didn't even break a sweat.'

I felt warm. Rivulets of blood were creeping out of my wounds and soaking my clothes, each one tingling and burning. 'I really didn't come here to fight you.'

'I know. You came here to join us. Not to infiltrate, but to genuinely, wholly, completely embrace this.'

'Yeah, no,' I said. 'That's sort of the opposite of why I'm here.'

Kingsley sighed and let his head drop. There it was, the frustration at having to deal with me. He was wondering why I had to be so bloody awkward and not just do as I was told, I was sure of it. As you might have noticed, people have that reaction to me a lot.

I turned around again, making sure to keep my shield up and focused behind me, and tried to look nonchalant as I made for the exit. Behind me, I could hear the sound of work boots scuffing over floorboards as the group shuffled around to keep me in sight. I didn't want to risk turning around, but I could tell from their footsteps that they didn't follow me into the bar proper.

The bar area was empty, as predicted, the front door double locked. A locked door isn't much trouble when magic's involved, but I really didn't want to drop my shield and the pain from my quadrillion stab wounds would probably keep me from being able to multitask in the old spell department.

Something heavy clattered onto the carpet behind me. A key.

'Take it,' Kingsley said from the doorway to the back room. 'It's yours. All of this is yours, if you want it. And eventually you *will* want it. When you do, you know where we'll be.'

I had comebacks locked and loaded, but there was a sureness to his tone that stopped me short of unleashing them. He wasn't telling me anything The Rider hadn't already told me, and that spooky son-of-a-bitch had done a much better job of it. But still, it seemed the number of people who were convinced it was only a matter of time before I turned magi-fascist was destined to grow.

Slowly, I picked up the key, being sure never to break eye contact with Kingsley. He nodded again, silent, as I unlocked the door and slipped out into the street. In one of my smarter moves, I took the time to lock the door behind me before I pulled out my phone.

I triple-tapped the power button, triggering the SOS function. Running was off the cards, but I could sort of amble somewhat fast down the road, and by the time that turned into a slow limp I was a couple of streets over.

Taking one last look to make sure I hadn't been followed, I ducked behind an array of over-stuffed wheelie-bins and hunkered down. It wasn't until my knees hit the cold pavement that I realised I still had my shield up. Letting it go was like exhaling, and my head started to spin. Everything went white, and I'm pretty sure I dragged my cheek across every damn brick of the nearby house as I collapsed.

Lesson learned: I'm shit at being a spy.

Three

'She set me up.'

Charlie didn't deem that worthy of a response beyond a weary grunt, but then I had been repeating variations on that theme almost continuously since she had picked me up. I had no idea where she had procured the van and its driver, but then that was why I had wanted her as my handler again – I could count on her.

I heard the rip of an adhesive dressing being opened. 'Right pectoral.'

Flexing my fingers, I flicked some power up to my chest, dispelling the flechettes that still sat lodged in my skin there. Almost instantly, she pressed the dressing down over my wounds. The van took a hard left and the back of my head bounced off the metal frame.

'You get this guy off Uber or something?' I said, wincing.

Another dressing packet tore open. 'Don't blame me, he's one of yours. Grabbed the first warlock who didn't look busy. Right shoulder.'

Again, I dispelled the lingering needles as she applied the bandage. 'When did I get so gullible?'

'You've always been gullible, you idiot.'

I shook my head. 'Not like this. I let myself get too chummy with her, I got careless.'

'Look, before you get all maudlin and self-defeating, do you want to maybe take a moment to make sure you've got the right of it this time? Ribs now, shallow breaths if you please.'

Charlie was showing remarkable restraint in saving her *told you so* for later. She had never been on board with me making nice with Kaitlyn van Ives, and with good reason considering her actions against Whitehall. I hadn't been either, at first. When did I start thinking of her as a friend, lowering my guard and letting her inside?

'That's enough,' I said, slapping Charlie's hand aside. 'You put any more of those things on me and I'm going to look like a walking duvet.'

'These are nasty spells, Parker. Each quill is hollow, like a gutter, letting the blood drain through it. I can't just leave them there.'

A low grumble bubbled in the back of my throat, but I nodded that she could continue. 'I'm proud of them, in a way.'

'Pardon?'

'Kingsley and his lot,' I said. 'Making the most of what magic they have – I'm not sure I would have been ingenious enough to think up a spell like this.'

She shrugged, which I took as a sign to mean that the conversation was over. Evidently, she wasn't in the mood for a treatise on the practical application of limited magical energy. Can't say I blame her.

We spent the rest of the drive in silence apart from her clipped instructions of which body part to dispel next. By the time we got back to our little hideout she had plastered over every leak with no small amount of skill. She was already out the back of the van as the driver hit the handbrake, however, wasting no time in disappearing into the building. I gave her a bit of a head start – wasn't quite up to moving just yet anyway.

I heard the driver's door open and close and then a young man popped into view out the rear doors. He was in his early twenties with dirty blonde hair and a growth of stubble on a long jaw with more angles than an Escher painting. His eyes were electric blue, but the left one had a blown-out pupil that made him unsettling to look at.

'The pair of us have not been formally introduced. Wolfgang Engel.' His voice was soft and deep, a no-nonsense rumbling whisper that put years on him. Until he said his name, I didn't catch the accent. The Germanic sharpness of the W cut through, though.

'Jameson Parker. Thanks for being my getaway driver.'

He smirked and held out a hand, helping me down from the van. 'It was not much of a getaway. Do you need more assistance?'

'I think I can make my own way from here, thanks.'

The young man dipped his head in a gentle nod and went about busying himself with something around the front of the vehicle.

I didn't remember recruiting anyone who wasn't British, but then I wasn't the only one bringing people into the fold. How many of the people in this little outfit did I actually know, anyway? Clearly not enough if I hadn't heard about a handsome German knocking about the place.

Once I was certain I had given Charlie enough time to breathe, I followed her into the building. She wasn't hard to find – one corner of the main dance floor, where the bar had once been, had been cleared of cots and supplies. In the free space that afforded, someone had set up some battered desks and maps of the city and some interesting technical contraption that I could barely comprehend. Judging from the wires and plugs, it was a number of laptop peripherals all daisy-chained together. As I approached, she was trying to untangle one specific cable from a bank of phone chargers.

'This is a better look for you than slumped against the wall, Chaz.'

Her nimble fingers were working on untying the sort of knot that always forms in a cable the moment you turn your back. 'You looked better without all the blood.'

'Are you angry with me?' I asked. I went to sit on one of the tables but thought better of it.

'Yes,' she shot back. 'No. I'm angry in general, I think. That was a stupid move, just walking right in because van Ives said it would work. It was a stupid move *and* an obvious trap. And I should have talked you out of it the moment you filled me in. That's what I'm *for*.'

'Charlie, don't beat yourself up over this.'

'Oh, I still blame you,' she snarled. The plastic peeled off under her nails, but the knot refused to budge. 'You should know better. But I should also know that you *don't* know better. What was she up to, Jim?'

I crossed my arms. 'I don't know. I could go ask, I suppose, but I doubt she'll still be where I left her.'

'She's too smart for that.'

'Agreed,' I said. 'But I'm thinking her motivations aren't what we should be focusing on right now. I'm still curious about The Aegis as a group.'

'Because she sent you to them to get fucked up?'

I frowned and took a moment to think before I answered. 'It's not that. People kick the shit out of me all the time, and if that was Kaitlyn's goal then she could have easily done that herself. But even *their* goal wasn't to do that, not really. The way they were talking, they were trying to tough-love me into unlocking my potential as a wizardy warlord or something.'

'You think that's why she sent you, maybe? Wasn't that what The Rider wanted you to do too?'

'No chance she's working with The Rider,' I said. 'But the way Kingsley was talking, I don't think I'm the first warlock to track them down. He wanted me to think I was, but it was all too rehearsed. How many warlocks have signed on with us, do we have a register or something?'

With one final grunt of effort, Charlie slid the cable from the tangled knot and plugged in her phone. Carefully, she balanced it against the amassed peripherals and began tapping away on a clicky portable keyboard. She squinted at her phone's display. 'Not as such, but I can ask around.'

'I want to know how many we've lost, specifically. And how.'

'That's a bit grisly.'

'Well, if Kingsley has tried his techniques on other warlocks, chances are that some of those casualties aren't.'

'Aren't what?'

'Aren't *casualties*,' I said. 'And if that's the case, I want to know about it before the spells start flying. If it's not the case, then we're just back where we were before. I'd be fine with that.'

'You going to track down every supposed corpse, are you?'

I shrugged. 'At least I'll feel like I'm doing something.'

'This is the urge that gets you filled with holes, Jim.'

She had me there.

My chest itched under my bandage, and I scratched at it for a moment. 'How's Preston doing?'

'She'll live, apparently,' Charlie said. 'So, there's a bit of good news for you.'

'I'll take what I can get, I suppose.'

It wasn't the weakest smile I'd ever done, but the one I managed to persuade my face to put on was pretty close to it. The world was trying *really hard* to make me more responsible and grown up, and I wasn't a fan.

I reached out and brushed a finger against the back of Charlie's hand. There were a lot of things that had gone unsaid over the years, but considerably more in the last few weeks. Now wasn't the time to say them, and even if it had been she was in no place to hear them, but I hoped even a little gesture would do for now. She didn't say anything, but she didn't pull away either.

When the moment was over, I gave Charlie the space to work and took myself away to the one room with a working television. The staff room had been the only room we had found with working plug sockets, and we had powered the rest of the building through the *incredibly safe* practice of plugging a hundred extension cables together and into one socket. The other socket was reserved solely for the television.

I hadn't watched any actual television for years – give me my Netflix and my Pirate Bay, thank you very much – but someone had made a case for keeping track of the rolling news cycle as a way of mapping out how Whitehall was reacting to things, and it seemed like a good idea. And it was, if you discounted how utterly depressing it is to watch twenty-four-hour news coverage.

Personally, I found it kind of meditative. The world is always just on the edge of completely caving in on itself, but it never quite happens, does it? Most of the other warlocks can't manage to look at it that way, so every now and then I like to drop by and shoo them out, get them back out into the much less depressing triage area.

Today, a couple of warlocks were sat watching the news quietly. I didn't feel like disturbing them, so I grabbed a can of Panda Cola from a pallet by the door and found myself a seat out of the way.

Parliament was in chaos, but then when is it not? Whitehall – the magic one, not the mundane one – largely operated independently from the government as a whole, but technically the PM was in full control and that meant the state of things would ripple through. Currently, the government was on its third Prime Minister in as many months, which clearly meant things were going badly. That was good for us, at least for now.

But knowing how Whitehall was doing wasn't the same as knowing how the other warlocks were doing. Or the minor talents. I could have called Paul or Ania, asked them for a check in on how their efforts were going elsewhere in the country, but I couldn't think of anything they could say that would make me feel better.

Christ, being part of a rebellion sounds pretty miserable when I see it all spelled out like this. No wonder I had been so keen to let Kaitlyn talk me into playing spy – it was something different, something exciting. It was something where I had no idea how it would end, unlike everything else these days.

Because I knew how *this* all would end, and the more time I had to think about that the harder it was to think about anything else.

A breaking news banner flashed across the screen. Correction: four Prime Ministers in three months.

We had been very lucky lately. A few clashes with Paladins notwithstanding, most of the violence so far was from trying to make peace with other mages. Whitehall had already been in the process of restructuring itself when the Vault fell, and it was clearly still struggling to find its feet. When it did, that was when things would get bad.

I finished off my Panda Cola – flat and unpleasant as it was – and started wandering again. They haven't made the stuff for something like ten years, so I wasn't really sure what I expected. We'd found the pallet here when we moved in.

There was a room off of what was now the triage that had, at one time, been the ladies' bathroom. It had been hollowed out for some reason when the building had been abandoned, and some optimistic warlock had tried to turn it into a bulletin board of sorts. I think his idea had been to try and keep people focused on the *good* bits of warlocking – keeping people safe, kicking magical monsters in the teeth, that sort of thing – but no-one had really taken to looking at it that way.

Whichever warlock he was, he'd stopped updating the board with fresh news clippings recently, but it was still packed with all the weird and wonderful stuff that crawls out of the dark when it thinks no-one is looking. Some of it were minor-level nuisances that could be dealt with easily – a squonk infestation in Dorset, coblynau sightings in Cardiff, that sort of thing – but the majority were getting depressing to look at. Flesh-eating ghouls in Hereford, leshies in the New Forest, a dragon in the running to be mayor of Durham. Not one of these issues was written plainly on the page, but a learned eye can read between the lines.

The other warlocks hated looking at this board. I think it reminded them that the world was turning to shit now a civil war was starting to brew. Me, though, I loved it. The uptick in all this rotten shit reminded me that even shackled as we were, we'd been doing some good. Gave me something to look forward to on the other side of all this as well – *look at all the things you can look forward to fixing once you get out of this bad patch.*

When did I become such a goody-goody? Disgusting.

Charlie found me there, staring at the board and generally letting my mind phase out of existence for a while.

'You alright?'

I took a deep breath and stared at the ceiling. There was a water stain on one of the polystyrene panels that looked like a fried egg. 'Trying to slow my brain down, make it work smarter.'

'Stop yourself wandering into dangerous places half-cocked?'

'I'm not a miracle worker. How did the research go?'

'I *am* a miracle worker, so…' she said, trailing off for a moment to hand me a folded sheet of paper torn from a pocket notebook. 'Behold, the list of suspicious casualties.'

Taking the paper from her, I unfolded it slowly. 'It's blank.'

'Yep,' she said. The smile she had been holding back flushed across her face. It was infectious. 'I checked the numbers, and we've barely lost anyone. Lots of injuries, but when you actually look at the numbers, we've only had a handful of deaths, and they are all accounted for. Did you enjoy the dramatic reveal?'

'Was it really necessary?' I asked. Her smile had taken full hold on my own face now, and I could feel it kicking the weary sadness out of me second by second.

'Yes. I think we all need to be reminded of the exact level of how bad things are, no more and no less.'

I'd missed that little mischievous twinkle in her eye. 'Doesn't help us make sense of all this, though.'

'Actually, I think it does help a little,' she said. The notepad emerged from the back pocket of her jeans, and she leant it against the wall to scribble something onto a fresh page. 'I've been mapping out how badly things are getting…'

'What a lovely hobby.'

'Shut your face,' she said, not looking away from the paper. 'At the top we have The Rider and his alleged apocalypse, but that's not happening soon.'

'Not *soon* soon, but soon enough. And—'

She waved me off. 'And all our problems come from him trying to prepare for it. A crucible to forge warlocks and stuff into stronger people, blah blah, monologue, blah. We know he wants to be at the head of some unified community of mages to stand against this vision he showed you. Right?'

I nodded and found myself staring into the shadows in the corner of the room. There was nothing there. 'More or less.'

'But there's a step missing.'

'Are you sure about that?'

Tearing the sheet from the pad, she held it up in front of my eyes. Scribbled onto the surface, a spidery and complicated flowchart seemed to map out The Rider's known motives and plans. I say *seemed* because good luck trying to make out more than the odd word of Charlie's frantic chicken scratch.

'A civil war weakens, it never strengthens. If The Aegis are his catspaws, then them working to split the magical community and turn it back to some supremacist bullshit doesn't work.'

I squinted, trying to follow her drawing. 'Wait, I get what you mean. Kingsley is actively countermanding Kaitlyn's attempts to create unity – assuming that she is actually doing that.'

'Whatever else she is, we've got nothing that says she's not doing that,' Charlie said with a shrug.

'Just also trying to make me walk into unexpected arse kickings.'

'We've all had that urge,' she said. 'Stick to the facts.

'*Goddamit*,' I shouted a little too loudly. 'They're a feint!'

'Exactly!'

'She wants us looking one way while he's off doing something else while we're distracted.'

Charlie gave me a very slow clap, crumpling up the paper as she did so. 'It's the only thing I can think of that even remotely makes sense.'

Remotely was the right word, there was a lot of supposition, assumption, and blind guesswork here. But it made sense. The Rider had never been shy about wanting to bring every mage together for one purpose, his purpose, and it didn't make sense that he would think he could do that by tapping into old prejudices. The fascist playbook works, I suppose, but you need a long run up to get a decent chokehold – it's not like we have a military to go installing a junta for him.

He needed strong, committed, *focused* mages on his side. If Kingsley's little gathering became a mainstream movement, we'd end up with quite the opposite – disparate, self-interested, isolated wizards with no care for stopping this supposed apocalypse The Rider likes to harp on about.

'If we're focused on his right hand,' I muttered. 'What's the left hand up to?'

Charlie sucked her teeth. 'Something worse?'

'Probably,' I said. 'But what flavour of horror pie is he dunking his thumbs into?'

'Lovely imagery there, Jim. Just beautiful.'

I wasn't listening. My attention had wandered over Charlie's shoulder and back to the bulletin board. A long list of our neglect, of things we had abandoned. Of things we had been *distracted from*.

'I need a different list, Chaz.'

'Of course, whatever you need.'

'It's going to be a big one,' I said. 'I'm going to need the names of every warlock we've recruited, and their case history.'

'Jim, even if we had only recruited like three warlocks, the case history would be ridiculous.'

'Yup,' I said. 'But you can get it all, right?'

'Well, most of it, sure, but—'

'All you need to do is gather all these haystacks. Let me worry about plucking out the needle.'

Charlie wanted to look annoyed, but I had her. I'd gotten her swept up in my excitement – she wasn't the only one with infectious personality traits. 'How are you going to do that then, smart arse?'

'Easy,' I said. 'I'm going to get a magnet.'

Four

There are a lot of charities that deal in helping the homeless. The fact that it takes a charity organisation to remember the basic human decency that the government has clearly forgotten is a polemic best saved for another day, but the appropriate issue that such a system raises is knowing where to look to find people.

On the one hand, this can be very helpful – no centralised databases means that people on the run from abusive shitbags can hide quite easily – but that level of protection does make it much harder for legitimate searches to turn up anything.

Magic, at least, let me narrow things down a little. I couldn't rely on thaumaturgy or your traditional tracking spell for this – no DNA to target the spell with – but a bit of loose scrying could at least narrow down my options. My attention was drawn to the centre of the city, and I hit the jackpot on my second attempt.

The shelter had been erected in the sports hall of a local secondary school. I'd expected something depressing and bleak, but I was pleasantly surprised to find that this wasn't some lingering Dickensian nightmare. The rows of cots that had been laid out had spawned an ecosystem around them, one full of keepsakes and belongings, all spilling out to make each little nook feel far from the clinical sterility I had expected.

I worked my way down one of the rows of these cots until I found my target.

Bennett had seen better days. His salt and pepper hair was more salt than pepper now, grown out into the awkward stage between *professional businessman* and *CBD evangelist.* Lounging across his cot, he had a battered paperback open in his left hand while the right was walking a stunted pencil up and down between his fingers. The cover brought a cheeky smile to my face – it was some mid-90s mass market fantasy garbage with a woman in a chainmail bikini wrapping her arms around a dragon.

'Don't judge me for my reading habits,' he said, spotting me over the top of his book. 'The dead deserve the right to lose themselves in whatever hobbies they want, guilt free.'

'Maybe, but you're not exactly dead, are you?'

Bennett snapped his book shut. 'To the rest of the world I am, Parker. How did you find me?'

'Whitehall killing off one of the few people with the brains to keep a bunch of rowdy ex-wizards in line? Didn't sit right with me, I figured they'd just archive you until they needed you again. Honestly, I'm a little disappointed to find they didn't just tuck you away in some menacingly surreal village somewhere.'

'Portmeirion was fully booked. Did you seriously track me down just to throw dated references at me?'

I shrugged. He must have seen something in my face that I hadn't intended to reveal, because he swung his legs off the edge of his bed and signalled for me to sit down. I did, and he waited patiently for me to speak.

'How much do you know about how bad things have gotten lately?' I asked.

'Nothing,' he said. 'When I was forced out, they cut me off from everything. Legally I no longer exist, which makes it hard to reach out to anyone I could call in favours from.'

'I suppose that was the point.'
'Exactly.'

Not a great start. 'Long story short, then. There's a war brewing, but I think it's all a smokescreen for The Rider. I think he's trying to hide his actions in the fallout.'

'Amongst the warlock work that isn't getting done, you mean.'

I snapped my fingers. 'Exactly.'

'Can't help you,' he said. 'I've been out of the loop too long.'

'Honestly, anything would be a good place to start. Your info might be out of date, but it could point us in *a* direction at least.'

Bennett let out a tired sigh that put about a decade on him instantly. We'd never been friends, but I had respected him and, I hoped, had his respect in turn. As, essentially, a warden he had been fair enough, and while there was still a not-insignificant part of me that wanted to rub it in his face how easily forgotten his loyalty to Queen and country had been, a bigger part of me couldn't help but feel sorry for him.

I'd been in the same boat not so long ago – struck down from a position of power and authority, humbled and made to watch as some shit in a nice suit kicked down my sandcastle. It's a boat full of thumbtacks and salt, tortured metaphors and humiliation. You could do your best to hide that – and Bennett had done a very good job of it – but with one sigh my former boss had let me know exactly where he stood.

'Fine,' he said. 'Pick my brain.'

I took out my phone and showed him a couple of pictures of the noticeboard. 'We've got a sort of informal surveillance board. Keeping track of all the warlock work we don't have the time to deal with anymore. I was wondering if anything on there might stand out to you.'

Taking my phone, he took a moment to zoom into the pictures and read a few of the clippings. 'There's a lot of them.'

'More and more every day.'

'No, that's not what I mean,' he said. 'I mean, that's a lot of exposure. There shouldn't be even close to that many things getting noticed.'

'Well, Whitehall is kind of busy right now. Maybe they haven't had the time to cosy up to the papers to kill the stories.'

Bennett let out a derisory snort and zoomed in on one specific clipping. 'What I mean is that this noteworthy stuff was all but eradicated by the time I was removed. That was the whole purpose, use warlocks to deal with the dangerous, the obvious, and the dangerously obvious. Once you had finished bringing order to the country, the fast trackers would take over.'

'Paladins,' I said. 'They've rebranded.'

'To a fucking stupid name,' Bennett said. There was a cold flash in his eyes. 'Point being, you'd all just about done your jobs. If there was any chance there was still a bloody dragon hiding out on the moors, we wouldn't have been preparing to pull the trigger on the transition.'

He showed me that same clipping that had caught my eye back in the hideout. I scanned it again. 'Because every paladin is going to be too green for a long time to deal with a dragon.'

'Or a werewolf, a leshy, a barghest. They'd be able to handle squonks and pixies and the like, but it would take a lot longer than was available to prepare them for proper beasties.'

'So, you're saying we'd nearly wiped the slate clean for them to start afresh on?'

'Pretty much.'

I narrowed my eyes, pocketing my phone quickly. 'It all backslid too fast to be natural. I was *right*.'

'In my formerly expert opinion, yes.'

It was a small win, but it was enough to get my engines firing again. It was still too early to say for sure that this was the right track, but Bennett had confirmed enough of my suspicions that my confidence was building. The current that had been dragging me forward since the Vault had slackened enough for me to start getting my bearings and regaining some measure of control.

'It's a weird thing to do though, right?' I asked. 'That's, like, chapter one of the *horrid baddie handbook*. The Rider at least thinks he has more noble goals.'

'If that's the case, maybe his definition of noble is different to yours.'

'Obviously,' I said. 'But if he's all about ends being justified by means, those means need a justification. What purpose does all this chaos serve for him, and why concoct a load of bullshit political intrigue to keep everyone distracted from it?'

Bennett crossed his arms and kicked back onto the cot again, all but pushing me to my feet. 'I don't know, but it'll backfire somehow. I bet he thinks he's got this all corralled away from his ultimate goal, but if his hands aren't actively on the reins then it'll get away from him.'

'And then we'll end up fighting a war on at least two fronts.'

'Which you'll lose.'

'Which we'll lose.'

There wasn't much about The Rider that I believed, but I did put trust in his overall aim to deal with the alleged apocalypse. The methods, agree to disagree, but the goal of saving wizard society didn't smell of bullshit to me. Getting all the malevolent magical monstrosities pushing their boundaries could very easily lead to a much sooner catastrophe without anyone actively working against it. Which meant there was something I was missing here, something vital to understanding his intentions.

What I needed was to compare notes with Charlie, but there was no way she had enough time to cobble together what I had asked of her yet. Maybe I could track down one of the nearest reports, ask it directly what got it all belligerent – but then I would just be rolling on back to my usual gung-ho self and would probably end up with my teeth shoved down my throat.

Best to let this all just sit for a moment, to simmer in my brain.

I caught Bennett looking at me with an eyebrow half-cocked. Before all this, he had a way of moving his eyebrows at me like he was loading a shotgun shell in an action film – an aggressive and sobering bit of visual punctuation. This movement wasn't that, but it still snapped me out of my own thoughts.

I fully cocked my eyebrow. 'You're thinking something.'

'I'm thinking I don't recognise you,' he said. 'You look tired.'

My laugh was vicious, unexpected. '*I* look tired? Bennett, mate, you look like the anti-matter universe's Rip Van Winkle. The last time I saw someone in as big a need of a kip as you, he'd spent the best part of a week raving his way around the entirety of Ibiza. He had more coke in his system than an advertising executive.'

'Sound like a fun guy to know,' Bennett said. 'Even your quips are a little forced. Is it really so bad out there that you are being forced to *be serious*?'

I nearly threw up in my mouth. 'There's not a power on this earth that can make me serious.'

His eyebrow un-cocked, but I could see that he knew I was right. Clearly, there was a lot he didn't know but I couldn't bring myself to tell him everything. How do you tell someone that you've seen the future and it's a big naked dude climbing out of the Aegean to fuck things up? I mean, yeah, I had told a couple of people that, but they had a bit of a run-up – Bennett would be going in cold. Looking at him now, he had enough to deal with.

I steered the conversation away from business and into the thick sludge of small talk. Bennett wasn't really into it, and neither was I, but I had to find a way to kill some time. Small talk was a skill I had once been proficient in, but everything had been big talk for so long I found myself floundering. Before long, Bennett excused himself and I realised I had outstayed my welcome.

On the way out of the door, something began to itch in my brain. It was a sort of skittering static, like a trillion baby spiders had hatched beneath my scalp. It put me on edge – obviously – and I found myself holding my muscles tense whenever I passed a shadow. The Rider was overdue one of his smug visits wearing Robin's face, and damn him if the notion of such a visit hadn't already started to programme my anxiety to kick in.

After a minute the itch subsided and The Rider was a no-show, but the anxiety would linger for at least an hour. He could be anywhere, essentially be any*one*, so the idea that he wouldn't know we were on to him caved in on itself, leaving a big black hole of trepidation. For all I knew, he could have watched my entire conversation with Bennett. Hell, he could have *been* Bennett.

The weather had turned biting cold, so I ducked into a little coffee shop and bought the cheapest, blackest, most tar-like brew to just hold and keep my hands warm. Picking at the polystyrene cup, I started thinking over what Bennett had said one more time before being interrupted by the insistent buzzing of my phone.

I pulled it out and checked my notifications – a text from Kaitlyn van Ives. The absolute brass balls on her, honestly.

'*Sorry,*' it read. '*Would explain, but you'd still hate me.*'

Not a great apology, if I'm honest. I've got years of experience crafting a good one, and this missed the mark by a mile. I squeezed the damned phone so hard I felt the screen would crack before I forced myself to put it away and take a long gulp of my horrible coffee.

People were watching me.

I'd clocked them when I first came in – heads turning and conversations halting immediately – but I had chalked that up to your typical regular clientele mindset, stare at the new guy. For a fair few of them, that had certainly been the case. They went back to their drinks and stopped paying me any attention. A few rows down the room, however, a table of women was watching me with great interest. I don't know whether that interest was malicious in nature or not, but considering the shape I was in I wasn't in the mood to take any risks. Back out into the cold I went, fully expecting them to follow me.

They didn't.

I took a few sharp turns just to be safe, doubled back on myself, made it difficult for them to keep track of me if they were indeed out to get me. Once I felt my tracks were suitably covered, I slumped into a cold metal bench inside a colder bus shelter and let myself breathe.

You stupid fucking idiot, I found myself thinking. *You're letting that obnoxious corpse get in your head. He's making you paranoid.*

It might surprise you to hear, but that little pep talk did very little to calm my nerves.

There was a tiny knife in my wallet. It wasn't long or sharp enough to function as a weapon or anything, but it was great for whipping up a quick spell circle in a pinch. Chalk is better, but dear god, the mess.

Extracting my knife, I engaged in a morsel of vandalism, carving a small circle into the ageing paint of the bus shelter. Millie Thatcher had taught me a couple of runic spells to help calm the mind, and while they had served as the basis for this one, I'd made extensive modifications. I carved out her runes, my additions, and filled the circle with my own power, letting it cook for a few seconds. Then I drew it all back in quickly, one big hit of rejuvenating energy.

My senses all fogged over for a moment before switching back on in ultra-high definition. It was like a reboot of my operating system, an enema flushing out all the bilge that was sloshing around in my brain. I sat there, slumped against the frozen steel of the shelter, panting while everything finished coming back into focus.

Much better. I'd purged the paranoia and the anxiety, now my head was clear enough to actually *think* about things instead of just filling up with them.

I grabbed my phone to check the time and found a set of emails awaiting me, all from Charlie. She had worked fast, pulled a whole mess of files, and forwarded them to me in batches. I started idly swiping through them, letting the details wash over me.

The details. Something was off about the emails themselves, not the files, but I couldn't quite latch onto it. Probably didn't matter anyway – the files were all there, that was what I needed. I just needed to find the ones that matched up with what Bennett had been saying.

A cursory glance backed up what he had been saying: the closer we got to the present day, the fewer major casefiles were being generated. It didn't take me long to find some files that directly shut down some of the problems that were on the noticeboard too, and with a thoroughly decisive resolution to boot. You don't kick some magical beastie's arse this hard and have it come rocking back this quickly. Either every warlock was padding their files, or this was my smoking gun.

That was enough proof to justify a little excursion, right? I wasn't being gung-ho or reckless, I'd done enough to paint this as a serious enough problem that we should look into it.

I clicked off the files and called Charlie. She answered on the first ring. 'Where the bloody hell have you been?'

'Out, you know that.'

'You've been unreachable for hours, you dickhead!'

'I think you're being a bit dramatic,' I said as diplomatically as I could. 'It's been like one hour, tops.'

'Try five.'

I snorted. 'God, you do exaggerate. Anyway, I've looked over the files you sent, and I've got a plan.'

'Jim, you can't just swan back in and—'

'We pick one of the cases that definitely shouldn't be up on the board, solve it, and then ask the beastie why it's causing trouble. I figure that will give us a direct line to The Rider.'

Charlie grumbled to herself. 'I... Fine, yes, that's not an entirely unworkable plan. I'm going to go ahead and guess you had a specific file in mind.'

'Actually, yes, there was one that caught my eye.'

'It's the dragon, isn't it?'

I managed to stifle the chuckle. 'Despite my reputation, I don't always make the worst choice just because it is also the coolest. Besides, I prefer to steer clear of politics.'

'You're seriously not going after the dragon?' she asked. I might as well have told her I was a flat-Earther given the sheer level of disbelief saturating her words. 'It's relatively close, all but a suicide mission, plus *a dragon*. Doesn't sound like you to just leave that alone.'

I put on my haughtiest tone. 'It's called *personal growth*, Chaz. Besides, I picked something even closer and just as cool.'

'Ah, here we go,' she said. 'I sense a catch incoming. What do you need from me?'

'A lift.'

She was very accommodating, agreeing to pick me up with only another five or so minutes of borderline playful insults. As soon as she finally hung up, I checked the time. She was right, I had been out a lot longer than I thought – several hours more. A little concerning, but I was pretty sure I'd just let things get away from me while I was reading or chatting with Bennett. No big deal.

Charlie rolled up about twenty minutes later, once more accompanied by Wolfgang who was driving a non-descript estate car. I didn't recognise the vehicle, but I caught glimpses of some heavy-duty warding inscribed on the tyres, so it had to be one of ours. Did we have a motor pool now? We were one pair of camo underpants away from becoming a legitimate *organisation* at this rate.

Wolfgang didn't talk, and neither did Charlie save to ask me where we were headed. I gave them the address and let the journey remain silent – I wasn't in the mood to push things, the wounds from earlier were starting to pulse painfully.

I was surprised how quickly Wolfgang got us to where we were going. The address wasn't one I recognised, and I had been working out of Humberside City for years. He, by all accounts, was fresh off the boat but already had a solid knowledge of the spiderweb of streets that made up the city. He drove with such confidence that I almost started to believe he was bullshitting me, just driving to wherever the hell he wanted in such a blasé manner that I'd just accept it as where I really wanted to go after all. But, no, he took me to the exact place I had expected.

If the homeless shelter that Bennett had been forced to live in represented the end stage of falling through the cracks of society, this estate signified the point where people start to stumble. The houses had the look of an old mining town about them – uniform terraces that opened out right onto the pavement – bought up by the council and neglected for decades. The once beige pebbledash walls had turned grey from years of air pollution and miserable northern rain, and even if the sun had been shining, I suspected it was always going to be dark and dreary down here.

It is possible that I'm being a little overly critical.

'You want to tell us which case you picked, then?' Charlie asked. She was trying to play the upbeat comrade as she had on the phone, but the illusion lost a lot of lustre when I could see the cold worry in her eyes.

'No,' I said. 'If I did, you'd only want to come in with me.'

'Need I remind you what happened the last time you went into a potentially dangerous situation alone?'

'You needn't. But staying out here *is* being backup. If things go wrong in there, I won't want to be fighting indoors.'

Charlie frowned at me. 'Why?'

'If I tell you that, where would the gripping drama be?'

I slid out of the car before she could answer, though I did catch an approving smirk from Wolfgang. Curtains were twitching from several houses as I made my way to number 17 and hammered the knocker. Through a frosted glass panel in the door, I caught some movement.

There was the rattle of several chains being removed, equally as many locks being undone, and the door opened slowly.

Five

The inside of the house was much less depressing than the outside. The smell of fresh paint and plaster hit me the moment I stepped inside, barely masking the woody scent of the furniture. The décor was a strange mishmash of styles that really shouldn't have gone together, but liberally applied throw rugs and plush pillows smoothed out the edges enough to counter that.

The resident, a woman in her early twenties with lank mousy hair and eyes greener than fresh-cut emeralds, was already midway through pouring me a cup of tea before I had finished navigating my way to a cosy armchair. The cup rattled against the saucer as she handed it to me.

'You're a warlock?' she said. Her hand was hovering over the sugar bowl.

I held up two fingers and she dutifully dropped a pair of cubes into my drink. 'I used to be. How could you tell?'

'You all have that same look about you. I've seen enough of you to notice.'

'How many of us have you run into over the years?' I took a sip of my tea. It was cold.

'Three or four. I think I scared them off after a couple of visits.'

I put on my best soothing smile. 'I find that hard to believe.'

'You should see me on my bad days.'

Laura Irvine had been the obvious choice for our first attempt at getting a line on The Rider, or had been as soon as I saw the file. Despite her being firmly on what had once been my patch, I'd not heard a word about her for my entire time as a warlock. There had always been other warlocks on duty in Humberside, but they had never been shy about their casefiles before.

Taking a closer look at Ms. Irvine's, however, it didn't take me long to work out why she was an exception.

'From what I've read, your bad days are hardly your fault,' I said.

She smiled meekly, too unsure of herself to make eye contract. 'That's what they all said. But even the ones who believed it didn't stick around. I thought you guys had forgotten about me, or written me off, or something, if I'm honest.'

'When was your last visit?'

Without ceremony, she rolled up the sleeve of her shirt and started counting a latticework of scars as if it was just another everyday activity. Brush teeth, get dressed, count the criss-crossed keloids littering your forearm. 'It's supposed to be every six months, but I think the last visit was closer to nine.'

'Is that why you've felt comfortable enough to let loose lately?'

Her expression changed in an instant, snapping from meek and friendly to harsh and aggressive. The light seemed to land on her differently as well, finding sharp angles where there had previously been smooth curves. 'Comfortable? I haven't been *comfortable* since this was done to me.'

'Done to you, that's an interesting choice of words.'

This was the real reason I couldn't have Charlie in here with me. According to all the files, Laura Irvine was a victim, and I wanted to believe that. The thing was, if the files were to be believed then talking to Laura was ultimately akin to chatting with the monkey. I needed to talk to the organ grinder.

'Yes, done to me!' she shouted. 'This condition, *this affliction*, I had no say in it!'

I shrugged. 'You could have been more alert, listened to all those posters they stick up around universities. You know, the ones about never leaving your drink alone, not letting handsome fuckboys with more dick than brains somehow outsmart you with one beer.'

The whites of her eyes had grown darker, leaving the green irises to shimmer starkly. 'How *dare* you! You come into my home and blame this on me? I was spiked! *Violated!* There's not a day goes by where I don't remember the *abuse* I was forced to endure!'

'Yeah, sure, I suppose,' I said. 'But maybe you led him on a little, you know?'

Ok, so, I am very aware of how shitty this line of interrogation makes me sound. Don't get confused here, victim blaming is trash-tier behaviour. But I needed her angry, and the best way I knew to do that was to poke at the wounds. It's not pretty, and it makes me feel like shit, but sometimes it's necessary.

With Laura, it was necessary.

My last little outburst of vintage man-o-sphere gobshitery did the job. It got in deep under her skin, tickled the insecurities that were nestled in the back of her mind like brass bells strung on silk. The ringing permeated her, and she snapped.

Those gleaming irises snapped, breaking apart like spider webs as her pupils blew out. The sharpness of her features increased until every corner of her face looked like it could draw blood. Her teeth, formerly uniform and straight, lengthened into a predator's fangs, some going so far as to bite into her lower lip. Her general build didn't change much, but her stance quickly shifted to one that matched her new fangs – dangerous and volatile.

Her right hand shot out and closed around my neck, pushing me over the back of the armchair and down hard onto the floor. Swiftly, she dragged me across the exposed floorboards and up the wall until I was standing again, her torn eyes less than an inch from my face.

'You don't come here and cause Laura pain, oathbreaker. She is under my protection.' Even her voice was different, the cadence and emphasis fluctuating like a mangled cassette tape. Or like someone who had to struggle against their nature to keep hold of enough humanity to use something as civilised as basic speech.

'A funny sort of protection, seeing as you're probably the biggest cause of pain for her,' I said. 'But I apologise, truly. I didn't want to hurt her, but I needed to speak to you.'

'Convince me,' she said. *'Quickly.'*

I fidgeted and struggled in her grasp, reaching for my phone. I unlocked it and showed her the file I had left open. Her file. 'There's been an awful lot of buzz about you lately. Out on the town, being a nuisance, that sort of thing. Looking through your history, though, you're the model convict – keep to yourself, never go off the reservation.'

'I get bored,' she said. *'I go out. You are not convincing me.'*

'And you're not convincing *me*,' I shot back. 'Come on, I know how this whole Jekyll and Hyde thing works.'

She snarled and recoiled a little, as if the words caused her physical pain. *'Do not use that term. We do not like it, oathbreaker.'*

'Fine, we can argue the correct nomenclature later if you like. Point is, you wouldn't put Laura in danger, and you *know* that acting up like this does exactly that.'

Her breath was hot on my face, those sharp teeth holding a fraction of an inch from my face. Then, thankfully, I felt her grip loosen and watched as she pulled away. I wasn't sure whether I had just defused the situation or somehow made it worse.

For a moment, she paced in front of me with the attitude of a caged animal. *'I exist to keep her safe.'*

'You exist because some shit-hearted vagician spiked her drink.'

'And then I protected her from him.'

Her eyes were boring into me, but I was making progress. 'You tore off his cock and balls.'

'Root. And. Stem.'

'Exactly, and that's how I know something's up,' I said, swiping through the file. 'All these sightings *suck*. Your heart isn't in it. If you'd pulled this weak-ass pish when you first showed up, no way you'd get the chilling moniker of... What was it again?'

A menacing shiver ran over her flesh as every muscle tensed again, ready to pounce. *'The Beast.'*

'Oh yes. You're not Jekyll and Hyde, you're Beauty and the Beast. Come on, tell me what's really going on. I can help.'

The Beast froze in place, her face a twisted snarl of thought. I found that I was holding my breath, quite literally, to see if I had cracked that outer shell. The fact that I wasn't already in agonising pain was a good sign, but it wasn't entirely off the table just yet.

Just in case, I did one quick check to see what options I had in case a fight broke out. What I had said to Charlie was true, I didn't want to get into a fight indoors if I could help it. The Beast was exponentially stronger than me, and the angrier it became at me, the more Laura shed her humanity, the stronger the Beast would become. Even at the height of my game, I wouldn't have enough magic to go toe-to-toe.

But I could run. Blast out the wall or the window, make a heroic exit out into the street and into the waiting car. Proper Hollywood blockbuster spectacle.

As if reading my thoughts, the Beast stepped between me and the front wall. *'She does not know.'*

'Laura?' I asked, forcing my lungs to work again.

'Yes,' the Beast said slowly. It was considering its words more carefully, and it was clearly struggling. *'I protect her not just from the actions, but the knowledge.'*

Seemed I wasn't going to be Beast-food today after all. 'I know. That's why I needed to bring you out. A protector as skilled as you wouldn't have left her anything to be suspicious about.'

'I clean up before I release her from my embrace. She can live safe and free of guilt or worry.'

Just a little more. One last step. 'What are you protecting her from?'

A fresh spark of rage flared in the Beast, but this time I wasn't scared. I knew it wasn't me stoking this flame. *'He started coming at night. The first time, his lips were at her ear before I could act. He spoke to her as you did, grinding her, fracturing her. She knew he couldn't really be there, but his words still cut deep.'*

'Who?' I asked, though I had a fair idea.

'She never knew his name. I never cared to learn it. When I stared into his eyes as his pitiful life drained from his ruptured nethers, I saw no reason to allow him the dignity of a name.'

Of course, that sneaky son of a bitch. Showing up out of the shadows and wearing the face of my dead girlfriend was too good a party trick to keep reserved just for me – The Rider was tormenting poor Laura Irvine the same way. It must have been a double whammy for her too – wearing the face of someone who violated her in such a way just to delivery vicious mockery from beyond the grave? I'd like to see him claim this was for the greater good.

'How long before he proposed the deal?'

The Beast's eyes narrowed. *'How did you know about the deal?'*

'Educated guess.'

'I learned to spot him, to predict his movements. I could wrap her in my embrace and shut him out, but I could not force him away. He started to visit every night, for longer and longer each time. The strain of such regular and prolonged emergences started to take a heavy toll on her.'

'He waited until you were desperate and then snapped on the leash.'

'I AM NOT LEASHED,' the Beast roared. *'But I accept the analogy…'*

'What were the terms?'

'Amnesty,' the Beast muttered. *'For her. Provided I perform favours. They are juvenile favours at best, he does not expect me to cause harm.'*

Well, of course not. The Rider was too smart for that. Trouble bubbling away at the sidelines, that was just atmosphere, but the moment people started getting hurt was the moment something would have to give. Right now, we were far too busy dealing with ourselves, but if the things that go bump in the night start, you know, *bumping* then those with *ideals* would start making *decisions*.

I swiped through the file again. Charlie had been thorough enough to append any appropriate clippings that had been on the noticeboard, complete with terse observations. There were only a couple of additions for Irvine. 'But you do need to look like you might.'

'*Yes.*' The Beast had a low rumble to simply breathing now, like a chainsaw at rest, and venom started to sprinkle its words as it spoke. '*Pathetic, petty, thug work. Intimidation, not justice. It is beneath me, but I will not have him continue to torment her.*'

I put my phone away and slowly began to draw in some magic. The Beast had their eyes on me, but I was hoping that they were too focused on our conversation to realise I had a hand behind my back, rapidly signing out a complex somatic formula. The magic coalesced in my fingertips, making them tingle unpleasantly.

'I'm willing to bet you aren't the only one he's been coercing.'

'*I am not. There are times when we are forced to work in unison, myself and others. They are base creatures worth nothing but contempt, and yet I am forced to ally myself with them.*'

I shook my head. 'I'm seeing it now. You're the rock dropped in the water, the others you have to work alongside are the ripples. A big, terrifying thing likes you grabs the attention, then the lesser horrors ride your waves and keep the news cycle bustling.'

'*They revel in the destruction,*' the Beast said. She snorted with disgust. '*I have a higher purpose, they have none.*'

They were natural followers, though. The Beast wasn't someone you wanted on your payroll for longer than you absolutely required – always looking for a way out of its cage, it'd carve your throat out the moment it had the opportunity. The same was true of the other big beasties on the board. But things like coblynau, squonks, all those little mischiefs would gravitate to anyone with enough personality to get them in their thrall.

The *what* of all of this was starting to come together. Running down the files in my head, I could already see a number of ways The Rider could coerce the quieter monsters into fucking shit up for him, and that was before I even considered the deals he could have made with the ones that had already been chafing at their shackles. It was exactly the same methodology as what he had done with the warlocks, except in this case the warlocks had been serving as the Vault for the beasties.

People have a habit of thinking that the sort of mind that can plan a thousand moves ahead is some sort of chessmaster. I've never really agreed with that, though. Chessmasters have to anticipate your actions because they are playing a game with you – you're white, they're black, move and counter-move. If they play well, they win. But that didn't hold for The Rider.

This was dominoes. He was painstakingly setting us up, one by one, so a single flick would set off a beautiful cascade. For it to work, we all had to be perfectly arranged, each piece ready to send the next one tumbling.

The dominoes never win.

'You've been a great help,' I said. 'And for what it's worth, you have my sympathies.'

The Beast cocked her head to one side like a confused dog. *You will not try to prevent me from holding up my end of the deal? Our agreement with Whitehall—*'

'I don't work for Whitehall anymore,' I interrupted. 'No warlock does. Eventually they might get around to sending someone to enforce the old contracts, but not today.'

'I… appreciate that.' The beast struggled to get those words out, even more than her usual speech. *'You are the first oathbreaker to show understanding.'*

That pulled at something in my chest. The truth was, I did understand – the Beast hadn't wanted to be here, it was just some slumbering spark in Laura's subconscious before it had been mutated and violated by magic. It wasn't something with a drive to cause misery, but it was willing to go to the dark side if it meant keeping a promise. It was an idea, packaged and processed and pushed out into the world.

Despite the name, the Beast wasn't a monster.

But it was a liability.

I nodded my head ever so slightly in a respectful show of understanding, then I held out my hand. 'I give you my word, I will not try to get in the way of your deal.'

The Beast regarded my outstretched hand with confusion for a moment. Gingerly, it raised its own hand and awkwardly slid it into mine, shaking it with a grip so tight that I could feel my knuckles rubbing against one another.

It was then that I cast the spell.

Its hand clasping mine, I swung my casting arm around and slapped my hand onto the Beast's forehead. My fingers, sizzling with magic, pressed hard against the skin, nails digging into the skin, magic forcing its way through into the core of her brain. Visualising its path, I followed it beyond the meat and into the meta, the electrical charges that gave life to thought and feeling. Deep inside, I found the kernel of magic that had infected the poor girl, the mutation that unlocked the Beast, and I chained it.

Inside Laura's mind the Beast gnashed and fought me, trying to tear out my sanity with claws that weren't really there. I pinned it down, wrapped it in thick links of hardened steel fastened with padlocks, and I hurled it down into the darkness.

The smell of ozone filled the air and my eyes filled with tears. Once I blinked them away, I found myself staring into the terrified, but normal, emerald eyes of Laura Irvine. The sharp features of the Beast had receded, leaving behind the rather ordinary young lady. Her mouth flopped open and closed soundlessly a couple of times, her breathing erratic and uneven.

She pulled her hand out of my grip and skittered backwards towards the wall, screaming in terror. Hitting it hard, she pulled herself down into a tight ball and started to cower. The prison I had built around the Beast wouldn't hold forever, but it was sturdy enough to take that piece off the board for a while – shit, now I'm doing the chess thing anyway. To lock that door, though, I had to go right to the root, and that meant I'd had to take away Laura's very notion of bravery.

Until the Beast could break out of that prison, the poor girl would be in total abject terror. It would be unrelenting.

So, yeah, this was the real reason I didn't want Charlie coming inside with me. Getting into a big fight was certainly one of the reasons, don't get me wrong, but if I could draw a solid link between Laura and The Rider, I need to sever that connection immediately. I wasn't sure that Charlie would have been able to accept that call.

Looking at her now, I wasn't sure it was a call that I would be able to accept.

I left quickly, slamming the door behind me and all but running back to the waiting car. Charlie opened the door for me, leaning across the back seat to pull the release, but I hesitated to get in. The Rider had been denied one of his playing pieces, but it wasn't as if I had the time to shut them all down. A greatest hits tour of the Northeast was not on the cards, but it was clear that something would need to be done, otherwise what good was the living hell I had just left that woman in?

One deep breath later and I was in the car.

'I hope you weren't too bored, the pair of you,' I said.

Wolfgang shrugged and fastened his seatbelt. 'I had a nap.'

'And tried to chat me up,' Charlie said pointedly.

Again, Wolfgang shrugged, but this time he kept his mouth shut. Apparently, getting shot down by Charlie hadn't had a major effect on him.

'Fair enough,' I said. 'Anyway, think I've got enough here to make a pretty solid case that The Rider is the one whipping up the gribblies.'

Wolfgang frowned. 'Did we not already know this?'

'Yes,' I shot back. 'But now we've got proof. Well, not *proof* I guess, but definitely *authority* or something. *Confirmation.*'

Charlie had her head against the window of the car, her eyes closed. 'But what good does that do us? Do you know what he's trying to distract us from?'

'Not exactly. We won't be able to find that while all this noise is going on, it'll have too much cover. But if we can turn the volume down a bit…'

'How do you propose to do that?'

I ran my thumbnail over my fingers, feeling the last few prickles of the spell finally melt away. 'If we take this to the various factions, we could possibly get a ceasefire or something agreed, at least long enough to turn over a few rocks.'

'Do you think—' Charlie began.

Wolfgang interrupted her, slapping his hand on the back of the passenger seat. 'Quiet. Look.'

He pointed across the street at a car that was idling by the side of the road. It was long and blocky, an old-style Jaguar, painted a burnt gold. Four men were sat in the car, staring right at us.

I felt a twinge of panic tickle the base of my spine. 'How long have they been there?'

'Since just after we arrived,' Wolfgang said. 'Pulled up when you went inside, but they weren't suspicious until now.'

I leant forward to get a better look. 'Does anyone recognise them?'

They were just far enough away that I couldn't get a decent look at them. From this distance, they just all seemed to blur into four instances of the same pale, potato-faced goon. A brief glance with my magical senses confirmed my first thought, that they were under a glamour – something subtle enough to make you ignore them, but not heavy-duty enough to work as a proper disguise. That meant other wizards then, or possibly an arcane monster of some description.

'I can't really make them out,' Charlie said. 'But they definitely seem like bad news.'

As if on cue, the doors of the car opened in unison and the four men climbed out. I felt energy flowing past me and I looked to see Wolfgang massaging a nascent spell in his palm, his jaw set and his nostrils flaring. As the men took a step towards us, I began to put together a spell of my own.

As suddenly as they had got out the car, the men stopped. One of the two that had emerged from the back seat snapped his fingers to get the attention of the others as he pressed a finger to his ear. An earpiece maybe? He nodded a couple of times, clearly in response to someone's orders, then shook his head at the others. They turned around and left us be.

And went immediately to Laura's front door.

'We should go,' I said.

Charlie's hand gripped my shoulder hard. 'What? What about whoever it was you went to see in there?'

'They can take care of themselves,' I lied. 'But right now, those guys are pre-occupied. We can't be sure they'll find us quite so uninteresting once they're done inside. I don't want to get in a scrap with people I don't know anything about.'

'Never stopped you before.'

She had me there. I'd gotten into fights with much less provocation and planning than this, and there was no chance she'd buy the excuse that I was trying to be *mature* and *show growth*. But, likewise, I didn't want her seeing Laura in the state in which I had left her.

I didn't want to see Laura in that state.

'Then think of it this way,' I said, sharply. 'The woman in that house is a Hyde.'

'Jesus,' Wolfgang muttered.

'Yeah, exactly.'

Charlie's eyes widened. 'If they kick in that door…'

'They're going to get a face full of teeth, and once her blood's up she won't stop at just them.'

'Then we have to stop them, right?' Charlie said. 'Because she's got *neighbours*.'

Well, shit. My attempt to make a speedy exit, to put distance between me and my latest questionable action, had properly backfired now, huh? Given time, maybe I could come up with some smooth and persuasive reason about how her neighbours wouldn't be in danger, but in the moment my mind was blank. I'd sprinted into a fucking cul-de-sac.

'Ok, fine. Bloody *fine*, we'll stop them. Just give me a minute.'

In an absolutely masterful huff, I threw open the car door and stomped back out into the street. The potato men didn't seem to care, busy as they were trying to pick the lock on Laura's door. As I got closer, one of the men turned and flashed me a glare that practically screamed *don't try it, dickhead.*

So, I punched him in the face.

In the few seconds it had taken me to cross the road back to the house, I had weighed up my options and found that the best course of action was also the simplest. If they had just wanted in the house, they would already be battering the door in. Picking the lock meant they wanted to draw as little attention as possible. And what draws more attention than a fistfight in the middle of the street?

The man I had punched stood up slowly, pulling himself up to his full height. He towered over me, much taller on this side of the road than he had looked from a distance. Sneering down at me, his gaze had me rooted to the spot while the other three stopped what they were doing.

I clapped my hands together and made a big show of pushing some magic into my fists, making them glow and crackle. 'Which one of you *bitches* wants to dance?'

All of them, it turned out.

I'm not a great fighter, we all know this. That said, despite their size and bulk, these guys were shit at kicking my arse. Their punches were slow, meaty, but also wild and thrown in such a haphazard manner that I could have made them look like chumps if I had wanted to. That's not me doing some arrogant chest-pounding either, they were atrocious. This meant I really couldn't fight back – I needed them to make a spectacle of themselves, and even outnumbering me as they did, I'd be able to end that fight far too quickly if I tried.

They landed four or five thundering blows to my generously stationary form before Wolfgang, god help his soul, decided to ruin everything by helping me.

Whatever magic they practice over in Germany, it is brutally efficient. Discs of shimmering air slammed into each potato man in turn, hammering them with the force of a manhole cover. All four of them, spark out inside a second. Counting all my teeth, I looked up in time to see the handsome German glowering down at the men, muttering what I assumed to be Germanic swears under his breath.

'Are you alright?' he asked.

'I'm fine,' I said, brushing his hand away as he tried to help me up. 'That was all part of the plan.'

'Charlie said the same thing, but I thought—'

'That you'd come riding to my defence?'

'I *thought*,' he repeated, much slower this time. 'That you had something smarter planned than being a punching bag.'

I looked around the street. Curtains were twitching, but it wasn't enough. Maybe the sort of nosey old crone that is proud to stick a neighbourhood watch badge in her window would note down our number plates, but that wouldn't be enough to scare the potatoes off.

They'd wake up in a bit, dust themselves off, and then try again.

Ok, fuck it. I'd simplify the whole thing.

'Get back in the car, we're going to need to leave pretty fucking fast in a second.'

Confused, Wolfgang scanned the street for himself. 'It's quite as a tomb here.'

'Yeah, but we don't want it to be.'

One more spell, a nice and simple little thing. I pointed at the Jag, still idling on the curb, and made a couple of quick gestures. The engine dutifully exploded, shredding the bonnet and sending bits of spark plug and *something*-manifold scattering like shrapnel. Pretty sure a couple of windows got cracked.

I was, however, positive that all the curtains were twitching now.

Now, obviously, this isn't something you want to get into the habit of relying upon, but the brain of your typical mundane is very good at refusing to believe in magic. I'd drawn some attention, but it wouldn't last – they'd convince themselves of a very normal and decidedly boring reason for what they had seen. Provided no-one hung around to rock the boat.

Without a word, I once more went back to our car and strapped myself in while Charlie and Wolfgang stared at me, completely agog. As we pulled away, I could already hear the sirens in the distance – not a bad response time, maybe they *were* already on their way.

All that just to avoid the chance of disappointing Charlie. Maybe I should have trusted that she would understand what I did, see it from my side. Laura's beast wouldn't be able to stand up to The Rider, it wasn't built that way, and eventually he'd get it to do something truly heinous. I needed to close that door and lock it tight before he even started getting his foot in there. It was cruel, but necessary. It wasn't as if she was going to be like that forever, anyway. It was just temporary, long enough for me to get a handle on this.

Yeah, I don't think I believed that either.

Six

I had Wolfgang drop me off at home, and he was more than happy to oblige. Neither he nor Charlie said one word to me on the drive, and I can't say I blamed them. They'd probably work things out given a few more hours, piece together why I had been so peculiar in how we handled the potato men, and why I had blown up the car.

Charlie would probably go back, find Laura Irvine huddled in the corner and shitting herself, then come back and kick me to death.

Until that happened, I needed to take a moment to think. Shocking, I know.

Once it had become clear that we were going to be focusing our attention on Humberside City again for a while, I had made sure to put a few havens together just in case. Our secret hideout was the main sanctuary, obviously, but one of the perks of supposed leadership is the right to just fuck off when people are too bothersome to deal with. I couldn't do that if I was only able to kip on one of those communal bunks.

This haven was a shipping container slowly rusting under the big suspender bridge that marked the city limits. I'd thrown up a couple of wards to make it harder to notice, borrowed some space to make it a bit less pokey, even risked carting some furniture up there to make it feel a little less like a cold steel box.

Didn't work.

There's only so much you can do to make a rusty rectangle liveable, at least without a film crew and a daytime TV budget. What it lacked in comfort, however, it made up for in being the perfect place to sit and think. The acoustics of such a place have a way of turning any noise into that soothing, susurrous static – and that's before we get into the weirdness of how sound travels when parts of your location are *technically* hundreds of miles away from each other.

I took a few snootfuls of the cold, tinny air, undressed, and padded into the shower. I'd borrowed the bathroom piecemeal from a hotel I had spotted on the way into town. It had been shuttered during the pandemic, so I didn't feel like it was much of a risk to bolt an entire suite to my secret shelter. It was the one thing I couldn't compromise on – if you're going to be laying low in a metal box, you're going to need hot water.

It was a difficult set of hours to wash off, but I managed it. Wrapping a musty towel around me, I moved back into the main room, bare feet cringing at the change from shaggy bathmat to cold metal. I could feel my hair flash-freeze at the sudden drop in temperature.

'Parker.'

Kaitlyn van Ives was crouched by the entrance, hunched over a box of tinned meals. There was a clank as she stood up and a tin toppled out of the container.

'Make yourself at home, why don't you?' I said. 'Oh, but while you're here, I think you left something behind the last time we met. *Is this your honking big knife that you left lodged in my spine?*'

Her expression was dead, her eyes glassy. 'Tradecraft. It wasn't personal.'

'Yeah, well, it felt pretty personal to me.'

I ripped open a different cardboard box and pulled out a bag of fresh clothes – one of those vacuum sealable things that infomercials used to *love*. Breaking the seal, I yanked out some clothes and started to get dressed. Kaitlyn could have an eyeful if she wanted, I wasn't about to stand around in that temperature bollock naked and risk irreversible shrinkage.

'It was a calculation and it paid off,' she said, thankfully averting her gaze. 'No hard feelings.'

I stopped midway into doing up my fly and gawked at her. 'No hard feelings? *All* the hard feelings. My feelings, such as they are, exist in a state of permanent, unmalleable hardness. By the end of the week, scientists in the god damned Hardon Collider will be obliterating God particles against my feelings and powering the planet with the resulting explosion.'

'Parker...'

'And yes, I know it's *had*ron collider, and I don't really know what they do there, but I do know that thanks to you I've got a target on my back with those Aegis arse faces.'

'Parker,' she said again, her voice a little quieter. 'Aegis won't be a problem.'

I opened my mouth to throw another barb of disbelief into her face, but I stopped short. Finally, I let her expression register in my brain. 'Kaitlyn, what did you do?'

She turned her back on me. 'Followed through on the plan. Stopped the community from fracturing.'

'*Kaitlyn.*'

Her shoulders were trembling, and her voice started to break. 'People were starting to listen to them. No matter how much I clawed and politicked, I was losing the support of key members of the community. But then you went to talk to the Aegis, and we got evidence of how radical they are.'

'When they attacked me.'

'You have to understand, Parker,' she said, steel creeping into her voice. 'People might not like you, but they respect your part in taking down the Vault. It wasn't hard to spin that against them.'

'And force them out.'

Kaitlyn shook her head slowly, before staring back over her shoulder at me with one wet and bloodshot eye. 'And destroy them.'

I'm not sure I've ever had the air driven out of my body by a look before, but that one is a sure-fire contender for the title. There was a cold, dispassionate pride in that eye – it said that while this may weigh heavy on her conscience for a while, that was a burden she could bear.

'They aren't the first to attack me since this all started.'

'But they were the first with *standing*.'

'Get out.'

A shiver of anger washed over her, something deep and primal, but she locked it away before she turned around to face me again. 'I haven't even told you why I'm here.'

'I don't care. Get out.'

'Parker,' she said. 'With the Aegis gone, I've got the support of all the major factions behind me. I want to bring the minor factions into the fold next, get all those who are unaligned on board. We'll finally be in a position to put forward our demands.'

'You don't have all the major factions, Kaitlyn. You don't have the warlocks.'

There should have been an eye twitch or a snarl or something. I had caught her out with my signature brand of smugness, but she didn't appear to have any reaction to that. 'That's why I came to see you in person. You deserve to hear this offer from me. I want you to pledge your support, it'll put an end to any further dissent and unify the community.'

'Under you.'

'Well... Yes.'

'Well, you have all the treachery of a proper politician, I suppose this was only a matter of time.'

She blew some air out of her nose and balled her fists. 'God dammit, Parker. I've set the tone now. If you don't show your support, they're going to start expecting me to do to the warlocks what I did to the Aegis group. Anything less, and I'm weakening my hand before the first card hits the table.'

'Eat shit and fuck off, Kaitlyn,' I shot back. 'We've spent the last five years shackled to self-serving, double crossing, political snakes. The Rider couldn't charm us, and you're not going to have any better luck.'

'You're comparing me to *him*?'

'You're both trying to put yourself at the top of the pyramid, no matter what you say!'

Kaitlyn's eyes swivelled down towards my hands. I followed her gaze and found them shimmering with blood-red magic that I hadn't even realised I had called to me. I pushed it away, let the spell dissipate – god knows I didn't need to add yet another fight to my day.

She relaxed a little as my spell bled away, but she still looked uneasy. 'You'll be getting reports about the Aegis tomorrow, I'm sure. Read them. I'll be in touch.'

Turning sharply, she was out the door and gone before I could muster some quality new swear words to push her out.

There were a few ways I could think of that painted this as a good thing – it was a blow to The Rider for sure, supplanting him as the figurehead of the magical community – but I had to work hard for any positives to not immediately lose their lustre.

Kaitlyn might have been sitting on the throne right now, but I found it impossible to believe that The Rider would let her stay there. If his plans had included her at the head of his wizard army come judgement day, he'd have put his energy into grooming her instead of me. No, he'd find a way to strike back at her, and I couldn't see that ending any other way than utter carnage. All those cracks and fractures Kaitlyn had papered over? They'd be bloody *canyons* by the time he was done.

Maybe that *had* been his plan, it was impossible to say anymore. His scheme was so fucking inscrutable that trying to work it out just seemed to leave us with even less idea of what he was doing than when we started. Maybe that was where we were going wrong…

I had really thought the Aegis would be a bigger threat. They had The Rider's backing. More than that, they were his catspaws in this. They had been his main recruitment tool, especially when it came to getting me on side. It didn't seem right that he would just let them get obliterated so quickly, especially when they had barely even started trying to turn me.

My bed, a thin mattress of memory foam balanced on a stack of plastic crates, creaked as I fell back onto it and let my eyes close. I would deal with this in the morning, no point in letting it ruin what little sleep I'd be able to get. Nothing to be done until the reports started coming in.

Completely true, but I couldn't convince my brain to shut the hell up long enough for me to get even an iota of decent sleep. I did get several minutes, possibly even a full hour, of piss poor sleep, though.

Maybe, one day, I'd get to close off one problem before a new one reared its ugly head. It wasn't looking likely, but I'm nothing if not an optimist.

When I woke up, my phone was buzzing non-stop, having vibrated its way onto the floor. It made the container sing like a bell full of bees, which I think might have helped knock me back into the right mindset to deal with the mountain of shit that I knew was awaiting me. Thirty-five missed calls and enough text messages that the little notification bar had given up counting. I guess Kaitlyn hadn't been lying after all.

I wasn't going to call in for this, it was something better dealt with in person. Once I was back at the hideout, I could puff up my chest and spit out enough authority to calm things down and take charge. Couldn't do that on the phone, Charlie would probably hang up on me the minute I tried to do anything commanding.

But, once I was there, I could fix this. Easy peasy.

*

Of course, I fucking couldn't. Jesus Christ, have you met me?

I'd been in actual war-rooms with more calm than I was seeing at that moment in the hideout. A group of warlocks had gathered at one end of the room, clustered around Charlie and a couple of others I didn't recognise, shouting in a register only achievable by the extremely sleep deprived. Whenever things had broken down to this state, it had clearly been going on for a while if Charlie's expression was anything to go by.

Slowly, I took off my coat and draped it over the small banister that flanked the tiny staircase leading from the entrance to the main floor. I adjusted my cuffs, my collar, smoothed down my hair and the ever-bushier beard that had decided to make a home on my face, then drew in a little power and slapped my hand against the wall.

Pushing my power through the plaster, I sent it searching for the metal skeleton of the building itself. When the nightclub had been built, it had been at the heart of a redevelopment campaign for the whole area, no expense had been spared, and that meant there was enough steel embedded in the skeleton of the thing to sing like a campanologist's wet dream.

I gripped that skeleton and forced it to make the biggest "*dong*" this side of a Ron Jeremy convention.

For a split second, everyone in that building stopped shouting just long enough to shit themselves. I had rattled the load-bearing structure of the entire building, and now they had something to worry about that was a more immediately concern than haranguing Charlie – potentially getting crushed to death by falling masonry. Obviously, I had no intention of bringing the roof down on them, but they didn't know that.

'*Right*,' I shouted as the ringing died away. 'We're all going to take a breath and step away from the lady, or someone is going to get their nethers ensorcelled.'

The group stared at me with tiredness and more than a little confusion, but they took my warning seriously. A little shuffling ensued as they disbanded from a crowd into more of a throng, some even breaking away entirely and skulking out to one of the other rooms. Those that remained gave me enough room to authoritatively march through the centre and right up to Charlie and the people with her.

'Screening your calls?' Charlie said. 'I left you a lot of messages, you know.'

I shrugged. 'No-one listens to voicemails anymore. What the hell is going on?'

'Kaitlyn van Ives massacred the Aegis,' she said. 'Look.'

She grabbed a tablet from a nearby table and pulled up a video on it. It had the aesthetics of an Al Qaeda press release but the production values of a Netflix miniseries.

On screen, Kaitlyn van Ives stood in front of a stark red background, emblazoned with some log that was so sleek and simple that it could only have cost a fortune in graphic designer fees. She had the full Zapatista ensemble going on – black trousers, earthy-coloured shirt, a beret that looked like it was cut from the same material that carpeted dilapidated bowling alleys. Her wild red hair had been tightly plaited on the side and ran down over her left shoulder.

Her eyes were staring down the barrel of the camera, her face set. 'Earlier today, a group of radicals made an attack on the way of life we, as a community, are building. Jameson Parker, the very warlock responsible for the destruction of the Vault, met with these radicals on a mission of peace, and they attacked him. Brutalised him.'

The shot changed to one of me lying bleeding out in the street, blood dribbling out across the pavement. I still have no idea how they got that photo, but I'll never get the image of it out of my head. A bloody mound of shimmering needles, leaking fluid like human colander – it didn't even look like a person in that light, let alone me.

'Jameson Parker is not perfect,' van Ives continued. 'He and the warlocks like him are collaborators and there will be a price to pay for that, but it is not for one small group to decide what that price should be. We, as a community, must come together as one if we are to survive when Whitehall finishes regrouping. Breeding division, such as that sort by Aegis, is a far greater crime than collaboration. It's treason.'

'Fuck me,' I muttered under my breath. My blood turned to ice in my veins.

Again, the camera cut, this time to shaky chest-cam footage. At first, it was hard to make out what we were even looking at what with all the artifacting and the muddy darkness. Then, a bright flash lit the screen – a breaching spell, shattering a wall like glass – and things became a lot clearer to follow. A pair of men moved in front of the camera, backs to the lens, but they kept enough of a gap between them to let the cameraman document things.

There was shouting, a lot of it. Too much to really decipher in the recording, but loud enough to make the sound clip. Someone moved in front of the camera, and I recognised him instantly: Efraim Kingsley. His face was red with anger, and he was almost frothing at the mouth.

'This is too far, van Ives!' he bellowed. 'Even for you!'

From somewhere over his shoulder there was a blinding flash, then another. The voices raised to an even more undecipherable level as Kingsley shot a glance over his shoulder.

'God dammit!' he shouted off screen. 'Do nothing! Say nothing!'

But it was already too late. He could barely finish his plea before the screen was filled with the shimmering lights of combat, the screams of pain. The cameraman didn't capture it all, mercifully, but he got enough to turn my stomach – a flash of a man being roasted by pyromancy, a woman impaled against a wall by a spear of pure force, a whole group of people swallowed up by the ground below their feet and compacted into a watery ball of limbs and *meat*.

Kingsley was the last man standing, battered and bloody, defiantly facing down Kaitlyn's hit squad as they closed in around him. They blasted him down to his knees, his shield buckling under their assault, before they obliterated his head with one final spell. The cameraman moved back to the entrance and panned over the destruction slowly.

There are no words.

Kaitlyn van Ives found some, however, as soon as the camera cut back to her. 'We can't do this alone. The Aegis were not the shield of the magical community, but *we* will be. A united community is a strong community, and one that can stand up to Whitehall once and for all. Our loyalty lies with you, now you have to decide if yours lies with us.'

One more cut, this time to a full-screen view of the logo on a fluttering red flag. It was every psychotic revolutionary's dream broadcast, provided said revolutionary had watched V For Vendetta five hundred times.

Charlie threw the tablet back onto the table and stared at me, looking for some reaction. I'm not sure what reaction my face was showing, but my guts were having a very *violent* response to what I had just seen – I had to take huge gulps of air just to keep a lid on that squid.

'It's war,' I eventually managed to say, so quietly that even I struggled to hear it. 'Kaitlyn's starting a fucking war.'

'It's actually worse than that,' one of the people behind Charlie said. Now that I was closer, I recognised her as Sophie Preston, finally up and on her feet again.

I shot her a pained smile. 'Good to see you pulled through just in time to give me bad news.'

She was all business, glaring at me from beneath a sharp fringe that did its best to cover a very angry scar. 'People are asking if you were involved.'

'Because van Ives put my name front and centre.'

'Exactly,' she said. 'Smelled too much like a bit of spin for me to buy it, but some of the others have concerns.'

'Hence the mob.'

Charlie snarled. 'Hence the mob. Warlocks and the few free mage friends alike are making it very clear that they aren't on board with massacring other mages.'

'And neither am I,' I said.

'Well, they don't know that,' Charlie said. She was glancing behind me, no doubt watching the group for any signs that my commanding presence was starting to wear off. 'All they know is van Ives was here for a chat with you, you got hurt, and suddenly she's invoking your name as an excuse for a purge.'

'There's a reasonable amount of us who know that it's bullshit, but not enough,' Preston said.

I thought back to the text Kaitlyn had sent me, and to what she had told me in my secret hidey-hole. The woman on the broadcast was steadfast as hardened steel, but that wasn't the Kaitlyn that I had been with.

As her reach had grown, so had the scope of her activities, but I wasn't sure the realities had meshed well with her morals. She could play the part for the cameras, but I'd seen the weight of it in how she had talked to me.

Did that mean much? Probably not. Whether she was conflicted about these actions or not, the fact remained that she had transmitted a declaration of war, or something that was close enough to one. By putting herself as the main force opposing Whitehall, she controlled the narrative – anyone who didn't play along could be branded collaborators, she'd subtly laboured that point nicely. An old tactic out of an ancient playbook, but a classic for a reason.

I turned to Preston. 'I'm guessing you've got a good feel for the general mood of the gang. How many of them want to sign up with van Ives?'

'None,' she said. 'That's the problem. The angry sods aren't asking when we're going to sign up, they're complaining about it seeming like we already have and they were the last to know.'

'Or that we're about to,' I said, finishing her point for her. 'What the hell is she doing? First, we put this fire out, then, Charlie, I need you to get some boffins together so we can talk this through.'

'Look at you being all bossy,' Charlie said. 'I'll draw up a list.'

I gave her a nod, then a second for Preston, and turned back towards the crowd. The patience that I'd dragged out of them with my little warning was starting to boil away. They were pulling in close again, people awkwardly rocking as they prepared to let the rage and confusion back in, and the questions back out.

I needed to shut that shit down before it even started.

'All right, you horrible lot,' I shouted, using my best Cockney Sergeant voice. 'Calm your tits. Despite what that woman might have said, we're not signing on to anything. We're not working with Kaitlyn van Ives, and we're not condoning the wholesale slaughter of people just for disagreeing.'

'Bullshit,' someone shouted from inside the group. 'You had a meeting with her yesterday and suddenly she's *so concerned* when you get lit up that she commits a mass murder? You really expect us to buy that you haven't put us in bed with her, one way or the other?'

I spotted the owner of the voice. It was a man in his late twenties, dressed up like a stockbroker – expensive suit, braces, expertly trimmed facial hair – which was a look that matched his voice well. He was another mage I didn't know, but I could tell from the way he dressed that he wasn't one of the warlocks.

Once he was done throwing accusations, I started moving towards him. 'We're not in anyone's bed, pal. Yeah, I had a chat with van Ives, and yeah, I did look into the Aegis for her. I'm not exactly going to mourn a group of magic supremacists, but if you really think that I could—'

The man crossed the last couple of feet between us in less than a second, so fast that I didn't see the punch coming. He caught me clean across the jaw and succeeded where the potato men I had run into earlier had failed – he sent my head spinning and put me to the floor immediately. Then, before I could regain my composure, he was over me, shouting right into my face as the group closed around me.

'Who gave you the right to speak for us all, huh?' he was almost screaming. 'You're not the boss here, Parker. You're just the piece of filth that floated to the surface. You don't get to make deals with people's lives!'

I raised my guard, ready for him to drive a boot or another fist into me, but instead I saw him yanked backwards and away from me. As he staggered back, a man moved between us – Wolfgang.

'Let's not do something any of us will regret,' Wolfgang said, his voice level and calm. 'For now, there are no facts. Direct your energy to those you know are guilty.'

The other man deflated, his eyes glistening with budding tears. As his shoulders sagged, Wolfgang grabbed them and gently started to lead him away and out of sight. He risked a single glance my way, and I saw disgust in his eyes. Wolfgang might have stopped me getting my face mashed in, but he wasn't completely sold on me not deserving it either. Kaitlyn had done a lot more damage than I thought.

Charlie and Preston appeared next to me, helping me back to my feet.

'Jim,' Charlie said. 'Jim! Look at me. You ok?'

I blinked my vision back into focus properly. 'I'll live. People really are ready to jump to conclusions, huh?'

'We were hoping he wouldn't show up just yet,' Preston said, staring in the direction Wolfgang had led the man.

'You know him?'

Folding her arms, Preston puffed a strand of hair out of her eyes. 'I know him. He's Ariel Kingsley, Efraim's son.'

*

Things started to calm down a little after Ariel's outburst, almost as if he had sucked all the aggression out of the room when he smacked me in the gob. There were grumbles still, and no small amount of withering looks thrown my way, but for the moment Ariel was a good enough lightning rod to smooth things out a little.

I retreated to one of the office rooms where we would have our eventual meeting of the boffins, once Charlie finished assembling them. Preston kept me company for a while, making sure I was ok and filling me in on the sort of man Ariel Kingsley was – in short, a powerful one.

How I hadn't heard of him before, I wasn't sure. Perhaps it was because he wasn't on my patch, or maybe because free mages didn't really register to warlocks unless they were being a nuisance. Whatever the reason, hearing that he was a big figure in the magical underground was almost as big a shock as him knocking my jaw loose.

'How did he end up here?' I asked her as she shoved a desk across the room.

Preston slotted the desk between two others, putting the finishing touches on a makeshift meeting table. 'He didn't agree with his dad's politics.'

'No-one ever agrees with their dad on politics.'

'Right, exactly,' she said. 'You know he used to run fugitives across the border to Ireland? Word is that he managed to keep Whitehall off his back by throwing a lot of money at the problem. *A lot* of money.'

I massaged my jaw. It was clicking. 'And seeing as I've not heard of him, I'm going to guess he wasn't part of the Dark Times.'

'Nope, he's got scruples.'

'Rare breed, then.'

Preston disassembled a stack of chairs and slid them into place around the table. 'Yeah. He's not well-known, but the people who *do* know him are with him all the way. He's got enough clout to be a problem if he keeps pushing.'

There was a question hidden in her statement there: *What are we going to do about him?*

She had made a clear show of support for me when I arrived, but it would have been foolish to think that there wasn't some doubt rustling around in that banged up head of hers. Kaitlyn van Ives had just murdered a whole group of people who had been a threat to her power base, and Sophie Preston had been very deliberate in letting me know that Ariel was heading down the same path as his father.

And she wasn't sure whether that meant I was planning to kill him or not.

Mate, politics just *sucks*.

'Let him push,' I said. 'He's hurting. We've all been there, and we've all lashed out at the wrong person. There's so much glass in my house that I don't get to lob so much as a pebble these days.'

'He thinks you've made him a party to the death of his own father.'

Head hanging, I shrugged. 'He can think that if he wants. He can't prove it, because it's not true, but he needs someone accessible to be the bad guy. I've needed that more than once over the years. And if you... Well...'

I lost my nerve to finish the thought, but Preston managed to finish my thought for me anyway. 'I don't need to make you the bad guy for *this*.'

Pulling back her hair, she revealed the full extent of her scar. It was jagged and scorched, a good quarter of her face having been left a mottled black from the impact of the spell. I wasn't sure of the particulars of the spell that had struck her, but the state of the damage meant that the caster had been serious about killing us. There was blood leaking into the white of her eye still.

'Are you sure? Because that looks like it hurt.'

'Oh, like a *bitch*,' she said. 'Still does. Whatever they hit me with, I can *feel* the flesh around the wound necrotising. Doc says I'll need daily treatments for a while to dispel that, but the scar is here to stay.'

'Doc?'

'The mage that pieced me back together. He's not a doctor, but he's got a very long and *very* Polish name, so he needed an easy nickname.'

She let the hair fall back over her wound, but now that I knew it was there, I could still see it. I wasn't about to get all maudlin and start spouting *Dulce et Decorum Est*, but I was still going to feel a bit shit about it all. They had used her to get to me. Kaitlyn had used me to get to, well, everyone. This rising conflict was turning me into a focal nexus for all the sludge of this war.

I helped Preston finish setting things up just in time for Charlie and the array of supposed boffins she had chosen. They arrived in a surprisingly orderly fashion, a welcome change from the aggression shown in the group at large. I recognised a couple of them – warlocks I'd rubbed shoulders with back in the day, but never actively worked with – and of those I didn't I could still identify the stuffy gaze of an ousted handler. An Oxbridge education always outs itself, you don't need to wait long.

Preston and I waited until everyone had chosen their own seats before we sat down, sliding into lone chairs ignored by the others. Preston got a chair by Charlie and I had to make do sandwiched between a man with a chin so small that he had the rough shape of a human pencil, and a woman who looked like she crocheted her own earrings. Handlers, I guessed.

Once we were all settled, Charlie stood up. 'Thanks for agreeing to this, everyone. We need to decide how best to handle the van Ives situation, and we need to do it now. I think we are all in agreement of that.'

There was a grumble of agreement from the group, heads nodding slowly. The man next to me stood up to speak, his voice nasal and thick with compacted mucus. 'It doesn't seem like there is much to discuss, Charlotte.'

'Introduce yourself first, Lucas. Not everyone here is going to know you, despite what you might think.'

A brief but brutal sneer slithered across his face. 'Lucas Beaufont. And, as I was saying, Kaitlyn van Ives has backed us into a corner.'

'You think we should join up with her?' called a warlock from across the table. Long blonde hair, scruffy beard, a nose with more corners than a Formula 1 circuit. 'Oh, er, Bodhi Maltese.'

Beaufont's chin vanished even deeper into his neck. 'She positioned it so that, for all intents and purposes, we already have. No-one outside of this building will believe that we aren't already aligned with her, so why fight it?'

'Bro, we've been associated with bad juju for long enough.' Bodhi had a reputation for being laid back, until he wasn't, and I could already see that it was bang on the money as reputations went.

Off to my left, a woman with closely cropped ochre hair, black skin, and eyes that shone just a touch too brightly, spoke with a thick Welsh accent. 'Lara Mgune. Let people think what they want. I don't think any of us want to get involved with a war. We just let them fight amongst themselves, yeah?'

'That would be worse than taking a side,' Beaumont said. 'If we ignore this situation, we'll have both sides gunning for us in the long run, and no protection from either. Giving an official acknowledgement of our relationship with van Ives puts us firmly under her protection.'

Bodhi snorted. 'Puts us between her and the people who want her to *piss off*. No matter what she says, we'd just be her bouncers.'

I felt my eyes grow heavy from the boredom. The conversation went around in a circle for a long time – Beaumont amassed a couple of people that agreed with him, Bodhi got most of the others, and Mgune managed to convince a couple of others, but not enough to be a real contender in the decision. After the fifth or sixth circuit, it became clear that the argument wasn't going to budge without the three heavyweight votes that had, so far, remained undecided and silent.

Myself, Charlie, and Preston.

With no small amount of vanity, I positioned my own vote as the nuclear option. It was my name that had dragged us into this mess, my actions that had allowed it in the first place, and my reputation that van Ives was trying to co-opt. If I brought the hammer down, that would do a lot to blunt any opposing arguments.

Charlie was one of the most respected people in our group, so naturally her opinions had a lot of weight behind them. I was the figurehead, I suppose, but she was the one that actually got stuff done.

And as for Preston – she was our newest and most obvious casualty. There was a little tinge of celebrity there that would serve her well for now and give her a bit more clout than maybe she realised.

What I wanted to do was to let the other two talk first, temper my language around theirs, but judging from the looks on their faces they couldn't even make up their own minds about the issue. We were quickly approaching a point where I would have to speak up, but again that would push me further towards being a *leader*. I really, *really*, wanted to avoid that eventuality if I could. I didn't need even more responsibility.

Luckily for me, Mgune had seen which ways the winds were blowing, and was ready to throw her lot in behind someone else. 'She is using blackmail to bring us onboard. If we have to pick a side, I refuse to pick hers.'

That was enough of a consensus to let me weigh in. 'Now that we have thoroughly reinvented the idea of refusing to negotiate with terrorists, we need to work out what to do next.'

All eyes turned on me with a measure of confusion. The buggers had forgotten I was even sat at the table – doesn't do wonders for the ego, let me tell you. Beaufont was the first to regain his composure, drumming a solitary hand on the table slowly. 'I see I am outvoted. Very well, but you surely can't tell me that the actions of van Ives will do anything but foster more division.'

'On that, I actually agree,' I said. 'But she knows that. The act she put on for the cameras was just that, *an act*. If we push, she'll back down.'

Beaufont frowned. 'I've read her file, Parker. I wrote half of the thing, for goodness' sake. Kaitlyn van Ives is versed in information warfare, but she isn't known for empty posturing.'

'I've read the same files, but I also had an unexpected visit from her last night and let me tell you that she was far from the confident revolutionary she was playing in that broadcast. She was hurting.'

'That doesn't mean much,' Charlie said. 'You can hate what you're doing but still do it. That's common knowledge.'

I turned to Charlie to respond and saw the pain in her own eyes. Even knowing what a state she had been in after working with The Rider, it was easy to forget how much of the guilt and agony still had a home in her head. Even if I had wanted to argue the point with her, I wouldn't have had the heart.

'Not doing anything makes it look like we support her,' I said. 'And we've basically all agreed that isn't happening.'

'And doing the wrong thing sparks a civil war,' Charlie said.

'Not a fight then, something more… Christ, I can barely believe I'm about to say this… Something more *diplomatic*.'

It was Bodhi's turn to piss on my cornflakes now. 'We've never been welcome at any of the big sit-downs. We've had to do one-to-one meetings for a reason.'

'And those haven't gone well either,' Preston said, silencing the room for a moment.

I broke the silence again before anyone else could start building some momentum. 'Because they didn't have a reason to talk to us before. Now they're going to want answers.'

'Fair point,' Bodhi said.

Beaufont chimed in, but something behind Preston had caught my eye. There was a fly on the wall – an honest to God fly, just sat there on the wall of the room, rubbing its tiny little legs over its face. It was perched near one of the corners, resting in the shadows where the soft light from the overhead strip light barely reached.

Now, it's not like I'm the sort of perma-anxious twitchy guy who finds himself drawn to any movement in a room, not matter how small. That shit's exhausting. Still, I could *feel* the fly looking at me drawing my attention, and I couldn't pinpoint exactly why.

Whatever point the discussion had reached, it no longer mattered. My gut was flashing big neon warning signs at me, all because of a single bluebottle, and there had to be a reason for that. I reached out with my senses, scanning the room.

The other warlocks in the room muddied the waters a little – each with their own heady and spicy scent of magic rolling off them in irregular whorls. Pushing past that, I started to realise why the fly had been so conspicuous, and I immediately jumped to my feet, knocking my chair backwards.

Charlie's hand tightened around my wrist. 'Jim? What's wrong?'

I opened my mouth to respond, to shout at them all to get out while they could, but before I could say anything the world went white, and I felt the hot thud of an explosion throw me back against the wall.

Seven

A lifetime of getting on the wrong end of combat magic helps you hone some very specific reflexes. In this case, those reflexes helped me get a shield up in time to save my bloody life.

I had still hit the wall hard, my head cracking against the concrete and leaving me seeing stars, but judging from the state of the room I had gotten off lightly. The ceiling was gone, letting the dull morning light illuminate the carnage so gently as to make it seem like some sort of surreal diorama.

Preston had extended her shield around Charlie, and Bodhi had done the same for Beaufort. Mgune, it seemed, had tried to do the same for the others around the table, but she hadn't the time to get her spell off. The explosion had ridden the path of her magic, seeping through the pores of the spell as it formed and used her as a conduit. It turned her into a sort of Tesla coil, arching out of her and into the people in the room who couldn't make it behind a shield in time.

It had boiled their skin, melting flesh from bone, in the time it took to blink an eye. Mgune, somehow, had survived – a mosaic of crimson gashes carved into her skin. Her right arm was singed down to the bone.

While I tried to shake my brain back into place, Bodhi dropped his shield and vaulted over the cratered remains of the table to tend to Mgune. Preston followed shortly behind him, dropping to her knees at the woman's head and lifting it up a little.

'What...' Beaumont said, his voice barely a whisper. 'What... What... Fuck?'

My stomach roiled and churned as my balance failed me. I stumbled, but Charlie managed to get to my side in time to catch me. She gave me a look that echoed Beaumont's words. Bodhi and Preston, it seemed, were too busy with Mgune to give much of a shit about anything else.

'Thaumaturgically guided death curse,' I managed to say. 'Big one. Surprised there's any building left.'

Beaumont's eyes were wide and glassy, and his mouth was opening and closing in shock. He was staring at one of the corpses without blinking, unable to stop the image of it from burning into his long-term memory. Charlie detached from me and went to help him. Taking his head in her hands, she dragged his gaze towards hers, locking eyes with him.

'Guided by what?' she asked me, not breaking eye contact with the man. 'Teeth? Hair?'

I shook my head. 'A fly.'

Bodhi sprang to his feet. 'Not possible. A fly is too tiny to extract anything meaningful without killing it. You can't channel to a corpse.'

'It's more complicated than that. I think—'

Somewhere deeper into the building, another explosion rocked the foundations. The remaining chunks of ceiling, balanced on battered rebar, shook loose and fell down onto us. Before we could catch our balance, another explosion rang out even deeper into the building.

'Explain later,' Preston hissed, still holding tightly to Mgune's head. 'Fix this.'

She definitely had a point.

I clambered over the rubble and blasted the door to smithereens – no time for subtlety – heading out into the hall. There was dust here, but nothing major in terms of damage until I reached the more open areas. The closer of the two explosions seemed to have happened by the main dance floor, the general living space. A few stripped and smouldering carcasses told a tale of people completely unprepared.

Pushing down my fear and revulsion, I kept going, pressing onward into the next room – the makeshift sickbay.

There was nothing I could do to prepare myself for the sight of all those injured people being flayed to shreds by this dark magic. And, thankfully, I didn't need to. If I had been any later, though, I may have.

Two men were balanced awkwardly on a folding table, a glowing ball in their smoking fingertips. The light danced off their pained faces as they held it – Wolfgang and Ariel.

They'd bottled the explosion, summoned their shields around it and kept it contained. And now they were losing their grip.

Sprinting, I crossed the room and leant my own magic to their shields. Instantly, I felt the heat of the explosion on my fingertips, the nerve endings overloading and burning away. I had bought us a few seconds at most, but there was no way we could hold the spells for long. With enough energy we could force it back in on itself, implode the damned thing, but trying that as we were would just shatter the shield.

So, if the bastard thing wanted to expand, I'd let it expand.

'Give me control!' I shouted through gritted teeth. 'Let me shape it!'

If Wolfgang heard me, he didn't show it, but I felt him cede his control to me. Ariel hesitated a little longer, glaring at me as he tried to decide just how much I could be trusted. Then he nodded and transferred his control as well.

The spell weighed ten times as much now, making my knees tremble and my back buckle, but I only needed to hold it for a second more. I needed to pick the perfect point, weaken it just enough, let the energy fracture through…

The spell shattered in my hand as the explosion found its way through the patch of shield I had weakened. It had found the path of least resistance and punched through in force, shooting out of my grip with the focus of a laser. The concrete ceiling gave little resistance as the explosion shot up into the sky, harmlessly dissipating into the cloud layer.

My knees finally gave way, and I slumped down onto the floor. Ariel went limp and tumbled down next to me, leaving Wolfgang without a counterweight on the table. He went backwards, clattering off a medical cart, swearing under his breath the entire time.

We lay there, staring up at the ceiling and chuckling to each other. Magic does weird things to body chemistry even when you aren't actively messing with it – making you laugh at life and death situations is hardly unusual. In this case, though, I suspect it was more the sheer blasé nature of the whole thing.

Eventually, I sat up and risked a look around the room. There was structural damage, but it didn't look as though anyone had died.

'You reacted quickly,' I said. My throat was dry from the panic and the shock, making my voice hoarse and raspy. 'We lost people.'

'Figured,' Ariel said. 'The noise gave us just enough time to act, and we had the barebones of a theory.'

'We tried to do what you did,' Wolfgang said. 'We couldn't aim it without losing the stability of the spell.'

'Just needed a little more oomph to keep the walls sturdy,' I said, checking out my fingertips. They were singed, but no longer smoking. All the sensation was gone and I didn't like not knowing whether that was a symptom of holding that magic or of something much more long-lasting and unpleasant.

I got up first, helping up Wolfgang before holding out my hand to Ariel. He grabbed it – a little harder than necessary – and let me hoist him to his feet. Thankfully, and somewhat ironically, the sickbay seemed to be the least fucked up by what had been going on.

'Did you see the cause?'

They both shook their heads, but Ariel seemed to be at the limit of his goodwill for me, leaving the conversational duties to Wolfgang. 'Not precisely. The explosion originated in the shadows over there, but no-one was by that area that I saw.'

Obviously, this was a co-ordinated attack. Three explosions, carefully placed, taking out our whole base of operations? That was military precision, but not military means. Thaumaturgy meant wizards, but Bodhi had the right of it – you can't channel a fly, there's simply not enough to them to make the magical link.

And yet, someone had.

Ariel turned his back and set about helping the wounded. The explosion had been contained in the sick bay, but the other two had still done some damage even out here. Masonry had cracked, ceiling tiles rattled free – enough small things to make a bit of triage necessary. Wolfgang gave me a look that I couldn't quite understand, but when I returned it with a curt nod, he went to join Ariel.

Charlie caught me up as the ringing finally subsided in my ears and a very insistent pins-and-needles sensation was starting to creep into my fingertips. Her hair was matted with masonry dust and a trickle of blood, neither of which I had the wherewithal to notice earlier. She barked a few orders, mobilising those that were still shellshocked but upright, then came over and grabbed my arm.

'Come with me,' she said, pulling me across the room to a fire exit. She pushed the bar, threw the door open, and dragged me out into the cold. 'Mgune will live but we think we lost our best healers in the attack. Without them, I don't think we can save her arm.'

'None of this makes sense.'

Charlie brushed some hair out of her eyes. 'Doesn't it? Makes a lot to me. Kaitlyn did this, it had to be.'

'Exactly,' I said. It was still hard to talk, and the cold morning air wasn't helping. 'But I don't get why. And if I'm right about the how…'

'A fly as a thaumaturgy focus? I've never heard that done before.'

'Because it hasn't been. If it was even remotely possible, Guy Fawkes wouldn't have needed all that gunpowder. One mage with the hair off a fly's arsehole could obliterate the chain of command instantly. But that can't happen because a fly is a *fucking* fly. It's too small.'

Charlie's eyes narrowed. 'But you have a theory.'

'Yeah, but it's only *slightly* more plausible than suicide flies.'

'Go on. Tell me.'

I closed my eyes and tried to pick my words carefully. 'I saw the fly on the wall, seconds before it went off. It drew my attention, and so I reached out with my magic to try and understand why. It was incandescent, Charlie. It might have looked like an insect, but I think it was a creature *made* of magic.'

'Like a homunculus?'

'Kind of, but not really,' I said. 'Homunculi are extension of the mage who created them, and they're a pain in the arse to make in the first place. Plus, they're a mockery of life, so if you don't keep juicing them up regularly with power they just fall apart. Too high maintenance for your modern-day wizard.'

Charlie was chewing on her lip as she listened to what I was saying. Maybe I shouldn't have had the capacity to find that cute, but I did. 'Fine, but that doesn't rule out knocking one together for a suicide mission.'

'No, they have the same problem as a fly in that regard. They, magically speaking, *barely* exist. The universe doesn't give enough of a shit about them to put enough mystical magic melange into them to let you channel to them.'

'But you said—'

'I know what I said,' I interrupted. 'What I said was that it was *kind of, but not really* like a homunculus. Those are beings made by magic, this was one made *of* magic.'

I watched as Charlie tried to get her head around what I was saying, and I could see that she wasn't going to manage it. In fairness to her, I didn't really understand what that meant myself. I know a lot about magic, including a lot of the things that you aren't supposed to know anymore, but I don't know everything. My practical knowledge is limited, as is my understanding of the science of the craft. I know how to paint, but I don't know which beetles to grind up to make my pigments. It was more than a little bit possible I was talking myself in dangerous circles here.

But they were circles that made a little bit of sense, which was something.

Eventually, Charlie huffed with frustration and threw up her arms. 'Okay, I give up. What the hell does that even mean?'

'I think it means I need a car with enough petrol to get me to London. If we've got any left.'

'You can't just leave,' Charlie snapped. 'What about all of *this*?'

She gestured madly back towards the building, hands flapping almost too fast to see.

'I can help with that, or I can stop it happening again, I can't do both.'

Charlie's voice became sharp enough to cut glass. 'If you leave now, while we are in the middle of a crisis, people will think—'

'I don't care what people will think, Charlie,' I almost shouted. 'I've spent the last god-knows how long being told to worry about how I'm seen. All this politics shit is *getting in the way* of doing *anything*. I tried playing nice and building alliances and all that has done is get me filled full of holes, exploded, and made anyone who was stupid enough to join up an even bigger target than they were to begin with.'

'Jim, where's this coming from?'

Her question caught me off guard for a moment. I didn't have an answer for her, and the more I tried to find one the harder it was to spot even the faintest glimmer of a reason. The words had just bubbled up, and with them I could feel more fighting to get out too. I was going to vomit an epiphany which, you know, is probably very on brand for me when you think about it.

'I'm so *sick* of being at the centre of all of this,' I said. 'I was content to do my time, use what few skills my life as a shitty wizard had given me to help people as a warlock. To *atone*. And, somehow, we've gone from that to so many different people using my name to fuel their devious little plans. It's too much responsibility. Pin all your hopes and dreams on a different name and let me just *do things* to help.'

Even listening to myself speak, I had no idea where the words were coming from. There were echoes of frustrations there, but they weren't driving this. The attack had rattled me, but not enough to spin me out this far. Charlie's blank face staring back at me did nothing to help me cut through the confusion either, the fact that she still couldn't quite understand where this had come from just dragged me even further away from understanding.

'I can't be trusted to think,' I found myself saying. 'Why have people been trusting me to think?'

'You've done pretty well so far, that's why,' Charlie said. 'I don't really understand why certain people rise to the top, and the fact that you have doesn't make you responsible for how people use your name.'

I don't think it was her doing, but whatever force was pushing the words out of my mouth decided to back off, leaving us in an uncomfortable silence. Charlie had nothing to say to me, defused as she had been by my self-entitled moment of whining. On my part, what more could I say? Anything I added would either break the spell and send us into another argument or put me on the path to another empty apology.

She sighed and pulled a set of car keys from the pocket of her jacket, placing them into my hands. A thin plastic strap dangled from one of the rings, a university crest inked on both sides of the fold. I closed my fingers around the keys as Charlie gave me another inscrutable look and left.

*

Charlie's car was a Mini Cooper with a death wish, so it didn't take me long to realise that giving me her keys had been the most brutal bollocking she had available at the time. Seriously, every time I touched the accelerator, the damn thing made a grinding noise like it was about to spit pistons.

It made the journey down to London a terrifying one.

On a good day, you can get from Humberside to London in about 4 hours. This wasn't a good day, but I still managed the journey in a hair less than 5. That said, it may have taken me half as much time again to actually make it *through* London to my destination.

Greater London had been, unsurprisingly, the one secure fortress that Whitehall was able to maintain. Other cities, even big ones, had varying degrees of mage resistance, but being the centre of power for the British government, it had been possible to get the city locked down almost as soon as the Vault went offline.

This meant that, to begin with at least, even the most bellicose of wizards saw the capital as a suicidal place to rock up. But things change quickly while an uprising is working its way towards rising up. London was still a fortress, but only because both sides had just flat out decided that it would be. Mages didn't bother trying and Whitehall didn't really bother trying to stop them.

I'm going to bring up chess again – it was like one of those stalemate situations where you both only have your kings left and you're just impotently shuffling them back and forth. Or, even more accurately, that horribly British thing of trying to walk around someone on the street while the pair of you keep trying to walk the same way.

Oh, excuse me, no after you, I insist, I couldn't possibly, oh how silly we've done it again, ha ha ha.

The upshot of this is that I could get into the city very easily, but I was still somewhat wary of making it to my final destination.

Fawkes Folly had been intended as a sort of reference library for Warlocks, and eventually for Paladins, one assumes. I've probably rattled on about it before – a disused Underground station positioned directly below parliament, built in the very tunnels Ol' Guido used to try and blow up the king. Or so the legend goes.

Last time I had visited, I had made my way in through parliament itself, but even knowing that they wouldn't be looking for me I didn't want to take that risk. Instead, I took the much safer path of walking the tracks of the London Underground. This is, obviously, not very safe at all and should never be attempted by anyone with a working brain or any sense of self-preservation.

I think we've established that neither of those points apply to me, though.

The Underground has a lot of service corridors, which helped me along on my little wander. In truth, I only nearly got run over perhaps three times, and even then, I had plenty of warning. All that considered, however, my heart was utterly soaking in adrenaline by the time I reached the blocked off tunnel that would take me to Fawkes Folly.

The bricks had been warded heavily when the tunnel had been closed off, but time and neglect had allowed a lot of the magic to bleed away. What wards remained powered weren't terribly difficult to disarm; the threads of power that bound them together were thin as gossamer and just as easy to sever. It took me all of five minutes to make the wall safe enough for me to punch through with a bit of magical muscle.

It felt as though the library's collection had grown since my last visit, what with piles of loose books positioned all next to each set of shelves. Yet, judging from the dust and the lack of lighting, no-one had seen to make use of it.

I found a light switch and flicked it a couple of times to no response. Fumbling in my pocket, I found a formerly enchanted ring, now exhausted, and pushed just enough power into it to illuminate the gems in the band. The light burned away my night vision but was far more welcome.

People always seem to make researching stuff seem pretty easy, like all you have to do is sit down and crack open a book. They like to neglect to mention that the hard part is knowing *which* book to crack open. I had hoped the librarian would be around to help me – either willingly or via a little encouragement – but judging from the state of the place that wasn't looking likely. Instead, I was forced to fumble around for a while, going from shelf to shelf to find the section I was after. The fact that the library had such an impressively large collection of books just made my job even harder.

Eventually, I found the right shelf and skimmed the titles for something appropriate. They were all chained to their shelves with braids of cold iron that had been woven up their spines. This wasn't overly surprising –

the sort of magic I was hoping to research here was the blackest of the black, which is how I knew to look to Fawkes Folly for it. Any grimoire with this stuff in that had been scooped up by the Whitehall snatch squads would need to be squirrelled away somewhere they had complete control of, it was too dangerous any other way.

One by one, I leafed through the books until I found something that fit the bill. The first two books – a book of demonology bound in weathered flesh and a charred treatise on astral projection – were of no help, but I knew the third book would have something useful the moment I touched it.

It's always the third one, right?

The binding was tacky to the touch, as if the leather had been dunked in tar. When I cracked it open, cottony wisps of the same sticky substance strained to keep the book closed. Instead of that warm, woody scent expected of the pages, it was sharp and chemical. Incredibly foreboding, so you can see why I had a good feeling that it might have what I was after.

There was no title on the spine, nor on the front cover, but written onto the first page in a shaky hand were the words:

Πέρα απ ό την εμβέλεια του Θανάτου: Να Φτύσεις στο Μάτι του Θανάτου

Which is Greek, a language I didn't have the faintest clue how to read. Still don't incidentally, but I didn't then either. This is where having magic is great, though – you get to cheat. If you know the name of a language, a small incantation and a tiny fleck of power can shift your perception enough that you'll understand it as though you were born to it. Think of it like changing the language on your phone, but for your brain.

Small problem: you need to know the name of the language *in that language*. Luckily, we live in the future so I could just ask everyone's favourite datamining search engine to knock out that translation for me.

I closed my eyes and kissed some power into my thumb. Placing it against my forehead, I muttered the incantation and hoped I could do justice to the one word of Greek I needed to pronounce flawlessly.

'Ελληνικά,' I said.

There was a momentary blast of vertigo and then the words on the page made perfect sense to me.

Beyond the reach of Thanatos: To Spit in the Eye of Death

Pretty metal, right?

I skimmed that book for the next hour. It was, unsurprisingly, a compendium of potential ways to live forever, some more practical than others. Liches, vampires, deals with crossroads demons, rituals to summon Death and trap them in a big glass jar, there were *pages* of the stuff and all by different authors. None of them fit what I thought I was looking for, but they made for fascinating reading.

About halfway through the tome, I found the chapter I had been searching for. Growing up as a mage, it had been a campfire story, a magical conspiracy theory. But considering what I had seen at our hideout, I was willing to entertain conspiracy theories just this once.

I'm going to reproduce the important parts of the chapter here, in English, because if I had to read the bloody thing then so do you. Plus, translating ancient magical texts makes me feel a bit cool.

The Worm that Walks
Catalogued by Alcestis Chatzinikolaou

While chiefly a creation of Western European practitioners, The Worm That Walks is universally potent. It can be achieved in any environment save the most desolate wastes of the known world. The reagents are near-limitless and, in fact, the difficulty of this spell comes not from the mystical preparation, but the physical.

The body must be prepared to undergo the transmutation, a procedure that can take months. Insects must be applied slowly and in trivial numbers, allowing them to acclimate at such a pace that they can begin to form one colony. As their numbers grow, they will begin to consume the flesh of the host, and it is at this point where most of the attempted transmogrifications result in failure.

In watching one such transformation, I observed the extent of the agony caused by the procedure. He was a man of youthful vigour, midway through the metamorphosis when I encountered him. Open sores covered his mottled skin, and as I watched, I could on occasion see the flesh writhe and wriggle at the motion of the creatures beneath. From time to time an insect would pry its way out of one sore, flutter above the man, then re-enter via another. I visited upon the man for several hours, and his screams never abated.

I reached the conclusion that a singular kind of mind is needed, one in possession of a focused vision so acute that it can mute any agony. As a locust ate its way through the man's eye, he screamed so loudly that I heard his vocal cords tear. He would proceed to drown in his own humours.

However, in successful cases, the transformation is perhaps the most perfect of all ways to live for eternity. When the last morsel of a mortal body is consumed by the myriad insects, the colony absorbs into itself the vital spark of life that animates the human soul. That soul suffuses the creatures, seizes them, melds them together on a spiritual level. A human mind spread across a thousand, a million insects, each a part of a greater being but also an individual in their own right.

The possibilities of such an existence are endless! Time will not see the end of such a creature – if anything, the impetus that drives the constant reproduction of such insects will ensure a refreshing of their numbers. Likewise, this will allow fast recovery should any harm befall a section of the colony.

As such, the only conceivable method of destruction for a fully realised being of this form is to ensure every minute individual in the colony has been obliterated. While this would technically be possible, the size and number of the constituent insects would make such an endeavour impractical. Without vital organs or a central cortex, even a single larva would be enough to eventually regenerate the entire colony.

I believe this is as close to perfection as any of us could strive to be.

Fucking horrible, right? In even my darkest of days I don't think my mind could have gone to such depths as thinking it would be beneficial if I got eaten from the inside out by a whole host of creepy crawlies. What a great way to spend a summer, feeling all your squishy human parts being slowly eaten away. Ten out of ten.

And yet, if what the book said was true, an old conspiracy theory had given me the answer to the attack. It raised more questions, sure, but it did at least answer a couple too.

You can't use a normal fly to channel thaumaturgy, but if that fly is part of a larger organism then, perhaps…

A Worm that Walks would be a perfect thaumaturgical organism, it practically illustrated the entire concept in how it worked. Each creepy crawly, even when off on its own, is still connected to the whole – possibly even via the same type of metaphysical connection between a person and a stray tooth or hair. The controlling consciousness easily manoeuvre tiny, unnoticeable pieces of itself anywhere, the perfect target for some laser guided spells.

This put paid to the idea that Kaitlyn van Ives had been behind the attack at least. Maybe she had gone a little bit off the deep end lately, but there was no chance she'd let something this profane into her clubhouse. And that was if she could even *find* one – like I said, they were a conspiracy theory on par with the royal family being shape-changing lizards from another planet. These things were *rare*, you couldn't just do a few swipes on Tinder and find your perfect bug boy.

Who else had we pissed off, then?

I slammed the book closed and broke the braid holding it to the shelf. It snapped a lot easier than I had expected, probably a result of being in close proximity to such a gross piece of literature. You can insert your own jokey reference here, I'm not going to do it for you.

In any case, might as well keep the big book of horribleness just in case. If I was right about this, it wasn't as if I could memorise the entire thing. There'd be more in there I could use, no doubt.

Tracing my steps back, I retreated to the hole I had made my entry through and climbed back out into the tunnels. The book was heavy and sticky in my grip, the tacky fluid soaking into the fabric of my clothes.

Charlie was going to absolutely *adore* reading it.

Eight

I risked spending the night in the city, booking a room in a Bed and Breakfast so cheap that they stuffed the mattresses with the same sawdust they stirred into the porridge come morning. The book spent the night under my bed – I had considered leaving it in the car, but that would just be asking for trouble. This way, if someone wanted to steal it, they had to at least work a little bit to get it.

It did spend the journey back to the north nestled in the boot though. The thing was even more unsettling to look at in daylight, and seeing as Charlie was going to be in a mood with me anyway, I didn't think it was wise to ruin the upholstery of her car by keeping it on a seat. I don't think the car appreciated my gesture, growling and grinding its way back up the motorway at an even greater volume than the trip down.

I set off early enough to beat the traffic, which meant I made it back to the remains of the hideout before midday. On leaving, I hadn't wanted to take a proper look at the outside of the building. There wasn't much choice on the way back, and I could see that there was no way we could salvage it. Still, there were warlocks pottering about in the debris outside doing their best to prove me wrong.

Between the car park and the building itself, the boffin squad had taken up residence. Some larger bits of debris had been gathered together and stacked to make small benches, a table, that sort of thing. Charlie was sat there, watching the warlocks at work, accompanied by Bodhi and a very beaten-up Mgune.

'Oi oi, saveloy,' I said as I approached, slamming the tome down on the makeshift table. The masonry quivered a little before settling.

Charlie ignored me, turning away from me to give more of her attention to the warlocks working on the hideout. Bodhi did the same, though I did catch him giving the book a vicious side-eye. Only Mgune bothered to react.

'A book,' she said astutely.

'A big grotty grimoire, to be precise.'

She didn't look impressed. 'Is it important?'

'I think so,' I said, then nodded at the other two. 'I would much rather not repeat myself though.'

Mgune fidgeted on her stool. She swivelled enough that I could see her arm now, or where it had been. The blackened husk I had seen before was already gone, replaced by a ratty duffel bag sewn to her shoulder. Quick and dirty healing magic, a regenerative cocoon. I doubted it would regrow a whole arm, but then I was never very good at the healing stuff.

She caught me staring. 'Nothing sterile survived the explosion, so a couple of the guys cast a purification ward on the bag. Not bad, really. Oh, and for reference? You won't have to repeat yourself. They're listening, even if they pretend otherwise.'

I opened the book for her, my fingers once again sinking into the gluey morass. The pages peeled open like a scab being ripped from skin. I had bookmarked the page on the beat, but *something* in the tome had ended up eating its way through the leather. 'There's our assassin.'

Peering over, Mgune started to read. She had barely cleared the first paragraph before she started laughing. 'You cannot be serious.'

'As serious as a terrorist attack.'

'Are you sure?' she said, skimming a few more pages. 'Because these things don't exist, and just because there's a chapter devoted to them in this book doesn't mean they do.'

'I'm not basing this solely off the book,' I shot back. 'I saw a fly being channelled. The only way that happens is if it's part of a larger whole. When I reached out with my power, I felt an incredibly strong energy, transformative in flavour. Granted, it's not conclusive, but it is compelling.'

Mgune turned the page with her good arm, wiping her fingers on the tabletop once she was done. 'Jesus, the procedure is *sick*. No-one would put themselves through that.'

'Let me see,' Charlie said, turning around to snatch the book. She flicked quickly through the pages. 'I've never seen anything like this.'

'Me neither,' I said. 'I'd ask the other warlocks, but something as revolting as that would have been big talk on the grapevine.'

'What does it mean?'

I crossed my arms and thought for a moment. 'It means that someone out there is making a play.'

'You mean The Rider?'

'I do,' I said, dropping my voice. 'This is proof that he's not just trying to get the magical monsters on side, he's using them as weapons.'

'Laura Irvine,' Charlie said. 'The goons that were aiming to storm her house...?'

'No, not them. My gut still tells me they're with Kaitlyn. The Rider has more subtle means to recruit. It's all pressure and coercion with him. He had his hooks in her brain for sure, though.'

Mgune slammed the book shut. 'We need to take another look at the big file of neglected warlock work. If you're right, there's no way one of these things gets into the country without leaving a trail.'

'Assuming it did come into the country,' I said. 'It's made of flies. The bulk of it could be sitting in a Spanish villa right now, just squirting out single insects to travel the world on its behalf. There's nothing that says it needs to be in Britain to hit us with thaumaturgy.'

'But to target us specifically would mean it at least knows of us, knows where we are. Or at least knows enough to lie in wait to hitch a ride to our hideout.'

'Can't argue with that,' I said. 'I'll go back through the warlock files, see if I can find any links.'

Charlie shook her head. 'No, I'll do that. I think your skills are best put to use helping the other warlocks.'

'What?' I spluttered. 'I'm not a builder. I struggle with Lego sets.'

'They're not building, dickhead. Look properly.'

Grumbling, I started watching the warlocks again. Shuffling around, grabbing debris, moving chunks of masonry a few feet. Looking again, though, I noticed the patterns. Yes, they were moving debris, but they weren't just dumping it out the way – there was a method here.

'Are they trying to erect a protective circle around the building?' I asked.

'Bingo,' Charlie said. 'The German made a point that now we know such an attack is possible, we need to defend against it.'

'So we're going nuclear, putting up a barrier that cuts the area off from magic entirely?'

'Only way we can be sure that another suicide fly isn't waiting on the wall.'

I squinted so I could get a better look of the circle they were building. The theory was sound – I've told you far too many times about how pentagrams work, I'm sure – but magic circles were rarely this large. Magic doesn't hold to the square-cube law really, but the bigger the spell the more power you do tend to need. The bigger a protection circle, the more ambient magic you need to shut out, and therefore the more magic you have to put in.

This is why they are usually used to keep things *in* – who really cares about the comfort of their monstrous magical prisoners?

But I had to admit, there were worse ideas they could have had. Typical wards don't work on thaumaturgy, and even your non-typical ones were hit and miss. Rune magic would probably have something to offer, but I was sure no-one present would know it well enough to make it worth the effort.

'Why aren't you three helping?' I said, not taking my eyes off the slowly forming circle.

Bodhi sniffed loudly and I noticed now that his nose had a new corner. 'Lara's not fit for it. Charlie doesn't know the art.'

'And you?'

'Me?' he said. 'I'm on reserve, bro. I'm a lightning rod and a battery all in one. When the time comes, I'm the one that charges things up.'

'You got the muscles for a circle that size?'

He shrugged. 'I think I've got enough to get it started, but I know I don't have enough to keep it running. We'll be rotating warlocks every hour to keep it topped up.'

Pretty ballsy move for a guy called Bodhi. Powering up that circle would drain him dry, burn out his magic for a few days if he wasn't careful. Then again, trust a warlock to jump in head-first when some dangerous potential sacrifice was put on the table. I'm pretty sure the only thing that had stopped some of the others from volunteering was the knowledge that fucking it up would leave everyone exposed to more attacks.

This was blitz mentality now.

I took my leave of the boffins and installed myself as head foreman of the construction project. No-one seemed to object, which I take to mean that I am a renowned expert on magical constructions. And, more importantly, the loudest person with the correct demeanour for bossing people around when the moment demands it.

Hey, if they want to hold me up as their poster boy, I might as well exploit it now and then.

For the most part, they knew what they were doing so my job was extremely easy. Whitehall didn't bother to recruit useless mages for the warlock ranks, after all, so it wasn't much of a surprise that I wasn't really needed. I was under no illusions as to why Charlie had wanted me watching over them rather than reading through the warlock work.

She was starting to doubt me.

Bringing up Laura Irvine in that conversation had seemed benign enough, but it was a signal to me that she had started asking herself some questions. It was possible she wasn't even aware what those doubts meant yet, or even what had caused them, but they were taking root. She wanted to be the one doing the research because, deep down, she wanted to find something she could use to justify whatever I had done that I didn't want her to know about.

Thing is, I was all but certain there was no way to get her to approve of trapping a woman in her own brain for the greater good.

In contrast with the chill in the air the day before, the sun was out today. It hung low in the sky, light skipping off bright stone and right into my poor retinas. I soldiered on for a while, but eventually I was forced into the shade to avoid a migraine. Closing my eyes, I placed my forehead against the cool bricks of a neighbouring building and tried not to spiral into overthinking.

'Penny for your thoughts?'

I opened one eye. 'Oh, just fuck off.'

Robin was next to me, leaning her shoulder against the same wall. 'Are you really not over greeting me like that, Jim?'

'Your mind games don't work on me, mate,' I said. 'I know what you're doing. I knew what you were doing before I got it confirmed by Irvine, and I'm certainly not any more susceptible to your bullshit now.'

'I'm not the bad guy here, Jim.'

'You drove an innocent woman insane, all to blackmail her darker half into drawing attention for you!'

'And then you caged her inside her own head, all but lobotomising her,' Robin said. 'I'd argue that is a much more tangible act of evil.'

'What I did was a mercy!' I shouted, turning on her. 'It was the only way to keep you out of her head.'

'Keep your voice down,' she said calmly. 'We don't want people to notice that you're talking to yourself, right? You can't save the world if you're locked up in the loony bin.'

'So, we're back to that then.'

Robin sighed and put on some puppy dog eyes. She had made an expression like that in my direction more than once while she had been alive, but it didn't fit her face now. It made her look like she was wearing a mask. 'Come on, Jim, we never left that. You know what my endgame is, and you know that you'll be there for it. You're already taking charge, and I'm really happy to see that. You've got a *ruling council*.'

'It's not a council.'

'Isn't it? You've got people hanging on your every word. Look at van Ives' masterstroke. Using your name to get people on her side? We both know that doesn't work if you don't have some major clout. Clout that, I might add, I worked hard to build for you.'

'And I don't want it.'

Robin shrugged. 'And I don't care whether you want it or not. It's needed to save the goddamn world, so suck it up.'

I allowed myself a moment to seethe. If there was one thing that I could say about The Rider, it was that he never changed his story – everything he did was some superbly intricate plan to put me in charge of the magical community so I could use them to save the world. The fact that I didn't buy any of that, that his methods only seemed to make everything immeasurably worse, didn't seem to factor into things. He simply wouldn't let me treat him as an enemy and it was infuriating.

'Tell you what,' I said, jabbing a finger at her chest. 'How about you just make use of the people who actually like you. You had Kingsley until you got

Kaitlyn to wreck his shit, so I'm sure you've got other lackeys.'

'Kaitlyn van Ives is going to mess everything up if she remains unchecked, Jim. If you believe only one thing I tell you today, believe that. Nothing she has been doing is following my design.'

'Bullshit.'

'That's your masterful retort, is it? You're just going to call *bullshit* with no evidence, disregard what I'm saying when I've only ever been honest with you?'

'Honest?' I half-shouted. I caught myself before the first syllable had finished leaving my lips, cranking the volume down a couple of notches. 'You're wearing my dead girlfriend's fucking face.'

'I'm not wearing her face! I am her, Jim! This is Robin you are talking to, mostly. I just happen to agree with The Rider on this.'

For far too long a moment, I found myself believing her. I wanted to. I mean, of course I did – for a long time I was certain she was the love of my life, and I still wasn't ready to forgive myself for her death. A lot of the nuances were spot on too; if we had been talking about anything other than this end of the world shit then I'm not sure I could have pinpointed any difference.

But we were. And I could.

'My Robin would never go along with this course of action, nice try.'

Her face fell and my heart ached to see it do so. That same disappointment had been frozen on her face forever because of what I did – seeing it again ripped at feelings I thought had withered away.

When she raised her head again, the red rings that highlighted her irises were glowing a little more prominently. 'Believe me or don't, Jim, that's your choice. But whatever you think, I know for a *fact* that the only way to avoid what I have seen is to get you ready. That's all I'm doing. You don't have to believe me, and you certainly don't have to like it, but you do have to accept it.'

'Nope.'

'Nope?' she said. 'Fucking *nope?* Jesus Christ, you really never change, do you? You really are the most irritating, frustrating, pig-brained walking arsehole I've ever met.'

That sounded a little more like Robin. 'I'm done giving your mind games the time of day. Piss off back to van Ives and tell her I'm coming for her. The pair of you have gone too far this time.'

'Be an idiot then,' she snarled. 'But I came here to warn you about Kaitlyn van Ives. Yes, I wanted to use her as a crucible to forge you into the man I need you to be, but someone else got to her before I could. I had that door slammed in my face, and you need to be prepared for what that means.'

'And what, pray tell, do you intend to tell me that means?'

She pulled herself up straight, her gait shifting and changing into one that didn't fit her body. I could only assume this was The Rider shining through a little more. 'It means there's no safety net for you here.'

'As if there was before.'

'Parker. My friend. You have no idea.'

And with that, she melted back into the shade of the building, leaving me alone to ponder her words. I do a lot of pondering, it seems, and I don't think it ever really achieves much. The sign of an anxious mind, too much pondering.

Did I believe what she had said? Not even a little. That little hint that I had been working with a safety net before – that, somehow, The Rider had been shadowing me like an overprotective parent, ready to swoop in when I fell over in the playground – was almost certainly just another mind game. I'd seen no evidence of any of that.

Other than how often I get my shit kicked in and yet I'm still alive.

Don't count that.

But even if that *was* true, Kaitlyn going dark like this still didn't sit right. It was sort of believable if I let myself think that The Rider could have co-opted her somehow, but not someone else. Especially not someone else who I'd had no inkling of beforehand. It was too convenient, a little too perfect an escape for her actions. Plus, she was too smart to get taken in by someone like that unless they were actively inside her brain.

Glancing behind me, I looked back at the group that Robin had called my *ruling council*. I barely knew two of them beyond their reputation, and yet still I trusted them. The Robin-Rider had been right about one thing – I had changed, enough to be able to trust again. It was bringing out dangerous impulses, like the one to actually talk to them about all this, but I still had enough smarts to know that was a bad call.

Hi, guys! Turns out the marauding ghost of the big bad has been talking to me through the form of my dead girlfriend. So that's happening.

I couldn't think of any way that could go down well.

Being that I was all fired up, I wanted to go out and continue my self-destructive pattern of seeking out trouble without thinking, but I had to reluctantly admit that now wasn't the time. Instead, I went back to my foremanly duties and let my pondering tick up to dangerous levels. Before I knew it, I was being pestered to give the massive magic circle my approval.

*

'We decided that was a bad idea and now you are wanting to go off and do it alone, making it an even worse idea?'

The circle had been active for about four hours, and Charlie's research had gone nowhere. Getting more than a little restless, I had finally pulled the trigger on the idea that had been birthed by my *extensive pondering*.

I'm going to ruin that word for you, that's my plan.

'Going to see them had been a terrible plan at first, yes,' I said, shuffling in close to her. 'But that was before Kaitlyn tried to blow us up with blood magic. We don't show up, she's going to spin this to her benefit.'

Charlie tried to roll her eyes and turn away, but I had carefully chosen one of the few safe parts of the hideout to have the conversation so that she wouldn't have the space to storm away – the stairs down into the booze cellar. I'd enticed her down into the basement with the promise of a medicinal vodka, and while we were perched on the stairs, shot glasses in hand, I had broached the topic.

I should have waited until she'd downed the shot, in hindsight.

'Then we go together, as a group,' she said. 'If those factions have got it into their head that this is some sort of UN of the magical underworld, we should treat it like that. If we don't, they're going to treat us like shit.'

'They're going to treat us like shit anyway,' I shot back. 'Kaitlyn's already in their heads, and they won't want to believe what I'm going to tell them.'

'Then what's even the point?'

Despite myself, Charlie was getting me riled. It probably wasn't her fault but sitting still was starting to make my brain itch. 'The point, *light of my life*, is to spray paint I LIVED BITCH all over Kaitlyn van Ives' manifesto.'

'You didn't even think this was her doing a couple of hours ago!'

'Well, a lot can change in a couple of hours!'

Our voices echoed off the cold stone walls, punctuated by the soft cracking of glass and the dripping of liquid. We'd pushed each other too far, too quickly – Charlie had closed her fist around the shot glass, crushing it into shards. I stared at her as she watched the blood start to trickle between her fingers.

'Did we always get this heated with each other?' she said softly.

'Probably,' I conceded. 'I am *very* annoying.'

'And stubborn.'

I couldn't help but smile. 'Please, that's confidence.'

Wincing, Charlie opened her hand and set about picking out the broken glass. The shards were big enough to be removed easily, and the cuts were thankfully superficial. Still, I stayed silent while she worked, not wanting to distract her. And, I suppose, not really having much to say. I felt a lot of the tension start to bleed away in the silence as well, which was a bonus.

'You called me the light of your life,' she said as she affixed an old dish towel around her palm. 'What's that about, getting all flirty all of a sudden?'

'I've always been flirty. It was a strategic flirt.'

'Hmm,' she said. Planting her feet, she rocked forward and all but buried her head in her hands. 'I'm worried, Jim. We've been struggling to make friends, now we're all turtled up. I don't like how this is going.'

I almost risked placing a hand on her shoulder, but I couldn't bring myself to do it. 'We're getting pushed out, but it's what we expected. Everyone expected it. We've got to make a statement, and I can't do that if people come with me.'

'But why?'

'Because if it looks like you agree with my shenanigans, people aren't going to believe you're the cooler heads keeping me in check,' I said. I *did* risk looking a little smug here, I was revealing my plan after all. 'I pull focus, make this all about me like Kaitlyn seems to want, and we're not going to have to worry about people trying to perform a fly-by on everyone else shacked up here.'

This was what my pondering had led to, the idea that a bit of potential self-sacrifice might be a good plan. Again, I wanted to try and turn this unwanted notability against the people who were trying to use it for their own ends, ram it down their throats until they gagged.

The decision had been easy once I saw the circle go online. I had honestly thought it would work after having given it the once over – the warlocks that had put it together had done an excellent job and watching Bodhi juice it up with his magic was intoxicating. The air shimmered and vibrated like molten glass, aurorae of vibrant purples flashing across the surface. It looks downright *majestic*.

But the moment Bodhi finished shunting the last motes of power into it, I saw the glaring flaw that everyone had chosen to overlook.

Everyone loves a good siege, but I feel like a lot of people forget how they end. Outside of big bombastic action films and TV shows, sieges end when the defenders surrender. Without outside help, you're fucked – little by little those outside your castle are going to starve you of food, of real hope, until all that's left is the bitter poison of believing that they might just show you mercy if you admit that they have won.

But they didn't win, not really. They sat there, cranking their hogs, while you beat yourself.

Sure, the circle would probably serve to keep us safe from thaumaturgical attacks, but every moment it was active the fear of the outside world was going to grow more tangible and oppressive. The longer we spent thinking about how we needed to be protected from the unseeable insect suicide bombs, the more we would start to see them buzzing around outside the bubble until, inevitably, we'd just never *do* anything about them.

I didn't tell anyone that I had had this epiphany. It was a little too pessimistic for public consumption and they wouldn't be able to hear it properly anyway. Sure, I could give a rousing tough love speech and calling everyone whiny little bitch-babies, but I didn't have the tools to chip away at this fear. Nor was it my place to anyway – I hadn't come up with the idea for the circle, and if I had going to be the one to talk down the idea, I had missed that opening by now.

No, better to let them have their comfort and just make sure that I was the outside help that they would need.

Fucking hero, me.

I'm not sure if Charlie managed to unpack my very brief answer into the long bit of poetic waffling I just gave you. Judging from the look on her face though, it was unlikely. 'Trying to keep up with the way your mind works is exhausting.'

'How do you think it feels from the inside.'

She let her head hang down and she shook it with resignation. 'Fine. I'm not sure how long the shield will hold anyway.'

'I don't know,' I said. 'Should be fine for a while.'

'If the warlocks on hand still have the magical muscle to keep it fuelled.'

'You don't think they do?'

Charlie shrugged. 'I'm not magical, I only know what I've seen with you. It's been a long time since a lot of these guys used magic regularly. All I'm saying is, I don't know if I'm as confident in the plan as the others are.'

Good old Charlie. It was always nice to be reminded that we shared the same brand of pessimism. Granted, mine was a bit more advanced than hers, but we shared the same core gloom. A little annoying, mind, that hearing the sadness hiding in her voice made me want to tell her that everything would be all right, that the circle was fine, that there was nothing to fear.

I forced that urge down – I wasn't about to start lying to her – but risked taking her hand in mine. 'Worst comes to worst, you know I'll keep you safe, right?'

'Jim, what's—'

'I know I don't do it very often, but try not to interrupt when I'm being serious,' I said quickly. 'Look, I can't make you a promise that the circle will hold, or that my plan will work, or really anything like that.'

'Really encouraging.'

'But after what happened to you with The Rider…' I trailed off, the words catching in my throat. For a moment, I thought Charlie was going to save me the agony of swallowing that lump, but she went just as quiet, reminded of how he used her. 'I'm not saying you can't look after yourself, but if you need me—'

'Ok, enough,' she snapped. 'Stop buttering me up and go get yourself nearly killed again. Once we've heard about you pissing off literally everyone, we'll come and smooth things over.'

She didn't want me seeing how much what I had said had touched her. Cutting me off mid-sentence, before I could say anything that couldn't then be unsaid, was probably for the best. Maybe all the talking with Rider-Robin had affected me more than I realised.

We exchanged a look that damn-near shattered the very flimsy wall she had just erected between us, then I shuffled over a little to give her the room to leave. She did so quickly and without ceremony, leaving me alone in the dusty darkness. I gave her five minutes, then slipped out of the building and through the perimeter of the circle.

Perhaps Charlie had a right to be worried – the circle was already noticeably weaker than it had been when Bodhi fired it up. I was able to cross the threshold without issue, my connection to magic snapping on like a light. I could give the others credit though: the circle did have enough heft to make me barely realise how much weaker I was inside it. That was some quality work.

Speaking of, it was probably time for me to do a fair bit of my own again.

Nine

I didn't know where the factions held their weird little congresses, and the only person I could bank on knowing had betrayed me twice already. Not wanting another knife in the back, I'd need to tap into one of the more deadly streams of intelligence – Zoomers.

It hadn't been long since I was walking a beat around this city, but it had been more than long enough for the landscape to undergo a total metamorphosis. My access to the underground society of mages and magic had been built around dingy speakeasies and illicit pop-up clubs – all of which were shut down now. Partly this was my fault, burning bridges and crashing parties at the behest of Whitehall, but a larger share of the responsibility lay on the removal of the Vault.

Which, I guess, is also somewhat my fault?

In any case, with the threat of getting gelded by the government truly out the window, the political activation of the underground had meant all those speakeasies and clubs had become obsolete overnight. Why skulk around in the shadows when the big bastard bird of prey has had its wings clipped?

All my old contacts were gone, signed up to one of the rising factions and just as likely to try and melt my face as take my call. Even if I was lucky enough to find one to take my call, they wouldn't tell me anything – all that politics and ideology would have dissolved any bonds they would have had with anyone outside their little echo chamber.

Not Zoomers, though.

See, they get a bad rap, but you can't deny the young know how to get shit done. I'd never taken an interest in the up-and-comers, the erstwhile apprentices of the lost generation, because Whitehall never asked me to, and I didn't want to put them on the warlock radar. They did things quietly, never caused a fuss, and honestly, I never gave them a second thought.

Until I met Millie Thatcher. She had lived hard for someone so young and, yes, she was absolutely shit at being a wizard, but it was impossible to claim she didn't have a heart of fucking granite and a mind to match. Don't get this twisted – I like my tomboy disaster goths to be Millennials, thank you – but seeing what she was capable of had switched me on to the younger generation, drawn my attention.

And in between trying to recruit what few of my peers weren't out to blast my sternum out through my arsehole, I had started mapping out the digital threads that kept all those baby magicians tied together. After some truly sobering realisations about how far beyond me modern slang had developed, I managed to immerse myself in the culture enough to pinpoint a few important locations.

Which is to say I sent a text to Millie and asked her to help an old man *do internet things*.

Long story short: turns out young wizards are into irony at a truly prodigious level. Between the docks and the shopping mall, a strip of wasteland was surrounded by what had once been an industrial estate but now was little more than a ghost town. They had co-opted it to come together and do what all young people with too much power and not enough parental supervision do.

They played Quidditch.

I know that sounds like bullshit, and before the Queen of TERF Island sends her corporate knee-crackers to come hobble me, let me clarify that I don't mean *actual* Quidditch. What they practice is a carefully choreographed display of superfandom, complete with home-made costumes and riding their brooms like hobbyhorses. It's truly a sight to behold, a command of spy craft that would make James Bond jealous as shit.

No-one on the planet would ever suspect these kids of having any magical talent at all. Except me, of course.

I'd been watching them for the best part of an hour now, lurking just out of sight at the corner of what had once been a warehouse for custom wallpaper. At first, they hopped around on their brooms, played the part, beaned each other in the head with a tennis ball someone had painted gold. Once they settled in, however, they dropped the act and got straight down to learning.

A pair of kids – and I'm saying *kids,* but they were all late teens or early twenties, I would guess – took on the role of instructors, arranging the others into groups of two before doing the rounds and showing them simple spells. It was fascinating to watch, the speed at which they each picked up the simple workings before experimenting on their own, branching out into more advanced workings of the craft.

One pair conjured a small dragon out of the flame of a disposable cigarette lighter, sending it on a controlled flight over their heads before rendering it back into flammable gas and enticing it back into the device's reservoir. Another duo was working on a spell that seemed to be designed to swap their physical appearances – a glamour of sorts, but deeper and with more permanence.

After watching long enough to get a decent read of their skill level, I thrust my hands into my pockets and started to cross the field towards them. Basically, I did the Columbo walk – obvious, hunched, a little goofy, absolutely no threat to anyone at all.

They clocked me before I was halfway across the field, but they pretended they hadn't until I was within shouting distance – at a guess, they were waiting to see if I was a homeless drunk coming to investigate some noise, or something *more*. When they got a good look at me, the whole group stopped what they were doing and turned on me.

'Don't let me interrupt,' I said, putting on my most disarming smile. 'I've got a few questions for you *upstanding* young mages. While I'd love to go one-by-one, I'm going to bet that your two instructors over there are the only ones that are going to give me the time of day, right?'

There was silence from the group, though a couple did nervously jerk their heads round to look at the pair that had been leading the class – a young man with terracotta skin and an equally young woman with the heft of someone who had just discovered the joys of weightlifting. The man waved the group's concerns away and walked towards me, hand outstretched.

I grasped it firmly, giving him the sort of uncomfortable shake dickhead recruiters do to make you feel disposable in job interviews. 'You would be the ringleader, I suppose?'

He shook back, grip only a tad bit less firm than my own. Confident. 'Not to be rude, but we're not saying anything until we know who you are. You could be a cop.'

'If I was a cop, I'd have to tell you. That's the law.'

'No-one has ever believed that shit, pal,' the woman said, coming alongside the man without offering a handshake. 'But treating us like idiots is definitely indicative of a cop.'

'I'm not a cop,' I said. 'I'm a warlock. Well, used to be.'

'A magic cop, then,' she spat.

The man smiled and took a half-step between me and the young lady. 'We all know it's a little more complicated than that. We're not interested in getting in bad with any of you lot. We've got our own causes, and I'm sorry to say, they don't line up with your civil war just yet.'

The kid was good, well-practiced. He'd given this speech before. 'I'm not here to recruit or conscript you, I'm here to make a deal for some information.'

'And why would we know anything that would be of use to you?'

I smiled. There it was, I had him hooked now. 'Because I've been watching your lot for a few weeks now. From afar. You've turned idle gossip into an art form, an almost uncrackable cipher. I think you lot have been playing a symphony on social media, disguising it all as total nonsense and hashtags.'

'Or,' he replied, a crooked grin creeping across his face. 'Or, we're just young, dumb, and full of cum.'

'If you think I'm going to believe that now, it's *shit* you're full of, not cum.'

His eyes narrowed, then he laughed and slapped my shoulder. 'You're all right, Old Man. I'm Walid, this here is Su-Yin.'

The woman's expression didn't soften, but she did go so far as to jerk her chin at me. 'Hey.'

Walid squeezed her shoulder then swept his arm out in an arc, signalling toward rest of the group. 'We call this Big School. A safe place for people to come and learn the sort of self-defence you need to know when a magical civil war is on the cards.'

'Self-defence?' I said. 'Like summoning a dragon out of a cigarette lighter?'

Su-Yin smirked like a wolf. 'Why make the lessons needlessly boring?'

'Fair enough.'

She nodded to Walid and walked around me and back towards her students. Practice resumed instantly, evidently her return signalled that I wasn't a threat to the group after all. Still, I could feel their eyes on me, nonetheless.

Walid slid into the welcoming smile of a used car salesman and gently led me a little further away from the group. 'I think she likes you.'

'She hides it well, if she does.'

'She doesn't trust easy,' he said. 'None of us do. When you get basically abandoned by the society, you've got to make your own, right?'

'Deep thinking for someone so young.'

'Mate, the world's been against us from day one. Frankly, you're the ones playing catch up.'

I liked Walid. His brash confidence was, I'm sure you'll agree, rather reminiscent of myself, and he talked with enough authority to get you believing he knew what he was talking about. But I also could tell already that he was going to be trouble. He was too friendly and far too welcoming – either he really didn't see me as a threat, which was foolish, or he was confident enough in his skill to take me out if I was, which was even more foolish. I'd played this game before, from his side of the board in fact, and it usually didn't go well.

He thought he had all the cards.

'Here's the deal,' I said. 'I need to know where those political nutters are holding their big congress or whatever they are calling it. Can you still call them pow-wows or is that racist?'

'Pretty sure it's always been a bit racist.'

I was playing the part of an ignorant elder, and the first step had been a success. 'Look, pretty sure you lot think you're above all that grandstanding and bullshitting. Or you weren't invited. Regardless, I know that you know where it's being held.'

Walid's smile dropped, his expression going from youthful and boisterous to entirely business. 'We're not spies or information dealers.'

'Today you could be.'

'Maybe, but we don't *want* to be,' he said. 'We know things, yeah, but they're for *us*, to keep *us* safe. The moment we start selling out, we become players in your world.'

'And you think you're safe because you're overlooked, that about right?'

He shrugged. 'We *are* overlooked. That can be something we resent, or something we can use for our benefit.'

'Sounds like you're just trying to haggle, to me.'

'Then you've not been listening.'

He didn't try to square up to me, but I could tell he had meant to put some punch into his words then. His stance shifted, his body turning in such a way that I could get a good view of the training going on behind him. The class was his leverage – and the fact he would make that implication told me that perhaps he wasn't as goodie-goodie as he was claiming to be. That meant there was a chance I could push him to make a deal.

'You'd be surprised how many people say that to me,' I replied, moving a couple of steps to position him between me and the group. 'But I listen just fine, and what I'm hearing from you is that you think your YMCA karate class can stand up to Cobra Kai. Fine, maybe existing under the radar has kept you safe this long, but someone *will* come knocking someday. I did, after all.'

'And I'm politely sending you on your way, no bad blood and no lasting sour taste.'

'Ok, we have a bit of an impasse here, built on one of us holding a faulty assertion,' I said. I'd found my way in, somewhere I could slide a hook into and twist until the armour buckled. 'You think you've got it all figured out, that you're secure and safe and hidden. I think your head is full of shit and you can't learn how to crush bollocks without an experienced bollock-crusher in your corner.'

'What?'

I chuckled. 'Sorry, I have a slight tendency towards gobshitery. The Spark Notes, then: you think you're negotiating from a position of strength, I disagree. If I prove I'm right, you give me the information I came for.'

'And when you're proven wrong?'

'You get another scalp to shore up that growing sense of security you've got there.'

Almost immediately, his eyes shot across the field to Su-Yin. Walid was unquestionably the big cheese of the group, but I recognised from his look that she had his ear. In fact, from the way the look lingered just a little too long, she had a little more than his ear.

His heart, if you missed the subtlety in my language there. Clearly unrequited, or at least unexplored, love –

it would always butt in where it wasn't wanted and right now it was colouring Walid's reasoning when it came to my offer.

Now, you see, a smart man would know that if someone like me makes you such a bet it's because he's got more aces up his sleeve that a Motorhead tribute band's best-of compilation. It's always a hustle, only an idiot would trust to chance. But a man who *thinks* he's smart will get caught up on trying to read you, working out whether you are bluffing or not. They'll also let things like pride and looking impressive for a girl get a seat or two at the brain table.

'You know what,' he said. 'You're on. Wizard's duel. I'll—'

I tutted and wagged a finger at him. I was going full condescending arsehole now. 'Not just you. Your entire class, at once, against just me. I want there to be no doubt that I beat you, *all of you.*'

Again, his eyes snapped to Su-Yin across the field. He knew that I was up to something now, but the need to hold his authority and allure was fighting him for control. It would convince him – you can't beat your own hormones, let me tell you.

'Deal.'

I clapped my hands loudly, drawing a little more attention. 'I knew you'd see sense. Go get your posse ready, I'll just wait here with my eyes closed and my back turned. When you're ready, come kick the shit out of me with any spells you happen to know.'

He gave me one last confused look, then jogged across the field to his class.

Now, I know what you're thinking – I name dropped Cobra Kai and now I'm going to flip that on its head and break out the old Mr Miyagi trope. But you're wrong. Sort of.

No matter how skilled you are with magic, no matter how much muscle you've got, the numbers game is still completely valid. The stories of dark wizards being brought down by legions of insufferable good guys all come from somewhere and, indeed, Whitehall wouldn't have been able to kick our arses so thoroughly if it wasn't true.

Have you ever watched The Pink Panther? Inspector Clouseau would get jumped by his manservant – a skilled martial artist – at the most inopportune moments and always win. Now, yeah, that's a comedy but it's not unfounded. The message is that you don't win by being the better fighter, you win by controlling the battlefield.

Or maybe that's Sun Tzu. It's easy to get those two mixed up, *The Art of War* and *The Pink Panther* – they're both classics, after all.

Anyway, with my back turned and my eyes closed I could just about hear the conversation between Walid and Su-Yin. Not the words themselves, but the general tone of things told me that people were getting on board nice and quickly. Everyone wanted a chance to test their new moves on the old man, as expected.

Reaching out with my power, I probed the capabilities of the group. Half of them were minor talents, so weak with magic that I could deflect their spells with a scowl, while the others seemed to have a fair amount of untapped potential. Walid and Su-Yin weren't especially gifted in terms of power, but their veins crackled with what power they could command – a solid sign that they had some skill with using what the good lord gave them.

All in all, a quarter of the group were worth worrying about, and I had no doubt that they knew they were the ringers. They'd lead the charge – and it *would be* a charge despite not needing to be – with Walid and Su-Yin at the head.

I drew in my power and held it tight to my chest, warming my heart and sending blood thundering to my extremities. Waiting still, I formed the spell in my mind, ready to let loose the moment they pulled the trigger on their attacks.

In all honesty, I have to admit that they came close to getting one over on me. They waited a lot longer than I had expected to start charging, and if one of them hadn't stepped a little too heavily I wouldn't have even noticed that they had been *creeping* up on me. The power profiles I had been studying were a clever trick, shadows held together by an impressive bit of prestidigitation. They had crossed half the distance between us by the time one of them bungled it, which wasn't nearly close enough to be any trouble.

Still, I acted quickly. Releasing my spell, I cast it down into the soil. It plunged down, past the topsoil and the roots of the over-grown grass, deep into the aquifer nestled at the boundary of the water table. I felt the cool water on its slow march through the ground, over towards whichever well or stream it would eventually burst to freedom, and I enticed it away. It followed my power up through the earth and into the dirt a few millimetres under the topsoil. At my command, it saturated that soil, reducing it to a muddy slop perfectly concealed by the still-solid topsoil.

The kids had no idea.

Su-Yin was the first one to reach my secret sinkhole, vanishing into the mud before she had time to realise that she had lost her footing. A couple of the students followed her in, their yells of surprise cut short by their disappearance below the surface. It was, however, enough to make the rest of the group scramble to stop themselves from following suit. I pushed the water towards them, dunking another few of them into the squelchy depths.

Despite the chaos, Walid and a couple of the more adept students had the wherewithal to cross the gap, leaping over my manufactured marsh with impressive agility. They hit the ground as one, rolling through their momentum and up to their feet, releasing a volley of magic as they did so. I span in response, wrenching my power out from the ground and up into a sweeping shield that knocked their attacks aside easily.

A momentary pause played out, the splashing of the confused and furious the only sound as Walid and his students sized me up. Again, I bided my time and let them make the first move. I didn't have to wait long.

Walid stepped forward, ushering his students back as he did so, drawing in a fresh wave of power. I could see the darkness in his eyes now, creeping to the forefront and offering him the strength to beat me. He knew the moves, the tactics, even the spells – but he'd not had anyone to teach him the *control*.

He unleashed a crackling torrent of energy that would have put a lot of hardened warlocks to shame with its sheer force. It had the wisps of life powering it, the stupid decision people always make when they let the darkness whisper to them a little too long. It was visually terrifying, and the flashing whip of magic was certainly strong enough to beat me into the dirt. But like in any fight, if you overextend, you'll throw yourself off balance.

Again, I knocked his spell aside, bringing my shield up at just the right angle to encourage the wild energy to another target. It slammed into the ground a foot away, kicking up turf and soil. By the time the dust had settled, I had closed the distance between us and twisted his arm up behind his back.

I know you've seen I'm not exactly great in a fight, but if you give me time to prepare, I can be pretty kickass if I do say so myself. Granted, I was in a fight with a group of what were essentially kids, self-taught and not exactly master tacticians, but I still made it look *good*.

The fight ended as suddenly as it had started. With Walid's arm locked, his students almost melted away, or at least their confidence. They dropped their guards and looked at each other with confusion, waiting for a new leader to step up. One didn't, and Walid let out a playful chuckle.

'OK, Old Man, maybe you do know a few tricks we aren't prepared for.'

I released his arm and slapped him on the shoulder. 'You're not bad yourself. These kids could stand to have a worse teacher than you I suppose.'

'Yeah, well, you won,' he said. 'So, I guess we're getting into the information brokering game. Give us half an hour, we'll get you what you need.'

The students slunk off, defeated and dejected. Some of them set about helping their friends out of my mud trap, the others headed to a pile of bags and coats that was arranged by one edge of the field. This second group pulled out a set of smart phones and started doing the exact sort of technowizardry I had sought them out for. I figured it would be best to let them work without hovering over them, so I found a comfortable bit of perimeter wall and perched there waiting.

After about ten minutes, the last of the floundering kids had been extracted from the mud. Walid and Su-Yin had been doing the bulk of the lifting, him with a little magic and her with pure strength. When the last one was hauled out, Walid looked the more tired of the two. He flopped onto the grass as a fuming Su-Yin, still caked in drying mud, stormed over to me. I shifted my weight, ready to roll with the oncoming punches, but instead she just sat down next to me on the wall and brooded for a minute or two.

'That was humiliating,' she said eventually. Her voice was low so that it wouldn't carry, but the frustration in it was thick.

'It was meant to be humbling, not humiliating.'

She shot me a look. 'Same thing. Some of us here have had to grow up faster than we should have needed to. It can be hard to remember we're not all masters of the craft yet. So, thanks.'

'I… Well, I wasn't expecting such a calm response if I'm honest.'

'Not going to give you the satisfaction of a tantrum. I'm young, but I'm not a bloody baby.'

I smiled. 'Never any danger of that.'

She let that hang in the air for a moment. 'You've caused a problem, you know.'

'I have?'

'Yeah,' she said. 'And if you're going to rock in here playing the wizened old codger card, it's going to go both ways.'

'I'm still not seeing how I caused a problem.'

'Bullshit,' she said, scooting up a little closer. 'Everyone saw Walid casting that last spell. Difference is, only the three of us – you, me, and him – know *how* he did it.'

Maybe someone in this little group knew a little about control after all. 'How often does he tap into the black.'

'Not often,' she said. 'But enough that it worries me. He doesn't believe in black magic, thinks of what he's doing there as a *limit break*. As far as he's concerned, it's just freak strength brought about by getting his arse handed to him.'

'Are things that bad that he hasn't even been taught the basics of Wearing the Black?'

'Yeah, hi,' she said, waving a hand around. 'You realise we only do this because there aren't any responsible adults around these days, yeah?'

'But you know.'

'First-hand experience. But let's not get into my sob story.'

I hadn't taken the time to really consider how the last few years would have affected the next generation. Even taking the time to look into them as I had, there was a lot more I hadn't even begun to consider – so much of our traditions and skills existed only so long as they were passed down from mentor to apprentice, and that should be extremely embarrassing for people as keen on fat books as wizards tend to be.

With a bit more context, I could see that I had misread Walid. Talented, skilled, protective, all of that was true, but he wasn't as confident as he had appeared. His glances toward Su-Yin weren't the furtive looks of young love – the more she talked, the more I realised that she was his conscience. That was a relationship I could understand.

'You keep him in check,' I said.

'He keeps himself in check,' she shot back. 'I just happen to help. But if he does slip... I know enough not to listen to that voice, and I don't think the others are strong enough to have it talk to them.'

I nodded. 'You don't think you can talk him down if the time comes.'

She shrugged.

'I've been there,' I continued. 'I had someone like you looking out for me, and she did a lot of good keeping me in line. But when words weren't enough, I had more hands-on help. I'll consider that your fee.'

'Fee?'

'For helping me with the information I need,' I said. 'I'll pay you back by stepping in when necessary. Oh, and keeping my distance when it isn't. I'm not interested in pissing in your cereal, you've got a good setup here.'

She looked relieved, and it surprised me that I felt a little serene myself. It was more of that same sensation I had first encountered dealing with Millie, something that was sorely lacking when it came to dealing with my peers. These kids were making mistakes, some of those mistakes pretty massive if Walid was any indication, but they were all their own – they had cut themselves off from the bullshit that Whitehall had pumped into our veins, and seeing how that was changing the way they developed as magicians was *fascinating*.

In any case, before she could say anything else, Walid interrupted our moment of reflection by thrusting a tablet under my nose. My eyes focused on a GPS map showing the grounds of a beautiful manor house just outside the town.

'That was easier than expected,' he said. 'Found it on AirBnB. Every room booked out by an account by the name of Neil Weaver. I think someone was trying to be clever.'

Su-Yin cut in, mercifully sparing me the humiliation of exposing my ignorance. 'How is that clever?'

'Neil Weaver sounds like a pretty normal name, right?' Walid said. 'But it's also the name of the principal founder of The Magic Circle.'

I couldn't help but laugh. 'We've used that organisation as a way to deflect suspicions from the magical community for years. I guess someone is keen on upholding tradition.'

'The place is called Dunningford Manor,' Walid said, zooming out the view a little. 'That enough for you to find your way there?'

'I'm not *that* much older than you, you know. I do know how Google works.'

I allowed Walid the cheeky little smirk. I'd kicked his arse so handily that I felt letting him snark it up in my direction was a suitable olive branch. Su-Yin pretended not to notice the gesture, but the moment Walid's attention was directed elsewhere she threw me a tiny nod of thanks.

He withdrew the tablet, slipping it under his arm. 'We good then?'

'I think so,' I said. 'You do good work though, far too good. Means I'll probably be back in the future when I need more snooping done.'

'We're not going professional here,' Walid said. 'Don't go thinking we'll be making a business out of this.'

I tapped the address into my phone, watching as the directions were calculated. 'Good, because I don't intend to pay you. Catch you later, kiddos.'

Ten

Dunningford Manor had a stellar rating on TripAdvisor and AirBnb, though the big brains who kept their critiques contained to Yelp were less impressed. Cold, airy, expensive, and *too many bidets* were their considered opinions.

Personally, my main complaint was that the driveway was ludicrously long.

My taxi rumbled past the gate ten minutes earlier, and it was only now that I was reaching the front of the house. The driveway had been windy and composed of loose gravel, the exact sort of setup to wreck the undercarriage of any vehicle daring to go above 10 miles per hour, and it didn't even have the good graces to break up the monotony of the view with a nice tree – just flat, perfect lawn as far as I could see.

Arriving at the manor, I paid the taxi driver a reasonable tip and sent him on his way. I had considered driving myself there, and the directions hadn't been difficult to follow, but I hadn't wanted to run the risk of turning up in an identifiably warlock car – they'd smell the magic that had seeped into the upholstery from a mile away.

The house did make the trip worthwhile, at least. A couple of centuries old, it had clearly undergone several rounds of modernisation over the years but never to the detriment of its appearance. In fact, the only things that marred the beauty of the place even a little were the few remaining marks of a long-since-undone remodel that had seemingly added a few bevelled columns to the building, reminiscent of Versailles.

I suppose, as a building, it adeptly summed up the magical community: beautiful, distant, self-important, and quite out of place in the modern world. No wonder they picked this place for their little tete-a-tete.

Taking a moment to smooth out any creases in my jacket just in case, I took the marble steps up to the main entrance. The main hall was vast but empty, though an unmanned reception desk did just awkwardly from one corner. A placard had been positioned above the little bell traditionally rung for attention; an arrow pointed down a nearby corridor and underneath it, in an obnoxiously curly font, *Weaver Party*.

Booking out all the rooms had made sense, but I hadn't expected them to pay off all the staff too. Don't get me wrong, I'm glad they did – last thing I needed was having to talk my way past a receptionist with a chip on her shoulder – but it did make me wonder what these guys were hiding. They didn't even want the *risk* of being overheard, and that said something.

I followed the corridor pointed to by the arrow, taking a couple of turns before reaching a pair of wooden doors, a slick honey-gold varnish giving the wood that regal shimmer. Another sign indicated that the place was reserved for the *Weaver Party*, so I placed my ear to the door to find out if I was about to make a very dynamic entrance.

I couldn't hear shit. The wood was far too thick.

One deep breath to bolster my nerves and I threw both doors open in as flamboyantly extravagant a gesture as I could manage, ready to strut in and interrupt some *goddamn politics*. Sadly, there was no party to crash.

Some enterprising soul on staff at the manor had laid out a number of tables, complete with place settings and silk tablecloths, but someone else had pushed them away from the centre of the room.

Instead, a high-backed wooden chair had been positioned as the focal point, angled towards the door, with napkins arranged on the floor around it like the markings on a clockface.

It was a familiar setup, albeit reproduced with less grandeur than the original quorum of the Magisterium. Whoever put this meeting together – and I had to believe it was Kaitlyn – was clearly pulling out all the stops to try and give it more legitimacy than it deserved, what with it being nothing more than a gathering of rebels, terrorists, traitors, and cowards.

She was using the visuals of the last attempt at a wizard government, and doing so shamelessly.

I walked the circle a couple of times, getting a feel for the arrangement. In the Magisterium, the central seat was reserved for the Speaker, the wizard that was setting the agenda for the day. The others would be arranged around the circle, a symbolic barrier between the heart of power and the supplicants come to make their demands. The more importance you had, the closer to the centre of the Speaker's eyeline you could stand.

It was a stupid and outdated way to do things, and we hadn't used it for the day to day. It was a theatrical endeavour, one we only bothered to trot out for effect, but it had a reputation. That's often more than enough to make people *think* you are doing things properly. That Kaitlyn hadn't chosen to waver from the laughably outdated overall design had me wondering which group she would be putting where on the circle – there wasn't a chance she would have held onto that feature if she wasn't going to use it.

After my third circumnavigation of the room, I crossed the boundary of the circle and made myself comfortable in the chair at the centre. I may not have been able to make a theatrical entrance, but I could damn sure set up an arresting visual for when the others arrived. By the time the factions started to show up I had made myself very thoroughly at home.

On by one they filed in, none of them seeming surprised to see me, filtering into their places on the circle as though they knew them by heart. That meant either that a memo had been sent around to which I was not privy, or Kaitlyn had been using this layout at her meetings for longer than I thought.

We really should have made the effort to attend sooner.

Kaitlyn van Ives was the last one to arrive. She had an honour guard of mages flanking her, clad in the same Zapatistan getup as she had been sporting in her broadcast. They looked very professional, every bit the modern freedom fighting force they purported to be. These guards closed the double doors behind them, blocking them with their bodies. Kaitlyn waited until they were in position before she began to slowly walk around the circle anti-clockwise, shaking hands and offering whispered greetings to everyone there.

Not once did she take her eyes off of me, though.

I stayed quiet and watched her orbit until she returned back to the start and took one step over the line of the circle. 'Parker. How fortunate you survived the attack. The second one, I mean. Two in as many days, someone really has it out for you.'

'Indeed,' I said, leaning forward in my seat. 'Good thing I have you looking out for me, then, right?'

An unreadable expression flickered across Kaitlyn's face. 'So, you've come to make our alliance all official, then?'

'Not exactly,' I replied. 'Seeing as the entire thing is a massive pile of horseshit, created just to con people into getting into lockstep with you.'

I had expected a reaction from the crowd, at least a gasp or something, but there was silence. A knowing silence – this wasn't news to them, it was a *given*. The only noticeable reaction came from the doors as a pair of new guards slid in behind the previous two.

Smiling, Kaitlyn started to close the distance between us. 'I told them the truth as soon as they RSVP'd, Jim. I just had to bring them to the table; once everyone was in the same room it became much easier to find our common causes, the lines we all needed to draw. And, hey, look, it even brought the warlocks to the table!'

'Not the warlocks, just me.'

She was right in front of me now and leant in close to whisper in my ear. 'The only warlock that matters. You'll see.'

Over her shoulder, I saw another pair of guards slip through the doors and into the room. Now, call me paranoid, but I was starting to get a little worried at that. If this influx kept up, Kaitlyn's men would outnumber the people from the other factions and they didn't seem to care, or even notice.

Kaitlyn pulled back from me and started to address the room again. 'We all know that, eventually, the Aegis would have been a problem. There's a lot of division in this room about what we should be doing, what the world looks like after all this, but I think everyone agrees that open conflict with Whitehall, at least right now, is suicide.'

There was a low murmur of agreement from the faction leaders. Some were more on board with her message than others, but even I had to concede that it would have been dumb as hell to step up to Whitehall while we were so divided. Even with magic on our side, they still had the numbers and the resources. They had, after all, already beaten us once.

'So, yes,' she continued. 'I manufactured a consensus and took out a problem. And now I've brought you all here to make sure those division are dealt with so that we have the strength to survive this.'

'Oh, come on, Kaitlyn!' I shouted. I needed everyone in the room to hear me if I was going to get in their heads. 'Surely even you can see there's no golden compromise here. Half of these groups alone are politically focused, pressure groups. You're not going to get them to agree to a show of force. The other half, sure, there's some militants in there, but do you think they're going to want to pull their punches to keep the others on side?'

There was another, louder, murmur from the group. Kaitlyn was swimming up river here, so I was very aware that I didn't need to win the argument, just throw enough rocks in that stream so that she couldn't beat back the tide. I'm not a great peacemaker, but I'm excellent at winding people up.

Annoyingly, Kaitlyn showed no sign of being concerned. 'You've never really understood compromises, have you, Parker? Those *golden* ones aren't real, they're not fought for and so only ever work in the short term. The real ones, the *lasting* ones, they're *bloody*.'

I'd missed it earlier – or I hadn't wanted to see it – but there was a wildness in her eyes as she said those words. The Kaitlyn I knew was terrifying when she had to be, but did so with a cold, calculated professionalism.

If she wanted to scare you, it wasn't because she enjoyed it, because she didn't. She did the bad things because they needed doing, not because they were fun.

But she *was* having fun now. Those wild, wide eyes and that smile so wide it looked like her cheeks would split, they gave her a malevolence I hadn't seen on her before. Not even when I had stood there and watched her tear the head off a vampire.

Maybe that was why I had been slow on the uptake, or maybe I really was incapable of conceiving what she was about to do. In either case, I missed any and all chances to stop her from pulling the pin on her metaphorical grenade.

With a snap of her fingers, the group of guards she had brought with her stepped aside, giving us all a free path to the door. Almost immediately, the handles rattled for a second before the heavy wooden doors burst inwards, smashing loudly against the wall. Standing in the doorway, seething and radiating the sort of rage that brought down whole kingdoms back in the dark ages, stood a hulking brute with torn irises and teeth like razors.

I almost choked on my own tongue. 'Laura…'

I guess that answered the question of what those potato men had been doing showing up at her house, but it raised some fresh ones too. Chiefly: what the *fuck?*

The Laura-beast took a couple of slow, powerful, horrifying steps into the room. Behind her, two more people I didn't recognise slipped out of her shadow. One was a young man, slender but with a roman nose and gleaming golden eyes lurking under powerful brows. The other, a short and withered old woman with one eye and, most unsettlingly, an extra knuckle on each finger. As they emerged, Kaitlyn and her people slipped behind them and out the door, erecting a spell to seal us all inside.

It was a slaughter.

The faction leaders tried to fight back, but it was clear that none of them had experience dealing with creatures of this scale and skill. Laura alone eviscerated one group before anyone could even react, moving onto a second and a third with such speed that spells were impacting about 6 feet away from where she was at any one time.

Laura went through the middle, but the other two went up the flanks. The young man torched the wizards to my right, spitting a gout of scarlet flame that burned so hot it roasted the skin away on his own cheeks, leaving smoking red scales behind. The old woman hobbled up my left, shrugging away spells as if they weren't even there, before wrapping her long fingers around the head of one unfortunate soul. She took a deep breath, drinking silvery wisps out of the man's mouth and nose. Not a few seconds later, she released him, his flesh now riddled with sores and pustules. She looked decades younger, and he fell limply to the ground.

The spectacle nearly kept me from bringing my shield up in time, bringing me very close to having my head ripped off by a single swipe of Laura's vicious claws. Still, her momentum was enough to knock me backwards, the chair tumbling, sending me to the floor. The back of my head hit the floorboards hard, sending my vision spinning for a second, but I had just enough wherewithal to deflect a second blow, and a third, letting her springboard off my shield and behind me and I got to my feet.

The other wizards were toast – even the ones that still lived wouldn't last more than thirty more seconds, and I was struggling to defend myself against one of the trio of terror. Maybe one on one, given the space to move and think, I could take each of them in turn, but not together. They'd overwhelm me and tear me to shreds.

And Kaitlyn had known that all along. The barrier spell wasn't for the benefit of the faction leaders, that was entirely to deal with me. Another trap, but this one wasn't for spin – she meant it.

What the hell was going on with her?

Laura lunged at me again, driving me back and towards the fire-breathing young man. He smiled and belched another burst of flame in my direction. The shield held, but not completely – the heat of the flames started to bleed through and I could feel the hair on my arms starting to singe. Somewhere behind me, I heard a horrifying cackle as the crone sucked the life out of yet another poor soul.

I was already getting tired and holding the shield against such an onslaught was draining what few reserves I had left. If I was going to survive this, I needed a way out and fast.

Scanning the room, I realised Kaitlyn had chosen well. The windows were huge, but the glass was thick, triple glazed, and lined with leading – it was breakable, but I'd have to drop my shield to do it, and then I'd be minced. There was only one doorway into, and out of, the room and it was sealed. The parquet felt as though it was laid right onto the concrete foundations, so there wasn't even a helpful basement to blast my way down into.

It was the perfect kill box.

Almost.

Another swipe from Laura cracked my shield and knocked me off balance. I stumbled, pushing what little energy I had left into the shield so that the follow-up spout of fire didn't roast me. My shield held once more, but in turning to block his attack, I spotted something. My salvation.

Behind him, set into the far rear wall of the room, was an ornate fireplace. A beautifully carved mantel, wide and deep pit for the logs, and, most importantly, what looked like a spacious chimney. Not overly glamourous as escape routes go, but you take what you can get.

I put every last ounce of magic I had into my shield and waited for the next attack. Seconds later, Laura obliged, using the young man as a springboard to come down at me from above, a strike powerful enough to drive me into the ground like a railroad spike. Again, she caught the shield, but this time I didn't even try to hold it. I let the spell shatter, haemorrhaging all the excess magic I had managed to push into it in a blinding flash of sparks. The hope was it would stun them long enough for me to make it to the chimney.

It was partly a success. Laura and the man yelped, covering their eyes and falling to their knees, but as I made my move, I felt a set of cold, bony fingers tighten around my throat. The crone, she had been so quiet I hadn't even heard her creeping up on me and now, her grip squeezing my throat closed, she had me dead to rights.

With a strength that belied her slender form, she turned me around against my protestations and locked eyes with me. The weathered old hag that had entered just moments ago was gone now and in her place stood a raven-haired, pearly-skinned pin-up from the 50s. Her lips were blood red, her cheeks flush, and that one eyeball was keen. A cold, emotionless smile spread across those plump lips as she began to drink from me.

I kicked at her and clawed at her hands around my throat, but it was no use. The more she inhaled the heavier my limbs started to feel. My vision fading, I lashed out with all my remaining strength and drove two fingers into her empty eye socket. I pushed until I felt bone, soft flesh squelching. She squealed in agony, as you might expect, and her grip loosened just enough for me to twist out of it and break into a sprint for the fireplace.

I crossed the room in less than a second, dropped into a slide, then launched myself into the chimney and started a hurried, scrabbling climb. There was no time to stop and breathe, no allowances could be made for safety, I just had to get up there as fast as possible and work out my next move.

My lungs burned, my forearms and back were cut from the jagged masonry, but I made it to the top in time to hear Laura tearing at the brickwork below me. Her powerful hands burst through the walls of the chimney, kicking up ash and dust, shaking me so much I nearly fell. Holding my nerve, I managed the last few feet and sloughed out onto the roof.

Laying there for a moment on the damp slates, I tried to breathe. The exertion of the climb had tapped me completely, but trying to suck in fresh air made it even worse, instead causing me to choke on the ash that had caked my clothes. The coughing and spluttering were eating into what little respite I had bought myself – it was too much to hope for that they would break off their pursuit just because I was on the roof.

Still coughing, I crawled across the tiles and over to some guttering. It was old, trusty iron that had been painted a hundred times, thick with weather-proof black paint. Gingerly, I took hold of the drainpipe and started to lower myself down. The brackets affixing it to the wall creaked worryingly with every inch I climbed, but it held, and within moment I was back on solid ground.

If I'd had a proper bit of teenage rebellion way back when, maybe I would have found the whole experience nostalgic.

I was behind the building now, and the view was not as pleasant as it had been from the front. The rear gardens were being renovated and most of the plants and grass had been relocated or straight up bulldozed. Piles of loose earth, muddy excavation pits, and stacked construction materials killed the classy vibe the front of the property had so expertly built up. On the plus side, it would give me marvellous cover.

Running wasn't on the cards, but I could just about manage a sort of lop-sided jog. If I could cross the garden and make for the trees that bordered the property, maybe I could disappear into the woods long enough that they'd give up hunting me. If nothing else, I stood a better chance of losing them that way than any other.

Weaving around the bulldozed earth, I kept glancing over my shoulder for Laura or her buddies, expecting them to appear in a window like the ghost in some gothic novel. I couldn't see them, which was a little odd. Laura had to have reached the roof by now, and they should have known that from there I wasn't going to head down the front of the building in case Kaitlyn and company were still there. It shouldn't have taken them this long to work out where I was going.

While peering over my shoulder for the fourth time, I managed to snag my foot and fell face first into the dirt. Cursing myself, I rolled over to find a coil of damp rope was wrapped around my ankle. Hurriedly, I tried to untangle myself, but every time it looked like I had managed to free myself, the rope slithered and knotted again even tighter. It didn't help that the damn thing was slimy and smooth, not at all like any rope I was used to dealing with.

Which made sense, ultimately, when I realised it wasn't a rope.

It was worms. Hundreds of them, interwoven and plaited just like a rope, but alive and writhing over me. I'm not ashamed to say I panicked and tried to kick them off me, but each attempt to shake them off just urged them to climb higher. They wrapped tighter around me, moving up my leg to my thigh, then onto my torso and up slowly to my already aching throat.

The tentacle of worms lifted me up by the neck, off the ground until my feet couldn't reach the floor. All I could do was watch as more worms – some thin pink strings, others fatter and grey – started to emerge from the earth and knit themselves into the heaving mass. They were followed by other creatures, things like slugs and spiders, things with more eyes than legs or more legs than braincells. Buzzing wings brought flies, wasps, hornets, crickets, all of them landing on the mass and locking together, merging.

As more insects joined, a shape started to emerge. A human shape. A man, his hand at my throat, staring up at me with eyes made of fireflies. His lips, a pair of rippling millipedes, parted to reveal a set of teeth made from the stingers of scorpions.

'Enough with the games,' he hissed at me. 'Your part is played, little man.'

He pulled me in tight, and I felt the tips of his teeth brush against the skin of my neck.

And then he exploded.

A shower of insects burst out of him, scattered into the air and the mud, peppering the garden beside me. For a moment, his hand still remained, tight around my throat, but then that too burst into a loose swarm. I fell to the ground again in time to watch him reassemble himself, rage causing the fireflies to burn even brighter in his face.

'You,' he all but spat with disgust, staring over me. 'Ready to come home at last, little bird?'

A volley of magic slammed into him, carving fist-sized chunks of bugs out of his form, sending him staggering. Then, as he sank to one knee, a bolt of pure cerulean energy obliterated him once more, driving insects into the dirt like buckshot.

Behind me, I heard the roar of an engine getting closer and I turned in time to see a van skid to a halt about twenty metres away, muddy water spraying from its tyres. Crouched on the roof, one hand gripping at the metal panels, a woman was brandishing a walking cane glowing with arcane symbols. She drummed the tip of the cane on the roof and the side door on the van slid open. Just to be doubly cool, she was clearly using magic to drive.

Ania Petrova glared down at me from the roof, magic crackling across her eyes. 'Fucking get in the van!'

I didn't need telling twice.

With every last tiny little morsel of life left in me, I pushed myself up and half-ran, half-crawled to the van while Ania was launching spells over my head at the creepy crawlies behind me. The door closed behind me as I threw myself into the back and the van wasted no time in speeding off, suspension crunching against the uneven ground.

The van drove hard and fast for what felt like half an hour, but was probably only a fraction of that time, until a shrill grinding noise signalled that the engine had heroically chewed itself to death ensuring my escape. As it drifted to a halt, Ania yanked open the side door and offered me a hand, pulling me out and onto the side of the road.

'Are you ok?' she asked. 'Sorry I could not get there sooner. I've been driving all night.'

I rubbed at my throat. If it wasn't bruised already, there was going to be some delightful marks showing up there in the next few days. 'I'll live. I think. I wasn't expecting you to show up, but I don't think I've ever been happier to—'

'Don't get too excited,' she said, cutting me off. 'When you hear what I've got to tell you, you might not be so happy.'

I sighed. 'Story of my life. Go on, hit me with the bad news.'

Ania leant onto her cane, suddenly looking much frailer than she had a moment earlier. 'The man of insects, I know who he is. He's Lucien De Sade.'

Eleven

Before Whitehall had thoroughly smashed us into the ground, Lucien De Sade had been the poster boy for the worst aspects of magical society. There was a lot of gossip about what exactly he did, how he did it, that sort of thing, but out of all of it there were just a couple of facts that everyone knew:

He was the pre-eminent sex wizard on the planet, and he was dangerous.

I took a moment to find my voice. 'Are you absolutely sure?'

'Parker,' Ania said, bristling. I had known the question would upset her, but it still needed to be asked. 'I'm sure. *Extremely*.'

'Are you all right?'

A low growl rumbled in her throat, her eyes flashing briefly with magic once more. Closing her eyes, she pushed it down through her cane and into the ground, making the sigils in the wood flare with light for a split second. 'I'll... I *will* be fine. There's a lot of bad shit to deal with there, and I thought I was coming out the other end. But seeing him again... It brought things back.'

'Brought things back, right,' I said, my tone a little sly. 'Brought back the ability to kick his arse into the stratosphere, you mean.'

There was a delay between her chuckle and her smile, it took a half-second or so too long to reach her face. She was trying to placate me, convince me that she was fine, but he was in there now, throwing open all the locked doors in her head. Ania didn't want me to know how much she was hurting.

Which made sense. Considering their history.

I've mentioned in the past that Ania had been one of Lucien's thralls. It was a while back, so I'll forgive you for not remembering, but even back then I didn't go into too much detail. I still won't – it's not my story to tell and there's no real way to do it without using *violent sexual imagery* – but what I will say is that De Sade graduated from the Crowley school of wizardry.

Aleister Crowley was a man of vision, which is not always as good a thing as you might think. He held that the most potent magical power was only accessible at the moment of sexual climax and that actions that let someone achieve that state were, therefore, magical rituals. This is to say he was a horny motherfucker who thought the words *magic wand* and *penis* were interchangeable. But he wasn't dangerous, not really. He was a curiosity.

Lucien De Sade took those teaching and twisted them with such vicious ferocity that could only be achieved by someone with his surname. He enslaved dozens of mages of all ages, all sexes, using them as living batteries for his magic. He was so vile in his actions that the Magisterium – you know, the council of big brained wizard bastards like me and The Rider – outright refused to ever consider inviting him to the table. It was the only thing on which we all agreed.

I don't know when he got his hands on Ania, how he broke her mind and made her one of his willing puppets, but I do know she was there at the end. She got a front row seat of Paul Renner putting so much lead into that profane sack of shit that he could pass as the world's largest pencil. Ania Petrova had watched him die, been at his side for a long time, so I was inclined to believe she was right despite how impossible it sounded.

'He *was* confirmed dead, though,' I said. 'And not confirmed as a pile of insects.'

Ania's eyes lost focus, drifting off into the distance. 'Paul held him down. He put his foot on Lucien's throat and emptied his magazine into his face. Lucien was laughing the whole time, even once there was nothing left to laugh with. His voice rang in my head for days.'

'And now he's a swarm that walks.'

'A what?'

'A swarm that walks,' I said, punctuating each word with my finger. 'A way to live forever by transforming yourself into a sentient mound of creepy crawlies. We've been theorising one might have attacked the hideout, but I'm thinking this counts as solid proof.'

'The hideout?' Ania's face went white. 'Is everyone okay?'

'Mostly,' I said. 'Only a couple dead, more than that injured. They're safe for now though, they put up a wall.'

'Explains why I wasn't able to reach anyone,' Ania sighed. 'I did try to warn you but I couldn't get through.'

'Yeah, about that. Not that I'm anything but happy to see you, but why *are* you here?'

Ania trudged slowly to the front of the van and bent over to place her forehead against the bonnet, hands clasped at the back of her head. She looked weary. 'Paul and I were in the West Country, hoping to talk a few of the more isolated wizards around. You know that, obviously, you asked us to go.'

'I did. Seemed like a low hazard job and you deserved a rest. Both of you.'

Another fake smile crossed her lips. 'And we got one, for a time. A few days ago, though, one of the people we were supposed to be meeting with turned up dead. I charmed the coroner and found out the cause of death – his tongue, the roof of his mouth, all the way to the back of his throat and part-way down his oesophagus were saturated with wasp stings. The report couldn't say whether it was anaphylaxis, suffocation, heart attack, or all three.'

'Jesus Christ.'

'Be thankful you didn't have to look at the photos,' she said. 'Anyway, we checked out the crime scene and it *stank* of sex magic. Smells like roasted jizz, unmistakable. Followed *that* all the way back to De Sade's new little secret sex cult. He wasn't there, but I persuaded one of his thralls to tell us where he was going.'

'And they said he was coming here?'

She made a pair of finger guns and pointed them my way, again without a glimmer of playfulness. 'Bingo. Paul stayed behind to dismantle the remains of the cult, but if De Sade is here, I bet he's already making a new one.'

'I think he already has…'

It would be so easy to accept that Kaitlyn's most recent actions were the result of some creepy vagician wriggling his grubby fingers inside her head. Maybe that was true, too – it would save me a lot of mental gymnastics in working out how to think about the woman I thought had been my, well, not *friend* but at least not enemy. The thing was, I couldn't make that determination just from knowing that De Sade was involved. It was just as likely that Kaitlyn was a willing participant in all this, that this was the planned endpoint of her entire endeavour.

Even if I wanted to let her off the hook with regards to responsibility, however, it was all but certain now that, whether willingly or not, she *was* working with De Sade. The more power she built for herself in the community, the more unsuspecting folk she would be sending right into De Sade's throbbing, penis-shaped fingers. His new cult would dwarf all his previous ones combined and put those remaining non-cultists firmly in the minority.

Oh, fuck me. Of course. *This* is what The Rider meant about someone muscling in between him and Kaitlyn. This unknown element was messing with the plan, he had told me as much.

'He's got Kaitlyn van Ives and her guys on his side, plus a couple of monsters.'

'Monsters?' Ania said. 'What sort?'

'A Hyde and two things I've not seen before. I saw them come to recruit the Hyde, but I didn't realise—'

'De Sade always did like to drink from the pool of outcasts. It's easier to break a mind that's already fractured from isolation or betrayal or fear. Makes for an easy hunt.'

I'd definitely set the stage for him to recruit Laura then, hadn't I? There's not much bigger a betrayal than leashing a person inside their own head to keep them contained and compliant. She was primed for a recruiting. Not that they would have known that when they arrived, though.

'Maybe, but I don't think it's just that,' I said. 'Those three are ringers, the sort of big guns you don't go through the effort of recruiting unless you've got a real use for them. Like you said, he'd want them too weak to fight back—'

'But using them as shock troops requires they be anything but weak,' Ania finished my thought for me. 'You're right, that doesn't really fit.'

'Theorising can wait anyway. We need to work out what to do next.'

'What happened in that house?'

'Kaitlyn consolidated power,' I said. 'She killed the leaders of every disparate group of free mages in the country, at least the ones with any standing at all. By the end of the day, she'll find a way to leverage that to make those leaderless factions fall in line.'

'And, by extension, give Lucien De Sade a big boost in supporters.'

'It never rains, but it pours, eh?'

I almost got a legitimate laugh out of her with that one, but still didn't quite manage it.

Pieces were starting to fit together. This puzzle was still not clear enough to make out the full picture, but I'd managed to find a couple of the corner pieces. Seeking out Laura Irvine had been the first step along a path I didn't know I was taking – I had been so focused on pumping her for information about The Rider I hadn't thought about her in the larger context.

Taking out my phone, I started to once again scroll through the files Charlie had sent me earlier. All the abandoned warlock work, and I'd been focusing on what could be *seen*. There had been a big rise in the overtness of these creatures without us to keep them trapped firmly in the shadows, and at the time that seemed like the most important point to consider. You see a dragon, you really *see* that dragon – you're not going to go counting exactly how many children the Smithwick-Joneses at number 15 had last week.

God, it was so obvious now. The Rider had been manipulating obvious displays, but if you really looked at them you could see they were all smoke and mirrors. Laura's beast had told me that itself, The Rider never asking it to do more than cause a little chaos. Loud, sure, and very visible, but ultimately harmless. This pattern fit with every single name on that list – dragons command a lot of attention, but rarely bother to really kick off; leshies are terrifying to bump into on a dark night, but they're more concerned with scaring you off than hurting you; and squonks are so pathetic that the only way one could hurt you is if you did a comedy prat-fall from slipping on its tears.

The fire-breathing man and the hag though, these were the sorts of predatory creatures that covered their tracks habitually. They would hide their crimes in the background noise of daily life, so steady and routine that the only way to notice they were there would be to track their activity all the way back to the start, to see the moment they slid into the statistics so you could pinpoint the differences they caused.

We'd been so busy looking at the peaks that we had missed the troughs.

Knowing to look for them, I could see those troughs now. There were a lot of them, far more than just the three that I knew were working for Kaitlyn. Not enough for an army, but enough for a problem, that much was sure.

Two bad dudes, tapping the same well from different ends. Difference being, The Rider was filling a water gun and De Sade was trying to cause a drought.

'Ania,' I said, unable to look at her. 'Did we fuck up?'

She blinked. 'Helping The Rider take out the Vault? Probably.'

'No, I mean since then.'

'What do you mean?'

I held my tongue while a car trundled up the country road, passed us, and vanished around a nearby bend. My nerves were still a little frayed from escaping sure death scant minutes ago and it took a lot of self-control to not just blast the vehicle to smithereens. It was soothing to see that Ania had tensed up the same way.

I took a breath. 'It just feels like maybe this is something we could have stopped, you know? We made a power vacuum and we have no idea who is sliding in to fill it. I'm wondering if the more we dig, the more we're going to find this all stems back to our... *my*... fuck up.'

'Add it to the list,' Ania said coldly. 'We're all fuckups, right? In my opinion, that's the real definition of a warlock. You killed your girlfriend, I let my boyfriend coax me into a doomed revolution. Who even cares at this point? Life is full of fucking up, they would have found their shot one way or another.'

'That's your pep talk? *We're all losers and we're always going to make things worse, so why does it matter?*'

She shrugged. 'It's efficient. You don't dwell on how badly you fail, you just keep pushing for a vicious revenge on anyone who laughs.'

'You add them to the list.'

'My list comes in several volumes. Like all good Russian literature.'

'Christ,' I said. 'You might actually be worse at this than I am.'

'Who cares?' she replied. 'We should get back on track. Where are we headed?'

That question again, another person turning to me as if I knew better than anyone else what to do. It had happened enough that the frustration of it all was starting to just merge with the baseline grumbles of living, losing its edge and just being a thing I would have to accept.

Didn't mean the question was an easy one to answer though.

'I don't want to get into an arms race with a bug man. He's got a head start there.'

'Ha,' Ania snorted.

'But... Kaitlyn van Ives, plus De Sade's monster minions, *plus* the confused and vulnerable free mages – that's a big force. That's march-on-Parliament levels of manpower she has there.'

'We always knew a war was coming, from the moment the Vault was taken out of the equation,' she said. 'We've never doubted that.'

I shook my head. 'No. But this is worse than even the Dark Times, this is a consolidated, cohesive unit. We go up against them alone, we lose, and we're not going to be able to drive enough of a wedge into any of the main groups now to pull off some clutch alliances to save the day.'

'Two options then. We capitulate to save ourselves, or we wait for them to crush Whitehall and turn on us, stamping us out.'

When she put it like that, the obvious next step would be to join up with Kaitlyn. Whatever strings De Sade had been pulling in Kaitlyn's head, the fact that she had put my welfare at the centre of her little political pantomime would give me some leverage amongst the rank and file. It wouldn't be enough to turn them against her no matter how I played it, but it *would* be enough to force her into an alliance of convenience with the remaining warlocks, let us ride out the upcoming conflict on the winning side. We'd be little more than lapdogs, but we'd be alive.

'No,' I snapped. 'I don't like either of those options.'

'Give an alternative.'

A bad idea flickered to life in my head, one so stupid and awful that, I hoped, it would manage to reach all the way around and tickle the back end of genius. 'I've got one, but we'll need to run it past the others first. If it's going to work, we'll need everyone on board.'

'Sounds suitably ominous. Back to the hideout then?'

'Can the van get us there?'

She placed an ear against the bonnet. 'Nope, it's fucked. But that's fine.'

'I'm not walking.'

'God, no,' she said, this time managing a laugh. 'I didn't drive up here in the van. I stole the van because my car wasn't bulky enough to be my magical murder tank. Left my car glamoured on the other side of this hedge. Always want to change cars when you've trying to lose a tail, you know that.'

Smirking, she led me towards a patch of hedge that looked a little thicker than the rest. Snapping her fingers, it vanished, leaving behind a dirt track and a car with the sort of angles you only got in the 1970s.

Hell, maybe they should be looking to Ania for leadership – she was showing me up with all this *planning* and *preparedness*.

*

'No, absolutely not. You're out of your fucking tree, Parker.'

Bodhi, despite still being visibly exhausted, was the first to summon up the ability to respond to my proposal. The others, every warlock we had left locally, as well as those out around the country, shared the same confused and dumbfounded looks. For the ones out elsewhere, they had the excuse of the slight lag inherent in all video calls, but the ones in the actual room had nothing. My idea simply did not fit in their heads.

Ariel Kingsley, sitting a few rows behind Bodhi, was next to shake off his confusion. 'I should have seen this coming from the start. Once a bootlicker, always a bootlicker.'

This broke the spell on the rest of the crowd, all of them erupting in shouting and jeering, naturally aimed in my direction. I let them get it out of their systems – it wasn't as if I hadn't expected it – waiting for a slight break in the din that I could seize and use to explain myself.

I think I wasted about five minutes waiting for that moment. When it didn't come, I slammed my chair against the wall as a sign that it was my turn to talk. That was much more effective.

'Look, I get it,' I shouted to the room. 'This feels like a step in the wrong direction—'

Ariel interrupted, pushing his way to the front of the room. 'You want us to slink back to those fuckers at Whitehall, tail between our legs, heads held high for the collar.'

Floating an alliance of convenience with Whitehall was not something I expected to go down well, but I did have hope that people would at least have the foresight to hear me out. Ariel was making that difficult. 'Have you not been listening to what I've said? We've fucked up and, yes, I take some of the responsibility for that, but the fact of the matter is—'

'—You've never been committed to this. You're blowing this out of proportion, making Kaitlyn van Ives sound like a bigger danger than she is so you can back out. If you think anyone is going to believe that another fucking bogeyman has just shown up out of nowhere—'

From behind me, a thunderclap of wood striking concrete interrupted Ariel. Ania stepped around me, her cane blazing once again and her eyes sharp with fury. 'Doubt Parker all you like, but do not *dare* to call my word into question.'

Some of the anger faded from Ariel's face as he took a moment to compose himself. 'I... Sorry, Ms Petrova. I didn't mean to disrespect *you*, and if you say Lucien De Sade is back from the dead then fine. But still, that doesn't mean we need to do *this*.'

'Stop interrupting and maybe you'll understand why this is exactly what we need to do,' she shot back.

Bristling, Ariel held up his hands and took a step back. 'Fine. You know what, say your piece, Parker. I'm sure everyone else will see how full of shit you are anyway.'

Ania stepped back behind me, gracing me with a delicate nod. It knocked a little of the piss and vinegar out of me, like my mum had stepped in or something, but it all came flooding back when I realised how much her support actually mattered to me.

Good grief, there's an image no-one needs – piss and vinegar flooding back.

'I thought you'd be all for sticking it to van Ives,' I said, resulting in an angry grimace thrown back my way. Before he could channel that into words and derail me again, I turned my attention to the rest of the group. 'We have grossly misjudged Kaitlyn van Ives, and we need to stop doing that right now. She earned her nickname, The Bane of Whitehall, for a reason.'

An arm snaked lazily upwards from the crowd and a woman stepped forward. She was heavily bandaged and one arm of her jacket hung empty. 'Perhaps Ariel does not recognise the signs yet, but I do. Van Ives betrayed us, hit us hard. Wounded us. She drove us to hide inside a magical shield. There is no chance now that she will not come for us sooner or later.'

Watching Lara Mgune speak, I could see quite clearly how much of a struggle it was for her to summon the energy to stand. She was almost having to lift herself, cradling her upper body with her remaining arm. The attack seemed so long ago already, which was stupid really. I should have lead with that at the centre of my argument.

'Lara is right,' I said. 'Either she takes however many of those horrible creatures she's recruited and kicks down the doors of Parliament, or she brings them here and crushes us inside this *impenetrable bubble*. Whitehall has to know they can't stand against that – they don't even know whether they can stand up to *us* if it came down to it – so they might just be open to a very temporary alliance.'

Ariel crossed his arms. 'And if they turn on us too, use this as evidence we are too weak to survive?'

'Then we get the shit kicked out of us a little earlier than we otherwise would have, secure in the knowledge that Kaitlyn van Ives and her magical murder squad are on the way to roast those duplicitous fuckfaces once the last warlock hits the dirt.'

'Not much of a silver lining, you're proposing.'

'The silver lining is that eating the shit sandwich might let us live. Not eating it means we get to greet death with clean teeth and minty breath. We'll still be dead, though.'

Despite my eloquence and robust command of the English language, the discussion deteriorated into squabbling several more times before people finally came around to my way of thinking. To Ariel's credit, he was one of the first to finally give in, going so far as to taking a step back from the frontlines of the debate. He didn't stop glaring at me but doing so in silence felt like progress.

No-one was happy with the idea – least of all myself – but ultimately everyone knew that we couldn't just leave things to chance. It was clear that I was right and we needed to make overtures to the same people who wanted us in chains so recently that we hadn't even had the time to come up with a suitable wartime slur for them.

After a couple of hours of further debate, I made my exit. People were talking themselves in circles now, putting too much energy into focusing on the worst-case scenario. That was good for me in a way, it meant that they weren't going to keep trying to put us on a different course, just prepare for any trouble. It was awfully depressing to listen to, though.

Charlie and Preston were waiting for me outside, neither looking particularly happy. Tucking her hair behind her ears, Preston spoke first. 'You're not going alone this time.'

'I wasn't planning to. But you're not coming.'

'I know that. I wouldn't go even if you asked — I'm going to be needed in case you're wrong and van Ives comes here first. We are closer.'

'Then—'

'She's here to referee,' Charlie interjected. She was holding her jaw tight, muscles flexing angrily beneath the skin. 'To stop me breaking your *fucking* jaw.'

Frowning, I looked from Charlie to Preston, then back again. 'Pardon?'

'I'll, uh, be over there,' Preston said. 'Out of earshot, not listening, but watching in case of violence.'

Sidling away, she moved further down the length of the building until, true to her word, she was out of earshot. Charlie watched until Preston was settled, then wheeled on me with an unexpected fury.

'Why are you doing this, Jim? Every goddamned time — it's like you can't just sit still for one minute, you have to go from stupid dickhead plan to stupid dickhead plan. Do you have a death wish?'

Her words were coming with such force that they made my own catch in my throat. 'I don't... Where is this coming from, Chaz? What's happening here?'

'What's happening is I just had to stand there for a few hours and watch you try and sell the idea of a truce with Whitehall. And what's worse is you actually made it sound like a good idea. You've plastered over all the danger of this, fine, but that doesn't mean it isn't still there.'

'Charlie—'

'You're *wounded* as it is! You need to just stop and think up better ideas, safer ones. Ones that aren't seemingly designed to end up with you dying horribly, alone, bleeding out in the gutter. I need you to do that.'

'Charlie, please just—'

'Whitehall could *kill you,* Jim.'

'Yes,' I said. 'But Kaitlyn *will* kill me, and you, and everyone else. De Sade will see to that.'

Frantically, Charlie shook her head. Her voice was breaking. 'Not everyone. Ania told me about his penchant for breaking people, using them up. He won't let everyone die when he can enslave them.'

'That's not—'

Her mouth opened and closed silently a couple of times as her eyes filled with tears. I'm not a total idiot, I could read between the lines, map out the fears she was wrestling with. After what The Rider had done to her, the thought of being put into a similar position could only have been gnawing away viciously in her head. And yet, of course, there was more there, something deeper.

She wasn't going to put it into words, and I *couldn't,* but we had reached a point where that unspoken bond, so rare and precious, was digging into her with more force than she could bare. I had given her too many things to worry about at once, a horrible melange of peril, drowning her, choking her. All of it centred on me and my wellbeing. Eventually, we would have to take the time to talk about this, to burst the bubble and face the contents, and seeing her as she was then made me wonder if it had to be that moment.

But, I figured, that would be too cruel. When I got back, maybe, and this was all over. If things go wrong, let her hate her dickhead friend for putting himself in danger rather than mourn the loss of the man she… Well, you know.

With great care, I placed my hands on her cheeks. 'This is my fault, Chaz. Or, if not *fault* exactly, certainly my responsibility. I made us all blind to Kaitlyn, to anything that wasn't The Rider. I all but gave them Laura Irvine in a nicely wrapped package, and I can't believe her other ringers would have been so bold if I hadn't let the warlocks take their foot off the gas.'

'You do know this doesn't have to all be on your shoulders, right?'

'Doesn't it?' I said. 'The Rider has been pushing me to become some sort of leader. Whitehall drilled us warlocks so hard that, left to our own devices, we're going to fragment and go our own ways. We're self-interested at heart – just look at how hard it was to convince them that we need to do this. They keep forcing me to the front, pushing me to make the hard choices, and I keep pushing back because I don't belong front and centre. But sitting back and waiting for someone else to step up has let Kaitlyn go this far. I can't—'

Her hands on mine, she pulled me close and silenced me with a kiss.

It was slow, sad, full of pain but also understanding. In that moment, I could have sworn that Charlie had some sort of magic in her, a light that she was sharing with me, warming me from within. She was giving me a reason to live, to fight even harder than I had been intending to. For the first time in days, I let myself just *exist*, let her drag me out of the world and into a place where it was just the two of us – one of endless potential and joy.

We existed there for an eternity. Then she pulled away, breaking the kiss and letting the world flood back in. I stood there, my forehead pressed to hers, breathing slowly and gently.

In the distance, I heard Preston shouting through cupped hands. 'It's about time! Jesus Christ!'

Twelve

I had intended to take Charlie with me for my sit down with Whitehall, but the surprise snog kind of killed that plan. There was no way I'd be able to play the room the way I needed to with her just constantly dancing across my mind's eye. That said, I did feel like having someone who knew the system well enough to back me up in the room was a sound plan.

While there were other options amongst our little group – as you know, we had our fair share of disgraced handlers – but if I couldn't have someone I could trust implicitly then I needed someone who would at least make the other side shit themselves.

Ergo, I took another trip to the homeless shelter.

Bennett had been reluctant to be of much help earlier, but walking into Whitehall with him at my side was perhaps the only way to get them to take my call. Or it would make them kill me all the quicker, it was sort of even odds there.

There was a palpable pall hanging over the shelter when I arrived. The people, hardly the most upbeat and active last time, were shuffling around listlessly, busying themselves with the sort of menial nonsense you can only find the willpower to achieve when trying to stay out of your own head. Stacking books, folding sheets, relacing boots, not a one of them had the capacity to even raise their head as I passed them.

A pit formed in my stomach, getting deeper and more consuming with every step, until I reached what had been Bennett's bunk. It had been roped off now, yellow and blue police tape wrapped over a stark white tent that had been set up to conceal, well, a *scene*. A couple of uniformed police officers were standing guard at the mouth of the tent, though the casual way they were standing had me thinking that they weren't alone. Perhaps it was paranoia, or perhaps there were a few more officers scattered about the room in plain clothes, doing a bit of spy work. Better safe than sorry.

I kept my distance from the officers, but I definitely needed to find a way into that tent. If Bennett was dead, I wanted to know how and why. Best case, it would give me another bargaining chip to throw in Whitehall's faces. A little callous, sure, but I was compartmentalising. Avoid a war, then mourn.

'Hey, Jim,' came a soft voice from behind me.

I didn't need to turn around, it was a voice that would forever live in my head rent free. 'Hello, Robin.'

'No insults this time?' she asked. Stepping around me, she put herself between me and the tent. No joy in her face this time, no playfulness. She was all business.

'Not in the mood,' I said. 'Banter has lost its appeal right now.'

She nodded. 'Because you're starting to see what I was saying is true. Ran into De Sade, right?'

She was blocking my view of the tent completely now, I couldn't help but lock onto her stare. 'You're always offering your help, right? So help me understand how a man like that manages to put together something like this without getting exposed.'

'Cheating death helps,' she said, allowing herself a single playful wink.

'It worked for you, I suppose.'

'Honestly, I don't know how he did it,' she said. 'Other than seemingly allowing me to lay the groundwork for him to steal. We've both been played for fools here, Jim.'

'Why are you still wearing her face if you're not trying to taunt me?'

She shrugged. 'You like her. It makes you a little more likely to hear me out, if just for a chance to see her face a few seconds longer.'

I moved a few steps away, resting my head against the cold white wall of the room. 'I'm not ready to accept that you aren't working against me here. What you did to Charlie—'

'Was necessary,' she interrupted. 'You needed pushing into the right frame of mind and causing her a little discomfort was—'

'That wasn't *discomfort*, that was a violation!'

'Yes, it was. But it was necessary.'

I took a couple of deep breaths and got myself back under control. 'I'm not ready to accept that. But, maybe, I'm willing to be civil.'

'That's big of you.'

'Very.'

'How does this *civility* work for you?'

I swivelled my head in a small nod toward the tent. 'I need to get in there. Give me a hand and I'll be more inclined to believe you aren't as shit as you make out to be.'

'No.'

'No?' I said, almost choking on my bile. 'Just a flat no? I tell you what I need to start, maybe, listening to you and you just—'

Rocking on her heels, Robin smiled. I'd seen that expression before, that coquettish little flush that would wash through her when she was teasing. 'I've got an easier way. Follow me.'

Without waiting for an answer, she led me out of one of the side doors and into the miserable corridors that wove through the rest of the building like an ant nest. They were easy to get turned around in, the monotonous grey blocks that made up the walls were only rarely broken up by a noticeboard or a bland poster, all no doubt very important but not very good as landmarks. Robin seemed to know where she was going, though.

It was only a small trip, and as I rounded a corner I saw her duck into a small room. The door had a cheap plastic plaque screwed to it that marked the place as a room for counselling, but the wall by the door was one large glass window, making it far too public for someone to share their intimate struggles. Following Robin in, I closed the door behind me and turned to find that I was nose to nose with Bennett's smiling, mangled, corpse.

I went beyond shitting myself – I was shitting *everyone*. I summoned the shared communal shit, the Platonic form of self-shitting that exists beyond the veil of perception, informing how we perceive reality itself. I was, in a word, *omnishitting*.

'See,' Bennett said. 'Bringing the mountain to Mohammed.'

'Hell of a way to confirm a death.'

Bennett's corpse was quiet for a moment, embarrassed. 'I think my... Condition might have had an impact on my social skills. I apologise.'

'It's fine,' I lied. 'Do you know how he died?'

Bennett shrugged. 'I've got access to his memories, but he didn't see his death coming. Painless.'

'But brutal,' I said, looking away from the face and surveying what remained of Bennett's body.

If they had killed him first, then Bennett had been shown mercy. The mutilation was severe – strips of flesh as thick as a pair of fingers had been torn from his chest. The wounds left behind painted angular and unsettling designs, circling around the rough location of his heart before passing under his arms and down his back. Further down, a bloody cavity was all that remained of his *gentleman's area*, ripped from his body root and stem. Similar designs as those on his chest were present on the thighs, wrapping around them like a hideous snake before travelling up and around the waist, joining with the others just above the buttocks.

To avoid losing my lunch, I tried to hold the images in my head as nothing more than sterile snapshots, little fleshy puzzles. It didn't work very well. 'This is ritual.'

'An old one,' Bennett said, staring down at himself. 'I'm struggling to find someone in here that recognises it.'

'All the dead people in human history, and you can't find someone with a clue?'

'Not so far, no.'

I frowned. A little suspicious, that. An issue for another time, though. 'I've got an informed hunch.'

'I'm sure you do.'

'We don't know who killed Bennett, but we've got two chief suspects.'

Bennett nodded. 'Whitehall and De Sade, I presume?'

'Exactly,' I said. 'And while I concede Whitehall and the Paladins are a shady lot, and massive scumbags, they wouldn't waste their time mutilating a corpse. Plus, if they had wanted him dead, they would have killed him when they pushed him out.'

'De Sade, then.'

'That would be my guess. Which, if that is the case, would mean that this killing was for more than pleasure or revenge, it had a purpose.'

I looked at the patterns again. They bore a certain similarity to a number of binding rituals I had read about during my awkward teenage years. Always wanting to rebel at that age, read the books your mentor tells you not to touch, crack open the *Unabridged Ars Goetia*, the one with the footnotes and the extra chapters. It probably wasn't for demons, too artistic and not nearly ragged enough, but there was enough to draw a connection.

I closed my eyes and reached out with my power, following my magical signature back through the labyrinthine hallways and into the main room. As soon as I passed the threshold my head began to pound and I found it harder and harder to hold my concentration. There was too much magic just floating in the air, categorising it was like watching a single speck of dust dancing in a sunbeam. Struggling, I pushed through – I needed a taste, some idea of what De Sade had been doing here. If I could work this out, at least a little, I could take it to the negotiating table and really stick the knife in with Whitehall.

The closer I drew to the murder scene, the harder I had to push. My consciousness bumped up against a huge swell of pressure, like a cushion of air that pushed me back as hard as I tried to force my way past it. Each metaphysical step closer was more strenuous than the last, and I could feel the magic in the air start to coagulate around me, slowing me down.

I reached the barrier of the tent and stretched out, ready to throw it back in the arcane world so I could get a solid look at what had been worked here. My fingers, or the manifestation of my power that functioned like fingers, brushed against the fabric of the tent and then, suddenly, I felt a shift in the morass of energy. There was something here, lurking in the tides of magic, and I had awoken it. The way the pressure moved and shifted, waves and tidal forces shifting around whatever this thing was, it made my teeth itch.

But I had to know.

Pushing myself just a little further, I began to open the tent.

Cold, tepid magic wrapped around my wrist, pulling me away. I felt it crawl up my arm, freezing my power solid and stealing my attention.

'Got you,' a voice echoed in my head, disrupted by the magic. 'Red handed and black hearted. *I cast you out.*'

The arcane equivalent of a haymaker clocked me across my face, knocking me off balance and stripping me of what little protection I had managed to muster against the pressure. My concentration in tatters, the tides took me, splashing my energy from pillar to post before spitting me back into my body. My legs gave way, my eyes rolled back into my head, and I folded like cheap tracing paper. Inside my head, I could feel my mind flipping levers and hammering on control panels, but no signals were reaching my body – I was a marionette with cut strings.

I managed to pry my eyes open after a moment, but that was as far as I could push things. Bennett's bare feet were inches away, backing up as another pair – shiny boots, no laces, Cuban heel – moved into view. Pivoting on their left foot, there was a flash of light and Bennett dissolved into the air like salt in water.

Feeling started coming back just in time for the owner of the boots to turn their attention to me, grabbing my arms and roughly twisting them up behind my back. I felt the cold bite of a zip-tie pulled too tightly, fixing my arms into an uncomfortable position, followed by strong hands yanking me up and into a sitting position. Those same hands gave me a couple of solid slaps to my face, bringing me back to myself.

I blinked my eyes back into focus to find a man crouching in front of me. He had the beard of a woodsman – wild and bushy – which was completely at odd with the rest of his outfit. He wore a perfectly tailored suit, the black-as-night blazer paired with a crushed amber shirt, an overcoat of ink-black pooling around those smart shoes. On the lapel, a sterling silver pin glinted in the soft light.

A paladin's badge.

'Been on a stake out?' I asked. My words may have been a little slurred, but my composure was recovering quickly now I wasn't trying to swim upstream.

The paladin dropped down from his crouch and onto one knee. He took my chin in his hand and started to turn my head left and right, taking a good look at me. His pupils were glowing the colour of burnt meringue – borrowed power letting him study the flow of magic. 'Waiting for you to come back to the scene of the crime. Exactly.'

'Murderers don't come back to the scene of the crime, dipshit,' I said, fidgeting. The zip-tie had already started to affect the blood flow to my hands, and I could feel pins-and-needles setting in. 'That's a TV thing.'

'Talk less.' he growled. 'Bennett may have been on the outs with Head Office, but he was still *respected*. He didn't deserve what you did to him, and I'll see you *burn* for it.'

'Okay now, hang on. I didn't—'

The tip of one of his smart shoes caught me in the stomach, driving under my ribs and forcing the air out of me. 'You were seen visiting him, his first visitor since his retirement. Suddenly he's dead. Is that supposed to be a coincidence?'

I managed to suck in just enough air to reply. 'Came to him… For help… Was doing so… Again today…'

'About what?'

'Needed someone to help me set up a meeting with Whitehall, actually. To talk cease fire.'

He snorted and rolled his eyes. 'Horseshit.'

It was enough. His eye off the ball for just a fraction of a second, I punched a quick flash of power through my veins, snapping the zip-tie and freeing my hands. I was up and on him in one movement, one hand on his throat to throw him off balance while I plunged a knee into his groin. He went down and I rolled over him, coming up in a rickety crouch of my own behind him. I drew in a bolt of power, fashioned it quickly in my mind into the form of a crackling restraint, and unleashed the spell.

I watched in slack-jawed surprise as my spell broke across his chest, scattering into a mist of impotent magic. Before I could react, he had closed the gap between us. A quick flurry of short and efficient blows put me back down, for good this time.

He stood astride me for a moment while I wheezed, then put his foot on my chest and applied enough pressure that I felt it was wise not to push him any further. 'Maybe it wasn't you.'

'Hang on, what—'

He twisted his heel against my breastbone. 'Your magic isn't the same as the sort that killed him. Lower potency, different flavour. Plus, if you could take Bennett then I shouldn't have been any trouble for you.'

'Bennett didn't know military martial arts,' I wheezed. 'That's what that shit was, right? The casual, efficient brutality of it gave it away.'

The paladin chuckled humourlessly but took his foot off my chest. He took a few steps back and held up his hands as a show of peace. 'Shows what you know. Still, trying the cease fire play makes me think you're up to no good.'

'You lot always think I'm up to no good,' I said, slowly getting back to my feet. 'But not this time. This is a genuine offer while we deal with a bigger threat.'

'And I suppose you're going to say the bigger threat is the one that killed Bennett?'

'Pretty much.'

His eyes lit up again, scanning me once more with that borrowed power of his. If last time it had been cursory, it was much more invasive this time around. The gaze lingered uncomfortably long at times, and all the while his expression was cold, unreadable. I felt the treacherous itch at the base of my skull, the one that made me want to draw in all my power and have another crack at him, but he had shrugged off my last attack so easily, and besides, I wasn't there to fight.

Just as that little itch started to blossom into something much harder to ignore, the paladin snorted again and gave me a slow nod. 'Oberon Kilbride.'

'What?'

'My name,' he said. 'That I'm telling you means I believe you enough to hear you out. Convince me and I'll take your offer to Whitehall myself.'

'Just like that?'

Another nod, even slower this time. It felt more than a little like he was taunting me. 'Just like that.'

I pushed down the itch. This might well be the best chance I would get to spin things for Whitehall – Bennett's death was a kick in the teeth, but getting the support of their man on the ground covering that death would give me more leverage than Bennett himself could have. Sad, but probably true, considering how Whitehall tended to work.

Deliberately and with careful consideration, I filled him in on everything I knew about De Sade, Kaitlyn, the whole twisted mess of it so far. The entire time, that face of his remained blank – there were moments where I found myself wondering if he was even listening at all, but then a frown would flutter across his face or a nostril would twitch in frustration at an appropriate moment. He had the very dangerous disposition of staying so quiet you found yourself filling up all the space around him with words, volunteering more than you originally intended. It's not a skill that meshes well with smart-mouthed gobshites like me.

'The files left behind by your civilian turncoats say Lucien De Sade is dead,' Oberon said as soon as I finished my tale. 'Incomplete, then.'

'Him still being alive is a new development,' I said. 'I've never seen anything like him, and if I'm right, neither of us alone have the oomph to stop him if he comes in force.'

Oberon folded his arms, the fabric of his coat pulling tight against unfairly prominent muscles. 'Which he will, if what you say is true. He has surprise, size, strength, experience, and unity. Our intelligence has made it clear to us that you don't have all of those traits in your little band of renegades.'

'And I know intimately which of those is lacking from your gang of boot-licking fascists.'

'I'm sure you think you do,' he said. 'We'll need to corroborate this information before anything is agreed upon, however.'

'Call me when you're ready to talk,' I said, turning to leave. 'You've got my number on file. Never bothered to change it.'

'Nuh uh,' he rumbled. 'You want this cease fire, you can make your case to the brass while we look for some evidence. You're coming with me.'

I stopped in my tracks and stared at him over my shoulder. The itch was back. It was telling me that he was like every other paladin – a self-aggrandising prick who was just pushing me because he enjoyed the thrill of power. They all had that chip on their shoulder, that need to prove that magic needed to be domesticated and sterilised, and anyone who embraced the chaos needed to realise how inferior they were to good, old-fashioned British bureaucracy.

They didn't need me to come in with them, they just wanted me to be on the back foot, to humiliate me into the subservient position. I could slap that smugness right off his face, remind Whitehall that we were their equals here.

But then, there wasn't any smugness on Oberon's face in that moment. Confidence, sure, laid on so thick that it was practically a wall, but none of that *seemed* to come from putting us beneath him. His military bearing, the calmness in his voice even when he had been threatening to burn me, made him stand apart from the other paladins I'd known.

That and, you know, the fact my magic just splashed off him like water off a duck's back.

If this cease fire was going to stand a chance in hell, I'd have to trust in the process. Everything about Oberon Kilbride painted him as a staunch professional, and if I wasn't going to take that first leap of faith with him then I might as well call off the whole thing.

'Okay, it's a deal,' I said. 'But if you're planning to take me all the way to London…'

'No need. We've got a place nearby. Follow me.'

Quick-turning on his heel, Oberon all but marched out into the corridors and back through the building to the main room. It was empty of people now, everyone I had seen on the way in had seemingly vanished while leaving behind what few worldly possessions they still had, as if disturbed in the middle of going about their day. The metallic tang of dissolving magic caught the back of my throat – it had all been one large glamour, that was the magic I had been struggling to push through. Oberon hadn't skimped when it had come to his stake out.

I barely had time to wonder where the real people had gone before Oberon led me out of the hall through a back entrance and immediately enlightened me.

At the back of the building was a loading dock, a relic of the centre's former life as a shipping warehouse. Piled up on the concrete were the remains of the centre's other residents. Like Bennett, their flesh had been flayed and carved into patterns that flowed into one another as though each corpse was a piece of some grotesque mosaic. Unlike Bennett, however, the bodies also showed signs of having been set upon by insects –

what flesh hadn't been torn off had been used as a canvas for the blackened welts of a million stingers swarming them.

Oberon stopped in front of the construction, staring at the carnage.

His voice was quiet when he spoke. 'I thought you'd want to see this first, to understand why you'll find the brass willing to hear you out.'

*

I wasn't sure whether it was bravado or a stubborn inability to change their thinking, but Whitehall were still fully entrenched in the same Field Office I had been attached to so long ago. We had been sure they would have closed up shop and pulled back to safer territory once the Vault went down, but more fool us, I guess.

In fairness, they had shaken things up a little. They'd moved the entrance, shifted the desks around a little, but it was otherwise just as I remembered it. A little disappointing to be honest, seeing as I had started thinking that I was going to be taken to some super-secret black site. But then, honestly, why had I expected anything different?

One big difference was in how short-staffed the place was. On my last visit, the office had been packed with handlers and warlocks and even a few fastrackers, but now it seemed like not even a third of the desks were in use. At those which were, tired and harried paladins were listlessly shuffling through folders or leafing through old books that I recognised as being pulled from Fawkes Folly. Overworked, underpaid, very underappreciated.

Good.

Oberon walked me to one of the empty desks and indicated I should sit down. 'You'll have no trouble from the penpushers. I'll be back with someone who's allowed to make decisions.'

Pretty bold of him to assure me I'd be safe from the paladins riding the desks – I was *the enemy*, after all – but then I got the impression that the statement hadn't been intended for my benefit.

Oberon Kilbride had cut an imposing figure from the moment he walked through the door. Following behind him, I had been perfectly positioned to see the heads turn, the eyes flick up from their work, all to watch this beast of a man move through the room calmly. It was weird and I didn't like it – paladins weren't meant to have a *presence* to them, and they certainly weren't designed to command respect, even amongst each other. They were *supposed* to be faceless civil servants with no personality, interchangeable cogs in the machine of government.

Even after he had left the room, it took some time for those rubbernecking at Oberon's arrival to return to their work. Where the hell had they plucked him from?

I settled in for a long wait. Whitehall may have made some changes, but changing the peripheral spindles and bolts doesn't do much to change the heart of a mechanism. If I knew Whitehall, and I did, it would take several phone calls before whoever Oberon had gone to talk to could even conceive of having words with me directly.

Unfortunately, that left me a lot of time to ruminate on what I had seen at the shelter.

Bennett's corpse, so completely rendered by The Rider, had been difficult to look at. Seeing what had happened to the other residents of the shelter was on a whole other level. It was so revolting that even now my brain doesn't quite accept what I saw, which makes the memory somehow a lot less traumatic to recall. It can take protracted efforts to get a mind to fully accept sights like that, a mental defence mechanism that I had no interest in circumventing.

But, that said, I did need to try and understand what De Sade could possibly have been doing. It certainly wasn't unlikely that he could have been just having a bit of old-fashioned fun by whacking out a quick atrocity, and the sheer level of viciousness that must have been involved gave some credence to that idea.

That didn't track with the patterns, though. De Sade was a vicious little fuck, but he wasn't the sort of deranged nutter that tried to make art out of human misery. He made power out of it, siphoned the agony to fuel spells. The ritualism of those designs spoke of there being more than *just* sadism at work, and while he had made Bennett a special example, the others hadn't just been an idle fancy.

I'd need to take Ania to the site, show her the corpses. The idea of exposing anyone to those things on purpose was a little nauseating, but if anyone would be able to give me some bearing as to where to look next, it would be her. Her knowledge of the man was going to be our greatest asset moving forward, and possibly my biggest bargaining chip when Whitehall bothered to come talk to me.

In what I'm sure was another powerful bit of testimony regarding his charisma or whatever, Oberon returned a lot sooner than I had expected. A few steps behind him, an older woman I didn't recognise was keeping pace. She had the blank, creased expression of a career politician, but her position in the Humberside office made it clear that, whatever her political aspirations, they had not gone well for her.

'Madeline Trask,' Oberon said, introducing her. 'Jameson Parker.'

Trask offered her hand, and I shook it. Her wrist was so limp that I was worried I'd snap it by accident. One of her eyes narrowed in scrutiny and she took one long, watery breath before she spoke. 'You look more well put together in your file. The life of a revolutionary is taking its toll, I see.'

'With what little respect you are due,' I said. 'I'm not going to rise to your bait. I'm not here to spar and banter.'

'Yes, Kilbride made that quite clear,' she said, flashing a look at the paladin. 'You're here to admit defeat and to beg to be welcomed back into the protective arms of the British government.'

Oberon growled. 'That is not how I put it, Ma'am.'

'You used diplomatic and formal language, Kilbride, as expected of you,' Trask said, waving away his words. 'But I'm far too old for all that nonsense. I've been around the block a few times, I know what all that bluster really meant. Parker, you have made more enemies than you can handle, so tell me why we shouldn't remain as one of them.'

Yeah, it was pretty obvious from the get-go that Madeline Trask was not coming into this with the intent of dealing in good faith. Still, if this was going to go down the shitter it wasn't going to be because I didn't give it a chance first. 'The fact that I'm willing to come and make a deal with the people that were feeding my kind to vampires for a few political favours should tell you what you need to know about how dangerous this new threat is.'

Trask bristled. I had kicked her high horse right in the danglers. 'A threat to *you*. You are a threat to us. We have no problems with this De Sade character.'

'Now *that* is some bullshit,' I laughed. 'Honestly, I'm surprised you could even say that with a straight face.'

'Parker—' Oberon began.

'No, no,' I cut him off. 'Whitehall might no longer have warlocks in its employ, but I know that one of the principles of replacing us with paladins was to make sure there was still someone around to do warlock work. *Maybe* that has fallen by the wayside what with our little conflict, but there's not a chance some sad analyst somewhere hasn't noticed the patterns.'

Trask sucked her teeth. 'You're smarter than you look.'

'I get told that a lot.'

'Some of our analysts have made a case that there has been a strange shift in the number of arcane-aligned aberrations, but there has been a distinct lack in compelling evidence to back up their assertions.'

'You have an eyewitness here,' I said. 'I've seen the very tip of the iceberg that's going to smash us like the bloody Titanic. We want to survive that, any of us, we need a radical course change.'

'An alliance would be a very radical change in direction indeed. Especially when we have just as much evidence that *you* are behind these… Irregularities.'

'What?'

Oberon leant forward. 'I've ruled him out.'

'You've ruled him out of the Bennett situation,' she shot back. 'Not out of anything else.'

'There's no connection to rule him *into* anything else, either.'

A cold look fell across Trask's face, but it had no effect on Oberon. He stared back, as intractable and calm as ever, reflecting her withering glare right into her rotten face. Eventually she let out a haggard sigh and turned back to me. 'Indeed.'

'Look,' I said, hoping I could defuse this tension before it got worse. 'Far be it from me to be the cooler head here, playing against type for sure, but De Sade is using the vacuum caused by our conflict to build his power. Seems to me that if we pull back on that conflict before he's ready, he'll be left exposed. We don't, he'll divide and conquer.'

'It is the position of Whitehall that if we can muzzle you wizards once, we can certainly do so again. De Sade is just another rabid dog like the rest of you were.'

Even Oberon rolled his eyes at that statement. Trask was toeing the party line like a true professional, parroting the statements she had heard from higher ups, all in the hope that it would let her ride their coat-tails up the governmental ladder. Hell, in another scenario it might even have worked. Kind of hard to make a name for yourself in the corridors of power if said corridors are full of murderous death scorpions, though.

I stood up, slapping my hands on my thighs to make a big British show of things. 'Right then, I can see I'm wasting my time here. I'll just have to go over your head. Thanks for absolutely shit all.'

'Now, now,' she snapped back at me. 'Don't take this personally. I don't disbelieve what you are saying, not completely, but there is a cost-benefit element to decisions here. You simply don't have enough capital on your side of the scales.'

'Were you a bank manager in a former life or something?'

'Investment banker, actually.'

That wasn't a surprise to me. There was no danger of getting confused over which colour tie she would be wearing to the Party picnic.

Oberon went to say something but stopped short, his attention pulled away by something on the far side of the room. It took me a little longer, but I noticed it too. Something had changed, a subtle shift in the background hum of the room. I couldn't quite put my finger on it until I realised, *there was no background hum.*

The field office had always suffered from poor ventilation. So many people, all rammed into one clandestine space designed to be overlooked, and no windows to crack open? The stink of body odour and sweat were a very real danger. Air conditioners – big rusted fans, hauled out of some supply warehouse that had been shuttered during the Cold War – had been bolted to the air vents to help keep things liveable. They ran constantly, bathing the building in a sort of soothing white noise that permeated deep into the gaps between the neurons in the human brain. It was something you heard in the same way oxygen was a thing you breathed – you didn't think about it until it was gone.

And it was gone now.

With the silence came a tangible foreboding, like in the moments before an earthquake hits. Even Trask could sense it now, and her realisation was now spreading out to the paladins working the desks.

My eyes were drawn to one particular fan, the central blades rattling gently against their bearing as they softly continued to rotate ever so slightly. Despite this, it felt as though the air was being drawn out of the room.

Oberon, his eyes locked firmly on the fan, moved to the nearest occupied desk and tapped his fingers on the surface, getting the occupant's attention. 'We're under attack. Stand ready.'

The paladin at the desk looked at him with confusion and opened his mouth to reply, only for a wet, bubbling gargle to escape instead. A single fly crawled out from the man's throat, up his face, and came to a halt at the base of his forehead. It turned around and started to stare at Oberon, purposefully wringing its front legs. The desk jockey's eyes rolled back into his head, and he went limp.

'Dear god,' Oberon whispered.

As one, the paladins at every other desk started to make the same gurgling noise, writhing and wriggling as another lone fly crawled out of each of their throats. Not one of us – myself, Oberon, nor Trask – could do anything but watch in abject horror as each fly crawled into the same position between each paladin's eyes.

Oberon's eyes were flashing with magic again, and I followed suit, reaching out with my own power to try and make sense of what I was seeing. Strands of power were snaking through the air vents before spreading themselves thin and reaching out to each of the insects. As it reached them, I saw, it wrapped around them, spiralling through their centres, and down through their legs like electrodes, burrowing into each paladin's head.

It was a web, criss-crossing the room at chest height, making it impossible to move without hitting at least one strand. I don't think it takes a MENSA candidate to realise that disturbing that web would not be wise or healthy.

Trask, bless her soul, proved that point for me with enormous haste, though.

I don't blame her for moving in for a closer look. I doubted that, as a politician, she had been gifted with some measure of magic. She had no way of knowing that by taking those few steps closer she would tickle so many threads. Myself and Oberon knew, of course, but there wasn't time to stop her. She tripped a number of those strings while moving to the nearest paladin, who greeted her by springing to life, hollow eyes boring into her. Grasping hands closed on her throat and gnashing teeth closed in for the kill.

Oberon kicked the husk so hard that I heard bones break and it went limp. He grabbed a stunned Trask by the shoulder and pulled her out of the husk's grasping fingers, pushing her behind him defensively. 'He doesn't want us leaving.'

I started drawing in my power. 'No, he doesn't. Son of a bitch is building an arena.'

There was a rumble from the air vents and a tidal wave of bugs began to pour into the room. They skittered down the walls, across the floor, buzzed through the air when they could, all pooling in front of us behind several of those magical strands. It bloated up into the shape of a human, those same firefly eyes igniting when they were done.

De Sade smiled. 'Welcome to Thunderdome.'

Thirteen

The revolting swarm slithered a little closer, baring whatever chitinous collection of thoraxes he had decided would be teeth today. 'Jameson Parker. You get where a draft wouldn't. An irritating trait to cultivate.'

I didn't give De Sade the reply he had been wanting. Instead, I unleashed my power, a crimson lance, tempered to pierce the swarm and explode, scattering him across the room. It would have worked too, but De Sade jerked his wrist, puppeteering a husk in front of my spell. It penetrated deep into the husk's shoulder before exploding, turning his torso into a cavernous mess of dripping meat.

Spiders began to scramble from the flesh.

'Nice try,' De Sade said. 'But don't waste your energy rattling the cage. This snare was not meant for you, but the mousetrap doesn't distinguish between the genera of rodents.'

From beside me, I felt the tingle of stagnant power roiling. Oberon was seething quietly. 'You killed them.'

'Yes,' De Sade said. 'To prove a point. This is your Hiroshima moment, Mr Kilbride. Parker and his warlocks have had theirs, and this was intended to be yours. This is the moment Whitehall realises the futility of trying to resist me.'

'You're making a mistake if you think you can scare us into surrender,' Trask all but shouted, pushing her way past Oberon. Her face was flush and her neck was already bruising from her close encounter with a husk. 'You mages are all flash and bang and pageantry. We figured your game out years ago.'

De Sade's cold eyes turned on her. 'I could have killed you too, you know. There were plenty of opportunities for a part of the colony to slip inside your ear, to chew through the soft and succulent flesh deep inside your head, to carve tunnels in your grey matter. You would have been dead before you could even blink, dancing on my strings. So, *watch your tone.*'

Trask didn't miss a beat. 'And yet you didn't. All talk from another pompous wizard trying to put himself on a pedestal.'

'Idiot,' De Sade spat. A couple of small beetles fell from his mouth. 'I don't use the Hiroshima analogy lightly. That was as much a message as this is. What good is a message with no messenger to deliver it?'

'We won't be your messengers.'

I shot a glare at her. 'He doesn't want messengers. He wants *a* messenger. Did you not hear him invoke Thunderdome?'

'Three enter,' Oberon said. 'One leaves.'

De Sade tried to give us a slow clap, but the crawling mass of insects didn't make much of a sound when they collided. 'Realisation begins to dawn, I see.'

'I'm not exactly a fan of Whitehall,' I said. 'But I'm even less of a fan of you right now, Lucy. If you think we're going to fight to the death for your amusement—'

'Obviously not,' De Sade interrupted. 'I predicted a few adjustments would be required to the format. Besides, I have comrades in arms who are *itching* for a good fight.'

I felt the magical energy in the room shifting and probed it with my power. The web was moving, lensing away from the centre of the space and opening up an arena of sorts. A second clearing opened towards the entrance and the doors opened, a pair of familiar faces stepping through.

The first through the door was the young man I had seen spitting fire. The skin around his mouth had started to regrow, raw flesh creeping down to cover some of the exposed scales. But it was the woman behind him that really drew my attention.

The hag, or whatever she was, had clearly been furnished with a few more meals since I had last seen her. Gone were any signs of age – the wrinkles, the pallid flesh, all of it – and in their place sashayed Morticia Addams: Pirate Queen. She was still lacking an eye, but she had managed to make the empty socket look like it was forever frozen in the middle of an alluring wink. Still, it wasn't enough to make me forget how she had been before, nor how deadly she could be.

'Last one alive gets to deliver the message,' De Sade said. 'And they'll do so with the correct level of terror in their eyes so that I can be sure everything is understood correctly.'

Our opponents in this tag team deathmatch started to circle us on the far side of the makeshift arena. Clambering over the desks, the hag's hungry eye flicked between me and Oberon, seemingly ignoring Trask for the moment. The man, on the other hand, had his sights set firmly on her.

'Bit of a ragtag bunch,' Oberon said, calmly removing his jacket. 'Which one do you favour – wyrmkin or the moroaică?'

Of course, he knew what they were, bloody perfect golden child of the New Order. Not wanting to let the side down and reveal my ignorance, I chose quickly. 'Moroaică. I'm not one for the heat.'

I mean, obviously the fire breather would be the wyrmkin, yeah?

'Shame,' Oberon said. 'I wasn't bred for high temperatures either, but I did give you the choice. You ready?'

'Not really.'

He shrugged. 'Me neither, but I don't think they're going to want to wait.'

As if those words had been a signal, they stopped circling and came for us.

Oberon broke off quickly, zipping past me and making straight for the wyrmkin. He caught it a little off guard, throwing off its timing and reaching it just as it started to spit one of its vicious gouts of flame. The paladin brought a fist up under the creature's jaw, knocking its head back and sending the fire arcing up to the ceiling.

I remembered the hag almost too late. This was the second time she had managed to sneak up on me when I knew full well to be prepared, as if she was able to cloud her memory in my mind as long as I couldn't see her. Last time, I had only noticed as those horribly long fingers closed around my throat. This time, I came to my senses just in time to duck and recoil away, coming around to face her.

Her lips, that plump redness that contrasted with the papery white skin, were twisted into a smile that showed too many teeth. The corners of her mouth pulled back too far up the cheeks, too hungrily, and as she grew closer whatever beauty there had been in her face was twisting into something out of a sleep paralysis nightmare. Again, I ducked under her grasping fingers, rolling to the side and tapping into my power.

I let loose an uppercut of my own – shaping raw magic from underneath her, sending it skyward. The force bent her backwards but her feet didn't move, they remained firmly planted on the ground. Her spine, though, that kept going, cracking at a sharp right angle and letting her torso flop backwards until the rear of her head could almost kiss her ankles. Then, naturally, her head rolled back up, bringing the torso with it, until she was standing upright once again.

That was me out of ideas then. Sure, I could hit her again, harder even, but you see someone who can have their spine snapped in half like a KitKat and not even complain? Why waste the effort pounding them?

If I had heard of these *moroaică* things before, that would have been something. A bit of adrenaline pumping and my brain would probably recall something, not so with an empty memory bank though. Where had De Sade even found this woman anyway?

Wrong questions. I had to focus, keep my mind in the fight. How was it wandering so much, in the middle of a life-or-death situation no less? I could feel my attention wanting to slip further away, to start picking apart the name, to try and determine from the inflections in each letter which country it might have come from, which parts were modular and interchangeable. A gendered suffix, perhaps? Fascinating.

I don't even give a shit about etymology.

Shaking the thoughts away, I came back to myself in time to once more slap her hand off my throat. No wonder her movements were so slugging and sedate, she did her hunting in the minds of her victims. But even knowing that, it was hard to keep my attention focused on her. I needed clarity.

A flash of heat singed the hairs on the back of my neck, and I turned in time to see the wyrmkin drive Oberon through a smouldering table. Very WWE.

With my eyes off the woman, she was already starting to fade from my attention. The cloud was creeping in – there was no way I could fight like this. I had to wake the fuck up.

Oberon and the wyrmkin's fight had moved away from me again, spreading chaos across the far end of the arena now. The splintered tables remained however, fire still dancing across the wood. Reaching down, I pressed my palm against the nearest shard and let the pain receptors do their work. Nothing is going to sober you up quicker than flipping the emergency switch in your brain with a bit of sudden agony.

The fog lifted and I could think again. I needed to keep her back, off balance. Maybe I didn't know how to beat her *yet*, but if I hit her long enough and hard enough her armour might start to buckle. If I could just get her to betray her soft underbelly...

Brute force wasn't working, so I turned to the elements. I wove my magic through the air, lassoing the smoke and ash from the nearby fires and bringing them to bear on the moroaică. Her expression changed again, becoming much more bestial and wrathful than it had been, and as my portable smog cloud whipped around her, I saw she was becoming hesitant to move. One grotesque hand was up over her face, shielding her one good eye, and it seemed as though the idea of pushing through was giving her pause.

Out of nowhere, Oberon collided with my back. He knocked me off-kilter, breaking my concentration and forcing me to abandon the spell. The smoke whirled around the moroaică for a second or two more, then span away into the air.

'Fight's not going well,' he said. He was bleeding from his mouth, his beard a matted mess of drying blood and burnt hair. Despite this, he was up before me and hauled me up with him. 'Yours?'

'Can't hurt her, but I can slow her down.'

'Is she not slow enough?'

And with that, he was gone and back to his fight. Turning back to mine, I saw the moroaică rubbing the last of the ash out of her eye. It was dripping blood and the white had started to turn red to match. Wincing, she screwed up her face and shivered for a second and, when she opened her eye the blood stopped flowing and it was back to how it had been moments before. Healed, youthful, keen.

There it was, her vulnerability. She could heal easily, I'd seen that twice now, but she couldn't hide the price she had to pay this time. Perhaps I would have missed it if I hadn't known what she was, or at least how she worked, but I did. Her victims gave her youth, vigour, strength – all finite resources, and she was using it to heal.

A single hair on her head had turned to grey as she healed her eye, and it had told me everything I needed. I pressed the attack.

Switching back to blows of force, I hammered her as hard and fast as I could. Without magic of her own to block or deflect my flurry, all she could do was take it and regenerate. She tried to get her fingers into my head again, lure my attention away, but my blood was up now and she couldn't get purchase. Quickly, she gave up that tactic and turned all her focus into survival – resetting bones, sealing cuts, untearing tendons.

I couldn't hit her hard enough, I didn't have the reserves. My assault had pushed her to a standstill, caused her to drain perhaps twenty years from her stockpile, but putting together so many spells so quickly was an impossible tempo to keep up. She noticed that too, lunging at me the moment I started to slow, ducking between two spells and coming up inside my guard.

This time, I couldn't bat her hands away. They closed around my throat and she immediately shoved me down to the floor, mounting my chest and pinning my arms with her knees. Evidently, she had remembered my previous trick. Her greying hair – now a stylish shock of it that fell down over her empty eye socket – tickled at my face and I felt her grip tighten and my life start to leave my body.

My fingers reached out, desperate to find something, anything, that I could use to fight back. Splinters of table, scorched papers, cheap plastic ballpoint pens, I couldn't manage to get a grip on anything I could use. I was done, there was nothing.

I didn't see Trask coming. Helpfully, neither did the moroaică.

The bureaucrat rose up behind her and brought something down hard on the back of the beast's head. The moroaică hissed and uncurled one hand from my throat, lashing out backwards and catching Trask across the face, sending her sprawling and making her drop her weapon. It clattered to the floor, inches from my fingertips – a simple office hole punch.

My fingers crept towards it, nails digging into the floor for traction as the moroaică brought her hand back to my throat. Leaning in closer, she pressed her lips against mine for an instant, and I felt some energy, some putrid and rotten magic, trickle down my throat and affix itself to my heart. She pulled her lips away, and with it I felt all the years I had ahead of me go with them, every moment a glistening droplet of saliva dangling from the tender string that now linked us.

I wanted to stop fighting and let it happen.

Instead, I dragged the holepunch into my hand and smashed the saucy bitch upside the head with it. Twice. *Three goddamned times.* Again and again, until she had no choice but to release her hands from my throat to protect herself. Then, with what little energy I had left, I managed to push her back and off my chest, down over my legs, all so I could kick her away.

The intention had been just to make space, but as she stumbled backwards I saw where we were in the arena, and so whenever I tell this story to other people I usually tell them that this was entirely to plan. She fell back, right to the edge of the arena and into the spiderweb of magical tripwires that bound the husks together.

I don't know how many she set off, but the husks descended on her like ants, swarming her with terrifying ferocity. Each individual blow didn't seem like much of an inconvenience to her, but they added up, too many fists and teeth for her counter. Through the throng, I could actually see the years melting off of her under the assault.

Then her composure broke. Her chilling calmness shattered, and with it went the last dregs of her stolen youth. Age didn't slow her down, though, if anything she was unburdened now, driven by the realisation that she was on the back foot for once. Lashing out with one hand, she struck at a swathe, carving through them like a scythe. Bodies fell and bones broke, and although they tried to get up and return to the fight, they could do little but twitch and writhe impotently where they lay. With ferocious speed she hit out again and again, scattering the husks' broken forms across the arena.

Breathing heavily, she stepped back into the arena. Her shoulders were slumped from exhaustion, her silvery hair lank with sweat. Under a sharply arched brow, her eye locked on me. If you're going to shit yourself, it's a look like that which is going to make you do it.

I had nothing. What magic I could draw on now was limited, having blown my wad on pummelling her down moments ago. If I was lucky, I could slow her down for, perhaps, a few seconds but then we'd be back to going toe-to-toe. That wasn't a fight I could win.

A single droplet of black blood dribbled from the corner of her mouth, ran slowly down her chin, and dropped to the floor. I did my best to ready myself, drawing in what power I could grasp and hoping against hope I could weave it into something useful.

With a sneer, she turned her back on me and stormed across the arena to the door she had entered through. Scything through the husks at the doorway, she risked one last withered glare at me before making her exit.

I'd hurt her. Perhaps not much, and certainly not enough to do any lasting harm, but more than she had been expecting. That black blood was her own – ancient and clotted, not vibrant like the youth she had stolen – and that was enough to give her pause. Of course, it probably also meant I had made a new enemy for life.

Another one for the list, I suppose.

There was still a fight going on, though. With the moroaică gone, I could finally turn my attention towards Oberon and the wyrmkin. Or at least get a front-row seat.

Their scrap had only gotten more physical. My tussle with the hag had been tactical, strategic, and this was the exact opposite. Watching the paladin and the wyrmkin fight was like watching two ancient barbarians laying into each other – they were demolishing the room itself as much as each other.

Oberon was battered and burned. Most of his shirt had been scorched away, slashes of charred cloth revealing the sickly red of burned flesh beneath. His nose was broken and one eye was starting to swell shut, both of which were adding to the blood all but pouring from his mouth and into his beard.

But he had given as good as he had got, and then some. The wyrmkin's jaw was broken, hanging slack and lopsided, a few of the scales knocked loose. One arm was tucked in close to his body, protecting ribs that I had no doubt were cracked if not completely broken, and his breathing was ragged and laboured. Each breath was accompanied by a weak crackle of flame and a splutter of thick smoke.

The paladin had dropped into a boxer's stance, ducking under the weak and slow swipes from the creature, only to deliver lightning blows to its undefended ribs. Oberon had pushed his power into his fists, making each blow hit like a sledgehammer. Still, the creature weathered the blows well, upping its own pressure until, with a single lucky jab, it seized the paladin by the throat and lifted him off the ground.

I started to move, picking up speed so that I could throw my weight into the side of the wyrmkin's knee. If I could hit it just right, I could shatter the joint, tear a ligament maybe, and give Oberon the opening he needed to finish the thing.

Turned out I wasn't needed.

Instead of struggling, the paladin swung his legs up and around the neck of the creature. Then, letting the weight of his body do the work, he let himself fall back, swinging down like a pendulum and flipping the wyrmkin, driving his head into the floor with a sickening crunch. The creature went limp as Oberon released him, falling into a heap as the paladin, panting, pushed himself up to his knees.

My skin crawled as I felt the ambient magic in the room retreat. A quick probing told me that De Sade's web of strands had dissipated, seemingly a signal that he was willing to accept his little Thunderdome was at an end.

As when all good fights end, everything went still for a moment.

'Message sent and received, I do believe,' De Sade said. He had slithered his way over to Trask who was laying in a pile of broken furniture. 'I doubt I could compel you to fight each other?'

'You fucked up,' Oberon growled. 'You've made an enemy of the government of His Britannic Majesty.'

'Oh dear, how dreadful,' De Sade said, his millipede lips curling into a mocking smile. 'What a terrible… Tactical… *Blunder.*'

With that, the swarm broke apart and made for the air vents. I almost want to say that, hidden somewhere inside the cacophonous buzzing, I could hear De Sade cackling as he made his exit. That's probably not true though – would have made for a really dramatic end to a big fight, mind. Possibly a little too moustache-twirling, though.

Oberon gave De Sade a moment, no doubt making sure this wasn't some ruse and he was about to swoop back in. When it became clear that things were over, he fell face first to the floor, utterly spent. I dashed over to help, but he managed to lift a meaty hand to wave me off.

'I'm fine,' he mumbled. 'Or will be. Tend to Trask.'

I frowned. 'You don't look fine. You're literally steaming.'

And he was. It would have been easy to mistake for smoke from his burns, but the steam was rippling from untouched areas too, from his taut muscles. They almost seemed to be shrinking a little, evaporating as I watched.

'Main rule of first aid: tend to the quiet ones first. I'll be fine.'

He had a point. With my limited medical knowledge, I gave Trask a once over. She was breathing, she had a pulse, and apart from a couple of cuts and a very large bruise coming into prominence across her face, she seemed to have avoided much in the way of injury.

'She'll live,' I said, slumping down onto the floor. 'So, think you can sell Whitehall on a cease fire now?'

Oberon chuckled. 'It'll be a lot easier now. I think De Sade showed his hand too soon, it's going to cost him.'

'Maybe. I'm not sure.'

My lips were still tingling from the moroaică's kiss, my neck was aching. I wanted to take this as a victory of sorts, but I couldn't shake the feeling that we had still, somehow, played right into his plans.

'What do you mean?'

I managed a shrug. 'He didn't sound like someone whose master plan had been derailed, did he?'

'Bravado,' Oberon said. 'Trying to get a last parting shot to save face.'

'Perhaps.'

With a noise that betrayed a Herculean amount of effort, the paladin rolled over onto his back. 'You'll have your alliance, Parker. Take the win.'

My gaze drifted over to the crumpled corpse of the wyrmkin. The sheer effort needed to bring him down, that was more than could be asked of even some of the most powerful warlocks. It was certainly beyond what I had seen of most paladins. That was before the moroaică was factored in, and how I didn't so much beat her as drive her to a stalemate.

If Irvine had been here, we would have been toast.

If De Sade really had an army of these things brewing, an alliance with Whitehall might truly not be enough. His message had been clear, but what message had we sent him? It was certainly possible that Oberon was right, but good luck convincing an eternal pessimist to look on the bright side of things, pal.

*

Oberon and Trask rested for half an hour or so before they left. The paladin was of the opinion that Whitehall would react more strongly to his testimony if he were there in person to give it, and Trask was in no position to argue. Despite the fact the beefy paladin looked as though he had been hit by a freight train, I needed longer to regain my footing than he did.

Once the Whitehall contingent were gone, I had a mooch about what was left of the field office. As a base of operations, it wasn't salvageable – the furniture was utterly fucked, and whatever enchantments had been worked to boost the size and subtlety of the location were already starting to break down.

I didn't need another safehouse, though. What I needed was information. Charlie and the other handlers on our side were a fantastic source of intel, but they hadn't heard of whatever De Sade had turned himself into. Perhaps given the names they could come up with something actionable on moroaicǎs and wyrmkins, but I didn't want to rely on having the combat lumberjack around to give me those names in the first place. Oberon knew them, which meant Whitehall knew them, which meant they had to have *something* worth adding to our woeful databank.

The problem with government agencies is just how much they love paperwork. Filing is an art form to these people, and decidedly uncivil wars have been fought over who gets which clerk to sort their documents. Seven places for everything, and everything in seven places. It's a remarkable piece of accidental data security – can't steal shit if you don't know *how* to look for it.

My approach was to just scoop up whatever I could find and hope it would end up being useful. The paladins that had been all but shackled to the desks had to be working on something important, and it couldn't all have been related to kicking warlocks in the bollocks. If we had managed to put together a bulletin board of possible warlock-work, they had to have gone at least one step further.

Using what little magic I could muster, I borrowed some space from *somewhere* and made the pockets of my jacket a little more roomy. Then I spent about ten minutes stuffing every scorched and bloody scrap of paper I could find into them, making sure Charlie and her boffins had plenty to sift through to keep themselves busy.

When that was done, I turned my attention to the dead wyrmkin again.

He looked in worse shape dead than he had done alive. I tried not to look him in the eye as I searched his pockets and patted him down, but that was difficult. With his head twisted in a peculiar direction from his broken neck, his empty eyes seemed to be perfectly placed to stare at me in judgement.

He had a key fob in his pocket for some fancy car that championed keyless entry. There was also a wallet, a mobile phone, and a pair of condoms. I'd expected something, I don't know, a bit less *normal* for a creature that could breathe fire and chokeslam a man the size of a brick shithouse.

In his breast pocket, however, I found something a little more interesting. It was a metal token, about the size of my thumb. On one side, carved into the metal, an intricate and elaborate design of swooping lines, harsh angles, and abstract shapes coalesced into something that had the vaguest hint of a family crest about it. On the other side, a message had been inscribed.

"*You are my blood by apathy alone. You will never earn my respect, whelp.*"

Oof, right?

Hate mail from abusive parents aside, there was nothing else of worth on the wyrmkin. I dropped the token into my pocket alongside the last few papers I could scratch together and headed out. Naturally, I commandeered the ridiculous car that corresponded to the corpse's key fob, too.

I should have gone back to the hideout, but something was bothering me. There were a number of potential reasons for why Irvine wouldn't have been at De Sade's stupid Thunderdome, and I didn't like any of them. Even the most benign, that bringing her would have made it possible to send a message owing to everyone dying, was hardly a comfort.

Her house was closer than the hideout, so doing a quick drive-by to silence my worries wasn't really a detour or anything anyway.

The street was somehow even quieter than it had been on my last visit. It set my teeth on edge a little but was also kind of a positive. The car I had acquired was the sort of rich man's wet dream that has to make itself known to everyone around it. Loud, flashy, a little too low to the road. It was engineered to turn heads and twitch curtains, and while it was fun to drive, it was going to get my class guilt going if I thought anyone in this road would see me.

Irvine's door had been left slightly ajar. The lock was intact, but evidently the care they had used getting in was not required for the exit. I took a quick look around and then ducked inside.

Perhaps unkindly, I expected some little shitehawks to have had their way with the place by now – you leave a door unlocked for long enough, *someone* is going to notice. I was wrong, however. Apart from the airy chill of a place that had experienced a couple of days of uninterrupted drafts, the place was exactly as it had been when I was last there.

Carefully, I moved through the hallway to the sitting room. It was still pristine, a perfect little diorama of normalcy. I wasn't sure what I was expecting to find – or even if I was expecting anything at all – but it wouldn't be here, not in her sterilised and safe place to interact with the outside world.

I opened a door at the back of the room which entered out into the rest of the house. The backstage area. The change was sudden – if the sitting room had been the airy-fairy lovey-dovey domain of Irvine the human being, the backrooms had been given over to the beastly part of her. It wasn't as though it had been redecorated with human entrails, but the chaotic nature of a Hyde's mind had seeped out into everything. The place was a mess, but a curated one, with things carefully arranged in just the absolute wrong way.

There had to be something here. The further I moved into the backrooms, the more I could taste a sort of stale magic on the air. There was no reason for her to have anything magical – Irvine had been as mundane as they come before getting dosed – but I still had to fight off the urge telling me that this was an invasion of privacy.

But there had to be a reason she hadn't been at the field office.

The sensation of magic led me up the stairs and into what, at one point, had been the guest bedroom. It had been a long time since Irvine had last had someone crashing at her place, and the Beast had found a new use for the room. The bed had been snapped in half and stacked against the wall, leaving an open space on the floor for a truly ridiculous number of newspapers. They had been scattered about the room and were full of holes where words or even entire sentences had been cut out.

Little bit murdery.

There was an old-fashioned vanity at the foot of where the bed had once been. The mirror was long gone, no doubt shattered in the middle of a rage, and in its place a scrapbook was sitting on a little stand. It was one of those photo albums you get to document a child's first few years, and even knowing from her file that she'd never had a kid, that sort of sight in a place like this made my blood run cold for a moment.

Approaching the book – because obviously, I'm not going to leave a creepy thing like that uninvestigated – I saw that on the surface in front of it was a letter. This was the source of the magic I was feeling. It was perfectly normal, with the only real sign of any malevolence at first glance being the fact that it was typed up in comic sans. Studying the magic a little closer, however, told me there was something to it beyond the writing.

Okay, so, here's another thing that's going to make me sound like a reckless idiot – I grabbed the letter. Kids, don't go grabbing weird magical shit without knowing what it does first, not unless you are a highly trained professional/dimwit like me. I figured it wouldn't be too dangerous though, otherwise it wouldn't have ended up so neatly placed.

As soon as I touched it, the words on the page changed, moved, until they spelled out a different message entirely. A Charlatan's Cipher – some truly basic hedge magic that keeps information protected so that only those of a magical disposition can read it. Useless for any real sense of security, and not normally so tainted by the fetid stink of dark magic.

The letter read:

I can cure her of you, you of her. I can certainly free you from the chattering spirit that whispers in her ear when you aren't there. What sort of a creature would use threats to bring you to its side?

Don't worry, it can't read this letter – the loathsome thing can't come near it. You could use it to ward the damned thing off entirely, keep it on your person like a sort of talisman, and you would be well within your right. This is a gift I offer freely, without any expectation.

But I would still like to ask, no strings attached, for your assistance.

Play the part. Do what it wants, keep it sweet, and all I would ask you to do is read what I send you with an open mind. For fun, you'll have to find those messages first. You are not the only person getting a letter like this, and writing a fresh one to all of you each time would be a bit impractical.

Keep an eye on the newspaper. You'll know what to look for. When you're ready to commit, I'll know to come for you.

It wasn't signed, but it wasn't difficult to work out which shitbag would use such flowery language like that. Plus, the handwriting was atrocious – probably the first time the old teachers' favourite saying was accurate: it looked like a spider with inky feet had crawled across the page.

I cracked open the scrapbook next, flicking through a couple of pages. Seems I had found what the newspapers were for – the Beast had taken those clippings and pasted them into the book, arranged them so that words and phrases from a hundred different articles all matched together to make one coherent diatribe.

Flicking through, I found a page different from the others. It was still made up of clippings from the papers, but only letters this time. No words this time, just a weird jumble of seemingly random letters and a few symbols. Trying to read it made my eyes lose focus, a little like staring at a magic eye picture, but dragging them back into focus made me see it in a whole different light.

Not a magic eye picture, but ASCII art dragged kicking and screaming into pre-digital media.

If you don't know what ASCII art is, then you're not nearly enough of a nerd to be reading a book about a wizard. But, in short, it's images made out of the letters and symbols on a keyboard, like a weird mosaic. It can be very effective, in a Matrix-esque *I don't even see the code anymore* type of way.

It took me a moment to dial my eyes into the picture. Some of the symbols weren't arranged correctly, and some still seemed to be missing, as if some issues of *Build Your Own Horrifying Murder Manifesto* had gotten lost in the post. But once I saw it, the image it was trying to paint was unmistakable, and horrifyingly familiar.

An enormous hand rising out of the Aegean Sea.

Fourteen

'I think you're reading a little too much into this, Jim.' Charlie was holding Irvine's scrapbook in her hand, turning it over and over again, squinting at the picture. 'I mean, I guess I can see the fingers? But how can you be sure this is the Aegean?'

I pinched the bridge of my nose in frustration. I had expected a little more support, if I'm honest. 'Because this is the image The Rider showed me. The exact image. Except, you know, put through a printing press or whatever.'

I had taken the book back to the hideout, but hadn't wanted to take it inside. There had been the smallest doubt in my mind that perhaps I was seeing things, and I had wanted Charlie to come and validate that I wasn't being a big dumb idiot before I tried to explain to everyone what it meant. However, her perched on the hood of my expensive new car and doubting me – while a bit hurtful – still had the desired effect.

It got me fully believing what I was seeing.

She closed the book carefully and set it down next to her. 'Jim. Obviously, I believe you. I'm still worried about you though.'

'I'm fine, Charlie. Don't go getting all soft on me just because—'

'Don't you dare weaponise that kiss, you dick,' she snarled, but there was a little amusement in her eyes. 'Just because I got sick of dancing around that issue doesn't mean I'm all domesticated. I can still kick your arse.'

I opened my mouth to make a smart and cutting quip about how it would be more like *licking my arse* because she did all her lashing out at me with her tongue, but I stopped myself. Obviously, not a very appropriate joke, but you'd be surprised how adept my mind can be when it comes to self-sabotage.

'Then don't make me,' I said instead. 'This is big news, right? It sets De Sade as the guy behind The Rider's big apocalypse. If we can work out how to stop him, we can stop all of it.'

'That's a lot of connections to make from one picture, though.'

I threw up my hands. 'What else could it mean?'

'I know you never had the patience to deal with all the intel I had to spoon feed you over the years, Jim, but you have to *interpret* data before you act on it.' Her tone had risen a little sharply, and she brought it back down. 'You might be right about it, that's extremely possible and likely given it being you and all. But, just, let me look it over first?'

Things really had changed between us. The words were the same, the playful jibes, but there was a softness in her tone now. Before, she would say what needed saying whether it had a chance of hurting me or not, but now that barrier was gone, and she was very aware that her words had more weight. I'm not sure whether that was good or bad, but it did put me a little off balance.

'Fine,' I said. 'But do me a favour and don't let anyone else see that thing. If… *When* you reach the same conclusion as me, I want to make a big deal about showing it off. I want people raring to do something about it, not pondering what it means.'

'Like I am, you mean?'

'I can trust you not to let all that *thinking* go to your head, though. The others… They're still weak from the bombing.'

A strange flash of emotions crossed Charlie's face. Pride. Sadness. A bit of happiness maybe? All a little confusing, but it didn't end with her being angry with me, so I took that as a positive.

'I… Thank you, Jim,' she managed to say, and I could see she was a little choked up.

Before I could respond, she had slid off the bonnet of the car and headed off into the hideout.

Charlie was the best in the business, there was no doubt about that, but she was refusing to grasp what this meant. The Rider had shown her something very similar to what he had shown me, and it had broken her for a good long while. Now, I suspected she was doing everything she could to avoid thinking about it. Totally understandable, but it was slowing things down.

The image was still front and centre in my mind, it had been ever since The Rider had shown me. Plus, you know, seeing a buff guy as big as a continent haul himself out of the sea is going to stick with you. The absolute awe and existential terror of the whole thing is hard to shift.

I had given the other pages of the book a bit more of a skim before I had handed it to Charlie – I'm not one for doing research, but I'm not a complete prat. The rambling manifesto managed to use a lot of words to say very little, putting a lot of emphasis on *rebalancing the scales* and *the slumbering auditor*. Without the context provided by the picture, it was indistinguishable from the bilge you find being spouted on YouTube by self-identified philosophers and unhinged Alt-Right mouthpieces.

Even with the context, it didn't do much to tell us where Irvine was, or why De Sade had been so reserved at rolling out his forces. It did make it clear that he had more on his mind than simple conquest, however.

Taking him out of the picture – would that really be enough to hit the brakes on The Rider's prophesied apocalypse? If I was right, it just might be.

Maybe then the cruel son of a bitch would stop tormenting me with my dead girlfriend.

I sighed and felt the weight of the world settling onto my shoulders again. It was becoming impossible to remember how old I even was at this point, all this stress was making time into this indistinguishable ball of, to use the scientific term, *bleh*. Good thing magic tends to give you a few extra years on your natural lifespan.

Just as I was about to head in, Wolfgang emerged from the building. He looked exhausted, but still kept a spring in his step and his eye bright. He'd been popping pills of some kind to keep him going, I suspected – something laced with magic, if the tremors in his fingertips were any indication. He spotted me and jogged towards me, raising a hand to offer me a steaming flask.

'Understand you had a run-in with a moroaică,' he said. 'You'll want to drink this.'

I took the flask from him and eyed the contents suspiciously. 'What is it? It smells like rotten seaweed.'

'Potions don't seem to be very popular over here, I've noticed.'

'It's the smell,' I said. 'No-one ever makes these things smell like something you'd want inside your body.'

He laughed. 'It's called White Dahlia. Won't get you back the years she managed to drain from you, but it will lessen the physical shock.'

'She didn't get much out of me,' I said. The potion was bubbling quietly and looked to have the consistency of bricklayers' mortar. 'You sure I absolutely have to drink this?'

'I didn't think the British would be such babies when it came to a little medicine,' the German said with a smile. 'It is not necessary, but it will help. No matter how many years she managed to take, the hangover is a killer.'

I shrugged and downed the disgusting liquid. It had lumps in it. There were granules that made their way between my teeth, gritty and crunchy like sand. It tasted like something you could grow in a jar under a teenager's bed, and the smell was so unpleasant that my nose shut down completely out of spite.

But it did what he said it would.

I hadn't realised how much the hag's kiss had affected me. After downing the potion I felt a little more awake, brighter, and that fresh weight had lessened enough that I didn't feel like my knees would give out from under me.

'Thanks,' I said, picking some offending gravel from between my teeth. 'That actually might have been worth the taste.'

Wolfgang took the flask from me and sealed it with a cap produced from a pocket. 'An entirely selfish act, I assure you. Thought if I told you the bad news in the state you were in, you might end up just putting a gun in your mouth.'

'I appreciate the concern, but you may as well hit me. I live for bad news at this point.'

'I managed to persuade a couple of warlocks to go through the notice board with me,' he said. 'I figured it might be helpful to work out what sort of creatures were getting recruited. Outside of the three you've already seen.'

'I'm going to guess bad ones.'

He folded his arms and pursed his lips for a moment. 'It's hard to say. Remember, we have no solid intelligence to draw from, it's just drawing loose conclusion from a pattern.'

'Your basic common-or-garden augury then.'

'One of the warlocks made that analogy too. Still, she seemed happy to have something to worry about other than keeping the circle up.'

'So, your results are unreliable and have a big old *citation needed* sticker attached, I understand. Might as well tell me anyway.'

'Glad we understand each other,' he said. 'Provided he has a way to make them work together, De Sade probably has enough creatures working with him that you could call it a horde. It's a motley crew for sure, a little bit of everything almost, and you mix that with van Ives and her followers—'

'You've got a force with enough variety it's impossible to properly prepare for. Got it.'

'There are a couple of positives at least. We don't think he could have gotten any werewolves or dragons on side. Probably nothing with faeblood either.'

'Makes sense,' I said. 'Werewolves are loners by nature and don't do well with authority. Dragons have their own games to play. And the fae…'

'Don't work for free,' he finished for me. 'What little we know of De Sade tells us he wouldn't pay their prices.'

I pressed the heels of my hands into my eyes for a moment. 'I suppose that helps. Takes *some* of the heaviest hitters out of the pool. But we're still outmatched, there's too many possibilities to prepare for.'

'I can drill people on the most likely prospects,' Wolfgang said. 'Make sure everyone has the same foundation. I've noticed that the experience level of each warlock is quite... Unique.'

'If you didn't know it when they brought you in, you learnt it only when they needed you to know it,' I said. 'Whitehall wasn't keen on us expanding our knowledge.'

'I know the feeling. One day I will bore you with the ins and outs of how things work back home. You'll appreciate the similarities, I think.'

There was something in his face that drew me to look at him a little closer. This foreign wizard, who had been content to follow along in our little rebellion, popping up out of nowhere and slotting in quite nicely. It hadn't been much of an issue before – and wasn't now, to be clear – but the more useful he made himself, the more conspicuous he was, the more he seemed to stand out.

'You've been a big help, Wolfgang.'

'I know,' he said, another tired smile starting to form. 'And it's making you question my motives, right?'

I shrugged. 'Not, like, *properly.*'

'Don't worry about it,' he said. 'I don't take it personally. And I won't lie to you, I am here for my own reasons. These troubles you've gotten yourselves embroiled in did get in the way of my goals, but I have been swept up in worse causes than this and I wasn't about to leave people in need when I could be of help.'

'Do I need to know what those reasons of yours were?'

'I doubt it, and I wouldn't tell you anyway. It's none of your business. I'm just a wizard in the wrong place at the wrong time, looking to help out. If that makes you uncomfortable—'

I shook my head. 'Everyone who has ever held the title of warlock was someone in the wrong place at the wrong time. I'm not about to start kicking up a fuss because you don't want to tell me your darkest secrets. You just started to stand out, that's all, and it got me thinking.'

'Like I said, no offence taken.'

His trembling fingers plucked a small box from a pocket, snapped it open, and grabbed a pill. Popping it, he tucked the box away again.

He seemed genuine, and he would have had to have been a remarkably committed sleeper agent to go this deep on helping us if he was out to stab us in the back. This was probably all Kaitlyn's fault again – I didn't even really suspect Wolfgang of anything, but her betrayal had me scrutinising everyone a little too closely now.

'You sure you're happy to give everyone a crash course on what to expect?' I asked.

'Sure,' he said. 'Moroaică are more common in Germany than here, for instance. There's no reason you warlocks should have any understanding of them. Likewise, I didn't know about Black Shucks or those weird squonk things until I came here. We can all catch each other up.'

How I longed for the days of dealing with something as simple as a Black Shuck again. 'Then you might as well get started. I'll have an announcement to make soon, and it's going to make everyone want to brush up on their bad-ass kung fu moves.'

'Fair enough,' he said, turning to leave.

'One thing before you go,' I called after him. 'If you know so much about moroaică, how do I kill one?'

He didn't look back. 'Easy. Wait for them to die of old age.'

*

Charlie took her time going over the scrapbook, but I didn't feel like complaining. More fighting meant more aches and pains to deal with, so I took the time to enjoy a nice nap in my new car. I could have gone inside and bunked down on one of the cots, but I didn't have it in me to talk to the group at large until I had something to say. Or, rather, something I could say with Charlie's approval. I could bring the warlocks on side easily enough, probably, but her voice would help with the others.

After I awoke, I watched the circle for a while as I waited for her to come back to me. We were down to the dregs now, the warlocks on the lower end of the power spectrum, and they were struggling to keep the shield charged. It would hold for another few hours, possibly even a day if we had a couple more people willing to chip in, but it was already having a hard time keeping out the ambient magic. A concerted effort would shatter it now, and soon it wouldn't take any effort at all.

If De Sade did want to hit us, he'd come then.

Idly, I tested the waters and tried to draw on my magic. The circle should have stopped me from doing that, but in its weakening state I was able to call on enough to make my veins tingle if not actually cast a spell. It was comforting to see that even after everything, I still had some juice available. But then, of course I did – I'd been practicing.

I let the magic run through my veins for a minute or two until I felt a little more awake, then I headed inside. Charlie had had long enough, and I was starting to get a little anxious waiting so long. I'd talked myself into thinking De Sade would come sooner rather than later, and now I had to do something about that.

Inside, the mood was grim. I'd managed to drive the memory of the attack from my brain, so seeing the building as it was – explosion damage and all – had me stall in the doorway for a moment. The dead had been cleared out, but the living had silently agreed to not mention the blood. Despite this, a sombre silence had washed over the place, accompanied by the sort of black malaise only found in the deepest of depressions.

Already it was clear why Charlie had been taking so long. As soon as she looked over what I gave her, she would have agreed with me, and that was a problem. I could talk the warlocks around to seeing the danger of the situation, the looming threat, that was the easy part. The hard part was talking them around in such a way that they didn't just immediately blow their own heads off.

Morale was so deep in the shitter that it had already passed through the U-bend.

I found Charlie using the remains of the bar as a table. She spotted me lurking and waved me over, doing her best not to look dour and miserable. Her face didn't wear sadness well, always trying to warp it around into some form of joyous smirk, and right now it was pulling double duty.

'Jim,' she said as I clambered up on one of the stools next to her. 'How much of this did you read?'

I shrugged my shoulders and leant forward onto my elbows. 'Not much. Enough.'

'We can't tell the others about this,' she said, dropping to a whisper. 'This is so much bigger than they are prepared to handle.'

'Come on, Chaz. They're adults. They don't need coddling.'

'You've worked alone too long. You know what morale is, but you don't really understand what it *does*, do you?'

I moved a little closer and placed my hand on hers. 'Sometimes I suspect you choose to think the worst of me. I'm not going to break their spirits, but they do need to know what's coming.'

Charlie stared down at my hand for a long moment, her fingers twitching a little as she longed to squeeze mine. Instead, she slowly withdrew her hand and scooted right up next to me, sliding the book across the table so I could get a closer look.

She started to flip through the pages. 'There's an entire battle thesis here, if you can read between the ranting. At first, I thought it was a typical psycho manifesto, but there are *layers* of meaning to it. It's ingenious in a way.'

'What do you mean?' I said, trying to read the pages. She was turning them too quickly.

'Somehow, he's found a way of cramming so much nuance into a passage that, depending on your mindset when you read it, you'll be led down a different path, so to speak.'

I frowned. 'So, what you mean… Like… No, I've got nothing. I have no idea what that means.'

Charlie giggled. A proper giggle too, like she used to do. 'I'll give you an example. Take this page here. When

I first read it, I thought it was just some waffle about Social Darwinism or Woke Culture or something like that.'

'Woke Darwin Culture.'

'Yeah, exactly,' she said. 'That sort of nonsense bilge. But then I tried coming at it from another direction, putting myself in the shoes of the intended audience.'

'Laura Irvine.'

She nodded. 'And other creatures of a magical disposition. Sending these messages through the newspapers means it can't just be for her.'

'Yeah, he said something to that effect in her letter.'

'So, if you read the same paragraph like a Hyde would, all angry and paranoid and with no patience for flowery turns of phrase…'

She stopped, evidently expecting me to give it a try. Not wanting to disappoint, I did my best to put myself in the mind of a Hyde. Thing is, I struggle to put myself in the shoes of other *people*, let alone hulking rage monsters.

Still, I tried.

I could sort of see what she was getting at. Forcing my mind to look at the words differently did make the meaning of the passages shift a little in my head, like trying to read a book when you're half asleep. I'd take in bits of a sentence and my mind would try to fill in the gaps, put together something useful. It made the text completely indecipherable, but I could feel *something* lurking just outside my comprehension. The further I could commit to the mindset, the more of these mental code wheels would click into place.

But I couldn't get there, not completely. 'Nah, you'll have to spell it out for me.'

'At least you gave it a try,' she said. 'But sure. If you read this with a Hyde's mind, you get directions, instructions on when and where to be for specific events. Provided I'm reading this right, your run in at that posh house was planned out here.'

'What about the whole Thunderdome thing? Does it say where she was for that?'

'Yeah,' she said, her voice even quieter. 'That's the bad thing. She was supposed to be co-ordinating with van Ives for *a full-hearted display of intention.*'

'Well, that doesn't sound especially promising.'

She started flicking through the book again. 'It doesn't. Especially if you connect the dots with some of the other ways I've tried reading the same passages. On the plus side, it's given me a sense of exactly what we are dealing with!'

'Which is?'

'Getting our arses kicked up and down the road like fleshy tin cans.'

I was rubbing off on her, she was stealing my downright poetic turns of phrase. 'Do we know when it's all going to kick off?'

'Not exactly, but it didn't sound like they were going to wait around.'

'Good.'

'Good? How's that good?'

I shrugged. 'Means they aren't working on an exact timetable, so I can go ahead and assume we'll have exactly as much time as we need to prepare. You follow me?'

My incredible logic managed to lock up her brain, making her mouth drop in confusion and her eyes bug out comically. I seized that opportunity to keep talking – I couldn't let her come back at me with *proper* logic and fully-thought-out facts or whatever, it would collapse my blind optimism that was already coming up with the foundation of some sort of plan.

So De Sade had put even more thought into this than anyone had anticipated, wasn't that just the usual state of affairs at this point? The rise of Whitehall had put a lot of plans, nefarious or otherwise, on hold in the magical community. It stood to reason that some people would just spend all that time stewing like big dumb nerds and overcomplicating their schemes, just waiting for the perfect time. Frankly, I'm surprised the death of the Vault didn't bring out even more of these dorks, a perfect storm of master plans and ambitious schemes, all bouncing off each other like spinning tops.

The best plan is always the first one you come up with, warts and all. It's pure, simple, probably quite direct. You don't build enough complexity into it that one misstep can throw the entire thing off-kilter. *That's* how you scheme like a professional.

And that was why, no matter how much planning and preparation had gone into De Sade's master plan, I was going to beat him. Easily.

All I needed was some phat beats.

Fifteen

I made the call before I went out to talk to the warlocks. Charlie had been right about one thing – well, many things, but one thing that is relevant right now – and that was the morale situation. If I just went out there and told them the full extent of everything, which they did deserve to know, then any preparation would be completely pointless. They'd expect to lose anyway.

I had to sugar the pill, and to do that I needed some help.

Walid and Su-Yin had been a little resistant at first. After my visit, they informed me, they had done a little more of that *spying* that they said they weren't interested in doing and worked out the scope of just how fucked everything was. My calling them up for help rang a little too close to offering a suicide mission for them.

I managed to talk them around – I had no intention of them being anywhere nearby when shit went down, and I certainly wasn't trying to hoodwink them into a fight to the death. The only things I needed from them were stacks of tech and some *sick tunes*.

After half an hour, I heard a knock on the rear fire escape. I opened the door to find Walid suffering under a Sainsbury's Bag For Life stuffed to the brim with cheap tech. He pushed past me and behind him Su-Yin followed with another two bags. She dumped them onto the floor and pushed a long receipt into my hand.

'We take PayPal, direct transfer, and I could be persuaded to take an Amazon gift card. And I'm going to want us square *before* you die a horrible death.'

I screwed up the receipt and made a show of stuffing it into a pocket. 'I'll get right on that. Did you get everything?'

Walid groaned and dropped his bag next to the others. 'No. You asked for a condensed Pink Floyd concert but, like, where do you even go to get a smoke machine? We got what we could get. This isn't exactly what we do.'

'We don't *do* anything,' Su-Yin chimed in.

Walid blushed a little. 'But if we *did*, it wouldn't be this.'

I picked over the bags for a moment, shoving around the boxes inside. 'You still did it, though. And I guess you did ok.'

Su-Yin crossed her powerful arms over her chest and glared at me. 'We did better than ok. We did fucking amazing given the time constraints.'

'We weren't going to do it at all,' Walid said. 'But we've been hearing some things and, well, wanted to do our part.'

Honestly, I didn't like that news of De Sade and his army of horrible gribblies was starting to spread. No doubt a fair amount of that was from the man himself – he had shown a predilection for pumping up the *threat* whenever he could – but any leak of that kind had the potential to throw the warlocks off before I had had the chance to get them all fired up.

What I did like, however, was how this was bringing us allies. Sure, they were kids, and I wouldn't put them in a fight if I could at all help it, but if battle lines were being drawn it was helpful to know that not everyone was going over to the side of the man made out of literal flies.

I locked eyes with the kid. 'Moment of sincerity here, thanks. If you want to get gone, I can take it from here.'

Walid went to reply but Su-Yin shoved him out the way first. 'We'll be gone before the shit hits the fan. But *please*, you need us to set this all up for you.'

'I'm not *that* old!'

'Maybe not,' she continued. 'But judging from the setlist you requested, you're old enough that we might as well just skip the part where you get confused about cables or something and just do it for you.'

First of all, my musical tastes are above reproach, but I wasn't about to get into an argument about it. If they wanted to go about setting things up for me, that was fine by me. I'm not saying they *would* do it faster than me, but I most assuredly didn't want to do it anyway.

While they pottered off to plug everything in for me, I set about gathering the remaining warlocks. Some of them – like Mgune and Bodhi – still had a bit of fight in them, but most were starting to seriously flag. They still gathered on the dancefloor, as requested, with the minimum of fuss though. Ania was dawdling, however.

I hadn't checked in with her since I had come back from Thunderdome, but I had seen her storming around. She had clearly not wanted anyone interrupting her foul mood and, being a gentleman, I had chosen to honour that. But now that I was gearing up for a big dramatic briefing, I felt that everyone needed to be present.

As I approached, she gave me a look that could curdle milk. 'Not now, Parker.'

'I'm going to do a big speech.'

'And?'

I took a small step back. This was even pricklier than I had expected. 'It's kind of an all-hands-on-deck situation. One of those very important morale boosting things. Got some information about what's coming that I think everyone, including you, needs to hear.'

'Then you should wait half an hour,' she said.

'Why?'

'Well if you want *all hands*, you're going to want to wait for Paul.'

I blinked. 'He's coming? I thought he was—'

'Yeah, well, so did I,' she snapped. 'But *apparently* now that De Sade is crawling out of the woodwork properly, he doesn't trust me to handle myself. Condescending prick.'

'He's just worried about you, that doesn't mean—'

Again, she cut me off. 'It means he doesn't trust me. *It means* he thinks I'm a child. No-one knows Lucien De Sade like I do, no-one is as aware of the danger he poses or the tricks he has. *No-one is equipped to tell me I'm not prepared to deal with him.*'

I felt the magic crackling off of her, which put me a little on edge. To be able to call upon that much while the circle was still up, she had to be so angry that she was really reaching. Without the circle, it was possible she would have already started to overheat.

Ania must have seen my reaction, because she caught herself and gently released the magic. 'Sorry. I… There may be a couple of unresolved issues there.'

'He loves you,' I said. 'Lot of issues there.'

'He has a love *for* me,' she corrected me. 'Seeing me how I was after De Sade… I don't think he's been able to shift that image. It's made him protective of me, and I *do* appreciate that. But I think it also makes him forget that he only had to deal with the aftermath, I *lived* it. And I'm still here.'

'What's the harm in having him here to help?'

She sighed and laced her fingers behind the back of her neck. 'I went through a bad time, I won't deny that. He was a great help, still is, but if he's going to undermine me like this when things get tough again... It's like he thinks I can't survive without him, and it...'

Her voice drifted away, and I caught the look in her eyes. 'It reminds you of De Sade.'

'Yes,' she said slowly. 'That's unkind to think, isn't it? But I do anyway. Just another man claiming to know me better than I know myself.'

'Is it ironic that you're venting this to yet another man? I suppose that would mean I shouldn't go offering advice.'

'I don't need advice,' she said. 'Just some time.'

I nodded and gave her a small smile. 'Fine. But I still think you need to come to my little presentation. And, for what it's worth, having Paul here will help out more of us than just you.'

'I know that. I know. I just... Oh, forget it. Who even knows what I think any more? Give me a minute, I'll calm down and lurk in the back of your little performance.'

Doing my best look of understanding, I left her be and sauntered off to what I was very generously calling the backstage area.

Knowing that Paul was coming gave me a bit more pep in my step. We had some good warlocks here, sure, and a few average ones, but none I trusted in a scrape more than Paul Renner. Not the strongest, not the most magically adept, but by far the most dependable. Honestly, he probably wouldn't be turning any tides, but it still gave me a little boost that I hadn't realised I needed.

Walid and Su-Yin needed the best part of an hour to get everything set up for me, and I spent that time on my own, trying to work out exactly what I was going to say. By the time Walid came over to tell me that everything was ready, I had locked down a grand total of 0% of what needed to be an empowering and rousing speech. Then, in the ten seconds or so it took him to hand me the tiny remote control for the little sound system I had requested, I formulated something perfect.

I work best under pressure, as I'm sure you've noticed.

Taking one long breath, I hit the play button and let the first few beats of my soundtrack wash over me. If I was going to convince a lot of dispirited people to get their chins up, especially ones who didn't want to be cheered up, I was going to need to harness the power of pure, military grade, 1980's cheese.

So, obviously, *Eye of the Tiger*.

Stepping out onto the stage, I noticed that the music hadn't done much to lift any spirits. Sour, sad, stony faces were staring up at me, with Ania especially staring *through* me from the back of the room. It could very easily have knocked me off my game, made me stumble and fall down the slippery emotional slope of stage fright, but they wanted a leader. They wanted *me* to be their leader. And, you know what? If they wanted me as a leader then they were going to get exactly what they were asking for, in full fucking cheesy glory, blasting 80's hits and seemingly not giving a single solitary shit.

They had made their bed, now I was going to lie in it and really fuck up their pillows something chronic.

'All right guys, gals, and non-binary pals,' I started, Eye of the Tiger still thumping behind me. 'We've got a bit of a situation to deal with, and you all need to know what it is so we can break its bloody nose.'

Very little movement from the crowd there, not totally unexpected. Off to the side though, nestled amongst the other former handlers and Whitehall defectors, I caught Charlie giving me the most lacklustre thumbs up imaginable. It wasn't even upright, just the barest twitch of the thumb up and out of her fist. Even her smile, such as it was, was more out of pity than support.

But it was enough.

'Thanks to some exciting daring-do on my part, we've put enough of the pieces together to know what De Sade, van Ives, all the creepy buggers we've been collecting on the noticeboard like Pokémon cards, what all of them are up to. We think. Sort of. We know enough, is the thing, to know that he's been planning it for a long time, and that we're a target.'

A mumble of resignation from the crowd this time, I was losing them. That was fine, it was exactly how I expected things to go so far.

'De Sade has been building his little group of weirdos for years,' I continued. 'And he's got grand goals for them. This is a concerted, carefully planned, detailed set of events, each one executed to perfection. Plans and counterplans, ready for every eventuality. But you can't plan for the spanner in the works, and what are we other than the best pains in the arse that the magical world has to offer?'

That grabbed some attention. It didn't do much to change the mood still, but I at least had them listening properly now, perfectly primed for my charisma to start doing its work.

'De Sade wants a fight. That's obvious, right? He's gone all military and done surgical strikes and hearts and minds shit. All those wizards and whatever are going to rock up here expecting us to be entrenched, fortified, and raring to get fucked up. What they're not expecting, is for us to change the rules.'

More of them were listening now, just enough to make it worth explaining my plan.

It was simple, really. Elegant. Very *me*.

De Sade's plans had all hinged on him being in control. He had the element of surprise, the high ground, the strength of numbers. His attacks so far had all been designed to make us feel like everything was hopeless, and to turn that around I figured we needed to simply not accept we were having a fight. Kick the expectations out the window and just totally make shit up on the fly. Step one was to make sure the fight was happening somewhere that had the least resemblance to a battleground as possible.

There will be a few clever sods who will disagree with this, but to my mind you can't get much further from a warzone than an absolutely banging disco.

I know, it sounds ridiculous, but that was kind of the point. We'd been treating the building as a hideout first, then little more than a ruin after De Sade's attack. But it was a nightclub first and foremost. You don't have big fights in a nightclub. You have some scraps before the bouncers come in and pull you apart maybe, but how are you supposed to really focus on kicking the shit out of someone when you're surrounded by flashing lasers, UV lights, and music so loud the bass line overpowers your heartbeat?

Exactly. You can't. And therein lies the genius of my plan. We repair the nightclub as much as we can with whatever time we have left, plug in some heavy duty speakers and a whole load of really obnoxious rave lights, and we make sure the whole building is so wired up that a stray glance our way will cause seizures. Unconventional sonic and visual warfare.

They'll never see it coming.

I explained that to everyone with, perhaps, a little more eloquence than I have here. Certainly, with a lot more words and showmanship. It's a bit tricky to properly describe my natural charismatic delivery of such things using just the written word, so use your imagination. My audience did, for one thing – once I filled them in on my plan I saw a number of them looking around, picturing how the place was going to look once it was all set up. I could see they were struggling, however, so it was time for my big finish.

At the front of the stage, Su-Yin had placed a little foot pedal, a trigger to set off this big finish. I stomped on it dramatically, and a pathetic pair of firecrackers popped on either side of me, coughing out a shower of confetti so anaemic that I'd seen higher quality paper in one of those cigarettes teenagers buy from ice cream vans. It plopped unceremoniously to the floor, a sad tangle of crinkled paper, but it did at least correctly herald the activation of the new speakers.

Just a little taste of the full power of these rinky-dink Bluetooth speakers the youths had provided, cranked up to eleven and daisy chained around the building. Never before has the ground-breaking Belgian techno anthem *Pump Up The Jam* quite literally shaken the rafters. I let it play for a couple of seconds, allowed some of the dust to drift down onto a couple of awestruck heads, then stomped the switch again to turn it off.

Silence fell.

And then, laughter.

It wasn't a mocking laughter, though I would have been happy enough if it had been. Obviously, it's an utterly ridiculous plan, and I'm not so dense that I was taking myself completely seriously in my delivery. I had wanted them laughing – anything to break their depression and let them reset. Sure, it wasn't as if this was going to fix it all immediately, but dealing with depression, I have found, is like trying to fish on a frozen lake: you'll get nothing done if you don't crack the ice.

Let me tell you, the ice was well and truly cracked.

Once they managed to stop laughing, it didn't take long for people to splinter off and start coming up with ideas to help get the nightclub prepared. I didn't have time to really sign off my speech or anything, they had just decided to take my idea and run with it. That gave me a little hope – even if they still didn't think it would work, quite understandably, they were at least committed to going out in one hell of a memorable moment. Sometimes, that's the better energy to have anyway.

'Well, I see you've played to your strengths again,' Charlie said. She had climbed up onto the stage behind me and was watching the warlocks with a mixture of confusion and pride. Bit rich taking pride in my work, if you ask me.

I smiled. 'Got to give the people what they want, Chaz.'

'And the people want a life-or-death fight under a strobe light?'

'I mean,' I said, gesturing wildly at the crowd. 'Don't they? Better than letting them think about a straight up fight that they've already decided they'd lose.'

Another genuine giggle from her. I'm not going to be so bold as to say my shenanigans had a medicinal quality for her, but seeing her laugh even a little after what she had been through made my heart go all soft like porridge. That haunted look would return as quickly as it had gone, but for that brief moment I could see the old Charlie again. 'Come on, a couple of the more switched on warlocks want a word, apparently.'

Grumbling a little, I followed her off the stage and over towards the bar again. I had hoped this wouldn't happen, but it was always going to be likely. Even before I saw which warlocks she meant, I knew it would be any of the ones that had had direct contact with me – immune to my charms after having been vaccinated by my continued proximity, they'd want and actual *boring* plan.

Preston was there, Mgune, Wolfgang, Ania. Bodhi was conspicuous by his absence, but that was more than made up for by the scowling visage of Ariel Kingsley, though some of his negativity was being blocked by the mere presence of Paul Renner. He was the only one who bothered to welcome me as I approached.

'Parker,' he said. 'Hell of a speech. A little light on actual, you know, useful details.'

Ariel snorted. 'Oh, I don't know. How many wars could have been won if only they had blasted some *fucking music* at the opposing force. Hell, the only problem with Vietnam was the set list!'

Mgune rolled her eyes. Somehow she had found the time to tailor her clothes to account for her missing arm, adding a flowing sash that made a statement out of the missing limb. 'We all have our concerns, but sarcasm will achieve nothing.'

'It will achieve a better mood out of me,' he replied. 'But fine. I'll try to be civil.'

She gave him a warm nod of thanks. 'Mr. Parker, I actually don't disagree with your plan entirely. Controlling the battlefield through confusion will help to mitigate the clear advantages stacked against us.'

'Well it's nice to know someone can acknowledge my tactical genius, Lara,' I said.

She held up her hand. 'It is precisely the *tactical* part that I request you flesh out. We need clear goals – are we fighting to the death? How do we handle the creatures? If De Sade himself takes the field, how do we neutralise him? Without answers to these questions, we will fail to make the most of our own advantage.'

'De Sade won't be a problem,' Wolfgang said, cutting me off before I could answer. 'Parker has already set up quite a defence there.'

I blinked. 'I have?'

'Sure, though I don't suspect you did it on purpose,' he smirked. 'Ultrasonic repellers. I don't think your Spotify playlist really counts as *ultrasonic*, but if you play it loud enough, as you intend to, it should do the job well enough.'

Paul slapped his hand on the bar loudly. 'Oh, that's actually very clever!'

'I'm sure that's how Wolfgang knew Jim didn't intend it,' Charlie said, stomping on my heart for fun.

'Ok,' I said. 'Let's *pretend* I didn't intend it and explain it for the others among the group who feel embarrassed because they don't know what an ultrasonic repeller is.'

Wolfgang bobbed his head conspiratorially. 'Basically, ultrasound is unbearable to insects. As long as those speakers are belting out at full volume, all of De Sade's *bits* will struggle to get close. Coming inside will be all but impossible for them.'

'See,' I said, clapping my hands together. 'I'm totally a genius.'

'Quite,' Mgune said. 'But that only removes one piece from the board.'

'The rest we'll have to fight,' I said. 'We'll have to share out the knowledge as best we can. We've all seen weird shit the others haven't, so we're going to have to work out some round robin crash course or something. Basic appearances, weaknesses, top five most disgusting attacks, that sort of thing.'

Wolfgang raised a hand again. 'I've already offered to share what I know with everyone about moroaică.'

'We have no way of knowing what to expect from his forces, outside of Kaitlyn van Ives and her disciples.' Ariel was glowering again.

'And rather than focusing on that, I'm trying to lessen how big an impact that will have. We can't prepare for everything, and we don't have the luxury of putting this off until we have better information.'

'Van Ives is the real problem here,' Paul interjected. 'I've seen her fight. We might be able to play off the strengths and weaknesses of the creatures, but she and her compatriots are battle hardened wizards. Warriors.'

Mgune ran her fingers gently over the place where her arm had once been. 'I am aware. But warlocks were designed to bring down such wizards.'

'Warlocks were designed to take the beating from those wizards until someone more *important* was ready to step up.'

Preston leaned forward, bracing herself on the bar and pushing back her hair. The scar on her face was more pronounced now – the skin had an unpleasant black mottling that was creeping down her cheek, fibrous tendrils reaching out for fresh skin. 'We struggle with disorganised rabble, skilled insurgents will have little trouble locking us down.'

'I'll take Kaitlyn,' I said with a surprising amount of confidence. 'She's owed a word or two from me after all this.'

'The rest of us should pick our Big Bads,' Ania said. She didn't look overly interested in the conversation, picking loose splinters out of the runes on her stick. 'The others out there, let them fire at will. We're the big guns, we need targets.'

Paul frowned. 'I think you're underselling some of the warlocks out there, Ania. Any warlock who has made it this far can hold their own.'

'Maybe,' she said back. She didn't even look up at him. 'But if they were smart enough to be included in this meeting of the minds, they'd be here. They're not. They're out there eating up Parker's juvenile bullshit. We might be able to trust them with our lives, but we can't trust them with our *lives*.'

'I have to say, I kind of agree,' I managed to spit out, despite the heinous attack at my beautiful plan. 'They're tired and vulnerable, and the need for a morale boost shows that. They're in no place to listen to complex orders or anything, it won't make it past the primary warlock directive of *fuck up any shit you see that isn't you*.'

Paul sighed, admitting defeat. 'You know them better than I do, I guess. No point trying to pick our targets ahead of time though. Might as well just wait until we see what we're dealing with.'

'Literally what I was saying, but ok,' Ania snapped.

The group fell silent after that. We all knew the one topic we hadn't addressed yet, and it was clear that none of us wanted to bring it up. As long as we refused to talk about it, we didn't have to think about it. Nobody wants to talk about how many deaths are acceptable.

Except Charlie, apparently. 'We need to talk casualties.'

'Irrelevant,' Preston cut in. Her hair was back over her face again now, giving her a very moody teenage goth look in the dim light of the hideout. 'If withdrawing was an option, we'd be doing that instead of making a stand at all. It's not, so either we get them to pull back or we die here.'

'A touch morose there,' I said. 'But right enough. There might be a chance for a handful of people to slip out the rear during any attack, but we're not getting a big group of us out without drawing attention. We try to organise a general retreat, we'll get in each other's ways as much as anything.'

Paul scratched at his beard. He was trying to hide the concern in his face. 'We better win, then.'

'We'll win,' I said, putting on my best grin and whatever was left of my best pep talk voice. 'After all, with a plan this good, how could we not?'

*

With a bit more spring in their steps, the rank-and-file made quick work of the preparations. Putting the building back together so that it was secure might have been beyond them, but making it a serviceable place for loud music and laser lights was apparently easy. Do you know where to get tarpaulins at short notice? I haven't got a clue, but the warlocks apparently did. Huge black sheets, stretched across the explosion damage and held secure by pitons driven into the remaining masonry – they'd gone hard on putting together my vision.

After our little council, my cabal of mouthy magicians had made themselves busy elsewhere, steadfastly refusing to talk to each other. I could respect it as pre-battle rituals went – if you know in advance there might be some killing heading your way, you might naturally want to take some time to get into the right headspace for it – but even still, it did feel a little like I had been abandoned.

It's not like I saw any of them coming up with a plan to resist the slavering hordes of the Human Swarm.

Charlie was the one that hit me hardest. Fine, I grant you that facing down almost certain death was not the best timing to have a little chat about what that kiss actually *meant*, but I could have done with a little support. After the council ended, she had taken Ania by the arm and led her away before I had a chance to have a word with her, and I hadn't seen her since. It was probably a little petty of me to feel put out by that, but I did, so I guess I'm a little petty. Deal with it.

I spent my last hours making sure all the technology was properly placed and plugged in, like a roadie at my own funeral. Walid and Su-Yin had provided more tech than there were sockets for but buried somewhere in those bags had been a lot of extension cables. For a while, I watched the pair of them string up speakers, laser lights, confetti cannons, looping them back into one extension cord before adding a new cord to the great trunk and moving on to the next area. After they had done this six or seven times, I was grinding my teeth so aggressively that I just had to do something, anything, to dampen my anxiety. So, I took a role of electrical tape and started to wrap the connections points of the grand trunk.

Look, it's *probably* fine to stack extension cords, I'm not an electrician. What I do know is that the last thing I needed was for the whole plan to fall apart because of an electrical fire. And I needed something that would stop me thinking about Charlie.

When I was done, Walid and Su-Yin gave me a quizzical look but they didn't seem interested in broaching the topic. Instead, I sent Su-Yin the cash and told the pair of them to get gone while they could. They had a lot of attitude and bluster, and the conversation was very much a rehash of the one from when they had arrived, but this time I had to hold firm.

See, the thing is, speaking as someone who still remembers being in their very early twenties and having the magical capacity to bitch slap a werewolf into space, I knew that behind their sass was a lot of concern. Concern and more than a little excitement. Walid especially – he didn't want to be part of our fight, but he did want to prove himself, maybe even show off to Su-Yin, and he was still so young that the notion that he could *actually literally die* had a way to go before it would settle in.

Su-Yin was the same, I was sure of it. She hid it better, played up the chip on her shoulder, but she was the one coming up with the most excuses to stay.

Always more things to do that I was simply too old and decrepit to do myself. On another day, I would have been sort of proud that I had made such an impression after only one meeting, but not today.

If I hadn't pushed, the pair of them would have found some way to stay, to fight in someone else's battles, and probably die in them. I wasn't sure if that made them heroes or absolute idiots, but it made them people to watch for sure. *After* this was over, long after.

Even as I was kicking them out, I was worrying it was too late. Outside, there was a pressure in the air. It was subtle at first, a prickling across my exposed skin. It didn't take long to grow stronger, more obvious. The hair on my head started to tingle and rise from my scalp, and shooing the kids away I looked up at our crumbling shield. Its time was at an end.

The circle was shimmering brightly now, like a large soap bubble and just as fragile. That tingling I was feeling was more and more ambient magic starting to breach the surface, pressing against the surface of the shield and worming its way through wherever a weak strand of power could be found. There was still a chance that we could top it up, repair the holes, but that was energy that could be better used in the fighting.

I flexed my fingers and tested my magical draw again, just as I had earlier. After the tiniest delay, I felt the magic coming stampeding to me. It had torn another hole in the bubble, I was sure of that, but it didn't matter. As the magic thundered through me, I felt ready.

Ready to fight.
Ready to survive.
Ready to kill.

I took that last thought and pushed it away. There would be killing, and no doubt I'd have my part in it, but I wasn't about to let thoughts like that get their claws in. Not again. Any black magic getting used today would be under my careful and considered control. I had too many people counting on me.

That felt especially weird to say, come to think of it. Though what was worse was that I didn't hate the idea.

Gross.

My veins crackling with power, I looked up at the shield and formed a spell. More rips were forming, each making the surface of the shield weaker, letting more rips form and more ambient magic force its way through. We had minutes at best before the circle failed, and that would be the signal to De Sade that he was free to attack – hit them at their weakest, their most vulnerable.

Whitehall were never going to turn up in time, I'd known that from the moment Kilbride had offered to plead our case. Still, I had been hoping I was wrong. We were out of time, and trying to hold out for an overdue squad of reinforcements would just confirm to De Sade that we didn't think we could win. If we had any hope of surviving, we'd need to get him thinking that *we* had the upper hand, Whitehall or not. Anything else was a signal to him that we expected to lose.

And if he was waiting for a signal, I had a better one for him.

Holding the spell in my mind I reached my palm up towards the sky and snapped my fingers shut tight. In one motion, I released the spell and with it I dragged lightning from the sky, directing it to strike the crown of the circle. There was a bright flash as the lightning struck, a clap of thunder loud enough to burst an eardrum, and the magic that held the circle together started to burn away like tissue paper. Tiny glowing embers of power got caught in the wind, getting blown high and away, blinking out against the clouds in the sky.

There you go, you son of a bitch. Come and have a go if you think you're fucking hard enough.

Sixteen

'I can feel them. Arcane power in the north, something more primal from the south and west.'

Preston was calling down to us from the roof. The moment the circle came down, there had been a spike of panic inside the hideout, but she hadn't let it take hold. Immediately she had started barking orders as she climbed her way up the piles of debris, slid around a tarpaulin, and climbed up to her vantage point on the roof.

'He's left the east open for us,' I called back. 'Obvious trap, right?'

She tilted her head to one side. I felt the focus of her magic shift, homing in on what De Sade wanted us to think was empty space. 'Obviously. Just the bare minimum of masking going on.'

'It's a test.'

'It's a shit one,' she snarled. 'Pinpricks of power, buzzing around across a vast area. If you take the time to look at all, you can't miss them.'

'That's him,' I shouted. 'De Sade. Like all good and pompous generals, he'll let the cannon fodder hit first. He'll be waiting to pick off anyone who tries to run. Who's closer, arcane or primal?'

She screwed up her eyes, her focus shifting again like some invisible lighthouse. 'Primal. Oh... Oh *fuck*. It's big, Parker. Super fucking big.'

I threw my magic out to the south, then the west, feeling out for what she was seeing. It wasn't hard to find, the assembled heartbeats of De Sade's army of creatures, moving at a forced march. I could feel them weaving around the mundane inhabitants of the city, the people totally oblivious to what it was that had just walked by them. Some would pass for human, but no doubt the others had been glamoured by Kaitlyn or one of her disciples.

Honestly, it was a good thing that we had the hideout prepared. Without a bottleneck to slow them down, we were capital-F Fucked.

I whipped my magic back to me and turned to Preston. 'Inside, now. Get everyone ready. Send Paul out to me if you can, I want to buy everyone as much time as possible.'

She snapped me a mockery of a salute and disappeared back inside the building. Within a minute, Paul came sprinting out of the front door. 'You rang?'

'I'm getting all Sun-Tzu here, Paul,' I said. 'I don't want to spoil our surprise before they get inside, but I want them off-balance when they hit the door.'

He clasped his hands together. 'You're thinking artillery?'

'I'm thinking danger close,' I said. 'I'm thinking lightning barrage. I'm thinking—'

'Delayed blast fireball.'

I gave him the ancient and most traditional sign for *exactly* – putting a finger on the end of my nose and pointing to him. 'A few of them. You want to top or tails this?'

'I've seen your dossier, remember. Your fireballs are shit.'

'You can do the arrangement then, I'll tie the ribbon.'

With a grunt of agreement, Paul unclasped his hands and pulled them apart. A small sphere of bright, crackling flame sprang into existence between his palms, growing bigger as he slowly moved them apart more. 'We could have done this earlier, you know.'

'And trust they'd come for us while the spell held?' I said. 'Never trusted this spell to hold more than five minutes, if I'm honest.'

I reached forward and plucked the flame from between his palms. It was twice the size of a basketball now, but it weighed nothing. I wrapped my magic around it, layer upon layer, until the flames were frozen solid, glinting like gold. With a twitch of a finger, I upped the pressure, crushing the ball down until it was no more than a bead, before hurling it over towards one of the thoroughfares that led into our private little patch of land.

'How many do you think we'll need?' Paul asked, another orb already fully formed in his grip.

I seized it and repeated my half of the procedure. 'As many as we can do. Soon as the first creepy bastard comes into view, we drop everything and run. I'll do the honours when we're ready to slam the door.'

'You know, I probably shouldn't say this,' Paul said, inflating yet another fireball. 'But I've kind of missed this. Sorry I wasn't here from the start.'

'It's fine. You were doing things that needed doing. I mean, I even agreed with it all, that's how much it needed doing.'

'Still, I know it's been hard for you, coming to terms with everything.'

'What everything?'

'The whole leadership thing, I know how much you were trying to fight it,' he said, then winked. 'And Charlie. I hear you finally broke ground on that long overdue development.'

'Who's been gossiping?'

'Ania. Who else?'

'I didn't think she was talking to you right now.'

He grimaced. 'She's not, this was before. I think, my friend, the pair of us have a lot to talk about with the women in our lives when this is all said and done.'

'Dying might be easier, you know.'

'You can't play the cynic with me,' his voice was a little raspy, he was struggling to keep up with me now. 'You've been pushing back against the two things we both knew were going to happen from the very beginning, leading and loving. I think you're going to enjoy both, and you know why?'

'I swear, if this is about to get mushy…'

'Because I'm proud of you. Wouldn't be so proud if I didn't think this was where you've always deserved to be. You just needed some time to get there.'

So, yeah, not going to lie but that kind of hit me right in the feels. When a good man, a genuinely good person, tells you that he's proud of you, even after everything you've done, that has to mean something. I wasn't sure what exactly, but it meant enough to legit bring a tear to my eye. I couldn't even throw a sardonic retort his way, just a trembling smile as a *thank you*.

The moment was short lived, however. As I tossed one last bead over towards one of the thoroughfares, the noise of De Sade's forces started to become apparent. South and west, through the busiest part of the city and consequently the most open way to our hideaway – I guess the nightclub had figured they'd get more foot traffic through with a nice open entryway, but it made things difficult for us now. I hadn't even finished covering the whole area and already we would need to pull back.

I went to signal Paul, but he had heard the same noise I had and was already making his way back to the door. Following him, I took up a position close by, where I could see the approach but could fall back quickly when needed. Once again, I started drawing power.

'I'll get them ready,' Paul said, his head poking around the door. 'See you in a minute.'

He waited for me to respond but I didn't dare take my attention off the approaches. Paul didn't wait long, and I heard the door swing back as he pulled it to the latch and made his way inside. Couldn't close it properly with me still outside, but he clearly didn't want the noise of what was about to happen spooking the rank-and-file.

The call for lightning, the same spell I had used to collapse the shield, strained for release in my mind. It pushed and scraped and insisted, building up a sensation not unlike holding your breath for too long. Some spells are content to sit there and wait to be let loose, but this one was like a caged lion losing its patience.

Thankfully, I didn't need to keep it shackled for long.

A loose gaggle of men emerged from around the corner, moving slowly and calmly. They were the whitest of white bread men you could imagine, each identical to the other. A glamour, obviously, and not a very convincing one – though it probably worked well enough to get them through the mundanes, which I suspected was all it needed to do. There would be no need to disguise themselves once here.

I had expected them to start running when they saw me, but I was surprised to see that they kept their composure and stuck to their leisurely pace. That was fine, made it easier to time things correctly. As they moved closer, however, and started the last leg of their approach, their glamour melted away and I got my first look at the assembled horde.

Irvine was at the front in full Hyde-mode, scything from side to side across the others and keeping them in check. She was shepherding them, a sheepdog that no-one would dare fuck with, even the *things* that were following in her wake.

I've seen more things that go bump in the night than most, but seeing them in the day light just made it worse. The first couple of rows housed some sort of goblins – coblynau for sure, and maybe a few redcaps sprinkled in for good measure, plus some flavours I didn't recognise. They were kitted out in makeshift armour as goblins are wont to do, pots and pans and trash can lids, the usual, except for the smaller ones on the flanks, who sported no armour but plenty of war paint daubed over their blue skin.

They looked a little ridiculous, but I suspected that was the point. They could be deadly if you underestimated them for sure, but the ranks behind them held the real dangers and they were only just breaking their glamour.

I didn't recognise half of them, and those I did were mostly things out of dusty old tomes I hadn't read for a decade. Tall and powerful creatures the lot of them, moving with the gait of highly skilled predators, holding themselves in check through nothing but a great effort of will. At a quick glance I saw some sort of hulking brute with bulbous eyes and scaly skin, an eight-foot-tall rat-man with muscles that belonged on a bodybuilder, a sallow-faced man with skin the colour of old parchment and porcelain orbs where his eyes should have been.

Even with the crash course of information sharing we had put together, these were alien to me. The creatures they held in support were easier to put names to – not just the goblinoid things, but grey-skinned ghouls, bulbous plague elementals, all manner of things that moved as *swarms* – but it seems they had saved positions of authority for the truly rare gribblies.

Another line stepped out of their glamours, led by a youthful man with a long nose and lank hair who held in his hand a bundle of steel chains that ran to a set of collars fastened around the necks of a gaggle of listless children who walked behind him in perfect lockstep.

One more row shed their veil – wymrkin, judging from the state of their mouths – before Irvine called a halt, just outside the range of our little explosive traps. My heart leapt into my throat, so sure that we'd been rumbled. If she had spotted the beads, they'd be more careful going inside, the whole plan would shift and our advantage would shrink. But how could she have noticed them? They were insignificant beads, barely visible against the grass and scrub they had landed in.

'Warlock!' Her voice was cold and sharp, cutting through the air to reach my ears. 'Is this your surrender? I promise I will treat you with the same kindness you treated the girl.'

'No thanks,' I shouted back. 'But I was hoping we could maybe come to a diplomatic solution. I'm getting good at those.'

She shook her head. 'Negotiations are done. We all negotiated with Lucien, and he has proven more trustworthy than any of you. When he has what he needs from all of you, the power he will be able to summon will provide for all of us.'

'The bloody big head in the sea? That power?'

'You deciphered his letters, then?' she said. 'I see that you fail to understand them, though. Never mind, he will help you see.'

She licked her lips and slowly raised one arm before sweeping it downward and releasing the horde.

I let them run for a whole second before I summoned the goddamned lightning.

Unlike with the shield where one large bolt would do, I peppered the goblins with a salvo of rapid-fire electricity from the sky. It stunned them, arcing off their various kitchenware armour, superheating some of it so that it began to slough right off their bodies. They stumbled, sizzling and smoking, falling flat on their faces and writhing in pain. The row behind were undaunted, stepping over the vanguard without any care for their safety, letting the crack and crunch of bones ring out.

Just a little closer.

On the other side of the sizzling goblins, the creatures that had climbed over them went from a reserved charge to a full-on sprint. There we go, that put them close enough. Time to get things started with a bang.

I snapped my fingers and dispelled my bindings on every single fireball. As one, the beads snapped back to their full size, the flames lashing and roiling with life again, and subsequently exploded. The noise deafened me and the heat might have claimed my eyebrows. For the split second before the flash blinded me, I saw something that looked uncomfortably like a mushroom cloud.

Try as I might, I couldn't blink my sight back – opening my eyes brought a stinging pain that I realised would take a minute or two to clear – so instead I let my magic see for me. Reaching out, I felt for the creatures, tried to count their casualties. There were some, but not as many as I had hoped. The blast had scattered them, obliterated any sort of military cohesion or discipline in the ragtag group, but stunned as they were I could feel them starting to get back to their feet.

That was my cue to leave. I staggered blindly to the door and pulled it open, almost fell inside, and slammed it shut behind me. I was breathing heavily, and in the colder air of the hideout I could feel that the heat had done more than just flash fry my eyebrows – my skin was tender, overly sensitive to the slightest chill breeze.

Some arms snaked under mine and helped me find my balance. I felt lips at my ear. 'Paul told us what you had planned. I knew you'd need someone to pick up your pieces.'

'Charlie?'

Her arms tightened around my chest, helping to keep me upright. I'm sure the fact that the act resembled a hug was entirely coincidental. 'Hi, Jim. You ready to ruin some days?'

'I can't see, Charlie,' I whispered. 'The flash—'

'You'll be fine. Give yourself a minute. No way it was bright enough to cause lasting damage, just a little disorientation.'

Without seeing her face, I couldn't tell whether she was lying or not. For now, I chose to believe her. 'Get me inside. It's time.'

She struggled to move me – I'm not the lightest guy, and she's not exactly Wonder Woman – but she endured. My balance came back before my vision, though by the time we'd snaked through the corridors and into the main room of the building I'd got enough of both back to be able to walk on my own again.

You know those cool pre-battle poses you get in big blockbuster movies? That bit in Avengers where all the heroes are showing up ready to kick Thanos in his corrugated purple face? That wasn't the view I was greeted with on the main dancefloor. This was organised chaos, makeshift barricades of rubble, furniture, a few strategically placed magic circles, and warlocks and handlers spread out all over the place with no apparent rhyme or reason to their positions.

It was perfect. Exactly what I wanted. It's not like we'd be able to hold a formation once the beat dropped, so why start now?

Away and up the corridor behind me, I heard the creatures hammering on the door. Took them a little longer to get themselves together than I had expected, but that was as sure a sign as any that I had to hurry.

Sending Charlie off to prepare the other handlers, I weaved my way through the crowd and up onto the stage one more time. Snatching up the little remote for the sound system, I placed my thumb over the play button and waited for my cue.

To my left, Paul took up a position covering that flank, magic arcing between his fingers. On my right, Ania clambered up onto the stage, her cane smouldering with energy. It flared at the sound of the front door being ripped from its hinges.

Maybe I should have been scared, god knows the warlocks in front of me were, but I was smiling. A full, manic, dopey, ecstatic smile.

I had one last little trick to play, and it was going to be *sweet*.

My thumb slid over to the skip track button and clicked it a few times. We'd need a different soundtrack for this.

'You ready, Paul?' I said.

He shot me a quick thumbs up.

My smile grew a little wider. 'Charlie?'

From somewhere in the darkness, I heard her mumble back. 'Uhhh, yeah. Sure.'

'Ania?' I could scarcely move my mouth at this point, my smile was so painfully huge.

She didn't respond, but when I looked over to her, I saw she had a smile of her own suppressed. She knew exactly what I was doing. That moment held for an eternity until she deigned to give me the nod of approval.

'*All right, fellas,*' I roared, practically giggling. '*Let's gooooooooooo!*'

I hit the play button. The world exploded with sound and light, a bass line that was like a sledgehammer to the gut. I had saturated every last molecule of air with the perfect soundtrack to fuck their shit up.

Ballroom GOD DAMN Blitz.

They came thick and fast, wedging themselves into the corridor that let from the entrance. Over the noise and the lights, it was hard to keep track of what exactly was happening, and once the spells and the gunfire started it was harder still. Irregular flashes of light would illuminate brutal dioramas, catching creatures in mid-air or warlocks midway through casting a spell. I'd get a snapshot of a painted goblin socking an unfortunate warlock in the stomach, another of some lumbering thing with melted, waxen skin getting its head blown off. Frankly, it was impossible to tell who was winning like this.

One constant was Charlie, however, lit by the muzzle flashes of her handgun. She had leapt up onto a pile of rubble and was firing down into the melee in front of her looking, for those that had the time to risk a glance her way, like some ancient goddess of war.

Something whizzed past my ear, and even over the thudding of the music I heard the crack of bone breaking. I spun around in time to see a redcap crumple limply to the floor as Ania retrieved her cane from its face. I flashed her a look that conveyed my appreciation, but she just shrugged and switched her grip on the cane, turning her attention back to the rest of the fight.

I started picking my own targets – anyone I spotted making their way to the stage got taken down first, then anyone bearing down on any other warlock or handler I could see. Ania was doing a better job of sniping down the troublemakers than I was, but I managed to pick off a few as they tried to force their way up to me.

The monsters must have noticed what we were doing, because they started to group up, using their numbers like ablative armour. A group of *things* I didn't recognise at all formed themselves into a wedge and rushed the stage, carving through warlock and creature alike to reach us. Ania and I laid into them hard, bolts of force and javelins of energy obliterating them one by one. As the wedge started to dull, the ranks behind the tip started to hold onto the corpses of their comrades, making it much harder work for us to bring them down. A corpse can make a great obstacle, and the more successful we were at creating them, the more it was benefitting the ones that hunkered behind them.

They pushed their way within spitting distance, and too late I realised what it was they were actually doing. At the foot of the stage, what was left of the wedge dissolved, unleashing their cargo – the lank man with the squadron of chained children. In stark contrast with how they had been outside, however, those same children were *alive* now, gnashing rabidly with shark-like teeth as they strained against their chains. The man's slender hands released them, and the children pounced.

The kids were nimble, somehow able to leap off each other in the air and redirect themselves. This let them dodge what spells Ania and I could snap off on reflex, then split into two group and crash into us at the same time. They were heavier than they looked, knocking me straight to the floor and crawling over my limbs, pinning me to the surface of the stage. I felt too many teeth sink into my skin, sawing through the flesh and probing deep into the viscera below. One set cut the deepest, and I felt something snap in my hand and recoil up my arm like a window blind in a cartoon.

Fucking hurts, let me tell you.

I tried to scream, but one of the children had slithered up onto my chest and was staring down at me. It planted a hand over my mouth and leant in close, it's blank and empty eyes boring into me as its mouth formed into a toothy smile. Suddenly, I became very aware of just how many very important blood vessels were completely exposed, how vulnerable I was. This kid was going to tear my throat out and all I could do was lie there and take it.

Struggling and straining, I tried to get some leverage, to weaken the grip of the other little biters just enough to wriggle free, but it was futile. Their teeth had sunk so deep that any movement was agony, and I was sure that some of them had gone straight through me and actually nailed me to the floor. The one in my face brought their head down to mine, placing the tips of their teeth against my forehead and raking them, slowly and painfully, down my face to my chin. Blood immediately started to trickle into my eyes.

The head dropped out of view and I felt the sharp points of those horrible teeth pricking at the soft skin of my neck. Before they could pierce the flesh, however, there was a loud bang, a flash of light, and the child sagged limply on top of me. Another few staccato blasts and I felt some give on my extremities as well. A boot swung into view quickly, catching one of the kids under the chin, knocking them back and making enough space for me to scrabble back. I tried to snap off a spell, but an agonising burning pain shot up my arm, catching me by surprise. The owner of the boot interceded, and I saw now that the blasts were from a handgun.

Still firing, Charlie offered me a hand to pull me back to my feet. I let myself have a second to take a mental snapshot of the ridiculously badass profile she was cutting, then slapped my working hand into hers and got up.

Wasting no time, I grabbed her shoulders and turned her in the direction of Ania, hoping that there was still time to get the chompy little fuckers off of her before they could do too much damage. She had done a better job of holding them off than I had – she was still upright and had managed to wedge her cane into the mouths of three of the scampering shits at once. The others she was holding at bay with some weird curved knife that she was holding in a reverse grip.

She was, however, still only just holding them at bay. Charlie put a few bullets in them and they went down no problem at all. Ania took a breath, checked herself over for bite marks, then gave Charlie an appreciative salute.

My own wounds were bothering me. Aren't they always? My arm was bleeding badly, far worse than even Kingsley and his goons had managed. It was possible, even probable, that the kids had opened an artery, though I wasn't seeing it pump out like I would have expected. My spellcasting arm was limp and rubbery, I couldn't even twitch my fingers. They'd gotten to the tendons or something, completely slashed them. Charlie had saved my life, but the kids had made sure I was useless to the fight now – couldn't cast a spell, couldn't make a fist.

There was a voice trying to cut through the music. I looked up to see Ania gesturing at me wildly, but as soon as she realised I had seen her she immediately tossed her cane in my direction. Catching it on instinct in my good hand, I sort of stared at it like a big dumb idiot. Ania was shouting again, pointing behind me.

I turned. The lank man was on the stage, stooped over the corpses of the biters. He had a flute pressed to his lips, the metal burnished and blackened in places, and seemed to be playing some soundless tune. The kids started twitching.

Without thinking, I thrust the cane in his direction and felt it pull a spell from my mind. My arm snapped back like I had been firing a hand cannon of some kind, and a sliver of sunlight launched from the end of the cane, vaporising the man's head. He slouched down onto the pile of twitching biters and they soon fell still again.

I stared at the cane in awe. The runes in the wood were glowing yellow as I held it, my own power siphoning through the designs in a way I had never conceived. When this was all over, I needed to get Ania to teach me how to make one of these. It *ruled*.

Spinning it around in my hand for good measure, I offered the cane back to its owner. She waved me away and pointed to my arm gravely – evidently, I wasn't out of the fight just yet, then. If that was the case, I felt it was best I got my money's worth.

The incident with the bitey bastards had felt like it had taken forever, but it had all been over inside of a minute really. The fight off the stage was still going strong, people so intertwined that I didn't dare attempt to snipe at people with Ania's stick. I was going to have to go down there.

The *things* that had sheltered the lank man and his cadre of cannibal kiddies made for a decent set of stairs to get down quickly. The chaos hadn't managed to spill back out into the wake of the wedge, giving me a bit of freedom to push in deep and get swinging. Cracked a few skulls, blindsided a few gribblies, even had time to stare in appreciation as Paul just fucking chokeslammed the fish-man through a table before getting embroiled in a fist-fight with the buff rat.

Yeah, being in a big fight to the death kind of sucks, but where else would I get to legitimately say that someone *got embroiled in a fist-fight with a BUFF RAT* and keep a straight face?

A scream rang across the room, even louder than the music, and I felt something splatter across me. Someone else's blood. Going out on a limb, I suspected that Laura Irvine had taken the field.

Tracking the direction of the blood, I managed to pinpoint the Hyde as it ripped a man's head off and slam-dunked it down his neck hole. In its other hand, the beast was wielding a severed leg like a club, twatting the living fuck out of some poor handler. Just as it finished bashing his head in, a volley of spells rocked it, and Ariel Kingsley fought his way through the crowd to capitalise.

It was a feint. As soon as he was within range, the beast pivoted and moved so fast it was almost a blur, pirouetting around his attempted coup-de-grace and catching him behind the ear with a vicious haymaker. Kingsley was going to die if I didn't do something.

There were too many people between me and Irvine for me to risk a spell. Every time I had the shot, someone's head would pop into the way and block my view. Given our numbers disadvantage – and, you know, basic morality – I couldn't risk assassinating one of our own. But I wasn't going to be able to reach Kingsley in time either, leaving magic as my only option.

Thinking quickly, I pulled my aim upwards and blasted at the ceiling above the beast. My trigonometrical ingenuity notwithstanding, the rain of polystyrene tile didn't seem to bother Irvine too much but caused just enough of a distraction to let someone else pop out of the crowd and put themselves between Kingsley and certain doom. Probably a little selfish of me to feel a pang of disappointment that Kingsley wouldn't realise it was my spell that saved his life – would have been nice to be able to hold that over his head so he would stop being quite such a rotten shit to me.

The beast rose up tall and shifted its weight, ready to come down hard on Kingsley's unexpected saviour. He brought up a shield, but he didn't need it. Irvine pulled her blow short, jerking backwards as if having heard a sudden noise behind her. Making space between her and the warlock, she leapt back towards the entrance corridor, then cupped her hands to her mouth and let out a shrill screech that cut through the noise of the sound system.

As one, the creatures disengaged and pulled back to join her. This wasn't a fighting retreat – the withdrawal was so sudden and urgent that I caught a couple of the slower critters getting cut down as they moved away, no thought given to defending themselves. Those that survived pressed themselves against the walls of the room, leaving warlock and handler alike confused and surrounded. It was all a bit evocative of a Secondary School prom, boys and girls on opposite sides of the hall and staring at each other awkwardly.

The temptation was to think we had won, forced them back. I caught myself starting to think that, even. Other warlocks were already letting their guards down I could see, letting that combat high transition into uncharacteristic braggadocio. But they weren't watching Irvine holding the creatures back, eyes flitting wildly to keep track of targets. And, most tellingly, her tongue was sliding over her lips hungrily.

It didn't take long for the hammer to drop.

A chill started to roll across the room, air pressure dropping as a draft crept under the tarpaulins. Like fingernails delving into a crack, the draft peeled the taut sheets and quickly made the few loose areas larger – large enough for the draft to grow into a breeze, then again into a wind, and finally into a gale, all within the space of a few seconds. The sheets were ripped from their moorings one by one, whipped off into the air and out of view, letting daylight rush in.

Just like that, we had lost most of our home-field advantage. With sunlight saturating the area, the laser lights and strobes would be heavily muted, limiting their ability to put the creatures off balance. The same was true of the music, losing most of its punch without the perfect acoustics of the nightclub.

It would have been the perfect moment for Irvine to call for the attack again – we were fully visible, exposed, and easy prey. But she didn't. She didn't need to.

Perched on the roof, looking down on us through the blasted ceiling that was now uncovered, eyes glowing with a malign power, was Kaitlyn van Ives.

Seventeen

Kaitlyn hadn't come alone. Flanking her at the edge of the precipice were her disciples, all of them leering down at us like a firing squad. Even knowing that she was most likely going to make an appearance, I still found myself dumbfounded at the spectacle of it all.

People always change up their style when they switch sides, and I'd expected some sort of stripperiffic, leathery, quasi-fetish gear to come into play once Kaitlyn's allegiance to De Sade came to the fore. What I hadn't expected was for Kaitlyn van Ives to rock up to murder us dressed in a dress so high class it would have its own insurance policy. Silk the colour of red wine clung to her form, vamping her up in a much more effective way than just showing some extra skin.

Her cronies were dressed much the same. The women were in elegant evening gowns plucked from the pages of a boutique fashion magazine, the men in suits so sharp they could draw blood. As an ensemble, the group looked like they would be far more at home enjoying some grey-haired crooner belting out Sinatra covers than kicking the shit out of us.

They were thoroughly committed to the latter, however.

With a snarl, Kaitlyn launched the first attack, calling a storm of wisps around us, pelting us with raw magic. There was scarcely time to get a shield up before her disciples joined in, throwing spells of their own at us. More warlocks got cut down in the first few seconds of that surprise attack than had fallen to the monsters during the whole melee, skewered and scalded and atomised by a sheer concentrated torrent of spells.

Those of us who survived were driven back hard, herded like cattle into a frightened huddle. This did at least give us the ability to link our shields, kind of like Roman centurians but with less style. As our magics interlinked, I tried to look around the group for someone I could work with.

My first thought was of Charlie, but once I spotted that she was safe I forced myself to push that concern aside. She was at the back of the group, pushing down the heads of the remaining mundane members of our crew and keeping them safely inside our shields. That was where she would be most useful, as much as it pained me to admit – I wanted her counsel, but this was a very mage-heavy problem to address, and she'd be out of her depth.

Right now, I needed wizards.

Paul shuffled close to me, his shoulder brushing against mine. 'Should have seen this coming.'

'Should have enchanted the tarpaulins or something.'

'And leave us with less magic for the fight? I think you made the right call, just would have been nice—'

'To not get ambushed in our own fortress, I know,' I snapped. 'We need ideas on how to deal with that *now*.'

From over my shoulder, Ania spoke up. 'What I want to know is why the monster brigade is content to sit back and watch this. If they came at us right now, they could overwhelm us easily.'

'Please don't give them ideas,' I snapped. 'One problem at a time, please.'

'It's the same problem,' Paul said. 'They're hanging back to stay out of van Ives' way. Soon as they get tired, Irvine will hit us before we can retaliate. It's a one-two punch.'

Paul was right, the longer we left Kaitlyn wearing us down, the easier it was going to be for Irvine to mop us up. We needed a way to bust out of the kill box and put some space between us again, make it harder for the second blow to connect.

'We need to take Kaitlyn out of play, but I would prefer not to kill her if possible,' I said. 'Paul, Ania, you know De Sade's programming better than anyone. How do we overcome it?'

Ania shook her head. 'Quickly? Impossible. Took months of therapy to get my head on straight again.'

'Signal interrupt,' Paul said. 'Ania's right, you can't break the programming quickly, but you can confuse it for long enough to get a cheap shot or two in. That's how I brought this one in.'

I nodded. 'Right then. Here's what we do—'

'*You* are going to do nothing,' Ania interrupted. 'If you're going to play general, stick behind the front lines. That arm is going to be a liability now.'

She wasn't wrong, but it still stung a lot to hear. 'All right then, let me tell you what I need *you* to do.'

I was surprised, her somewhat brusque outburst aside, how intently she listened to my plan. In fact, there wasn't a single complaint from her or Paul, and the others huddled in our little magical testudo were nodding along as well. Evidently, I was becoming something of a tactical genius.

Ania nodded enthusiastically once I had finished explaining my plan and dropped into a crouch, ready to go the moment the opportunity presented itself. I gave her a moment, then placed the tip of the cane I had borrowed against my throat, pushing some magic into my voice, amplifying it.

'Kaitlyn!' I boomed. 'You've made your point! Call off the dogs and we'll talk terms.'

The bombardment didn't even slow. 'Bullshit!'

'If you need a white flag, I'm sure I could make one,' I said, slowly standing to my full height. The shield warped with me, weakening a little but it would hold long enough regardless. 'Just hear me out, all right? I'm admitting that you've got us over a barrel here.'

She made a hand signal I didn't recognise, and her underlings ceased their assault. They kept hold of their magic though, great waves of it radiating off them. This wasn't a cease fire, it was just a pause while they charged up. 'Surprise us all, Parker. Let's hear your terms.'

'First of all… Jesus Christ, hang on,' I winced, realising for the first time that the music was still blaring loudly out of every speaker in the place. 'Let me turn that noise off so we can think.'

Ok, it was a bit of an obvious move, but I think I sold it well enough. By the time it registered to Kaitlyn that this was all a sneaky bit of subterfuge, Ania had taken the opportunity to sprint across the room to the nearest speaker. Kaitlyn did realise though, peeling off a spell in the young woman's direction. Paul was ready to deflect it, however, giving Ania just as much time as she needed.

Ripping the speaker off the wall, I saw her send her magic through the grate on the front, deep into the diaphragm of the cheap electronic tat. With a movement of her wrist that was weirdly akin to someone wrapping candy floss around a stick, she drew the music out of the speaker, condensed it, and then slammed her palm against the wall.

With a bit of a kick from Ania, the vibrations rattled through the metallic substructure of the entire building. Like tuning a radio, she dialled it in, focused it on the exact section she wanted, concentrating all the energy on one spot. A millisecond before Kaitlyn's comrades could release the mighty blow they had been charging, a large section of the ceiling – the bit they were standing on, naturally – crumbled under their feet, sending them all tumbling down to the ground.

The next step needed to be just as fast – faster even. We broke the shield and charged before Kaitlyn and her crew could find their feet again, locking the wizards in the worst place for any spell caster to be – a fistfight. Without time to cast spells, even our former handlers could break a few skulls, and Charlie was emblematic of that – she was pistol-whipping the ever-loving shit out of one of Kaitlyn's goons already.

I didn't join that fight though, not with my arm. Instead, I slammed the cane into the floor and channelled its magic to throw the fresh debris from the ceiling backwards, into the amassed horde of monsters. The damage would be minimal, but it would make for a decent obstacle.

Kaitlyn was the real target, though. The other wizards, maybe they'd have some ass-kicking potential, but Paul and I had seen her rip the head off a vampire. We needed to stop her gaining any momentum. With her crew occupied, that was Paul's job.

Heading straight for her, he dropped his weight down and drove a knee into her neck, pinning her. 'Kaitlyn, listen to me. Listen to what I'm saying and think. You have to know you're being used here.'

She clawed and struggled under his weight, unable to find any leverage to move him. 'I *did* think that at first, but Master explained it to me. This is the only way forward for us.'

'Master? You know that's not how you talk, right? You *know* he's in your head.'

With a roar, she popped her hips and rolled out from under Paul's knee, flipping him to one side as she came up to her feet. Her elegant dress, now torn and dusty from the fall, managed to find enough of a breeze to flap around her legs angrily. 'I know that Master is the future, and that standing against him makes you fuel for the engine of change.'

She lunged, fast and vicious. Paul tried to deflect and use her own momentum against her, but she had too much going for her and shattered through his guard. Tackling him to the ground, they tumbled across the floor before coming to a stop with her straddling his chest, fingers digging into the skin under his chin.

My turn. I grabbed the cane again, switched my grip, and swung it like a baseball bat at the base of her skull. With only one hand, I doubted the blow would put her down, but it would at least give Paul a few more seconds before she started to remove his head. I needn't have worried, though, because she somehow knew what I was doing, an arm snapping up to block my attack before snaking around the shaft of the cane and disarming me. In one fluid motion, she rolled the cane over her knuckles and drove the point of it down at Paul's head.

He had already moved. The staff crashed into the dancefloor, cracking the already battered and scuffed surface, and for a moment I saw a look of concern flash across Kaitlyn's face. Paul, having somehow managed to slide down to freedom between her legs, placed a hand on her shoulder.

'I'm alright, Kaitlyn,' he said softly. 'You didn't hurt me.'

'I don't… What…' she stammered. She stared down at her shaking hands, and I saw that her eyes were watering.

'You've been violated,' Paul continued. 'He's warped your mind, made you act against your nature. You can feel that, and you're fighting it.'

She ran her fingers over the cracks in the floor. 'Impossible. I had protections. I'm protected.'

'He found a way. Listen and think. Listen to your own thoughts, they are telling you the same as I am.'

What was it he had called it – signal interrupt? If that was the case, it certainly seemed like Paul had really sent a jolt through her signal. I'd never seen her looking so confused, so unsure of herself. There was vulnerability in its purest form here, stripping away the powerful terrorist that we all knew, drilling into her soft core. It wouldn't last long – kick-ass, confident, and deadly were just who she was – but it would let Paul end this.

He removed his hand from her shoulder and pulsed some magic through it, ready to lay her out unconscious with a simple enchanted slap to the back of the head. Painless, quick, humane.

Before he could swing, she was up, turning on him, staring him down with eyes brimming with rage and fury. 'Nice try, Renner, but you don't have the charisma to trick me like that.'

She headbutted him, breaking his nose and sending him sprawling. Then, without even taking a breath, she wrenched the cane out of the floor, held it aloft, and called some lightning of her own.

I don't know how the rest of the fight had been going, but it was done now. Using the cane like a lightning rod, Kaitlyn channelled the energy down one arm, through her body, and out the other like a weaponised Tesla coil. Having done something similar before, I knew how effective it was going to be before the electricity hit me, but I had no idea how much it was going to *hurt*. The world boiled away for a moment, and when it started coming back to me I had nothing left, no tangible life force to do anything with.

Every warlock, every handler, we all hit the ground hard. Lolling my head over, I locked eyes with Paul for a moment, then Ania, and finally Charlie, each one of them groggy and broken.

I was dimly aware of the popping of lightbulbs and the fizz of speakers short circuiting. All that electricity had to go somewhere, I suppose, and after it had taken a leisurely jaunt through us it seemed to have arced its way through the wiring, melting what was left of anything electrical.

Our last line of defence against De Sade was gone. Not that it mattered, we had no fight left in us now.

I heard the click-clack of Kaitlyn's heels as she started to make her rounds, checking on which of us had survived her spell. She didn't say much, but she did manage to bark a couple of orders at her comrades, though I wasn't conscious enough to really make out words.

'Separate the wheat from the chaff,' were the first things I heard her say. 'Master will have no use for the dead and I'll accept the punishment for that. Ready the living, same as before, and keep them constrained. He'll be here soon.'

I heard more footsteps and grunts of exertion, the dragging of boot heels as people started getting moved around. My skin tingled with the sensation of fresh magic as Kaitlyn's underlings worked some spell to keep us all compliant. It ramped up the fatigue, made my limbs feel far too heavy to move. When it was my turn to be carefully filed away, the slender arms that wrapped around from behind my back and clasped over my heart seemed too lithe and spindly to be able to lift me. Still, they managed, and I felt breathing on my neck as I was dragged backwards along the floor.

In my ear, a voice like broken glass whispered to me. 'I regret not being able to taste of you again, mage. Oh, how titillating a taste you arcane ones are. Perhaps, if there is anything left after the visionary is done with you, I will take the remains. You owe me *years*.'

It was a testament to how fucked up I was that not even having the moroaică right up in my grill could elicit much of a response in me. I heard the voice, recognised it even, but I couldn't work out what to do with that information – there was a chasm in my brain and I had nothing that could bridge it.

The moroaică dragged me over to the other survivors and propped me up against the wall. Slowly, I felt the ability to just *exist* creep back into me, and I managed to start taking in the scene a little better.

Half the warlocks under my care were dead, fried into crispy black husks that crunched and cracked as Kaitlyn and Irvine's lackeys moved them out of the way. The others – which included, much to my relief, Charlie and Paul and Ania – were lined up near me in various stages of consciousness. Preston was at the far end of the line, somehow managing to struggle against the big buff rat I had seen Paul fighting earlier. He cracked her upside the head, and she went groggy and stopped resisting.

The buzzing of thousands of tiny wings signalled De Sade's arrival, the swarm of tiny insects sweeping through the large hole in the ceiling to join with the creepy crawlies that chose that moment to pry their way up through the floorboards. They swirled around each other, slithered over each other, and wove themselves into a human form once again – never gets any less gross to watch, let me tell you.

Actually, the grossest thing was seeing Kaitlyn and her disciples drop to their knees in front of this grotesque hive. Like, it was full on hands-on-knees, heads hanging kneeling. Sure, outside of Kaitlyn herself I didn't really know much about the people in her cell – what I did know was that gestures of submission and deference were not in their nature, and seeing their response to De Sade was highly unsettling.

Irvine and her creatures were, ironically, much less disgusting. They bowed their heads gently in respect, some more enthusiastically than others, but that didn't look coerced. It's a sorry state of affairs when hideous monsters are the things giving me the least amount of creeps.

A grotesque smile rippled across De Sade's face as he surveyed the scene. His eyes flicked across the corpses, counting each of them in turn before doing the same for those of us that survived. 'Little bird, attend me.'

Kaitlyn rose to her feet, her head still bowed. 'Yes, Master.'

'The corpses. Explain yourself.'

'They were resistant,' she said. Her voice was cracking, scared. 'I pulled my punches as best I could, but—'

'Do better next time,' he snapped. 'Still, enough have survived. I'm not *completely* disappointed in you.'

'I... Thank you, Master.'

He turned away from her and she instantly slunk back to her knees. It appeared as though, once out of his sight, she no longer existed to him, so focused he was on staring us down. Walking the length of our little line, I saw concentration on what passed for his face – I'd expected some egomaniacal gloating like a true villain, but the cold calculations he was clearly making instead were worse in a way.

Starting at the end of the row, he singled out Preston. She was still groggy, barely conscious, but his slimy hands hoisted her up to a standing position so he could get a closer look at her. Roughly, he grabbed her chin and turned her head left and right. 'Solid. Powerful. A sturdy reagent. We'll start with this one.'

His fingers gripped tightly at her hair, dragging Preston from the line and into the centre of the room. I tried to move, to get up and put a stop to this, but my legs weren't working now either, just twitching impotently in response to my attempts to move.

Once in position, De Sade wrenched her back by the back of her head, curving her body into an uncomfortable arch. Placing his other hand on her throat, he dug the nails into her flesh, making her scream. He held them there while he spoke. 'I suspect this will be of little comfort to any of you, but your sacrifices will bring a new age of peace. Eventually.'

With great care and attention, he started to carve his way through Preston's flesh. His fingertips, formed from the stingers of scorpions, sliced effortlessly through her flesh and clothes, flaying her with very little resistance. Her screams grew louder, ear-splittingly so, but if they had any effect on De Sade he wasn't showing it. To him, apparently, skinning a human being was no different than peeling a banana, at least in terms of the whole moral issue.

Preston passed out before he reached her navel, but considering the damage he had done that wasn't surprising. De Sade had scored out strips of flesh – the same gory design I had seen carved into Bennett and the others at the shelter – but he was muttering some incantation under his breath as he did so. As he uncovered more of her viscera, the blood shimmered with raw power, the magic in her veins being pulled to the surface and starting to flow messily through the channels and troughs carved into the woman's skin.

Bending her over, De Sade finished slashing at her flesh. The final strokes cut a small circle at the base of her spine, a place for that shimmering energy to pool at the end of its journey. He waited, his firefly eyes glowing greedily, as this reservoir began to fill. Preston's magic rippled gently, not quite a liquid but not a gas either, growing more colourful and vibrant even as the life was draining from her skin.

When his little well was sufficiently full, De Sade hunched over, placed his lips around the pool in a perfect seal, and swallowed Preston's essence. With a shiver of enjoyment, he dropped her body to the floor and snapped his fingers, ushering one of Kaitlyn's men to remove her. The channels carved into Preston's flesh were just meat now, all the magic gone from her.

A little way to my right, I heard Ania seething. 'You son of a bitch!'

'Little bird,' De Sade said. 'I hear you tweeting. It's time to fly home.'

Ania put up more of a fight than Preston had, but not by much. He had her up and in his grip in seconds, staring her down with his eyes barely an inch from hers. There was nothing but burning contempt on Ania's face, though.

'I'm not your little bird.'

De Sade smiled wider. 'You are all my little birds, always have been. Living at my pleasure, *for* my pleasure, and dying for a purpose beyond your understanding. Your minds are so simple that I know understanding this is beyond you, and it's why I'm not insulted by your rudeness.'

'And what if I spit in your face? Will you take offense then?'

'There are far fouler things beneath this *skin* than saliva. Take your place at my heel, like you were born to, and I'll share that with you when the time comes. There are plenty I can draw energy from to fuel the awakening, but you mean so much to me… It would be meaningful to me for you to be there.'

'Kiss my arse,' she snarled at him. 'I know how much you like that. Just fucking kill me and be done with it.'

'I had wanted you to be there,' he said, yanking back her head and placing a hand on her throat exactly as he had with Preston. 'The lengths I have had to go to so that I could amass the power needed to wake The Sleeper… There has been a lot of suffering on my part, knowing that I was incomplete. So many little birds were lost to Whitehall, and while I've recovered many of them you were the one I missed most of all. The most *skilled*.'

The Sleeper. He had to mean that big bald bastard lying deep beneath the Aegean, right? His whole mad-arsehole manifesto had been centred around that image, and if he was going to start wittering on about it now, there had to be a connection.

Would explain a lot. It's not much of a stretch to go from the ability to lend magic to having that magic siphoned off unwillingly, though I had never heard of it happening before. I'm not sure it needed to look so grossly sexual either, but sex wizards are going to sex wizard, I guess.

What really got me was the need for so much magic. The whole school of sex magic is about harnessing the power of others, but it's supposed to be explosive and climactic, orgasmic. To take that much into himself and store it like that, no wonder he turned himself into something so profane – he'd need to just to avoid burning up from the inside out.

But even having sold off so much of his soul for this power, he couldn't drive out all that humanity. His words may have been crass and slathered thickly with disgusting implications, but there was a genuine look of love in his eyes as he held Ania. Not love in the truest sense – he clearly didn't see her as a person – but the kind of warped jealousy that powers covetousness. For that moment, his loftier goals were secondary to his need to prove, once and for all, that Ania belonged to him.

I'd been so focused on the very inhuman parts of him I had forgotten to account for that. It made him beatable, and all it had taken to remind me of that was seeing him look into the eyes of the one that got away.

Just a shame, really, that this realisation was going to come too late for me to save Ania.

'I don't have the time to put you back in your cage, my little bird,' De Sade continued. 'But I can add your essence to the chorus, so that you can at least experience one last moment of bliss. Together, we can take what is needed from the remaining wizards, from Whitehall, and then I'll take you to Greece. There's nowhere more romantic for a final grand climax.'

De Sade's fingers started to dig deep into Ania's throat. Kicking and choking, she tried to pull away. Any distance she managed to gain was futile, filled quickly with flies and worms and locusts, all swarming to pull the bulk of De Sade closer. Even if she had wanted to scream, her throat was now so full of flies that it would have been impossible to get out any sound.

A blur shot past me and charged at De Sade. I don't know how Paul had summoned the ability to move at all, let alone so fast, but as he grew closer to the pair, he pulled a trinket from his pocket and triggered it with a gesture. A gleaming phantom blade shot out from the object, and he brought it down fast on the insects making up De Sade's arms. The cut was clean and the smell of burning chitin filled the air for a moment.

Ania fell to her knees, vomiting up all manner of insects, as Paul positioned himself between her and De Sade. Whatever force of will had gotten him up was already draining from him – he couldn't lift the blade and it hung limply at his side, the tip cutting into the floor.

'Enough,' he hissed. 'You've had your fun with her. Never again. If you want to summon an ancient horror from the ocean floor, you use me and leave her out of it.'

'Paul… Don't—' Ania sputtered behind him.

De Sade reformed his arms and grabbed at Paul. He swung the blade again, clumsily but with gusto, but the swarm of critters filtered around the attack, wrapping around his throat and wrist. I watched as Paul was lifted up by his neck, disarmed by means of a sudden twisting off his wrist, all while De Sade sneered at him.

'You always impressed me, Renner,' De Sade said. 'Such *virility*. The sheer force of will you possess will make for a powerful voice in the chorus. Provided you don't break first. Perhaps, my little bird, seeing your white knight broken will bring you to heel in time to save your life. One final sacrifice from you, eh, Renner?'

Everything I had, even a fuckton of things I didn't, I put into getting back to my feet at that moment. Searing pain mixed with chilling numbness, a hundred warning signs blaring at once, and yet somehow, I felt my limbs start to move. There had to be some power I could draw on, some last drops of magic in me that hadn't dripped out of the wound in my arm. How much blood had I lost? Surely not enough to stop me from saving a friend.

I was slow, and even as I pulled myself up I felt my knees giving out again, sending me sprawling. Pushing myself up with my good arm, I reached out for enough magic to cast something, anything, that would stave off the execution. Paul had managed it, dammit, so I bloody well could too. I had to.

But I couldn't.

I could only lie there and watch as De Said prepared to unzip one of my few friends and drain him dry.

Paul managed to turn his head a little, getting one last look at Ania as he did so. 'One. Final. Sacrifice. See you down the road, kid.'

Then, turning back to De Sade, he smiled and died as I always suspected he would.

Like a fucking hero.

Eighteen

De Sade had been so intent on watching the defeat in Paul's face, or the anguish in Ania's, he had forgotten the first rule of magic – always follow the magician's hands.

Dangling from the swarm's grip, Paul had somehow managed to draw on enough energy to drag another fireball into existence. Just as outside, the flaming sphere floated in the air between his palms, growing as he pulled his hands apart. It was the size of a football when he let it detonate; in such an enclosed space that was far more than enough to wreck everyone's shit.

The shockwave threw me back into the wall, and everyone else as far as I could tell. My head hit the wall hard, though, smacking me into darkness. I came around before the smoke finished clearing, but after Ania had had enough time to crawl over to Paul's remains and throw herself on top of him in tears.

When the fireballs had gone off outside, I had been able to avoid the aftermath. Now, though, I had no such luck.

The survivors – warlock, mundane, monster, and wizard alike – stumbled around in a daze, picking under the rubble in search of others from their side. None of what I was seeing felt real, like I was watching through someone else's eyes. There was a thumping pain in my head and the more it went on the more disconnected I felt from everything else.

Our hideout, such as it had been, was truly done for now. The explosion had finished the job De Sade had started not so long ago, turning the remaining architecture into a scattered collection of debris, rubble, and flame. The only positive I could see was that the man himself was gone, a burning mound of half molten bugs laying at the feet of Paul Renner.

I crawled closer, knowing even then that we needed to be sure. The books said as much – if a single fly, a worm, a *maggot* had managed to escape then it would be just a matter of time before De Sade would make his way back to full strength. That couldn't happen, I wouldn't let Paul have sacrificed himself for just a *delay* in the apocalypse.

The crawl was slow, arduous, painful. But when I reached the mound I put those feelings aside started just fucking *pounding* the shit out of the remaining bugs. Again and again, slamming my fist into the floor to make doubly sure that every last one of them was reduced to pulp. Then I fell back, exhausted, and felt myself drifting off into that restful darkness again.

When I woke up the second time, it was to the sound of masonry grinding over itself. A pile of rubble, large chunks of concrete and rebar, caved in on itself as I watched. From deep inside it tumbled a young woman covered in dust, bleeding heavily from a nasty-looking gash at her hairline, her face crisscrossed with small cuts and scrapes.

Through all of that, it's a miracle I recognised Laura Irvine at all.

The beast had retreated, leaving behind the terrified and stunned young woman. She got to her feet groggily and spotted me staring up at her. I saw her eyes widen as she looked at me, and she bolted in fear, clambering over rubble and vanishing out of view.

Again I passed out, and this time I didn't feel like waking up again.

*

I did wake up again, obviously. Would be hard to tell you this story if I didn't.

When I *did* come round, a woman in blue scrubs and a surgical mask was hunched over me, shining a light in my eyes.

'This one's alive and stable,' she shouted. 'Observation only, watch for changes. Low priority.'

And then she was gone, leaving me swimming in my own head for a moment as the latent starburst from her torch faded from my eyesight. Forcing myself into a sitting position, I tracked her to see where she was going.

Someone had dragged me outside of the ruins and onto what was left of the parking lot. Evidently there had been much less debris over here, and it had already been swept to the side, clearing out the asphalt to make space for a triage of sorts. Black mats had been arranged in rows on the floor, people having been dumped unceremoniously on top of them. No more than ten people in the same blue scrubs and surgical masks were flitting from mat to mat, tending to the injured and shouting clipped instructions at each other.

Past the mats, at the perimeter, stood people in smart suits and ties. Even from this distance, I could make out the glimmer of the pins on their lapels.

Whitehall had chosen to show up after all. Better late than never didn't really feel appropriate, though.

Sitting up, I tried to get my bearings. I didn't seem to be bleeding anymore, my arm heavily bandaged and strapped across my chest uncomfortably, and the thudding pressure in my head had been replaced with a distant burning that was easy enough to ignore. There was too much activity to get a decent look at the occupants of the mats nearby, but not enough to stop me from noticing the pile of body bags arranged on the other side of the perimeter, being loaded one-by-one into the back of a non-descript transit van.

Behind me, the scraping of chair legs on asphalt alerted me that someone had settled down at my back, but I didn't turn around. Kilbride sighed, and I heard him lean forward, forearms resting on his knees. 'Feels like it would be a little tactless to say we got here as fast as we could.'

'Didn't expect you at all, if I'm honest,' I said. My eyes were welded to the body bags. There were so many of them.

'The Prime Minister agreed to the ceasefire,' he continued. 'This one actually listens when you speak.'

I shrugged. 'Then they'll be out by next week. Not that it matters, just look at us. People were saying this was going to be the start of a fresh dawn, but—'

'It's better than it looks. I won't lie to you, I know you can take it – a lot of warlocks died today. You've got to temper expectations and look to the triage. Everyone that makes it to a doctor, no matter how fucked up they are, that's a victory.'

'I watched a good man torch himself to bring us this victory,' I said. 'Doesn't feel much like one to me.'

'That will be harder to deal with.'

I thought he was joking at first because, well, I would have been. He was dead serious, however, and once again I felt sure that he was speaking from experience. Maybe later, if I could ever get my head together enough after this to care, I'd work out his deal. Maybe not.

For now, all I had to do was...
Oh god.

I was up and moving before I even realised it. In the distance, I could hear Kilbride shouting after me, but I wasn't listening. Scanning the faces of the dying and damaged as I ran past, most of them too bloody for me to even recognised, I slowed down only when I spotted familiar features. Three, four, five times I had a false alarm, and the sixth one nearly ended me then and there – I showed up as they started zipping up the body bag, making me push past them to get a good look.

Mercifully, Charlie was on the mat next to the corpse. She looked in about the same shape as I was – her nose was broken, a menacingly black bruise was forming under the skin, and one eye had swollen shut – but she still managed a smile when she saw me.

I'm afraid I was very uncool, practically leaping next to her and pulling her into my arms. She hugged me back, a vise grip that made the bones in my spine pop pleasantly. We were probably both doing a little cry, as you do. Very lovey-dovey moment, all the trimmings.

Eventually, and with much reluctance, we broke off the hug. I nearly shat myself when we did – Kilbride had caught up and was looming a few feet away, waiting patiently for me and Charlie to finish our tearful reunion. He had his hands in his pockets, nodding at Charlie. 'I did try to tell you, she's fine.'

'I couldn't hear you,' I said. 'And even if I had, would rather hear it from her anyway.'

He shrugged. So fucking nonchalant. 'You'll have to wait a little longer then. There's a nasty crack in her jaw, she's not supposed to talk for a while.'

'I'll talk if I want to,' she grumbled from between clenched teeth.

I looked back at Charlie. She had a habit of setting her jaw when she was stressed, grinding her teeth and clenching so hard she could crack them, but the whole presentation was just *off* now. Just a little bit off centre, slightly slacker than usual, a couple of small but irregular lumps where they shouldn't be.

'Jesus Christ, Charlie,' I said. 'I didn't mean… You've… I'm just so sorry.'

She started mumbling and gesturing, an impromptu game of charades being rattled off far too fast for me to keep up with. Too shellshocked to say anything, I just let my eyes glaze over and watched her as she signed out fucking War and Peace or something.

Eventually, Kilbride stepped in. 'I don't know exactly what the lady is trying to say, but with her permission I'll do my best to interpret.'

Charlie stopped, frowned, then gave him a curt nod.

Kilbride nodded back, then continued. 'You're blaming yourself for what happened to her, and that's not helpful. You are not responsible for all the ills that befall her, only the good. Thinking anything else makes you one self-centred, arrogant, obnoxious son of a bitch. There's a war on – help people get back on their feet, don't fret about others putting them on their backs. That about right?'

A playful snort signalled that Charlie approved of his interpreting skills, and she even pointed at him while staring at me as if to say *pay attention, dickhead*.

'So, it's officially a war, then?' I asked.

'The PM said as much herself,' Kilbride said. 'Only way she could justify sending paladins to *help* warlocks. In fact, not to be rude, but we need to have a word with you. In private.'

'I knew you were lurking around for a reason. This the sort of talk that starts with a sack over my head and ends with car batteries hooked up to my unmentionables?'

His expression turned grave. 'No.'

'Then I suppose we better get it out the way then. Lead on.'

I said my goodbyes to Charlie – awkwardly, especially as she couldn't really respond – then let Kilbride escort me across the camp and over towards the other paladins I had seen when I awoke. They had been deep in conversation until they saw me, at which point they clammed up instantly and stared as if I was some fascinatingly ugly deep-sea fish caught miraculously strolling about on land. Kilbride shot them a look and they parted, letting us through the perimeter.

A full-blown crisis centre had been erected on the other side. Tents, trucks, the sort of things you'd expect to find at the staging point for a ground invasion, not for a scrap at a nightclub. I wasn't sure how they even managed to fit it all in given the limited space.

Kilbride guided me towards one of the larger tents, off-white canvas stained with mud and its guy ropes bolted to the concrete. He pulled back the flap and ushered me inside. It was stark inside, just a folding table with a couple of old books piled up on one side and what looked like a corpse draped across the middle.

A man in a pinstripe suit a few paygrades above that of the paladins was tinkering away beside the corpse. He had some sort of magnifying instrument and was hunched in close, seemingly scanning every inch. He had rolled up his shirt sleeves and I could see dry blood on his forearms. When we approached, he gently placed the magnifier down next to the corpse and wiped his hands clean on a rag hanging from a hook nailed into the side of the table.

'Jameson Parker,' he said, offering a now-clean hand. 'Milton Reese-Burrell, deputy Prime Minister.'

I declined to shake his hand. 'A little hands-on for a politician, aren't you?'

'Was only appointed this morning. With things the way they are, the PM felt this was going to need a permanent liaison, but with there not being a cabinet office for magical insurrections… Well, the short of it is she figured I'd outlast her premiership.'

'Good for you,' I said. 'What do you want?'

'I need to know what our little friend here was up to.' He reached over and moved one of the books. It had been stacked on top of a small glass jar, inside of which rattled a tiny little gnat. He flicked at the glass. 'Horrid little thing, but ambitious.'

'You should destroy that thing at once.'

He flicked the glass again. The gnat landed on the bottom of the jar and stared out at him. 'We will, when we are done with it. We're not even sure it's involved – perhaps it's just an innocent insect in the wrong place at the wrong time. But the PM, in her infinite wisdom, wants to actually *understand* what happened here, especially if we are to avoid a repeat in Parliament. This young lady's body tells an interesting story, for instance…'

He picked up the magnifier again and hunched back over the corpse. With slow and considered movements, he followed the channels that had been carved in the skin, starting at the navel and moving up, around her chest, over her shoulders, and up to her throat. To my shame, it was only then that I realised whose corpse it was.

I turned on Kilbride. 'Is this a joke? Did you drag me down here just to watch some posh twat ogle a friend's body before it even gets cold?'

Reese-Burrell slammed the magnifier down on the table. 'I am indeed a *posh twat*, Mr Parker. I am thoroughly misliked by my colleagues at the House, and I'm told that working with me is not unlike the experience of extracting a candiru without anaesthetic. But what I also am, Mr Parker, is someone who has a modicum of understanding regarding the life of an outcast. I am, quite frankly, the only person left with a connection to Whitehall who will give you so much as the time of day, so it would be prudent not to make an enemy of me. If you don't mind, that is.'

'You're violating the corpse of Sophie Preston, a warlock under my care!'

He took a long, slow, deep breath and placed his palms together patiently. 'I am performing an autopsy. You've been through serious trauma, so I'll overlook your insinuation. Please, take a minute and calm yourself.'

'You're not a fucking coroner,' I spat. 'You're a politician.'

'I was a coroner, once' he said. 'A very good one. The one that got called for years whenever something unexplainable ended up on an autopsy slab. Then someone got it into their pedestrian head that the government needed an expert more closely on hand, and so a bit of electoral sleight-of-hand later and I'm the MP for a town that consists entirely of empty second homes for other MPs. Then the deputy Prime Minister. Then the liaison between the legitimate power in this country and the loud, uncouth, anarchistic children that court chaos at every turn. That would be you. Now, compose yourself and help me with my examination.'

It's rare, as I'm sure you'll be aware, for me to find someone who likes the sound of his own voice quite as much as I do my own. Reese-Burrell was certainly muscling in on my turf in that regard. But at the same time, knowing that Whitehall were taking this seriously now did help a little. Seeing one of my friends under a microscope was sobering and my immediately reaction was to kick this guy's teeth down his throat, but if we were going to finish nailing this coffin lid down, we needed as much information as we could get.

'Fine,' I said. 'I'll be the bigger man. How can I help?'

He smirked and went back to examining the cuts on Preston's flesh. 'How magnanimous of you. I need you to tell me what you saw of these marks.'

'I saw De Sade flense the fucking skin off her until she died, does that count?'

'Yes, horrible, certainly. But the *purpose*, if you please.'

I looked at Kilbride who just shrugged at me. Guess I had to play ball. 'Some sort of ritual magic. Drained her power right out of her.'

'Ah, yes, of course,' Reese-Burrell said. He rolled Preston onto her face and started to study the wounds on her back. 'So this would be the siphon, I see. Quite ingenious, though I've never seen this result in death directly…'

'You've seen this shit before?'

His head flopped from side to side, his fingers tracing the well in the small of her back. 'Not exactly. It's evocative of an old Witchfinder rite, the Quietus Maleficarum. No-one's performed that for hundreds of years, of course, far too barbaric for these enlightened times.'

'More barbaric than ripping out a tooth and threatening to use it to make your heart explode in your chest?'

'The Quietus Maleficarum purges the body of its connection to the arcane realm. The theory, as I understand it, is that by opening certain ley lines on the body—'

'We don't need to discuss the theory,' I snapped.

'Of course, the facts are more important,' he said, unbothered by my interruption. 'Anyway, this isn't the Quietus, the whole point of that rite was to render a witch able to stand trial and, ultimately, face execution in the eyes of the Lord. Tell me, what was the culmination of this ritual?'

'He, well… He sort of *slurped* up her magic. Right out of the hole.'

'*Fascinating.*'

I was getting ready to lose my patience at this point. All of my shits were gone, and while I recognised the need to be civil and play the game to keep our new allies on side, this was taking the absolute piss. We didn't need to write a fucking academic paper about this, we needed to do *something*. Working out the specifics of what De Sade had done would be very helpful, no doubt there, but this was more than just *science*. People had died.

Kilbride must have seen the desire in me to kick off because he put himself between me and Reese-Burrell, a subtle gesture that he wouldn't let this go too far. 'So, he's after more power? A traditionalist then, with traditional and predictable goals.'

'Not quite,' I mumbled, swallowing my frustration. 'Look, there's this *thing* asleep at the bottom of the Aegean. He wants to wake it up.'

'Ah, an apocalypse,' Reese-Burrell said. 'If you had led with that at the start, perhaps we would have had our alliance in time to save a few of your lives, hm?'

That was it. I lunged for the little fuckface, grabbing across the table to take him by the tie and choke him. Again, Kilbride made his presence felt by bodychecking me off balance and out of reach of Reese-Burrell. I stumbled, but I kept my balance and turned on the beefy paladin, already sending out feelers for enough power to lash out with.

There was that irritating calmness again, the stony glare of pure composure. It worked though, and I stopped listening to the voice in my head telling me that it was time to pick a fight. What little magic I had summoned – barely enough for a spark as I was, truthfully, far too hurt to truly consider a fight – fizzled out. Kilbride stared, unblinking, until he was sure I was good, then turned and slapped Reese-Burrell across the face so hard it sounded like a gunshot.

'Be civil,' he said. 'We're all aware that the only reason the apocalypse gets any credence now is because we've seen the damage De Sade is out to cause. Enough prodding.'

Reese-Burrell didn't rub his cheek, but there was anger barely contained in his eyes. 'Very well. I believe I've heard enough from our *good friend*. You may both leave. In the spirit of our alliance, I'll have my notes sent to you when they're ready, Mr Parker.'

Before I could respond, Kilbride took me by the shoulder and marched me out of the tent and back to triage. He led me to Charlie once again, finally leaving me with her long enough for some of my anxiety and worry to start to dissipate.

I didn't tell Charlie about what Whitehall was doing with Preston's body – she wouldn't have understood. Hell, I think I've made it clear that I didn't really understand. They were playing catch-up, and they had their ways of doing that I suppose, but as much as I needed her reassurance that this was on the level, I couldn't give her that burden right now.

For now, I could take some solace in easing her burdens instead. Maybe Kilbride was right and I couldn't blame myself for what had happened to her, but I was going to make sure I took the time now to do my part to help. The Rider had scrambled her brain, De Sade had smashed up her body – either I blamed myself for putting her in the way of that harm or I did something positive and *helped*.

In a show of huge personal growth, I chose the latter. We didn't talk, obviously, but we sat together and watched the sun for a bit, watched it slowly set. We watched the doctors purposefully shuffling from mat to mat, helping where they could and bagging where they couldn't. We watched them tend to people we knew and those we didn't, but each of them at that time *felt* like family.

Eventually, night fell and some annoying paladin fired up some huge floodlights to keep the triage area well lit. By this point I had just about come to terms with Reese-Burrell, the alliance, all of that stuff. My mind was sorting itself out and I was starting to shake the shock and confusion of everything.

Sighting a few of my little council out amongst the living helped with that – Lara Mgune had come out of things surprisingly well, though they did have to dig her out of a pile of debris. Ariel Kingsley had taken a beating, and his survival was a little touch and go, but he was going to pull through. It surprised me how much I cared about that, if I'm honest. He was a dick, but he was our dick.

Excuse the phrasing.

A lot of that burgeoning optimism fell apart when we found Ania, though.

She had taken herself away, back into the ruins of our hideout. A rather skittish looking paladin, a young man scarcely into his twenties, was milling around nearby and wrapping hazard tape over every point of ingress he could find. Every now and then he would wince in response to a distant *thwomp*, followed by the sound of rubble shifting. He raised a hand to stop us, but thought better of it and stepped aside as we approached.

The noise led us to the sight of Ania, blasting the ever-living shit out of the rubble. She had been crying but judging from the dry tears on her cheeks she had moved on from sadness and through to anger. And, you know, the fact she was just fucking obliterating loose masonry was a bit of a clue as well.

Cautiously – not wanting to be mistaken for a shapely pile of rubble – I took a few steps into the room. I felt Charlie fall into step behind me, using me as a human shield – from a place of love, I imagine. Ania flicked her wrist and shattered another pile of stones, then let her shoulders droop and flopped down to sit on the floor.

'Looking for my cane,' she said. She had her knees pulled up and was hugging them, her head resting tiredly atop. 'I don't think van Ives took it. Must be buried under all this.'

I sat down next to her. Somehow, it was harder getting down than it had been to get up. 'Can you make another?'

'Sure, I could,' she shrugged. 'Don't want to. Was Paul's idea, and…'

'I didn't know.'

'Why would you? When they finally let me out of the hospital, I wouldn't let him come with me when I went in for physio. He wanted to, obviously, but he didn't overstep. Instead, I came home one day to a fucking tree branch on my doorstep and a note telling me to make staves cool again.'

From behind her knees, I caught the barest glimpse of the saddest smile I had ever seen. I think I found myself copying it. 'That's a really roundabout way to get someone a gift. The IKEA of arcana.'

'He wanted me to remember I was more than damaged goods,' she said. 'I think he wanted to get me something to show he cared, but didn't want me thinking I was incapable. I liked it, anyway.'

'I've never known anyone quite so willing to help as him, that's for sure. One of the best men I've ever known.'

'Fuck off,' she muttered.

'What?'

'I said, *fuck off*,' she roared, jumping back to her feet and snapping off another blast of power. 'He was an arrogant, condescending, patronising, perverse jerk! He latched onto me the moment he got me out of De Sade's clutches all those years ago, and why? Because he had decided in that moment that there was no way I could succeed without a man looking out for me. The only difference between him and De Sade was that one of them would look you in the eye while he fucked your life.'

'Ania, I don't think—' Charlie tried to say, but the angry woman shut her down.

'Don't you start. You and your perfect love story ending. The pair of you fuck about with your *banter*, and somehow the gods let it all play out nicely for you despite every opportunity for it to turn to shit. You don't have the memory of watching Parker immolate himself to save you, *without you even asking him to*, do you?'

I stood up slowly. 'He was saving your life.'

'I didn't ask him to! I *never* asked him to! He gave me more of a life than I ever thought I would deserve. At some point I was supposed to be able to return the favour, to properly thank him. He robbed me of that! *It's not fair!*'

The tears were back now, and with them came angrier and more destructive blasts of power. Over and over, she slammed spells into rubble, hammering a crater into the floor. I think she was screaming as she did so, but honestly it was hard to hear anything over the jackhammering of her magic.

It took a great effort of will to stop myself from interfering. I'd been where she was now – after Robin, I was lost for a good long time – and that was why I was sure she wouldn't want to hear platitudes and *advice* from me. There might be a time later for that, but throwing my opinions into the mix right now would just give her something else to lash out at. There's only so much space in a human heart for emotions, and sometimes you have to let the pressure out so you can start to rebuild.

I managed to convey all that to Charlie with a look, I'm not exactly sure how, and she resisted her own urge to get involved. Instead we just watched her pound her arcane fists against the wall until they came back bloody, metaphorically speaking, and slumped against the remains of the wall, exhausted.

Before I could think of something safe to say, Ania's eyes lit up. With a renewed energy, she threw herself to the floor and started scrabbling through the broken wood and smashed brickwork, hurling chunks of it aside. From the wreckage, she managed to retrieve a heavily charred length of wood, about the size of her forearm. As she held it, wisps of smoke formed on the surface, then a familiar set of sigils started to light up on the wood.

'You found it,' I said, stating the bloody obvious.

She was staring at it, watching the sigils pulse and sputter. 'It's broken. I suppose that's fitting, considering…'

'The other half is probably still here. We can find it and—'

'No thanks,' she said. The wand – seeing as it didn't feel right to call it a cane now – vanished into a pocket and she was already pushing past me to leave. I watched her go, feeling very much not great about the whole thing.

It dawned on me that there would be others like her. A lot of warlocks had died today, and the whole point of this endeavour had been to help bring them back into the world, to force them to make connections. There was going to be a lot of mourning, and people were going to look to me to know what to do next.

I, of course, had no bloody idea.

Charlie's hand found mine and squeezed it tight. When she spoke, it was quiet, and the words clearly hurt her. 'Do all your wizardy types have such *big* feelings?'

'The nurture of the beast.'

'Nature.'

'Not in this case,' I said. 'Chaz, what are we supposed to do now?'

She smiled sweetly at me and shook her head as if to say: *I don't know.*

'That's very helpful. Neither do I.'

'Good thing you don't have to work this all out on your own then, huh?'

Nineteen

My council – which I only now realise was a term I had started to use in a non-ironic fashion – was heavily depleted. Wolfgang and Bodhi were missing, Preston and Paul were dead, and Ania was very much not in the right headspace. That left me with myself, Lara Mgune, and Ariel Kingsley to try and work out what our next move was going to be.

The paladins had *graciously* allowed us the use of one of their tents. I suppose it was a show of good faith, treating us like equals for once, but it still felt wrong. The three of us held off on business until we had put up enough wards to put our minds at ease.

'Thanks for coming,' I said, doing my best to get comfy on one of the folding chairs the paladins had left us. 'I know we all have a lot of wounds to lick right now, but—'

Ariel interrupted me. His voice was flat, cold. 'De Sade can't be allowed time to regroup. If he comes back, he'll come back hard.'

'Provided Renner didn't kill him,' Mgune said. 'I know the paladins believe he still lives, but I am not so sure that anything could survive so potent a cast.'

'I'd like to think that way,' I said. 'But we can't take the chance. If one insect survived, De Sade survived. Whitehall half suspects they might have bottled up his last surviving gnat, for what it's worth.'

Ariel folded his arms. 'It's worth very little. If anything, the idea of one speck of him surviving just makes it more likely others did too. We need to counter-attack now.'

'With what forces?' Mgune had leant forward, but her voice was still calm and warm, not reproachful as I would have expected. 'Attack where? De Sade achieved his goal, perhaps not completely, but he's sufficiently weakened us to the point where we can't stand against him. And even if we could, we've never located any of his bases. We started this on the backfoot, and we are still there now.'

'Yes, we already know that,' I said. 'It's how we move forward from that starting point that we are here to discuss.'

'Use the paladins,' Ariel said. 'If they're really going to commit to working with us on this, let them use their manpower for good for a change.'

I frowned. 'You'd trust them?'

'No, of course not. But they have the numbers that we are sorely lacking right now, right?'

I opened my mouth to respond but my attention was drawn by a gentle vibration from one of my wards. Someone was lurking just outside the flap of the tent, eavesdropping. Pressing a finger to my lips to silence the others, I reached out to my ward and triggered it, detonating a web of magical strands and causing them to restrain the nosy bastard.

A swift yank, mentally, and the eavesdropper stumbled inside, landing on his knees. He looked up, seemingly a little amused.

'Spying on us, Mr Reece-Burrell?' I asked him.

He beamed smugly. 'As the government liaison, I felt it only fitting that I should attend this meeting the moment I heard about it. Locking me out of one of my own tents though? I'm sure that was in error. Or jest.'

'It wasn't,' Ariel growled.

'Ah, that's a shame. I thought we were all trying to be *civil* here.' If Kilbride had been in the room, that would have worked as a great clapback. Or should I say *slap*back. Ha ha.

His shoulders bobbed up and down for a second, then the politician was unbound and already getting back up to hit feet. In his hand he had a small pen knife stamped with the same badge he wore at his lapel. Enchanted knife for, essentially, an enchanted rope. I started to wonder what other preparations he had arranged, knowing he would be spending time with us magical folk.

'Civility at this stage may be too optimistic,' Mgune said, attempting a diplomatic tone. 'But I assure you that we can all manage to avoid being *openly* hostile.'

Reese-Burrell pressed his lips together, making them barely more than a thing line. 'Excellent. Now, had I been invited to this meeting as I should have been I could have prepared you for this news. As it is, however, I am afraid I must tear off this plaster quickly. While I appreciate the initiative in attempting to come up with our next step forward, your kind will be playing second chair to us in matters of strategy.'

'Excuse me?' I asked.

'There has been a *re-evaluation,*' he said, and he was rubbing his palms together in a way that somehow was just utterly infuriating. 'The alliance stands, you don't need to worry about that. But after your thorough drubbing here, the scales are far from balanced. We have the lion's share of the forces, the equipment, the resources in general. It's only fitting that we take the lead.'

Bile rose in me, but surprise was completely absent. This was always how it was going to go, at least once they had the upper hand. Everything was an equation to them – if they could lean on you they would, it was just the nature of the beast. Sure, Reese-Burrell was being the smuggest shit ever about the whole thing, but not because he thought he had gotten one over on us. There wasn't enough of the gloating for that.

I managed to swallow the urge to break his face, but Ariel was struggling. Leaping to his feet, he knocked his chair over backwards and jabbed a finger in the politician's face. 'You two-faced bastard. This was always the plan, wasn't it? You just wanted to kick us when we were down, boot everyone back into the doghouse. This isn't a cease-fire, it's a fucking betrayal.'

'Calm yourself, Mr Kingsley,' Reese-Burrell said. He was doing his best to look calm and composed, but he was recoiling from the young man's finger as if it had been the barrel of a gun. 'It's just a little administrative reshuffle, it's hardly driving a proverbial knife into your equally proverbial back.'

'You're going to play semantics right now? At the scene of a literal massacre?'

A little roughly, I stepped in and put myself between Ariel and Reese-Burrell. 'Let it go, Ariel. Whitehall have the right of it here – we might have been the first target, but they're the biggest. They're taking the most risk, they get the right to call the shots.'

He rounded on me, and I was sure he was about to throw a punch my way. '*Seriously?* I was just starting to think that maybe, *maybe*, you weren't some bootlicking wanker. But you're going to side with *him*?'

'I'm acknowledging the facts of the matter,' I said calmly. 'We don't even know how many warlocks are left alive, let alone able to fight. Kaitlyn van Ives is still knocking around out there, and she has a lot of mages on her side, more than we had *before* this. Any way you slice it, paladins are going to be on the front lines more than us now.'

Ariel was seething, so much so that he couldn't find enough breath to form the words to respond to me. The utter disbelief at the situation had thrown him so hard that he totally locked up. This *would* end with him throwing a punch – lashing out was the only option he had left really, an emergency response that his brain could send out while it scrambled to understand what was going on.

Mgune placed a soothing hand on his shoulder. 'Now is not the time, Ariel. This is warlock business and should not be explored in front of *friends*.'

She angled her head around Ariel's so she could stare pointedly at Reece-Burrell. It took him an embarrassingly long amount of time to get the hint, but once he did so he dutifully took his leave. 'Perhaps you are right. I shall give you a moment to *leash your dog*, so to speak. Then, I expect, we can have a more productive discussion.'

Mgune's hand stayed on Ariel's shoulder until Reece-Burrell was gone. Then, in a single swift action, she conjured up a barely visible dome of energy to dampen all sound trying to escape the tent. She subsequently utilised this advantage to smack Ariel right across the face.

'Be smarter,' she snapped as he rubbed at his cheek. 'You would not have lasted a week as a warlock.'

'Because I'm not a bootlicker?'

She rolled her eyes. 'Because you are ruled by your pride. Deference is a shield, not a humiliation. Explain it to him, Parker.'

I gave her dampening field a cautious prod with my magic before I spoke, just to make sure she had done as thorough a job as it appeared. 'Honestly, Ariel, if you think anything I said in front of that pompous fuckbag was sincere you are far too naïve to survive in this world.'

'What?' Ariel blinked.

'Look, I know you're not naïve. You fought Whitehall in your own way, but you never had to deal with them directly. There are ways and means to deal with bureaucrats that just don't work if you confront them directly.'

'Whitehall always think they are in control,' Mgune added. 'They were always going to see the ceasefire as an admission of weakness on our part. A necessary act of magnanimity on theirs, and a way of humbling us.'

'But you agreed with them,' he said.

'To *their face*,' I replied. 'I mean, obviously, that was all fucking lies. If Reece-Burrell really thinks I'm going to let them guide me back into my prison cell via the backdoor, he's sorely mistaken. You play non-confrontational though, you slip off their radar.'

'They are looking over here, watching what this hand is doing,' Mgune said, holding up her hand.

I threw up one of mine. 'They don't even think to look over here.'

The rage started to bubble off Ariel, replaced with a flush of embarrassment and a touch of wounded pride. I couldn't blame him – no-one likes being shown they know fuck all about something. He slumped back into his seat, head in his hands. 'This has been a very long day.'

'It has,' I said, taking my own seat again. 'So, my vote is we let Whitehall take over and just do what we want anyway.'

Mgune shrugged. 'I am all right with this plan.'

'Fine, okay,' Ariel said. 'But we still don't know what that *is*.'

'Right now, I think we've shown each other that we need to take the time to grieve,' I said. 'I wanted us to get the jump on whatever De Sade or whoever is going to end up doing, make sure we have thoroughly stomped the fucking head of the snake into the ground. But I think it's pretty clear that we're no good for it like this.'

With tired groan, Mgune sat down too now. 'The urge to strike back is strong in my heart. My head, however, says we should heal first. It's not a path my heart is fond of, but I believe it's the right one.'

'That's going to take a long time,' Ariel said. He sounded completely deflated, and I couldn't help but feel sorry for him.

'It will take as long as it takes.'

I felt the buzzing of my phone in my pocket. Slipping a hand in, I hit the button to silence it – whoever it was could wait. 'And we can use Whitehall as armour while we work through things.'

'Some alliance,' Ariel chuckled grimly.

'An alliance of necessity,' I said. Again, my phone was buzzing. 'Don't worry, I'm sure they've got a tent on the other side of this camp that's full of hot-blooded paladins talking about ripping our bollocks off as soon as they don't need us anymore.'

'As if they have the prowess to manually remove a testicle,' Mgune said. 'Most would quail if offered the opportunity.'

'I didn't mean it literally.'

'Oh,' she said, a little disappointed.

For a third time, my phone buzzed insistently in my pocket. I snatched it up angrily. 'Excuse me, I need a cigarette.'

'Do you smoke?' Ariel asked.

'I might do,' I said, and excited the tent.

Outside, I found a place in the camp that seemed secluded enough to not have to worry about obvious eavesdroppers. By the time I found that place, I was up to my fifth missed call, all were from the same number that I didn't recognise. I ran a search for it on the internet, just in case it had been flagged somewhere as a call centre – I didn't need to talk to someone trying to hard-sell me a credit card or a premium dating package right now.

The search came back clean, but before I could dial the number they had the decency to call me back for a sixth time. This time, I answered immediately. 'Whoever you are, get to the point. I'm having the shittest day.'

'You utter arsehole,' came the reply. 'You could have just *asked*. Yeah, sure, we might have said no but still, we're on your side. It's not like we needed coercing.'

'I think you might have the wrong number.'

'Don't try and fob me off, Parker,' they said, and there was something in the way they said my name that made me recognise the voice.

'Su-Yin?'

'I told you, don't you dare try and play me for a fool right now.'

'Su-Yin, please,' I said. 'I honestly have no idea what you're talking about. Why are you calling me from this number?'

She went quiet. When she spoke again, there was concern in her voice. 'You really didn't know?'

'I *don't* know. Present tense. What the fuck are you on about?'

'We had a visit from one of your warlocks about an hour ago,' she said. 'Petrova. She said you'd sent her for some information. When Walid said that wasn't really what we did… She… Well, it wasn't pretty.'

'How bad?'

'He'll be fine,' Su-Yin said. 'Tapped into the black to bear the pain. Not happy about that, so don't start. More concerned with how your woman acted, to be honest. We're moving somewhere safe, hence me calling from a burner phone.'

Even on the run, she had the balls to call me from a burner just to give me a bollocking. I wasn't sure if that was brave or incredibly stupid. Maybe both? 'What information could possibly be worth such a reaction?'

'She wanted us to break into Laura Irvine's social media, email, everything.'

Great, Ania was on the warpath. Just what we needed. 'Send me what you sent her. I'll sort this.'

'Fine, but don't call us again. After this, we don't want anything to do with you and your shitty war.'

I ended the call. Su-Yin would cool down, or at least Walid would see reason if it came to that. They'd had a taste of the grown-up world of magical mayhem, and that wouldn't be easy to shift.

Ania was going to have to do a lot of apologising when this was over. Don't get me wrong – I've said before that I understand the desire to just completely self-destruct, especially when hurting like she was. I can't say I totally understood her choice of target though. Maybe it was because Irvine was the only identifiable member of De Sade's crew that would be easy enough to find? Personally, I would have opted to take out my frustrations on Kaitlyn, but to each their own.

Even if that was the case, was that enough to focus a roaring rampage of revenge on? It certainly seemed like that was Ania's goal, but I couldn't help feel like I was missing something again. Bit of a jump from distraught and grieving to wrathful and vengeful.

Su-Yin sent through a link to a cloud folder full of passwords and usernames for Laura Irvine. If this was the amount of info they could turn up in less than an hour, there was no way they'd be able to stay out of the game. They were naturals.

A couple of text documents were highlighted – metadata for photos posted on her Instagram page. The linked photos were innocuous enough, but the GPS co-ordinates tagged in the associated metadata pointed to a studio apartment in a complex in the city centre, rented under the name *Lauren Virvane*.

Coming up with aliases is a skill, all right. Not everyone has taken the time to build it up.

In this case, Irvine's substandard skills were going to lead to a very angry warlock turning up on her doorstep any minute now. And, if she was lucky, a very charming, handsome, and charmingly handsome one arriving moments afterward in time to save her life.

*

Charlie had wanted to come with me, but I had done the heroic thing and begged her not to. I didn't think she would be in any danger – Ania was hurting, not psychotic – but if I was right, more eyes on her would just compound the hurt.

Virvane's apartment was in the basement of the complex. It had all the hallmarks of being put together by a greedy landlord wanting to find a way to scrape a few coins together out of nothing. It had its own entrance for one – probably advertised as a real selling point and not, as I suspected it may have truthfully been, a holdover from when the apartment had been home to the building's septic tank.

I found the door ajar, the lock having been burned out with more care and subtlety than I had been expecting. That was a good sign. Inside, the omens turned a little darker. The door didn't lead straight into the apartment, instead it opened into a long corridor, all breeze block walls and painted concrete floors. In the distance, a rhythmic hammering noise was being made even more sinister as it echoed its way down to me.

Because, of course, things weren't done being dramatic and stressful, oh no.

Moving down the corridor, I didn't pass any other doors. At the very end, it opened out into a staircase and one sad little door – creaky and rusted metal, like you'd expect to see on a boiler room, not a living space. The lock on this one had not been so carefully burned out; three great chunks had been blasted out of the side of the door at varying points up its length, causing the metal to buckle. They were still smoking.

The hammering noise was coming from within – because of course it was – and I pushed open the door slowly, hinges creaking, and cautiously entered. Stepping through the tiny vestibule, I saw Ania throwing spell after spell at what I assumed was the door to the unit's bathroom. Each cast filled the small living space with phosphorescent light and a sound so loud I could feel my bones shaking. She was in a frothing rage, her screams melding with the impacts of her spells.

I picked my moment, waiting for a gap in her assault. 'Hello, Ania.'

She span, eyes wild, and loosed a ragged bolt of power in my direction. I'd been expecting it, so was able to bat it aside calmly. It struck a cabinet behind me, shattering the wood and causing a small waterfall of tinned food to clatter down onto the floor.

Those wild eyes grew wide, her face ashen. 'Parker… I… Sorry, I didn't mean…'

'It's fine,' I said. 'I've been there. Not quite sure I understand what you're doing, though.'

'She needs to pay, Parker,' Ania said. She looked back over her shoulder at the door, and I saw her tensing up again. 'De Sade is gone. I can't blame Kaitlyn. But this *piece of filth*, she made the decision of her own free will. A lieutenant to that *monster*, not through coercion or control, just by choice. She's next in line. '

This time she threw her foot into the door, stomping on it just above the handle. Not quite as loud this time, but it still set my teeth on edge. 'Maybe you're right. Not a great visual is it, though, gunning someone down while they cower in their toilet. Paul wouldn't want that.'

'Wouldn't he?' she asked. 'I think he'd be fine with it.'

I scowled. 'That doesn't sound like the man I knew.'

'What did you actually know of him?' she whispered, her eyes drifting over to the space at my side. 'You were friends, sure. But he and I are family.'

'What I know is that when I went off on a mad magic bender because of something traumatic, he was the one that brought me back to myself.'

'That was then. Whatever he wanted then doesn't matter, I'm going to see that he gets to rest peacefully. I owe him that much. He wants this to end, and I'll end it for him.'

'That's the second time you've used the present tense to talk about him. You do know he's dead?'

Her eyes started to water. 'Dead but not gone. Not yet.'

A great pit formed in the depths of my stomach. I was putting the pieces together, and I didn't like them.

Closing my eyes, I reached out with my power, crept inch by arduous inch around the room, feeling for something that didn't belong. There was a coldness, like the chill of someone walking over your grave, and I latched onto it, pulling it forward and into the open. It resisted, strained against me, but I'd caught it on the back foot.

With one last effort of will, I dragged it out into the light.

Paul materialised out of the air, stunned and a little confused. He stumbled, bracing himself against the wall as he regained his balance. 'Jesus Christ, Jim! Did you have to be so rough?'

'This isn't funny,' I shot back. 'This isn't fair on her. End this now.'

'That's what we're doing,' he said. 'Ania and me, together. Irvine is the last pillar of De Sade's movement – one of his generals. Killing her now will make sure I didn't die in vain.'

'You son of a bitch. How *dare* you use her grief like this?'

I didn't even feel the punch coming. Honestly, I had no idea how angry I was until I felt my fist swinging at his face. What surprised me even more was that I actually connected, smacking him into the wall and bloodying his mouth. I didn't have much time to reflect on that, however, as I was instantly hit full force in the side by a glimmering lance of energy by Ania. It lifted me off the ground and drove me down, quite fortunately, onto the unmade bed across the room.

'Leave him alone!' she screamed. 'Why are you trying to deny him his rest? I don't understand!'

'That's not Paul,' I managed to splutter. 'You know it isn't. You're smarter than that, you know how The Rider operates.'

Paul clicked his jaw back into place and made his way over to the bathroom door at a leisurely saunter. Crouching down, he slowly turned the knob and the door clicked before swinging open. 'There we are, the end is in sight.'

I sat up slowly. Cowering in the bathroom, huddled up on the base of a shower, Laura Irvine was whimpering and crying, pulling her legs up tight and hoping against hope that this was all a bad dream. As Ania stepped into the doorway, Irvine tried to scuttle backwards, pressing herself tight against the wall and blubbering with abject terror.

'Ania,' I croaked. 'Not this. Not in cold blood.'

'Yes this,' Paul snapped. 'This stops a war before it truly starts. Every figurehead of De Sade's movement gone in an instant. They need a leader; we can't let them have one.'

With great difficulty, I pushed myself back up onto my feet. 'Then we take her in.'

Paul rolled his eyes. 'And put her where? Hand her over to our new friends in Whitehall? Warlocks kill, that's what we do. We're not the police, we're assassins. That's how we help, that's what we do.'

Ania started to draw in power, one final burst to put an end to this. 'The hard choice. The lasting choice.'

'Ania, I've been in this moment, same as you. I've used the pain as an excuse, and if that was the real Paul right there he would be telling you how much that fucks with you. You do this, you let the black in – you let instinct and reaction overshadow reason, and when you calm down you'll have to live with that for a long time.'

'I know all about that,' she said. 'I tracked a werewolf once, did you know that? Everyone knows that. Tracked it, killed it. It was just a man, an innocent man that got a bad break of it. But I killed him, because letting him live would have let him cause more harm.'

I was moving closer, step by quiet step. 'Yeah, I've heard that story. You wanted to try to save him, but Whitehall said no.'

'And they were right to push me, as Paul is right to push me now. This has to end. *It has to end before it can start.*'

Seeing she was about to unleash her spell, I lunged the last couple of steps. I grabbed her shoulder and pulled her aim off-target, yanking her out of the doorway and back into the main room. The spell arced wildly, crackling out across the room, up and over the ceiling, until I brought it to bear on Paul. It struck him centre mass, sending him sprawling. Before he even hit the floor, Ania tried to dash to him. Pulling her close, I wrapped my arms around her and held her still.

'Look at him,' I whispered in her ear. '*Really* look at him.'

When he stood up, it wasn't Paul that was staring back at us. It took even me a moment to recognise his real face, being so used to seeing him wearing the guise of someone else, but those red-ringed eyes have a way of sparking the memory pretty quickly.

The realisation washed over Ania, and I could feel all the power that came of her rage start to drift away, replaced by crushing sadness. Now I felt like the cruel one, robbing her of what had been, in some small way, a chance to say good bye to Paul Renner. Even knowing that wasn't the case, feeling her sobbing quietly in my arms was far from a pleasant experience.

'I really did think we were on the same page at last,' The Rider said.

Ania was done now, without the rage to drive her she had completely descended into shock. I set her down on the bed and turned back to The Rider. 'I won't lie, you pull strings well. You really had me believing that maybe some of what you were saying was true.'

'It's all true.'

'The facts are true,' I said. 'But the theories? This whole greater good shit? You whispered in Laura Irvine's ear, drove her mad to try to get what you wanted. You were doing the same to Ania. You violate grief and fear. Even if you are right, even if this is necessary to prepare for your alleged apocalypse, this is beyond the pale.'

Now it was his turn to twist in rage. 'I am doing what needs to be done! This is an opportunity I didn't foresee. Yes, I thought the only option was to prepare an army for the end of the road, but why not end it before it starts? One dead young woman, one traumatised, but that's a small price to pay!'

'Then give her the choice!'

'And if she makes the wrong one?' he roared. 'What then? We just let the world burn because we didn't want to hurt a few feelings? Your blindness utterly astonishes me.'

'You were right about one thing,' I said. 'It *is* time to put an end to this. Your interference needs to end.'

'You're going to fight the dead, Parker?'

My eyes snapped to Ania. 'Let her go. We'll end this together.'

'She was never in any danger from me. But I'm not letting Irvine go.'

'We'll see.'

He nodded slowly and gave me leave to move Ania. The grief had locked her inside her head now, far too lost in memory to function.

And he claimed she was never in any danger from him!

I led her outside and a little way up the corridor, setting her down on the cool floor well out of what could conceivably have been a splash zone for any magical throwdown to come. She didn't deserve such pain, and she most certainly didn't deserve to see what was going to happen next.

Once I was sure she was secure and safe, I returned to the apartment. The Rider was limbering up dramatically, air boxing and flexing. I walked right past him and into the bathroom. Irvine was still cowering, though confusion had overshadowed fear by this point.

'Hello,' I said, crouching down in front of her. 'Do you remember me?'

She nodded. 'The one who locked me away.'

'I shouldn't have done that,' I said, looking away. 'I was scared of you and didn't think before I acted.'

Irvine shook her head slowly. 'I understand. My beast, she tries to protect me but what's good for me is not often good for others.'

'She picked this place out for you, didn't she?'

'Yes,' she said. 'A safehouse, in case any one of her paranoid delusions would come to pass. She just wants to keep me safe, that's all.'

'That's why she joined up with De Sade, isn't it?'

'Safety for us, not safety from us. It spoke to her.'

'The Rider's right, isn't he?' I said. 'She'll go back to De Sade.'

'Not if I don't let her. I can't control her all the time, but I can talk to her, reason with her.'

'You can give her the choice.'

'Exactly!'

I stood up, smiling. Irvine started to unfold, perhaps starting to realise the danger had passed. A bit of that calmness and serenity flowed back into her, and I could see that she trusted me to see her safe.

Which is when I killed her. Quick, painless – she didn't even see it coming. A surgical bolt of magic between the ribs and into the heart. Without a sound, she slumped over onto the floor, a trickle of blood gurgling up from her throat. I left the room, closing the door behind me.

'You really do amaze me, Parker,' The Rider said. 'After all that bluster, you still see things my way after all.'

I pushed past him, staggering over to the apartment's kitchenette and running some cold water into my hands, over my face. 'Go fuck yourself.'

'But—'

'No, you listen to me,' I interrupted. 'You are right, there are times when hard choices need to be made. Maybe Laura could talk her beast around, but you're right – the stakes are too high.'

'Then why not let Ania—'

'Because you didn't give her the *choice*. You misled her, violated her. All you do is mislead and treat people like pawns. Well, fine, you wanted me to be a leader, I'll be a leader. I'll take on the burden of those hard choices, but I'll do it with my eyes open. No more of your games, none of this lurking over my shoulder wearing the faces of people from my past. You can fuck off, and I'll let you go because, while your methods are vile, I do believe your goals are honest. The one honest thing about you.'

'I see.'

My stomach was roiling. 'You had better. I see you again, we have this fight for real.'

'If I'm right, what you've just done will mean we'll never have to see each other again.'

'Good,' I said. 'Get out.'

He did, fading away into the air like a fine mist. I gave him a moment, reached out with my power to make sure he was gone, then sat on the bed and had a little cry.

It was that sort of a day, I guess.

Twenty

I took Ania back to the smouldering ruins of our hideout and left her in the care of the other warlocks. They didn't ask where she had been or what was wrong, and I wouldn't have told them even if they had. None of their business. She didn't need judgment right now, or even sympathy – just a place to feel what she needed to feel.

Share the pain.

I needed some of that myself.

Charlie tracked me down within minutes of my return. She didn't even try to talk to me, just waited until I had handed Ania over to Mgune before taking me by the hand and leading me silently out of the camp and off towards the main street. I confess I had sort of slipped into a kind of fugue by that point – didn't even have it in me to make a charming quip. Too many thoughts rattling around in my fat head.

She all but marched me to a small park nearby – more of a forgotten patch of greenery that had been lucky enough to inherit a bench – and sat me down. Again, without a word, she left me there for about five minutes, before returning with a paper bag. Gently, she placed it in my hands.

'Drink that,' she said.

Confused, I opened the bag. Inside sat a tiny bottle of whiskey, the ones you get someone as a novelty gift. 'What's this?'

'You look like someone in dire need of a drink. I don't really like the idea of using alcohol to deal with problems, but I reckon it has its place.'

I cracked open the bottle and gulped it down. It was barely enough for a mouthful. 'Chaz, I need something from you.'

'I know,' she said, squeezing my hand. 'You want me to tell you that you did the right thing.'

I blinked. 'How—'

'Jim, come on. I've known you for years, I can read your face. I don't know what it is you've done, but I know it's serious enough to make you, well, *serious*. Must be a big deal.'

'I think we neutered De Sade's whole plan today,' I said. 'He's probably dead, his main lieutenants are dealt with. Everything The Rider showed us is off the table now.'

'Well, that's good, right?'

'I killed someone.'

She nodded. 'Not the first time.'

'But the first time it was a choice,' I said. 'The others were accidents, instinctual, self-defence that sort of thing. I've got excuses for them, at least ones I can tell myself. But this…'

'I understand.'

We sat in silence for a while, me lost in thought while she rested her head on my shoulder. One of Charlie's greatest qualities – and one that I would probably benefit from learning myself – is knowing when it is better not to say anything at all. Coupled with that, however, is knowing when it's time to break that silence. You kind of need both.

After a while, she nuzzled in a little closer. 'If you want, I can take your mind off things.'

'Yeah?' I asked.

She nodded. 'You can file the apocalypse away now, confine the costs to a spreadsheet in your head. We've still got the problems of Kaitlyn van Ives, the resurgent population of arcane creatures, not to mention Whitehall.'

'Thanks. Just fill my head with new worries, that'll really help.'

'Stops you worrying about the old stuff though, right?'

I very nearly almost laughed. 'I suppose. At least they are all smaller problems than the literal end of the world, right?'

'Exactly,' she said, pushing herself upright again. 'The joy of rebuilding.'

'With an ally whose only refraining from planting a boot on our neck because they think there's a bigger enemy out there.'

'An enemy that you probably just took out of play.'

'Yep.'

'See?' she said, beaming at me. 'Much more pressing things to worry about.'

I pulled her in close and planted a kiss on top of her head. 'You are an atrocious counsellor, you know that?'

'I'm the counsellor you deserve, Jim.'

So, sure, I'd put aside thinking about whether what I had done had been right, at least until I had the time to spare worrying about it. There was always going to be something more important going on than introspection, I guess.

I hadn't even considered how all this would affect things with Whitehall, but now Charlie had reminded me I was already spiralling into dread on *that* front. We'd been holding our own before, but that had been very hit-and-run, limited engagements while they tried to understand what was going on. In one smooth move, my attempt at forging some sort of alliance had shown them how weak we currently were.

In a way, I suppose it was lucky that there was no-one to report that the danger was over. Maybe I could spin things on a little longer, keep them jumping at shadows until I could work out what to do? Sounds like a great idea, I know, play your new allies for fools. Great foundation for some meaningful diplomacy.

We had lost too much to see it all end so quickly, though. Paul, Preston, all the others – I wasn't going to allow their deaths to be overshadowed by those who survived ending up back under Whitehall's boot. I guess it was time to be the leader The Rider had wanted me to be, at least partly. Mages didn't need an army ready to fight an apocalypse anymore, but they were going to need legitimacy, authority, and above all they were going to need *friends*. I'd always known that, but I'd thought that was someone else's job to sort out.

Seems like no-one else was up to the task, though. Sorry state of affairs, but what are you going to do?

'Got a few ideas brewing,' I said. 'Think I can keep the wolves from our collective doors for a bit.'

Charlie smiled. 'Yeah? Want to give me a hint?'

My hand closed around something in my pocket, a metal token. I ran my thumb over the intricate design engraved into the surface. 'Going to make friends with the biggest wolves before they get hungry.'

Epilogue

Walid hadn't driven cross-country before. He'd travelled like that before, but it had always been someone else doing the driving, buying the petrol, concentrating on the road. It was a very different experience having to actually drive for so long.

Having to stop for petrol had been unexpectedly welcome. Not so much the price, which was draining what limited funds he had left, but being able to blink without worrying it would lead to a crash was such a sublime sensation.

He privately conceded that he was probably overreacting. That warlock had scared the shit out of him, and Su-Yin's anger at it all, while somewhat comforting, did just keep dredging it all back up. It had been all she could talk about for the last few hours. Standing inside the little petrol station shop was giving him such much needed respite from that too.

Through the glass front of the shop, he could see her in the passenger seat of their car, drumming a tune on the dashboard to whatever dad rock banger was on the radio. She looked beautiful.

Walid shook the thought away. There was no point pining over her, that issue had been settled already, albeit not out in the open or very directly. It was stupid to let it re-open itself. He could, though, treat her to an extra-large chocolate bar – not as a display of love, obviously, just as a thank you for taking care of him.

If she happened to read it as a display of love though, and happened to react to that in a positive way, such as a cute little smile or something... A kiss maybe? That would be too much to hope for, wouldn't it?

Lost in thought, he didn't notice the man sidle up next to him. 'A difficult choice, I know.'

'Pardon?' Walid said, blinking out of his stupor and turning his attention to the man.

'Picking a chocolate bar,' the man said. *He was young and handsome, with an easy smile and warm eyes. His voice had the sharply operatic cadence of a German, softened a little from speaking in English.* '*I'm rather indecisive myself when it's something so important.*'

'*Is chocolate important?*'

'*It is if you're a German,*' he said. '*Or, rather, when you're a German who's trying to nonchalantly strike up a conversation with someone. I need information.*'

Walid groaned.

Once. He had done a bit of information gathering literally one time and now people were already seeking him out to make his life more difficult. '*I don't—*'

The man shook his head and interrupted. '*Before you lie to me, let me just be clear about something. I will pay you for your time, and you can be assured that, should you enter into a contract with me, no-one will every come through me to find you.*'

Interesting turn of phrase, Walid thought. "Should you". Not quite a threat, yet still functioning well as one. '*Tell me what you want to know. I guess, maybe, I can help a little.*'

The man smiled. '*I need to know where I can find a young woman named Millicent Thatcher.*'

Epilogue: Part 2

An insistent dripping in the dark. Blood pooling, mixing with salty tears and casting spirals on the ground, trickling towards the drain.

Alone but not lonely. Quiet but not silent. Dead but not gone.

She was ready to fade away. The endless struggling, the torment of clawing through each and every day, it had weighed far too heavily. Constant conflict, arguments, eternal anxiety over her own actions. Surely, she deserved to rest now.

But like this? Dying is dying, but didn't she deserve some dignity in the act? Was she the one thinking that, or was it the Other, her constant companion with its voice ever at her ear?

Impossible to tell now, of course. It had been easy once — her thoughts were calm, kind, pedestrian, while its thoughts had been vengeful, passionate, compelling. Over the years, they had carved a warren in her mind, as no doubt she had in theirs, tangling it all together so that no-one could pick apart the twine. Even now, with the last moments of her life drip-drip-dripping away, there was no way to know.

Why had no-one helped her? That was never explained to her. This condition was inflicted upon her, that surely meant it could be undone. No-one ever offered that option, though. No-one except for him.

She hadn't believed him, but the Other had. It thought like a child, those thoughts she could pinpoint as not her own. It believed, it trusted, provided it was what it wanted to hear. She did the opposite. But now, at the end, she saw some of the logic in how the Other worked.

After all, those with noble ambitions had only ever kept her caged at best, murdered her at worst. Lofty ideals to mask base cowardice.

But to barter, quid pro quo, tit-for-tat — a simple transaction for mutual interest. It was simple and it was, in a way, childish, but it was unburdened. If she had the chance again, she would be in concert with the Other.

And, she realised, she would have that chance again.

Dripping in the dark. Blood pooling. Something watching. Something new.

It didn't speak, it didn't need to. She knew the words it would have said, the question it would have asked. She knew how she would answer. It would be a contract, but a fair one, an honest one. The price was straightforward, the rewards clear.

If she would sign her name, pledge her life, it would return to her one to pledge – quid pro quo, tit-for-tat – and do for her what those with nobility would never even attempt.

It would set her free, as promised.

Gladly, she would give her name. A new one would form in time, but when she would awake, lying on her side on the floor of a small bathroom and basting in blood and tears, it would be a rebirth.

Laura Irvine's eyes opened.
Laura Irvine was dead.

Thanks For Reading

I hope you enjoyed the book (if you made it this far then I'm going to assume you at least didn't hate it), and I'm very thankful for you taking the time to read through Jameson Parker's fourth big adventure.

If you enjoyed it, or even if you didn't, please consider writing a little review. Writers can't grow without constructive feedback, and pretty much every comment received will give me something to work on in the future. This is especially useful for series like this one; I want to make sure I'm giving you what you want to read, after all!

So, please consider [leaving a review on Amazon](#) or [Goodreads](#) if you want, and if you're interested in keeping up to date with what I'm doing and future releases you can find me at [@stevetheblack](#) on twitter or even sign up to my newsletter from my website at [stevekpeacock.com](#) (you'll get first pick when it comes to giveaway, exclusive content, all sorts of things like that!)

Printed in Great Britain
by Amazon